M000240304

IMMINENT THREAT

A THRILLER

DANIEL DICK

◆

Black Diamond
Publishing

This book is a work of fiction, except where it's not. Apart from the well-known locales that figure in this narrative, all names, characters, places, and incidents are products of the author's imagination or are used fictitiously. Any resemblance to actual events, locales or persons living or dead is entirely coincidental.

Copyright © 2019 by Daniel Dick

All rights reserved. No part of this book may be reproduced, scanned, or distributed in any printed or electronic form without permission.

ISBN 978-0-9864959-2-2

♦ Black Diamond Publishing

Dedicated to the unsung heroes who serve
under extraordinary circumstances
to protect and defend us all.

Warfare is ordained for you, though it is hateful unto you; but it may happen that ye hate a thing which is good for you, and it may happen that ye love a thing which is bad for you.
– Qur'an 2.216

The enemy of my enemy is my friend.
– Old Arab Proverb

Part I

A CALL TO ARMS

1

ABDUL SAQR WAS finally ready to act. Thousands would die as a result.

Two years ago a Palestinian banker turned mujahideen had come to him with a dream; a dream that had, at first, seemed foolhardy. Who was this man, Sayyid? Abdul suspected the Palestinian suffered from a type of madness not uncommon to those living in the occupied territories. He had tried reasoning with him, but the man refused to be dissuaded. That he was intelligent, there was no question. And his plan of attack, though risky, was inspired. Ingenious even. But impossible.

Weeks later, after many long discussions, Abdul was convinced the Palestinian's plan could work if—and only if—they could persuade the others to cooperate.

That was the key.

Two years later, standing at the edge of the estate's grand terrace, he watched the deep red of a Mid-East sunset as it spilled across the horizon. "Look at it," he told Kamal, "Allah has set the sky ablaze for us."

Kamal, sitting close by at a large table, made no comment.

Abdul continued to stare at the blood-red sky, his hands gripping the iron railing, knuckles whitening. "It's a sign of what's to come," he said.

"Perhaps it is nothing more than a sunset, Abdul." As a young engineer, Kamal was not prone to romanticizing his commitment to jihad and it displeased him when others did so.

Letting go of the railing, Abdul turned. "What is it?" he asked, the fervor gone from his voice.

"The time for rhetoric is over," Kamal replied.

Abdul nodded, ignoring the young man's impertinence. He walked over to the table and sat down. "You're right, the time for rhetoric *is* over. Have you finished all the necessary arrangements?"

"I have. And the council has given their consent?"

"Yes."

Abdul had assembled a diverse group of influential men—both Arab and Persian, Sunni and Shi'a—to help carry out Sayyid's plan. The men, their political goals as varied as their places of birth, formed a powerful entity with contacts situated in every corner of the Muslim world. Working together, their potential was without limit, but they had needed convincing; their distrust and dislike of one another presenting an almost insurmountable obstacle at first. After much debate though, the council had ultimately agreed to lend its support, each member endorsing the attacks for their own selfish reasons.

"We send it then?" Kamal asked.

"Yes, send it now. And pray to Allah that our Arab brothers in America succeed."

Kamal nodded and opened his laptop. He logged onto a server account he had piggy-backed the day before. He had never used the account and would not use it again after tonight, guaranteeing the email would remain untraceable. Next, he retrieved an encrypted text file that sat on his desktop and attached it to the email. He carefully typed in the address where the email would be sent and double checked it.

Abdul peered at the computer screen over Kamal's shoulder. "You are sure it's safe?" he asked.

"We have gone over this," Kamal replied. "It's safe. The Americans will not get to it." He paused, then added: "Not in time to make a difference."

2

WITH A SINGLE keystroke, the email began its journey.

Racing along a strand of glass no thicker than a hair follicle, the email passed under the city streets of Damascus at the speed of light. On the outskirts of the city center, where the fiber optic cable ended, it was transferred to a microwave tower, then ferried through the air down the Helbun Valley from one tower to the next.

Fourteen kilometers to the east it reached a satellite uplink station where it was finally relayed to an orbiting communications satellite. The email was now on its way to New York City, the entire process having taken only seconds. But what neither the sender nor the intended recipient knew, was that a second satellite had intercepted the email by capturing the spillage from one of the microwave towers outside Damascus.

ES 79 was one of more than a hundred spy satellites belonging to the United States Government. Overseen by the National Security Agency, the satellites were tasked with intercepting all possible human communication: emails, cell phone conversations, texts—all of it collected and relayed to ground stations scattered across the globe. Several million discrete communications were collected every half-hour by the network, codenamed ECHELON.

22,000 miles below ES 79's orbit, in the English countryside of North Yorkshire, sat RAF Menwith Hill. Home to over 1,300 American personnel, it remained an RAF base in name only. On-site sat 32 giant radomes housing extremely sensitive antennae aimed toward the sky. From afar the radomes resembled giant mushrooms sprouting from the lush countryside. Radome thirteen was currently receiving the data feed from ES 79 which had captured what would later be referred to as *The Damascus Letter*.

Deep below ground, software programs called "sniffers" sorted through the millions of intercepts. The programs, running on Cray supercomputers, searched tirelessly for keywords, email addresses, and text patterns that might lead to the discovery of vital intelligence or potential threats. Although not as powerful as those at NSA headquarters, the Menwith computers were capable of over one hundred billion calculations per second. Encrypted, and having originated in Syria—a state sponsor of terrorism—The Damascus Letter was priority-selected and fed into the computers less than an hour after being intercepted. Several minutes later multiple keywords and phrases on the NSA's watch list were identified in the text.

Red flagged, the email was immediately forwarded to NSA headquarters with a level three security designation: *Urgent Attention Required.*

3

AT GEORGETOWN UNIVERSITY in Washington DC, professor Akil Hassan broke off his lecture without warning.

Stepping out from behind his lectern, he walked to the edge of the stage, paused for a moment, then jumped down with the grace of an athlete. As he walked up the center aisle, a mounting crescendo of chatter began to fill the auditorium. His first-year PolySci students looked to one another, searching for an explanation, wondering what was happening.

At six-three, with a taut physique and short cropped hair, Akil could be an intimidating figure when he wanted to be. He was well aware of this. A highly decorated CIA officer, he had conducted covert operations overseas for more than a decade. Recruiting agents and infiltrating the treacherous breeding grounds of the jihadi, he had worked most of the Middle East at one time or another: Egypt, Syria, Yemen, Beirut.

Then the CIA had fired him. In a heartbeat, his career was over.

He had crossed a line. He knew that.

Now he taught part-time at the university, having finally come to terms with the fact he was no longer a part of the CIA. Accepting this new reality had been a painful process and he'd be the first to admit that teaching political science was a poor substitute for his life as a spy. It wasn't that he didn't enjoy teaching. He did. But ever since graduating from The Farm, he'd been unable to picture himself doing anything else. He missed the adrenaline rush of operating in hard-target countries and meeting with agents. The work required a particular mindset and a unique set of skills, all of which he possessed.

He'd tried working for private contractors, but found their commercial ethos unpalatable. Without knowing what to do next, he'd ended up teaching at the university.

Halfway up the aisle Akil pivoted to his right and faced the student who had caught his attention. The student he'd targeted—this wasn't the first time he had done this—wore a black leather jacket and a trucker-style baseball cap. A sketch pad sat in the student's lap. He was shading in the jawline of a lop-sided skull, a bullet hole etched in its forehead.

It wasn't the dubious art work that interested Akil, it was the oversized headphones the student was wearing. He could hear the music bleeding from them now. Industrial metal of some kind. German maybe. The volume was obviously maxed out, which explained why, despite the entire class having come to a halt, the student remained oblivious.

Akil waved his hand in front of the student's face in order to get his attention.

The student looked up, surprise making his eyes widen.

Akil smiled, then reached down and pulled the headphones off the student's head. Rapid-fire guitar and crashing symbols ricocheted off the walls and ceiling of the auditorium to the delight of the class.

"Hey!"

Akil gave the student a well-honed look that stalled any further complaint. "You're going to want to listen to what I have to say, Mr. Sobel."

With that, Akil turned and walked back down the aisle towards the stage, the headphones still in his hand, the umbilical cord trailing behind him. Akil didn't look back, only listened as Mr. Sobel—realizing his professor wasn't joking around—jumped out of his seat, scrambling to release the headphones from his smart phone in time.

He was too late. As the cord's tension peaked, Akil felt the momentary tug as the headphone jack ripped free of the device. No doubt there had been some damage done, but that wasn't his problem.

Hopping back onto the stage with cat-like ease, Akil tossed the headphones into a metal garbage can he'd placed there earlier. The sound of the headphones clanging to the bottom of the receptacle provided his exclamation point. Message sent—not just to Mr. Sobel—but to the entire class. He was serious, and so was his subject matter.

With the stage set, Akil carried on: "America and its citizens are in grave danger," he said, his voice projecting to the back of the room. "Far more than we realize. Somewhere in the world Islamic terrorists are plotting against us, planning to kill more Americans in the name of God," he said. "Al-Qaeda. The Islamic Brotherhood. ISIS. Take your pick. The list is extensive."

Holding the projector remote in his left hand, Akil cued the next slide. A man wearing a green headscarf to hide his face—an AK-47 thrust above his head—was yelling on a crowded street.

"These soldiers of God, these jihadi or freedom fighters—whatever label you apply—are a minority in the nation of Islam. By definition, marginal, and yet extremely dangerous. Driven by religious fervor and a political will born out of a growing sense of humiliation and desperation, they continue to embrace acts of terror. Some are small, yet deadly. Acts of opportunity for instance, like driving a vehicle into a crowd of innocent civilians. Others are much larger. Operations planned out and executed with sophistication and precision; the kind our imaginations cannot fathom until they unfold before us in horrific fashion."

Akil triggered the next slide.

The smoldering image of an obscured Manhattan skyline—choked with smoke and dust—filled the media screen behind him. Working his way across the stage, Akil cross-faded the image onscreen with a quote from the Holy Qur'an.

> *O Prophet, urge the believers to fight. If there are twenty patient men among you, you shall overcome two hundred, and if there are a hundred, they shall overcome a thousand unbelievers, for they are a nation who do not understand.*
> – Qur'an 8:65

"Allah has clearly willed the jihadi to take up arms against us—the unbelievers. Christians. Jews. Atheists… Red Sox fans."

The class broke out in laughter.

"Even other Muslims," Akil continued. "It's a holy war. That's what the jihadi preach to their young Muslim brothers. It doesn't matter that in doing so they distort the words of the Prophet Muhammad."

With one arm resting on the lectern, Akil took a moment to assess his new students. The young men and women looking back at him were mostly first year undergraduates. Innocent still; naïve in ways they could not yet perceive. It seemed a lifetime ago that he had been in their shoes, initially at Brown, then that all-important first assignment overseas with the Agency. As he looked at their young faces he began to isolate and register each one individually, memorizing them. Cataloging them.

Old habits die hard, he thought.

"I was born in Lebanon, but grew up here in the United States," Akil said. "Thanks to my parents, I speak fluent Arabic. As a result, I've had the chance to live and work in the Middle East. More than once I've sat down and shared a meal with those who have preached hatred against America."

Akil engaged the remote.

Several Arab faces popped onto the screen behind him.

"The zealots portrayed in our media are not the crazed caricatures you've been led to believe. They're far more dangerous. The ones I met were extremely articulate, organized, and resourceful. I can assure you that the recruiting drives are working. The number of radicals is growing. Innovative financing schemes are being put in to action so that new terror operations can be funded. Nine-Eleven may feel like a distant memory, but these terrorists are determined to strike at us again in dramatic fashion. Right here. On American soil."

Akil stepped away from the lectern and moved slowly across the stage once again.

"Take this into consideration," he said. "Islam is the fastest growing religion in the world. The only religion still increasing its numbers. Nearly one out of every five people on Earth is Muslim and more are converting every day. If present trends persist, that number will increase to one in three by the year 2030. There are over three thousand mosques in the United States alone and anywhere from four to six million Muslim men, women and children. Since 1950, the Middle East's population has more than quadrupled. And more importantly, the number of active jihadi has spiraled upwards."

Akil switched to the next slide.

> *We have never targeted an American target or American*
> *interests despite its hostility. Until now we did not. I*
> *am talking about now. In the future, God knows.*
> — Senior Hamas Leader

Akil watched his students shifting in their seats, whispering asides to one another. By delivering tonight's lecture, he'd hoped to create a jumping off point for the rest of the course by sparking debate. The last thing he wanted to do was bore his students. Better, he thought, to provoke them.

"Let's do the math," he told them. "The probability of a WMD being unleashed in a major American city by a terrorist cell is what?"

He scanned his audience but there were no takers.

"Twenty percent?" he asked.

"Thirty," a girl near the front offered.

Akil stepped back behind the lectern and gripped it with both hands. "Let's say that over the next ten years twenty separate groups will try to get a biological, chemical or radiological weapon into the country, and that each one of these groups will have a one percent chance of success in any given year that they try. That seem like a reasonable assertion?"

A few students acknowledged the point.

"If we do the math, and I'll save you the trouble," he said, smiling, "the chance that just one of these groups will succeed during the next ten years is about seventy percent."

The lecture hall erupted into a low rumble again.

"But let's alter the formula slightly," he offered. "If we think that in this day and age of technological advancement and terrorist savvy, that each of these groups reasonably has a two percent chance of success, the probability of a single group unleashing a WMD rises dramatically.

"How high? Mr. Sobel?"

Akil watched the young man as he struggled to come up with an answer. "Ninety percent, Mr. Sobel. It rises to approximately ninety percent over ten years."

A collective gasp rose from the audience.

Bingo!

Akil stopped talking because his students were no longer listening. They'd broken into a frenzied debate amongst themselves as to whether or not the numbers could actually be true. It was precisely the reaction he'd hoped for. The extent of America's vulnerability was a well guarded secret, but not for the terrorists. They knew the odds better than anyone. The threat was real. Hopefully the passion his students were exhibiting now would carry forward into the coming weeks of more academic-based study.

Akil glanced at the clock on the wall to his right. It was half past nine. "Now that I've adequately alarmed you all," he said, "next week we'll begin studying the root causes behind this upsurge in extremism and touch on the socio-political history behind it. For now, you're free to go."

And with that, Akil turned and left the stage, file folder in hand.

4

THE MAN SITTING at the back of the theatre watched as the professor darted out the stage-side exit. The door opened onto an interior hallway that eventually led outside. He knew this, not because he was a student at the university—he wasn't—but because he had checked every entry and exit point hours earlier.

Getting to his feet, buttoning his jacket, the man started to make his way down the aisle. He cut a clean path through the stream of students traveling in the opposite direction, taking his time, not wanting to follow too closely.

He'd been sent to deliver a message, and it was a message best conveyed in private.

5

IN NEW YORK City, Sayyid al-Rashid Ibn Muhammad sat in his rented apartment eating a late breakfast of pita bread, hummus, and labaneh drizzled with olive oil. He sat on a wool blanket spread out on the floor instead of using the table and chairs the apartment had come with. Eating like this reminded him of mornings spent with his father back home in the occupied territories.

As he poured another cup of tea his laptop chimed to life on the nearby kitchen table. The soft harmonic tone signaled the arrival of the email he had been waiting for. Only one person had been given the address, so he already knew who the message was from. What he didn't know, is what the message said.

Getting up, Sayyid placed his dishes in the kitchen sink, then hurried over to the computer. He had bought the laptop online two and half weeks ago, then set it up himself. He'd made sure not to surf the internet or contact anyone—not yet—making only the necessary preparations. Then he'd waited patiently, knowing how important it was to stick to the plan and not be lulled into a false sense of security. The watchers had increased their numbers threefold. They were relentless. He had to be cautious.

The subject line of the email was straightforward: *Good News.* He smiled, then wondered if he was being premature.

Clicking on the subject line, the email popped open. It was blank, as expected. He downloaded the attachment the email had come with, prompting the computer to ask for an encryption key. Without the correct key—a sequenced combination of 16 numbers and letters—the contents of the attachment would remain locked, an impossible scramble of symbols with no discernable meaning.

Kamal had followed his instructions well.

Summoning the key from memory, Sayyid typed the numbers in to their respective boxes, each combination representing a surah from the Holy Qur'an. The light signifying hard drive activity pulsed green for a few seconds as the email was transformed into readable text. A moment later another window opened with the message inside.

فمن بين يديك الآن.
أبناء عمومتنا جعلت كل شيء ممكن. انهم أتمنى لكم التوفيق في مساعيكم
لديك سعيد عيد الشكر. نشر كلمة الله.
الهدايا الخاصة بك سيصلون قريبا.
١١

He read the text carefully, then exhaled. It was good news indeed. The council had agreed to let him carry out his attack without restriction, and with its full support. He would strike the first blow on Thanksgiving Day, less than forty-eight hours from now.

"*Insha'Allah,*" he whispered to himself.

God willing.

6

AKIL EXITED THE theater and headed cross-campus to the Leavey Center parking lot. Outside, a late November snow storm was gathering force and threatening to lay siege to the city. The bitterly cold winters along the east coast had taken a lot of getting used to and he still missed the warmth of the Mediterranean and the handful of cities he'd lived in and operated out of. The Mid-East had become a second home and it's where he'd made a name for himself with the Agency. In fact, his last year overseas, in Lebanon, had been one of the most enjoyable and productive assignments of his career.

News of the transfer had reached him in Khartoum just after Easter. He was to be stationed out of Beirut in early May with orders to recruit as many assets as possible. His family had fled Beirut when he was still a child and he had not been back since. The civil war that had torn the country apart was long over and the city had undergone an impressive renaissance. Arriving on the precipice of the summer months, he quickly reacquainted himself with the city, spending time in and around the cafes, always with his ear to the ground, getting to know its inhabitants. Its operators. And when he could find time, he traveled north to Tripoli to do the same.

The ancient city had seduced him the first time he laid eyes on it, with its natural beauty and understated grace. Tara, unfortunately, had the same effect on him.

Tara Markosi.

No matter how hard he tried he could not purge her from his memory, even now. He had tried, more than once. He couldn't think of Lebanon—or his current circumstances—without conjuring her image. He had engineered their first meeting to look like an accidental run-in, but it was she who had found him first, cornering him at a diplomatic reception. She asked him what he did for a living and he'd lied, the way he'd been trained. He told her he worked as a freelance journalist because that's the cover he'd been given. The conversation, which went back and forth for nearly an hour, ended with a promise to meet for coffee the following day, and it wasn't long before the two of them started seeing each other on a regular basis.

She was a pleasure to talk to—charismatic, intelligent, her eyes warm and inviting. The affair was consummated a few weeks later on a hot and humid Saturday afternoon, the sound of a nearby market filtering in through the shuttered windows of his rented apartment. Soon they were spending their weekends together, taking refuge under the shade of Eucalyptus trees or wiling away their afternoons holed up inside the apartment. He had known she was trouble that first night—knew, even then, that he should walk away. Better yet, run. But she fascinated him. That was the problem.

Eventually, he'd recruited her as one of his agents, which had always been the plan—the impetus for their relationship from the very beginning. In the end, he had broken the rules for her. Because of her. He shouldn't have done it. He knew that then and he knew it still. Would he have done it differently, he wondered, knowing what it had cost him?

A powerful gust of wind broke Akil's reverie and he pulled his coat tight around his neck and shoulders to keep out the wind. A moment later he felt his body tense ever so slightly. Years spent in the field had given him a highly tuned sixth sense, and something or someone had just set it off.

Raising his head, Akil conducted a quick sweep of his surroundings, moving only his eyes from left to right. He spotted nothing unusual, but the uneasy feeling was still there. He reacted by not reacting.

Thirty feet up the stone path he turned left and headed toward the new administration building. As he turned, he checked his peripheral and spotted a possible tail out of the corner of his eye. He had been trained to spot surveillance, avoid it too, but that was when he was still part of the Agency. As an associate professor he was no longer in the habit of running counter-surveillance.

Not wanting to let his pursuer know he'd been spotted, Akil cut across the grass and approached the administration building at an oblique angle. Running the length of the building's south wall was a massive slab of tempered glass. The architectural feature, which he'd admired on more than one occasion, acted like a giant mirror under the right conditions. Tonight, with snow already on the ground, those conditions were ideal. The glass allowed him to see nearly fifty yards over his shoulder without turning his head. The harsh angle at which he was skirting the building limited his scope of vision, but the move was necessary to prevent his tail from figuring out what he was up to.

He managed to catch sight of his pursuer for a precious few seconds. More than enough time. The man carried himself like a trained professional, but had ventured too close. He was in his mid-to-late twenties, lean, tall, wired. Fair-haired. Akil didn't know him, but he recognized the face, recalling it from the lecture. Back row, third chair in from the aisle. He'd figured him for another curious grad student, possibly someone on an athletic scholarship.

Akil continued on as if he were unaware he was being followed. He was trying to figure out who would want to surveil him, but with no easy answer and no time to speculate, he put it out of his mind.

It was time to seize control of the situation. Edging past another building, Akil spotted the entrance to the underground parking lot forty yards ahead and quickly slipped into the gap. Although out of sight, he forced himself to maintain a regular pace. His footprints were clearly visible in the snow, and if it appeared he had started to run, his pursuer would know he'd been detected.

Instead, Akil walked as fast as he could without breaking stride. His heart pounding, he calculated seven or eight seconds until the man following him rounded the corner and regained line of sight.

Three...four...five...

On the count of six Akil reached the reinforced metal door that led down into the parking lot. He slipped inside, the smell of urine engulfing him. Was this guy running a passive surveillance operation, and if so, why? How many were there?

Akil held the heavy metal door open just a crack, waiting for his tail to rush around the corner. As soon as he saw his pursuer, he let the door close and bounded down the concrete steps two at a time, hoping he'd be followed. His limbs vibrated with the sudden rush of adrenaline his body had dumped into his bloodstream. His fight or flight responses were at their peak now. Despite the danger, he felt loose. He knew he was out of shape and out of practice for this kind of thing, but he couldn't help relishing the thrill of it. It was something that had been absent the past two years of his life and he missed it.

Controlling his breathing the way he'd been taught, he opened the door to P2 and dug a pen out of his file folder. He gripped it tightly in one hand like an ice pick and looked around the parking garage. Square concrete pillars stretched off into the distance. The garage contained a handful of cars, but as far as he could see there was no one around.

A floor above him he heard the exterior door being jarred open. On cue he let the door he was holding slam shut, then moved around the corner to his right. Standing in an empty parking stall, he placed his back against the cool concrete and let the file folder he was carrying drop to the floor.

Listening to the man rush down the stairs, his feet hitting every step in a tippety-tap rhythm, Akil quickly slipped off his own shoes and waited.

There was a brief moment of silence followed by the sound of metal on metal as the door to P2 opened. Akil resisted the urge to peek around the corner as he counted off the seconds.

One-one-thousand…two-one-thousand…

The telltale sound of rubber-soled shoes gripping the polished concrete was scarcely audible, but it was enough to tell him what he needed to know. The man was moving away from him.

Akil edged forward—readying himself—then peered around the corner. He could see his pursuer, six, maybe seven feet in front of him. In his stocking feet, Akil lunged forward without making a sound. He locked his left arm around the man's neck from behind, pulling back hard. Next he drove his fist into the man's kidneys, delivering two rapid-fire blows, then shifted his weight and swung the man across his hip—using his body for leverage—bringing him down on the bare concrete with full force.

The man landed on his back, the air trumpeting from his lungs. Without hesitation, Akil spun around and jammed his knee down on the man's chest, holding the ballpoint pen to his throat.

"Who are you and why are you following me?"

The young man struggled to catch his breath, but Akil kept his knee in place. An inch lower and with a little more force he could easily sever the sternum and kill him.

"You have three seconds," Akil said.

"I'm with the Agency," the young man stammered.

The Agency?

"You're lying."

"Check for yourself."

Akil looked around quickly, half expecting more assailants. There was no one. He dug around in the man's jacket for his wallet. Finding it, he looked inside. The guy was telling the truth. He was CIA.

"Why are you following me?"

"Your name's Akil Hassan, right?"

Akil pressed his knee harder onto the man's chest, feeling the rib cage compress. "Answer my question."

"Bill...Bill Graham sent me," the man shot back, pain accenting his words.

Akil instantly recognized the name. Bill Graham was Director of the CIA's Clandestine Services and his old Chief of Station in Cairo.

"Why'd he send you?" Akil asked, staring into the young man's eyes.

Before he could answer, the young man broke into a coughing fit.

Akil eased his knee off the man's chest so he could breathe. "Go on."

"He said he wants a word with you."

"That's it?"

"He wants to meet tomorrow at The Blarney Stone. It's—"

"I know where it is," Akil said. "What's he want?"

"I don't know. Nine PM. He said it was important."

The young man was still struggling to get up as Akil retrieved his file folder and shoes. His car was one level down. As he opened the door to P2, the young man called after him. "What do I tell Bill?"

"Tell him he's lucky I didn't kill you."

7

JALAL MAHMOUD STOOD shivering outside a Wal-Mart in Jersey City.

Stomping his boots on the ground to generate body heat, he slipped his hand inside his ski jacket, resting it on the Qur'an he carried with him. He asked himself the question again: *Am I ready to kill for God?* It was not an unusual question to ask in his situation, though tonight there was a new urgency to it. For a long time, he had felt ready. But could he carry through with it? Could he actually do it?

When he was seven, Jalal changed his name to Jordan—like the basketball player—in order to fit in with his friends at school. Back then he had been small and somewhat shy. The other kids had teased him and called him names. Bullied him. But they were the only friends he had, so he'd done what he could to fit in. That was then. Now he was proud to call himself by his Muslim name.

He wasn't afraid anymore. He had new friends.

Born and raised in Brooklyn, Jalal was the only son of Yemeni parents who had emigrated to America shortly after their marriage. They were loving parents, hardworking and determined to make a good life in their new country. His father, Aziz, drove a cab while his mother took care of the house. They sent him to public school along with the rest of the kids in the neighborhood, and on weekends they took him to the local mosque to learn his faith. His parents were happy to be Americans, proud even, but they didn't want their son to forsake his religion. His heritage.

As Jalal grew into adolescence, he became more and more isolated from his classmates at school. They didn't understand his religion, and he didn't understand their contempt for its traditions. They taunted him, but he didn't give in. He felt frustrated though, his religion demanding one thing and his friends another.

Growing more despondent, Jalal was befriended by a local sheikh at the age of thirteen. The sheikh could see that the boy was vulnerable and he'd reassured him with kindness. He treated Jalal as a peer and not as a child. He took an interest in Jalal's ideas and encouraged his adherence to the laws set out in the Qur'an and the Hadith. Because of this, the two had grown closer as friends. Eventually, the sheikh had taken it upon himself to personally instruct Jalal in the teachings of the Prophet Muhammad.

More and more Jalal began spending his free time at the mosque. After school, he and the sheikh would sit and discuss questions of faith over tea in one of the mosque's back rooms. In the company of the sheikh, Jalal slowly acquired the sense of belonging he had longed for. The new refuge was in stark contrast to the suspicion and scorn Jalal sometimes experienced as a Muslim on the streets of New York. The racial slurs. The not-so-subtle discrimination. The message he heard was loud and clear. He didn't belong.

As his hostility toward the United States grew, his sense of isolation was tempered only by his mounting faith in Allah and the kinship of his

Muslim brothers. It wasn't long before Jalal began defining himself not as an American-Muslim, but as a Muslim living in America. When Jalal's parents saw their only son taking an interest in his faith, they encouraged him. They were happy to see him embracing his religious heritage. But they had no idea the extent to which their son had turned against their new home. Had they known, things might have been different.

Jalal's transformation was not an accident of circumstance though. The sheikh had carefully shepherded the boy, taking pains to educate him about jihad. They discussed what it meant and explored its origins in the Qur'an. Waging jihad, the sheikh explained, was part of being a good Muslim. It was a responsibility. Then, one day, the sheikh, who had propelled Jalal into a strong embrace of the Prophet's teachings and a burgeoning belief in the necessity of holy war, asked something extraordinary. He asked him to stop attending the mosque.

At first, Jalal was disconsolate with the notion. The mosque was his refuge. How could the sheikh ask such a thing? The sheikh tried to explain that the will of God is not always clear. He promised Jalal that his schooling was far from over, that he would continue to give him books to read and videos to watch—that they would still see each other, just not at the mosque. The sheikh also told him that his parents could not know about any of this. True, they were good and honest Muslims, but they didn't see that there was a struggle for the survival of Islam or understand that it was God's will that all Muslims fight for that survival. For these reasons, the sheikh advised, it was better not to discuss their relationship in case his parents forbid them from speaking with each other. This being the last thing Jalal wanted, he agreed to keep their relationship a secret.

Not going to the mosque was difficult and lonely at first, but Jalal had faith in God now, and the sheikh was true to his word. As the years passed, he kept in close contact. The sheikh explained how America had become the number one enemy of Islam, that it supported Israel and suppressed the will of Muslims in their own lands. The fate of Islam was increasingly at risk, he said, and the only way Islam would survive was if its enemies were defeated.

Jalal's devotion to Islam was all he had, and he didn't want to see it destroyed. That was why, when the sheikh told him that warriors were needed to serve the will of God, he was desperate to join the ranks. The sheikh went on to explain that being a *mujahid* sometimes required great sacrifice, and that with that sacrifice, came great rewards.

Jalal understood. Without hesitation he had told the sheikh that he was not only willing to die for his faith, but that he *wanted* to die for it.

8

AT FIRST GLANCE The Blarney Stone wasn't much to look at, but it was just the kind of place Akil favored: uncluttered, the wood polished to a fine sheen from regular use, the low rumble of conversation—not loud music—filling its interior. It was the kind of place where local residents gathered and where you could still sit and have a quiet conversation among friends.

Entering through the front door, Akil scanned the bar's interior. Seeing that he was the first to arrive, he moved to the back and took a seat near the emergency exit, making sure he had a clear view of the entrance.

When the waitress stopped at his table, Akil ordered a scotch. It was true that Muslims were forbidden to drink alcohol, but despite this, many still did. If not in public, then in private. Growing up as an American, Akil liked having a drink now and then with friends. It had never, in his mind, diminished his faith in God. On assignment, of course, when he was overseas, he stuck to the strict rule of Islamic law. But back home things were different and he was thankful for it.

Halfway through his first drink, Akil spotted his old boss, Bill Graham. He was on the opposite side of the street carrying an umbrella angled just enough to obscure his face. Bill had been appointed Director of the CIA's National Clandestine Service six months ago, the promotion capping an already remarkable career. In contrast, Akil had been expelled in disgrace from the same fraternity two years prior. The fact he'd been let go still hurt, and he didn't like the prospect of being reminded of what he'd lost. But if Bill said it was important, he felt he owed it to him to show up and hear what he had to say. Bill would have done the same.

Entering the bar, Bill stuck his umbrella in a bin by the door and headed toward Akil's table. Tall, well over six feet, Bill had an Ivy League air-of-sophistication you sometimes saw in older gentlemen who still believed in the class system. Bill Graham was no cliché though. Born of a wealthy family, he'd chosen to labor in the mean streets of the world's backwaters and back alleys for over half his life, and it gave him a quality of character that separated him from most men. In certain circles, he was considered a legend, and rightfully so. Coming away from their first meeting, Akil had not known what to make of his new Station Chief. At the time he had been a raw recruit, fresh from The Farm in Virginia with a budding reputation for reading people quickly and accurately.

But that first day on the job—meeting Bill—he'd found himself at a loss.

Arriving at his Cairo hotel, Akil had found Bill waiting for him in the lobby. Plainly dressed, he looked unremarkable as far as Akil was concerned—nothing like what he'd expected. That was his first lesson, even if he didn't realize it at the time: assume nothing and expect the unexpected.

His flight out of New York had been routed through London and Frankfurt, then on to Cairo. He had been traveling eighteen hours, and unable to sleep on the plane, had planned on freshening up at the hotel, maybe even grab a few hours sleep before reporting in.

But that wasn't going to happen. Something approaching an apology was given as Bill explained that they had an urgent appointment to keep.

Can't wait. Leave the bags, the hotel will take care of them.

I'm parked out front.

It was like this that Bill led him back out into the mid-day heat, the two of them climbing into his beat-up Toyota sedan.

Driving towards the outskirts of the city, through an endless stream of cars and motorbikes spewing dark plumes of smoke, Bill didn't utter a word. Twenty minutes later they had left behind the office buildings and tourist dives and entered the Cairo you never saw in brochures. Akil kept checking over his shoulder to see if they were being shadowed by the State Security Services. At The Farm, they had pressed upon him the importance of counter-surveillance techniques and they remained fresh in his mind. But he knew better than to question his superior, so he sat quietly, observing the passing scenery, checking his side mirror from time to time. If they were being followed, he assumed Bill Graham wanted it that way.

As they left the paved road dust came in through the open windows and swirled around.

"AC is broken," Bill informed him.

Akil had nodded, happy to have the dusty breeze if nothing else.

Farther from the city center they passed houses made of reclaimed cinder blocks and scraps of corrugated metal. This is where the Islamic Brotherhood recruited—the shantytowns of Manshiet Naser, Bulaq Al-Dakrur, Helwan, Walda.

Then, after several turns down twisting alleyways and truncated streets, an open field dotted with mounds of rotting trash came into view.

The smell hung heavy in the air.

Akil wondered what this trip was all about, but kept it to himself.

At the far end of the field were a number of abandoned cars that had been stripped bare and left to bake in the sun. Bill drove onto the burnt grass and eased them toward a group of idle police cars around which a handful of Egyptian officers were grouped. Bill stopped the car well short and turned off the engine. The police officers eyed them suspiciously but carried on smoking their unfiltered cigarettes.

"Get out," Bill ordered. "And don't say a word."

Akil got out of the car. Bill followed suit, then walked over to the assembled police officers and showed his State Department ID to the nearest man, stating he was an official from the American Embassy in Cairo. The Egyptian officer took the ID and studied it carefully. Akil wondered if the man could even read English. Probably not.

The officer told Bill to wait and walked over to his superior who was standing near a distant pile of trash with several deputies in attendance. They looked to be investigating something, though Akil couldn't tell what it was.

The officer in charge did not seem pleased with the prospect of company. He looked at Bill's ID, then spit on the ground. The spitting seemed an ominous sign, but a second later the officer waved Bill over.

Bill greeted the officer with perfect Arabic and an exaggerated deference to the man's rank. As he did this he discreetly handed over of a large sum of Egyptian pounds. The officer deftly received the payment and pocketed it.

The fleeting transaction had been conducted with such grace and sleight of hand that Akil barely recognized it for what it was.

The Egyptian turned and barked an order to his men. The deputies, with the urgency of underpaid civil servants, slowly headed back to their parked cars as Bill motioned Akil to join him.

As Akil got close, he spotted the reason the police had ventured out here in the oppressive mid-day heat. A dead body lay at Bill's feet. Half buried in the refuse, the naked body showed clear signs of exposure. It was a young man. Middle Eastern. Egyptian, most likely.

The smell of rotting flesh was overwhelming.

Bill used his foot to gently kick away some plastic bags that had drifted onto the corpse, obscuring it. "Take a good look," he told Akil.

Akil had seen dead bodies before, but not like this, not tortured and discarded like trash, left to rot under the heat of an Egyptian sun.

He forced himself to look, not wanting to show any sign of weakness. He keyed in on the cigarette burns that had been inflicted on the man's genitals, noting that the man's arms were frozen awkwardly behind his back, preventing the body from lying flat. Rigor mortis had set in. He'd been killed while he was still tied up, then dumped afterward.

"He was working for us," Bill said, "passing information on the Islamic Brotherhood. His name was Assam Sadiq."

Akil felt queasy. The victim's mouth was stuck open, the tongue having been cut out. "Was he yours?"

"Ran him for eight months. Lost contact three weeks ago."

"I'm sorry," Akil said, noticing now that two fingernails had been torn from the victim's left hand.

"Don't be. He was in it for the money and he got careless. I warned him several times, but he wouldn't listen."

The words, spoken over the dead man's body, seemed harsh. The man had obviously suffered a great deal.

"Don't let emotions cloud your judgment," Bill said, as if sensing what Akil was thinking. "It's business one hundred percent of the time when you're out in the field. If not, you start to lose perspective. And that can be dangerous."

"It's just—"

"The practice drills are over, kid. This is what you signed up for. This is the real thing."

"Of course," Akil said, glancing at the body one more time. "I think you've made your point."

Bill stared at Akil for several seconds, his eyes unflinching. Finally, he turned and strolled a few feet away, studying a row of dilapidated shacks that sat at the far edge of the field.

"Your file says you grew up outside Seattle."

"Yeah, near Tacoma," Akil said, joining Bill.

"Couldn't have been easy being an Arab kid up there," Bill said. "White bread town the way I remember it."

"It wasn't that bad."

"We both know that's a lie." Bill dug a pack of Marlboros from his pocket. "What did they call you in school? Sand nigger? Camel-jockey?"

"Something like that," Akil said. "What's it matter?"

"It matters." Bill knocked a cigarette free from the pack and lit up. "But you showed them in the end, didn't you? High school football star. Full scholarship."

Bill had obviously gained access to his 201 file from Langley: the interviews, background check, lie detector results. But Bill didn't know the half of what he'd gone through. No one did except Akil's brother. He had worked hard to try and fit in at high school. Be accepted. By senior year he'd made the starting line-up for the football team, a sport he'd learned to love and still did.

"File says you attended Brown."

"That's right."

"Good school."

"I liked it."

"What did you study?"

"Poly-Sci. History. What's this about?"

"Completed your masters. Graduated with honors."

"If you already know the answers—"

"File says you applied to the Agency halfway through your dissertation process."

Akil nodded, waiting for Bill to go on.

"Eager to start your new career?"

"That's not a crime, is it?"

"No," Bill said, pausing to take a drag off his cigarette, still staring at the dilapidated shacks across the field. "But it's telling."

"You think you've got me all figured out, is that it?"

Bill stubbed out his cigarette in the dry grass, then turned to face Akil. "All figured out? No, not yet. But I know people. That's the business we're in, kid."

"I like that. They should use that at The Farm."

"The point I'm making is, we both know you should be a natural at this. You've spent your entire life adapting to your surroundings, trying to fit in. You're driven. You're smart. But your instructors expressed some concern, said you were…a little *too* confident for your own good. All cock and balls is the way they phrased it."

Akil shook his head dismissively, but deep down he knew his instructors had a point. "I wanted to prove myself," he said. "Wanted to get noticed."

Bill considered Akil's answer for a moment, assessing his reaction to the repeated prodding.

"Confidence is a good thing," he said, finally. "But it's different out here. There's no room for the ego. It'll get you killed."

"I know I still have a lot to learn."

"You're damn right. In the field, humility is a strength, not a weakness."

"It won't be the same as running drills back in Virginia," Akil said. "I know that."

Bill stared at his latest recruit, his face a blank slate.

Akil stared back, not challenging, but not backing down either.

Having made his point, Bill cracked a smile and slapped Akil on the shoulder. "Alright," he said, "as long as we understand each other."

"We do."

"Then welcome to Cairo, kid. Now let's go grab a drink."

As they turned back toward the car, they passed Sadiq's lifeless body. As they did, Bill offered one last piece of advice: "You rarely get a second chance to make a mistake in this business. Remember that."

9

SECOND CHANCES? BILL was right about that. Akil had made one mistake and lost his entire career in the process.

"How you doing, kid?" Bill asked, sliding into the seat across from his former protégé.

"You look like shit."

Bill laughed. "I hear you're turning into a first-rate professor."

"That right?"

"I've been keeping tabs on you. You're earning quite the reputation from what I hear."

Akil sat forward and placed his elbows on the table. "Next time you want to deliver a message—"

"I know, I know," Bill said, raising his hands in mock surrender. "I'm sorry about that. The kid got carried away. So did you."

"He wasn't very subtle."

"You did quite a number on him," Bill said, raising his eyebrows. "Bruised sternum. Couple busted ribs."

"He's lucky it wasn't worse."

"He wasn't supposed to follow you, just deliver the message. He didn't listen."

"Whatever."

Bill was in his late fifties, but you wouldn't know it by looking at him. He'd worked his way up through the ranks as a case officer during the eighties and nineties, running agents in some of the most dangerous countries in which the CIA operated. He'd worked Moscow Station when the Soviets had the best counter-espionage crew the world had ever seen, and he'd beaten them at their own game. But Bill wasn't the kind of person who dwelled on past glories.

"What are you drinking?" Bill asked, taking off his jacket, making himself comfortable.

"Tell me what this is about. I haven't heard from you in almost a year. Then you spring this cloak and dagger shit on me."

"Just having a little fun, kid. Wanted to see if you still had the goods."

"I thought your boy wasn't supposed to follow me?"

"Did I say that?"

"I'm serious, Bill. What's this about?"

"Alright," he said, flagging down the waitresses. "I wanted to meet because I have a proposition for you."

Bill broke off as the waitress arrived at their table. "Two double Talisker," Bill said. "No ice."

The waitress took the order and left.

"What kind of proposition?" Akil asked.

"I had a talk with Anthony Marchetti a few days ago."

"About what?"

"About you."

"Me," Akil said, surprised.

"That's right."

Anthony Marchetti was the Director of the Central Intelligence Agency and a political appointee with no previous experience in the intelligence business. In two short years, he had swung the Agency in the direction of the President's agenda like a weather vane caught in a stiff wind. What the President wanted, the President got, and what the President wanted of late was smooth sailing into the next election.

"Must have been a short conversation," Akil said.

"I was touting your virtues. You tell me."

"You were playing to a deaf audience. That's what I think."

"I told him you were one of the best officers I ever trained. I told him you were an Arab who spoke the language. And I told him we should put you back in the field, that you were being wasted on a bunch of pimply-faced freshmen studying Middle Eastern politics."

Their drinks arrived.

"To old allegiances," Bill said, raising his glass.

"To old friends."

They drank, the tension between them fading.

"I want to bring you back into the fold, kid."

Akil didn't respond right away. He wasn't sure he could trust what he was hearing.

"I'm offering you a second chance," Bill repeated. "What do you say?"

Akil slumped back in his seat. He had dreamed of getting his job back for a long time, so long in fact, he'd convinced himself it would never happen. But here he was. "You're serious?"

"I'm serious."

"And Marchetti?"

"He objected, of course. Can't blame him, you broke the rules. No one's forgotten that."

"Neither have I."

Akil hadn't broken just any rule, he'd broken a cardinal rule of espionage. He'd gotten romantically involved with an agent he was running. He had been warned about the danger way back at The Farm, but when you spent your life living a lie—overseas and alone most of the time—it wasn't difficult to become attracted to those you met with in secret, especially a woman as beautiful and captivating as Tara.

Bill lifted his glass and inhaled the aroma of the single malt, then took a long slow pull. "I know you never lost sight of your mission. I taught you better than that."

"And I knew better than to get involved, but..."

"The important thing is, you got the intelligence, and you kept pushing for more. You took care of the business end first. Thanks to you we got our hands on some first-rate material. Had it been any different we wouldn't be having this conversation."

Akil nodded.

Bill looked around, eyeing the other patrons in the bar. "What was her name again?"

Akil didn't rise to the bait.

"Still carry a torch for her?"

"It was a long time ago."

"Alright," Bill said, sitting back against the worn fabric of the booth. "I'm putting my reputation on the line, kid. I want to make sure you understand that. I need you to understand that you can't cross any more red lines."

Akil downed his double measure of scotch in one go and said nothing. He wasn't going to apologize again, not after two years out in the cold.

Bill kept talking: "Marchetti doesn't want to do you any favors. Or me either, for that matter. But we've been intercepting all sorts of chatter lately. The Middle East is a hot mess. Newly minted mujahideen are pouring out of Syria, headed god-knows-where. Al-Qaeda is restructuring. ISIS is franchising. Truth is, I'm desperate for good men I can trust. I need you to recruit assets: Arabs who can blend in over there and search out when and where the next attack is coming."

"I don't know," Akil said.

"What do you mean you don't know?" Bill asked. "Don't play coy."

Akil hesitated, wary of getting his hopes up. "Marchetti won't go for it," he said finally.

"The threat levels are rising. There's another attack in the offing. Marchetti knows it, same as I do."

"What do you have?"

"I can't discuss the details here, but the signposts are popping up all over the place. Money is on the move. Chatter levels are high, as I said."

"And you think Marchetti is willing to look the other way because of that?"

"Marchetti promised me a certain degree of autonomy when I took on Operations. I intend to use that autonomy. The question is, are you ready to get your hands dirty again?"

Akil turned his head and watched the waitresses deliver a tray of drinks to a nearby table. Bill knew his answer already, knew it before summoning him here tonight; knew that he'd never truly given up hope, that he'd only been living a different kind of lie these past two years.

Knew too damn much.

Akil reached for his glass of scotch, realizing at the last moment that it was already empty. He pushed the glass toward the middle of the table and looked up, a smile spreading across his face. "So what now? he asked, feeling an unexpected rush of excitement.

"I already have the paperwork drawn up," Bill said, shuffling sideways out of the booth. He placed a pair of twenties on the table. "I just need your signature and we're back in business. Come by the office tomorrow morning."

"It's Thanksgiving tomorrow."

"I know, but we need to get started right away. And there's something you need to see. Can't wait."

10

JALAL COULD NO longer feel his toes, and his fingers had gone numb.

Where were they? They were supposed to be here by now.

Standing at the far edge of the deserted parking lot, sure he'd been forgotten, he thought about giving up and going home. But tonight was far too important for that. He'd waited a long time for this chance, and if it meant he had to wait a little longer in the freezing cold, so be it.

A few minutes later a car pulled into the empty parking lot. It stopped quite a distance away for some reason. All Jalal could make out were the headlights shining back at him. Blinding him.

He hurried across the slick asphalt, trying not to slip and fall, relieved to finally be getting out of the cold. As he closed in on the headlights, he suddenly realized the mistake he'd made.

The large block letters along the side of the car came into view one by one: *P...O...L...ICE.*

Shit! Shit! Shit!

He tried not to panic, but he didn't know what to do. Should he run?

No. Running would only draw unwanted attention; they would think he was guilty of something even though he'd done nothing wrong. He had done nothing at all. Not yet.

His mind raced but failed to find traction. What would he say if they asked what he was doing in a deserted parking lot this late at night? Was he waiting for a friend? What were he and his friend planning to do?

Without warning, he slipped on a patch of ice. Throwing his arms out, he barely managed to steady himself. Regaining his balance, he turned and walked toward the far exit, hoping it wasn't obvious that he'd been heading straight for the police car.

Halfway to the street, he began to feel a mounting sense of relief.

It didn't last.

The entire parking lot erupted in a swirl of red and blue light. Jalal's heart leapt into his throat. He looked over his shoulder—there was no longer any reason to be cautious—and watched the police cruiser wheel around and head straight for him. He began to pray. His chance to be a martyr was over before it had even begun.

He'd failed.

He held his breath, his emotions torn between fear and shame. Then the car's sirens surged to life, stopping him in his tracks. A second later, eyes closed, he heard the cruiser sweep past him.

Puzzled, he opened his eyes and watched the car snake out onto the street and disappear. He didn't know whether to laugh or cry.

A few minutes later a second vehicle pulled into the parking lot. It was an old Econoline van, the kind with the sliding side door. Its headlights blinked on and off once as it approached. It must be them, he thought, but he didn't move this time.

As the van sped to a stop beside him, a man jumped out. Still keyed up from his encounter with the police cruiser, Jalal instinctively stepped backwards, his hands rising up. The man grabbed him by the arm and threw a hood over his head, then pushed him into the back of the van.

Jalal stumbled as he got in, landing hard on the corrugated metal floor. The sliding door slammed shut behind him. As he struggled to get his bearing the van pitched violently over the curb and sped off down the street. In what direction, he had no clue. He didn't know what was going to happen next. He'd been told to wait in the parking lot—alone—and his brothers would come for him. The sheikh had simply told him not to worry. To have faith.

A voice came from somewhere above: "Relax."

"Where are we going?" asked someone else. Jalal had cousins in England and he recognized the accent straight away.

"Don't speak! You'll find out soon enough."

It was nearly as cold in the back of the van as it was outside. Jalal could feel the warmth of the person lying next to him, but couldn't see them. Everything was pitch black.

They picked up two more people and drove around for what seemed like forever before the mechanical stutter of a garage door signaled their arrival.

The side door slid open and a hand gripped Jalal's arm, gentler this time, guiding him out of the van. He was led across a concrete floor and told to put his back up against the wall. Another person was positioned beside him. He tried to figure out how many there were. Five, maybe six people he guessed from the sound of shuffling feet.

Where had they been taken? Who was in charge?

He had so many questions.

The lights inside the garage were on. He could tell because some of the light filtered in through the hood over his head. Then suddenly the light was eclipsed by someone standing in front of him.

He tensed.

Next, he felt the coarse fabric of the hood tugging hard against his nose and ears as it was pulled from his head. Once it was off, he struggled to adjust his eyes to the onslaught of light. He could see four young men lined up against the wall beside him. They were standing in a two car garage attached to what he guessed was a house. The smell of burnt motor oil saturated the air.

Two older men stood in front of them with automatic rifles slung over their shoulders. "Salaam alaikum, my brothers," said one of the men.

The young men standing against the wall replied sheepishly, but in unison: "Alaikum Salaam."

"We sleep here tonight, and with the blessings of Allah, we carry out our mission tomorrow. We will go inside now and sleep. Do not talk to one another or share your names. Do as we say and follow our instructions exactly. *Tayeb?*"

"*Tayeb,*" the four young men replied.

11

In Fort Meade, Maryland, it was early morning and the end of a long shift for Carl Price.

Carl was an analyst at the National Security Agency and worked in the operations building. Isolated on over nineteen thousand acres of land, the state-of-the-art facility looked like any other downtown office tower with its reflective glass exterior and steel-girded frame. But its appearance was a deception. Hidden behind this facade was a building within a building. What you saw from the outside was merely a shell comprised of two panes of bullet-proof glass with a hi-tech copper shielding and five inches of sound-deadening space in-between, preventing any electromagnetic signal or sound from escaping. The building was, effectively, a man-made black hole—a massive labyrinth of rooms, hallways and cubicles that were patrolled, monitored and sectioned off from top to bottom.

Every day for twelve years Carl Price had journeyed deep inside the operations building to dig through the millions of intercepts NSA received, looking for information that would be of value to the United States Government. And although the hours were long and the work was often stressful, Carl loved the challenge. It was one of the things that made him so good at his job. His highly tuned instincts and deft eye for pattern recognition, along with an extremely high IQ, had earned him a privileged spot amongst the NSA's top analysts. But what had started out as a passion for the work was slowly becoming an obsession. His life was beginning to telescope toward an unhealthy and singular focus—the search for what NSA analysts referred to as *the needle*.

What Carl really needed was a vacation, and he knew it. He thought about where he might go as he took a last drag off his Pall Mall cigarette and butted it out alongside the half-dozen others.

Bermuda, maybe. Yeah, Bermuda sounded nice.

Getting up off the couch, Carl left the designated smoking area and headed for the elevators. With three hours left on his shift, he was determined to get out of the Rubik's Cube on time today. Of course, he'd promised himself the same thing three days running without success.

Inside the elevator, he swiped his security badge and quickly descended two floors. On the way to his office, he encountered one of the many unmanned security portals that dotted the NSA's inner sanctum.

Carl swiped his security badge and entered the glass booth, beginning the tedious process wherein his personal information would be collected and checked against the CONFIRM system's database. Already, load cells concealed in the floor had calculated Carl's weight to ensure he was alone inside the box. Mercifully, there was no visual display of the information. His name was instantly fed to computers in the basement and cross-referenced against a list of authorized personnel. The computerized voice then prompted him to approach the eye scanner. The scanner recorded the pattern of blood vessels in his left retina and compared it with a scan already on file. Each retina was like a fingerprint; no two were exactly the same.

Carl wondered, and not for the first time, if a cigarette was worth this much hassle. He usually pondered this question several times each shift. The answer, sadly, was still yes.

As the green light flashed on the eye scanner, Carl heard the electronic locks of the security portal disengage. Exiting, he continued on to his office where his workload was mounting by the second. Millions of inputs were entered into the NSA computers from all over the world each and every day, but less than a tenth of one percent of them actually made it into the hands of analysts like himself. He and his colleagues were the final arbitrators of what constituted vital intelligence, and it was an uphill struggle just to stay ahead of the curve. Carl sometimes felt like a modern-day Sisyphus fighting a never-ending battle against worthless information. People who complained that they received too many emails at work had no idea how bad it could get. But every analyst worked towards the day when he or she would find that one input that offered actionable intelligence. The needle was out there; every analyst knew it, believed in it, and was looking for it. Carl more fervently than most.

Carl punched his password into his computer and called up an input that had been forwarded to NSA headquarters by the ECHELON station, Menwith Hill. The input had been forwarded almost two days ago but had somehow gotten lost in the shuffle. It was hard to fathom the volume of communication that existed today, never mind how much of it could be pulled out of thin air. Email and cell phone traffic alone continued to quadruple annually as technology became cheaper and more pervasive. No wonder the input from Menwith Hill had gotten misplaced, despite having been given a level three priority.

Fortunately, Carl had stumbled upon the email by accident and culled it from the pack. Seeing that the email had arrived in its original Arabic, he'd run it through a translation program before going for his break. With a fresh cup of coffee in hand, he read through the translated text at speed.

Once he'd finished, Carl immediately went to the top of the screen and read through the email again, slower this time, paying particular attention to the individual words and their potential meanings. As he stared wide-eyed at the screen—hardly believing what his eyes were seeing—his coffee cup slowly tilted forward.

Hot coffee began to spill over the rim of the cup and into his lap.

He sprang out of his seat causing more coffee to spill across his desk and keyboard. "Son-of-a-bitch," he muttered, wiping the milky liquid from his crotch.

Putting the coffee mug down, he ignored the spill and read the email through from top to bottom one last time. He wanted to make sure fatigue wasn't playing tricks on him.

It wasn't.

"Holy shit!" He'd found the needle. He'd found the goddamned needle.

Carl checked the date and time on his computer. It was Thanksgiving Day, but still quite early in the morning. Maybe there was still time.

God, let there still be time.

Carl knew that the email could turn out to be nothing, but his gut told him it was real. And he trusted his gut.

He began typing his report as fast as he could, outlining only the critical details. When he'd finished, he alerted his section chief and suggested an Arab linguist manually translate the email to corroborate his findings. The NSA might have the best translation software in the world, but there was no replacing a warm-blooded human being who understood the nuances inherent in a language more than 1500 years old.

Finally, he forwarded the email along with a cursory evaluation to the Director of National Intelligence, the Director of the Central Intelligence Agency, the National Counter-Terrorism Center, and two other agencies dictated by protocol.

Once the email had been sent, Carl stood up and took a long, deep breath. He needed another cigarette.

12

THE ROOM WAS small and the walls had been painted baby blue at one time. A kid's room, Jalal thought, but the color had faded and the windows were blacked out now. Two thin mattresses lay on the floor with blankets thrown on top.

Jalal had been billeted with one of the older men whose intense snoring prevented him from sleeping. Lying in bed, feeling restless, he managed to doze off for an hour or two in the middle of the night, waking sometime before dawn.

He was alone in the room now. He stretched his arms, then rubbed the sleep from his eyes. According to his watch, it was almost 5 AM. Climbing out from under the blankets, he got dressed, then quietly opened the bedroom door and walked down the hall toward the kitchen.

The man he had shared the room with sat by himself at the kitchen table. Seeing Jalal, he smiled and offered him a cup of tea. Jalal thanked the man whose name remained a mystery.

The tea was sweet—the way he liked it—and Jalal drank it quickly, gripping the ceramic mug with both hands to fend off the cold.

"How did you sleep, Jalal?"

"I slept okay. Enough."

"Good. Today you become a martyr to Islam."

"Insha'Allah," Jalal replied.

"Insha'Allah."

Each of them drank their tea as if to toast the idea of his approaching martyrdom.

"You must make sure you prepare as the Prophet instructs."

"I will," Jalal said earnestly.

"The others will be up soon, and we will perform the dawn prayer together. After that, someone will come and explain your mission to you."

Jalal nodded, excitement and nervousness mingling inside him. He had dreamt often of this moment, ever since the sheikh had given him the opportunity to become a mujahideen. In his dreams he was always strong and confident. Last night, and this morning, things were different. His nerves were unsettled. The thought of failure had wormed its way into his mind. His resolve, however, remained firm.

"The bathroom is down the hall," the older man said. "You should prepare now so the others will have time."

"Okay," Jalal said, finishing his tea quickly.

Jalal left the kitchen and walked down the hall to the bathroom. In order to be accepted into paradise, he had to first cleanse himself through ritual purification. If he didn't correctly purify his body and soul, he would not be allowed to enter paradise; he would not receive his reward from God.

Before beginning the ritual, he recited out loud the *Bismala*: *Bismi-llahi ar-rahmani ar-rahimi.* In the name of God. Most Gracious. Most Merciful.

Running water in the cracked sink, he began by rinsing his mouth out and cleansing his nostrils. He washed his hands thoroughly up to the wrist three times. His right hand first, then his left. He had performed this ritual often, but today he made sure to observe each detail with renewed vigilance. He would be with Allah soon and he wanted to make sure the Prophet was pleased with him.

Splashing cold water over his face—again, three times—he felt the momentum of the day building inside him, its power guiding him toward an inevitable end and a new beginning. He thought about the moment he would blow himself up along with the *kafir*—the unbelievers. It prompted him to recite a passage from the Qur'an under his breath: *Those who believe fight in the cause of Allah, and those who reject Faith fight in the cause of Evil.* It was a particular favorite, one the sheikh had recited often during their time together at the mosque.

Now he washed his forearms up to the elbows, as he had been taught as a child. It was hard to imagine he'd ever been so young. So naïve. His parents had shielded him for too long, hiding the truth about what was happening to his Muslim brothers and sisters in the Middle East and beyond. His parents had meant well—he was sure of that—but they were blinded by their new life in America. He feared for them. He feared that Allah would cast them aside on the day of judgment.

Passing a wet hand over the whole of his head, Jalal breathed deeply, knowing he alone could save his parents from the fires of hell. As a martyr, he would have the right to intervene on their behalf. They would see then that what he was doing was righteous.

Once he'd finished purifying himself, Jalal headed back to the kitchen to wait for the others.

Soon everyone was awake and moving about the house, each performing the ritual in turn.

They eventually gathered in the small living room before sunrise. Simple prayer rugs had been laid out on the floor and they stood on them facing east towards Mecca. Jalal prepared himself mentally to pray with an honest and open heart. He raised his hands toward his head, along with the others. "*Allahu Akbar*," they sang.

Then they began to recite aloud the opening chapter of the Qur'an:

In the Name of Allah, the Most Beneficent, the Most Merciful.
All the praises and thanks be to Allah, the Lord of the Universe.
The Most Beneficent, the Most Merciful.
Master of the Day of Judgment.
It is You alone we worship and You alone we ask for help.
Show us the Straight Path.
The Path of those on Whom You have bestowed Your Grace; Not the path of those who have earned Your Anger, nor of those who went astray.

13

MORNING PRAYERS TOOK almost an hour. As they were finishing up they heard the sound of the garage door opening. One of the two men in charge rose to his feet. "They're here," he said to no one in particular, hurrying down the hall to the back of the house.

Who is here?

The entire room eyed the hallway anxiously as the murmur of distant voices drifted into the room. Jalal strained to hear what was being said, but could only distinguish the odd word.

Two men he'd never seen before finally rounded the corner and entered the living room. One of the men was short, the other tall. The shorter man carried a large duffel bag in one hand, keeping the other hand tucked away in his jacket. His face was heavily scarred on the right side, the skin having melted into a morass of uneven ridges and crevices that navigated his jaw-line all the way down to his collarbone.

Jalal couldn't help but stare at the man—transfixed by his scars—then noticed too late that he'd been caught staring. He quickly averted his gaze, his heart skipping a beat. His eyes had met the shorter man's eyes for only a second, but it had been long enough to unnerve him. They were cold and unflinching—dangerous eyes.

The second man had no visible scars. He was tall and handsome with light colored skin and a sense of calm about him. Dressed in a white collared shirt, dark slacks, he didn't look particularly Arab or intimidating, and yet he assumed control of the group without so much as a word. The two men who had been instructing the young martyrs focused all their attention on him now. Jalal and the others stood taller as well, trying to appear more confident than they actually were.

"My name is Sayyid," the man announced in a soft, but assertive voice. He looked around the room at the young martyrs, smiling generously at each of them. "It is my pleasure to be among you on this auspicious day."

Sayyid moved to the middle of the room and asked one of the two men who had been in charge of the group to bring them tea. "Sit, please," he said, addressing those who remained.

Everyone sat down in a circle facing Sayyid. The man with the scars remained standing, his eyes surveying each of the young men in turn.

"My associate's name is Asad," Sayyid said, gesturing with his hand. "He is our explosives expert. He is going to fit you with your vests. With his help, you will be able to go into battle and perform your duty to Allah today."

Each of the young martyrs stirred at the sound of the word *battle*. Sayyid sensed their discomfort. "Do not be afraid," he told them. "There is only one death in this life, so let that death be in the path of God."

Jalal nodded his agreement, along with the others.

"The Qur'an promises that once you perform your duty, as you will today, a life of eternal happiness awaits you in paradise. First, you must put your trust in Allah. With Allah guiding you, no one can vanquish you."

The tea arrived.

Nine cups were poured and passed around. Jalal took his tea and placed it on the carpet in front of him instead of drinking it. His stomach would not be still and he didn't trust his hands to hold the cup without shaking. What he wanted was to hear more from Sayyid.

Sayyid took a sip of his tea. "We must let the enemy know that the blood and the minds of Muslim men—of Muslim women and children— are not for sale," he said. "Their lives will not be taken without a fight. The leaders in Washington and London make war against us in our lands, using the apostate regimes of Egypt, Jordan, and Israel. No more. The blood you spill today will land on American soil and directly impact American lives. The blood of its citizens will be on the hands of its leaders. Only then will they think twice of the contempt they show us."

Jalal and the rest of the young martyrs hung on Sayyid's every word.

"This is a just and holy war," Sayyid continued. "The Qur'an states that we must fight those who neither believe in Allah nor the Last Day; those who do not forbid what Allah and His Messenger have forbidden, and those who do not embrace the religion of truth. I can see that each of you is brave and strong and committed to your duty. Remember as you go into battle, that martyrdom is not something that is given to you…it is something that is achieved through action. It is the individual warrior who is committed enough and devout enough to perform his own personal act of worship for Allah that will be rewarded in the end."

Sayyid looked each of them in the eye as he spoke, his voice rising slightly. "There is no god but God and Muhammad is his messenger."

The group repeated the phrase. *There is no god but God and Muhammad is his messenger.*

"Good."

Sayyid stood and the rest of the group followed suit. "Asad," he said, placing his hand on the bomb maker's shoulder, "fit these brave warriors with their vests so that we can send them on their sacred mission."

14

ON THE MORNING of September 11th, Gamal Hassan kissed his wife and newborn child goodbye for the last time, though he didn't know it.

He had driven to work at the accounting firm of Greene & Associates, then hopped the subway onto Manhattan Island. A previous meeting with the First National Bank of America had been rescheduled for that day. Arriving early, Gamal took the elevator up to the 96th floor of the North Tower of The World Trade Center and waited in the reception area. Phone records later showed that he made several calls just prior to the attacks, the last of which connected him to an unlisted phone number registered in Amman, Jordan.

The number in Amman was eventually traced back to a freight company—Cornwell Transport—which FBI investigators later learned was a CIA front operated with the help of British Intelligence. The call lasted 43 seconds and ended abruptly when American Airlines Flight 11 struck the North Tower.

Akil had been on assignment and had not received the call from his brother. He learned of his death days later after returning from the West Bank. The news came as a shock. Denial was followed by anger, then guilt. In the end, tears of sorrow washed it all away, though it had taken years to transpire.

Akil knew his brother's story was not unique; there were hundreds of stories just like Gamal's. Knowing that, however, did not ease the pain.

The Agency flew him back to the States so he could attend his brother's funeral. On the flight home, Akil listened to the voicemail his brother had left for him at the number in Amman.

Akil, pick up, it's Gamal. Where are you? Hannah and I have been talking and we both think...well, we both think you'd make a great godfather to Michael. You listening to this? A godfather! Look, call me soon so we can—

The message ended abruptly.

It was the last time he had heard his brother's voice.

Gamal had been the closest thing Akil had to a best friend growing up. Moving from their childhood home in Lebanon to the suburbs of Seattle had been difficult. The two of them struggled through the transition together and formed a unique bond in the process. His brother's death had been hard to take.

Akil dealt with the loss by drowning himself in work—fourteen, fifteen hour days spent at Langley combing analysis, cross-checking field intelligence from Waziristan and the Northwest Frontier, whatever he could do to keep himself occupied. Months after returning home he still found it difficult to visit his sister-in-law and nephew. Hannah and Michael were a painful reminder of what he had lost. Despite this, he dropped by to see them at least once a week.

Six months later Akil requested to be reassigned overseas. He regretted the decision later, but at the time he convinced himself he needed to focus on his career. What he really wanted was to escape the memory of his brother's death.

Returning home years later, after being fired from the Agency, Akil cautiously began to make amends to his sister-in-law. For her part, Hannah welcomed him home and encouraged him to get involved in Michael's life. The boy needed a father figure, she told him. Who better than his uncle.

Akil had been willing to try, but the speed with which Michael had adopted him as a surrogate father frightened him. And for good reason. At the time he had hoped to be reinstated, which meant he would have to leave to go overseas again. How could he explain to Michael that one day he would be gone, for a year or two, maybe longer? Maybe forever, like his father. There was always that risk. How could he do that to the child?

Over time, however, the prospect of getting his old job back faded and he began to feel more at ease in assuming a larger role in his nephew's life.

Then Bill Graham had come calling.

15

AKIL ENTERED CIA headquarters with a renewed sense of purpose. Strolling across the checkered granite floor—his head held high—he savored his return from exile. He was finally back where he belonged.

He gave his information to the security officer at the front desk. "I'm expected," he said.

The security guard checked Akil's name against the list on his monitor, then handed Akil a laminated visitor's pass. "Here you go, Mr. Hassan," he said. "If you'll just proceed through the security gate on your left."

On the other side of the security gate, Akil spotted the young man who had tailed him after his lecture. Akil gave him a genial nod of the head.

"I've been instructed to escort you upstairs to Bill Graham's office," the young man told him.

Akil had to laugh. Sending the kid to ferry him upstairs was vintage Bill Graham. "I'll follow this time if you don't mind," he said.

The young man led on without the hint of a smile. Akil could hardly blame him after the other night.

Bill's office was on the seventh floor, along with Marchetti's. On the way there they passed by The Ops Center—an enormous room laden with blue carpet and staffed 24 hours a day by officers tracking world events and, more specifically, the CIA operations surrounding them. Akil slowed his pace, feeling the urge to go inside and soak up the atmosphere. The itch to get back in the game had come back with a vengeance.

As they rounded the last corner, Akil could see Bill waiting by his office door. The kid saw him too and peeled away without a word and headed back downstairs to whatever menial task Bill had created for him.

"You're a son-of-a-bitch, you know that," Akil said.

"So I've been told," Bill replied, the hint of a smile forming at the edge of his lips.

They entered Bill's office. It was large, its sheer size masked only by the stacks of books and papers strewn about. Akil still remembered the old days when Bill had regularly used his beat-up Toyota sedan as an office, despite being Chief of Station. Now he was head of Operations. A bureaucrat.

How quickly things change, Akil thought.

Bill adjusted the floor-to-ceiling blinds so that no one could see in. "How's Hannah doing?" he asked.

"Good."

"And Michael?"

"He's growing fast," Akil said. "You wouldn't recognize him."

"They don't stay young for long."

"I'm catching the shuttle to New York this afternoon. Hannah is throwing a birthday party for him."

"I won't keep you long. Have a seat," Bill said, motioning to the leather couch. He grabbed a manila folder off his desk and removed several sheets of paper. He handed them to Akil. "Sign these."

"What's this?"

"Same stuff you signed when you first joined up. Contract. Liability waivers. Usual lawyer bullshit. HR has marked off where you need to sign and initial."

Akil flipped through the legalese briefly before giving up. There was no point; you needed a cryptologist to decipher most of it, and in the end you either signed or you didn't take the job.

"You might want to run another background check on me," Akil said, joking. "I could have joined forces with the other side while I was away."

"Already took care of it," Bill said, his delivery offering no clue as to whether or not he was joking.

Akil didn't ask if he was serious. Instead, he signed the papers while his former mentor rummaged through the quagmire of file folders on his desk.

Finally locating what he was looking for, Bill handed Akil a photograph. "Recognize him?"

Akil studied the picture. "No. Who is he?"

"Name is Nasir Khan. Pakistani. Jordanian authorities picked him up trying to cross into Syria last week."

"What do we know?"

"He's an al-Qaeda go-between that was headed for Damascus. From what he's told us there was some kind of terrorist council set to meet there. No names, unfortunately. They were planning to authorize a new operation."

"What kind of operation?"

"We don't know."

"Where?"

"Kahn was just the messenger. He doesn't know any of the essentials."

"Have you finished questioning him?"

"He's still being interrogated, but it's been four days and he's told us nothing new. The well's gone dry."

"And that's all we know?"

"We know he was sent to give al-Qaeda's blessing. Chances are he wasn't the only one they sent."

"So al-Qaeda is taking a back seat on this one?" Akil asked.

"Hard to say for sure. Could be Khan's a decoy. But yeah, on the surface, it looks like they're not in charge."

"Who's running the show then?"

"That's just one of the things we need to find out."

"And where are they planning to strike?"

"Where indeed," Bill said. He grabbed his pack of Marlboros off the coffee table. "I'm sending you back to Lebanon to nose around, see what you can find out. You still have contacts there, don't you?"

"Sure."

Bill lit a cigarette. You weren't supposed to smoke inside, but old habits were hard to break and no one had the balls to tell Bill he couldn't smoke in the sanctity of his own office.

"Could be something big, could be nothing," Bill said. "Everyone's still on edge because of Rome. Mossad has given—"

The phone on Bill's desk rang.

Akil could see the flashing red light through the low cloud cover of strewn paperwork. The red light meant it was urgent. Bill stepped out of his chair and picked up the phone.

"Graham here," he said tersely.

Akil sat on the edge of the couch and listened to Bill's end of the conversation.

When?...uh-huh...right. Where did it originate? Damascus? You're sure?... really!...okay, fine, fine...no, I'll get someone down to NCTC right away to coordinate. ...Yeah, I have it here on my screen now...could be connected, too early to say...that's right...okay, thanks.

Bill hung up the phone and stood rigid for a few seconds as he internalized the information he'd just received. Then he turned to Akil, his face grim.

"What is it?"

16

JALAL WATCHED AS Asad unpacked the suicide vests and laid them out on the floor one at a time. Each vest contained a series of metal pipes packed with explosives. They were wired together and surrounded with ball bearings and scraps of metal to maximize casualties.

Once Asad finished laying out the vests, he removed his jacket and threw it to the side. The bomb maker was missing his lower right arm. In its place was a crude prosthetic fitted with a two-pronged metal hook instead of a hand. It looked old. About halfway up the prosthetic duct tape had begun to peel away at the joint. Asad pointed the artificial limb at Jalal and ordered him to come over and stand next to him.

Jalal hesitated, his stomach churning. Then he did as he was instructed. He would be first.

17

SAYYID HAD TAKEN refuge in the garage at the back of the house while Asad fitted the vests. His thoughts were weighing heavy on him. It was not the first time he had sent young martyrs to their death, and though he understood the necessity of it, he wished there was another way.

His people had tried to live in peace. They had tried fighting the Israelis too, and yet the land the Jews had stolen from them remained occupied. The country the Palestinians longed for was denied them. Everyone knew the peace process was a farce. The Jews would give the Palestinians as little land and freedom as the world would allow.

No. Action was the only way. Millions of people's lives were relying on him.

Two days ago he had received the email from Damascus giving him permission to proceed. Everything in New York had already been organized: the martyrs had been hand-picked, supplies had been gathered, targets chosen. The operation in its entirety had been in the works for more than two years. Dozens of people had already risked their lives to help guarantee its success, and more would risk their lives in the following days. As he prepared to take the first crucial step, Sayyid tried not to think of all the things that could go wrong. Whatever happened, he would stick to the plan. He couldn't afford to fail his people.

Asad entered the garage and walked over to Sayyid.

"Are they ready?" Sayyid asked.

"They are almost finished making the recordings," Asad replied.

The young men would record a declaration on videotape explaining why they had chosen the path of martyrdom. The confessions were, for the most part, unscripted. He had presided over them many times and knew that most martyrs believed their decision would make a difference. He hoped to God this time they were right. The responsibility for that would, of course, rest on his shoulders. On how he carried out the rest of his plan.

"The clothes? You made sure they fit?" he asked Asad.

"Yes. Don't worry."

Hard lessons had been learned at the hands of the Israelis and Sayyid was determined that they be put to good use here in America. Once the tapes were finished being made the young martyrs would change their clothes. He had chosen individual outfits that would help the young men blend in with their surroundings. Different targets required different looks, and attention to detail was the key to success.

Sayyid turned and faced the door leading back into the house. His voice became somber. "You see how they are, Asad?"

"What do you mean?"

"They're so eager to die."

"They are strong. Consider it a blessing."

"They're like lambs to the slaughter."

Asad did not respond.

"They seem to be of a single mind," Sayyid continued. "Their handlers have been very thorough."

Asad looked at his friend, concern showing on his face. "Many things in this world are not pleasant, but they are necessary, Sayyid. You know this. You have said it yourself many times."

"Yes," Sayyid said, staring at a vacant corner of the garage. "And it's true."

"Especially in war. Their task is not easy. There is no room for doubt."

"Of course. I know that."

"So why are you talking like this?" Asad asked.

"I wish it could be different. That's all."

"But it is not."

"No, it isn't."

"Their reward will be great," Asad said. "They will end this day in Paradise."

Sayyid gave a thin smile. "You're right, my friend. You're right."

"You are too sentimental sometimes."

"Don't worry," Sayyid said, clasping his hand on Asad's shoulder. "I am as determined as ever. Especially now, when we are so close. These young men are going to help us achieve our goal. Their sacrifice will not be for nothing. I promise you that."

18

SAYYID ENTERED THE living room with Asad and took another look at his martyrs. They had been chosen carefully and close attention had been paid to their individual needs and desires early on. Years of training and mental underpinning had completed the process. Like master craftsman, their handlers had molded them into warriors of God—true believers willing to lay down their lives when instructed. And though he detested some of the techniques, and much of the rhetoric employed by these men—these sheikhs and imams—Sayyid knew their methods were meant to ensure success.

"It's time," Sayyid announced. "You will leave the house one by one and approach your targets as we discussed earlier. The attacks must happen at nine-thirty. Together. We cannot give the Americans a chance to respond. Don't forget. Nine-thirty."

Asad stepped forward. "When you are in place, press the detonator three times and you will see your place in Paradise." Asad held up an extra detonator and demonstrated. "Three times to claim your reward."

"Jalal, you will be the first," Sayyid said. He took him by the arm and led him to the front door.

Jalal wore a large New York Giants football jersey underneath an oversized puff jacket which had been left unzipped. A large gold chain hung around his neck. At the front door, Sayyid stepped back and examined him from head to toe. "Excellent," he said after several seconds, "the clothes hide everything."

Jalal adjusted his jacket, suddenly self-conscious.

Sayyid placed his hands on Jalal's shoulders and looked into his eyes. "It has been an honor to have been with you today, Jalal," he told him. "Your Muslim brothers and sisters owe you a great debt of gratitude for what you are about to do. They will be by your side, as will Allah. Have faith, and you will triumph."

"*Shakran*," Jalal said.

"*Hamdulillah*," Sayyid replied.

"*Hamdulillah*."

With that blessing, Jalal exited the front of the house. There was a subway station close by and he'd been given directions and train fare, then told where to get off and what to do once he was in Manhattan.

Walking down the street, all alone, he was surprised at how heavy the bombs strapped to his chest were. The vest kept chaffing against his ribs, but he didn't try to adjust it. It would all be over soon. A couple of hours at most.

19

SOPHIE MARTIN SAT at her desk, inundated with paperwork. It had been almost fifteen years since she defended her thesis in International Studies at Johns Hopkins.

Has it really been that long?

She had mailed her application off to the Federal Bureau of Investigation that same day. The weeks that followed were anxious ones. Every morning she checked her mailbox for news—not of her grades—but of her application to the Bureau. She had made her decision to join the FBI after talking to a recruiter her freshman year. He made the job sound exciting, and more importantly, challenging. She never doubted her decision, despite her father's disapproval. He thought his little girl could do better. A career diplomat himself, he envisioned her working as an attaché, maybe becoming an ambassador one day—not a cop.

But every morning Sophie had gotten out of bed, gone downstairs and looked in her mailbox, undeterred. After several months without news, she began to worry that her application might have been lost. Or worse, rejected. Practical by nature, Sophie started to make contingency plans, crafting cover letters and tailoring her resume to fit different job opportunities. She did this half-heartedly until the morning she finally received the letter. It was printed on a single sheet of heavy-bond paper, the familiar blue and gold seal centered at the top.

She was so nervous she made her mother read the letter first. She needn't have been. She'd been accepted and was headed to Quantico. All she had to do was survive seventeen weeks of law enforcement training and physical abuse and she'd be an honest-to-god FBI agent.

A knock on Sophie's office door interrupted her reverie.

"Yes," Sophie said.

Jim Neville stuck his head through the doorway. "You wanted to see me?"

"Yeah," Sophie said. "You have that breakdown on Hamas' money laundering operation in Chicago?"

"Just dotting the I's and crossing the T's," he told her. "I'll have it to you by lunch."

"Alright, thanks."

Jim closed the door and carried on down the hall.

Sophie had been reading form a binder. She set it to the side and put her feet up on the desk.

Her first posting after Quantico had been Portland, Oregon. She'd kept her head down and worked hard, learning what she could from the senior agents. She still kept in touch with a few of them, the ones who didn't have a problem working with a woman.

In 1999 she was transferred to New York, the same year the FBI created its Counterterrorism Division. Sophie immediately wanted in, but she knew she wasn't ready. She took it upon herself to learn everything she could about counterterrorism techniques. For nearly a year she worked herself toward exhaustion, studying after work, signing up for internal FBI courses, getting up at 4 or 5 in the morning to prep for exams.

In March of 2001, she felt confident enough to apply for a transfer but was turned down. *No open positions at this time.* Then 9/11 happened and the CT Division was suddenly center stage and in desperate need of bodies. Two weeks later she was transferred.

Right away she began to put her training to good use. The hours were long and the work was endless, but she was happy.

Over the next decade, as many of her colleagues quit to go work in the private sector—often doubling their salaries in the process—Sophie stayed on and reaped her own rewards, if not in cash, then in mounting responsibility. The promotions came in a steady stream after that. She had earned every one, forsaking her personal life for her professional one. She couldn't remember the last date she'd been on. Her job had quietly consumed her life. But that anxious little girl who had checked the mail every morning to see if she'd been accepted to the Bureau had, over the years, risen to become a lead investigator inside the FBI's CT Division. And only weeks ago she'd been assigned to the National Counterterrorism Center in Washington, DC.

NCTC, as it was known, was the central clearinghouse for all intelligence gathered by the United States. Sixteen separate agencies fed their raw intelligence into it, including the NSA, CIA and Naval Intelligence. For Sophie, there was no better place to be, especially if you wanted to hunt down terrorists.

20

SOPHIE GRABBED THE stress ball off her desk and reached for the binder. Squeezing the ball in her left hand, she continued reading through that day's threat matrix. The daily brief listed the latest and most urgent threats facing the United States—both domestic and international—and was based on information gathered by NCTC's vast intelligence web. None of the threats listed today were categorized as imminent, so she moved on to the second binder: the SITREP.

SITREP stood for situation report. Every day the FBI's CT Division received hundreds of leads concerning potential terror threats. Many of these were attributable to everyday citizens reporting suspicious activity throughout the country. Much of the time—almost all the time, in fact—the leads turned out to be innocuous, usually the product of people's overactive imaginations. There were always the exceptions though, and the exceptions were what prevented attacks and led to arrests. Not paying attention to them could be deadly.

By the time the reports reached Sophie, each lead had been followed up with at least one phone call. Those leads that were not dismissed, were added to the SITREP and would eventually be checked out by an actual warm-blooded FBI agent or police officer assigned to the JTTF: Joint Terrorism Task Force.

Sophie started reading down the list.

There'd been a construction site burglary in Buffalo. Missing was an unspecified amount of dynamite, blasting caps, detonating cord and various power tools. She made a note to find out exactly how much dynamite was missing.

In Jersey City, men described as Arab-looking had been seen entering a house in the 8700 block of Smithwick. A neighbor claimed that the house had been vacant for weeks prior to the sighting, but Jersey police—conducting a drive-by—reported seeing nothing suspicious.

In Morocco, Doctor Abdul-Kadr Youssouf had attempted to board a British Airways flight out of Casablanca to New York via London, Heathrow. Having been placed on Homeland Security's no-fly list in 2008 for suspected ties to al-Qaeda, he was denied entry.

There were dozens of similar items, and Sophie kept going down the list until she had reviewed them all. Nothing screamed out for her immediate attention, so she got up and refilled her coffee mug. As she was doing this her office cell began to dance across the desk.

Bzzzzt. Bzzzzt. Bzzzzt.

The only time her office cell went off was when something was wrong. It didn't have a number you could call, per se. Instead, one of the techs had rigged it to NCTC's emergency alert system. Being a wireless device, it gave no details other than the time and date the alert had been posted. To access the classified information she needed to log on to a secure portal.

Putting her coffee down, Sophie returned to her desk. Her screen was flashing red. She hit the escape button and entered her security password, then waited.

A few seconds later a report from NSA filled her screen.

Codeword: ZARF

Email origin: Damascus, Syria. Intercepted: Menwith Hill (Echelon) 2037 Tuesday, November 24. Received: New York City, 1342 Tuesday, November 24. Recipient Identity: Unknown. Culled and translated: NSA (Carl Price), 0643 Thursday, November 26. Translation: NSA software systems.

Threat probability: Extremely high. Language patterns indicate coded message. Text follows...

21

BILL GRAHAM REACHED for his cigarettes. "That was Marchetti on the phone," he said, checking his monitor. "NSA just flagged an email that's got everybody bouncing off the walls. Says here the email originated in Damascus almost forty-eight hours ago and was sent to an "unidentified" in New York City."

"Your al-Qaeda go-between," Akil replied. "What was his name? He was headed to Damascus, right?"

"Nasir Khan. That's right. The initial impression from NSA is that this email is authorizing some sort of attack."

"Coincidence?" Akil asked, knowing Bill's default answer.

"No such thing."

"No such thing, exactly. So this terrorist council is for real."

"Looks that way." Bill used the mouse on his desk to scroll down. "Says here the attack is planned for today."

Akil was seated on the edge of the couch now. "That doesn't leave much time. Do we know the target?"

"No. Could be anywhere."

"Where was the email sent?"

"To a server in New York, but that doesn't tell us anything." Bill crushed out his cigarette in frustration. "If I can log in and check my email from half-way around the world, so can these sons-of-bitches. We have no way of knowing where they're going to strike. Or if the U.S. is even the target."

Bill found something new on his monitor and studied it carefully. "Feds are contacting the service provider looking for an address and ID on the recipient."

"I doubt they'll find anything," Akil said.

"It's a long shot, for sure." Bill turned off the monitor and walked around to the other side of his desk. "This is the FBI's ball to run with, not ours. But if it turns out to be the real thing—"

"Then we need to be prepared to cover our end."

"Look, I know you have plans. Michael's birthday…but I'd like you to head over to NCTC and hook up with whoever is running point on this. If the feds find something, I want to know about it."

"Sure, no problem," Akil said, hoping Hannah would understand. He'd have to make it up to Michael too, somehow, but this had always been the nature of the job. It's what made having a family so difficult.

"David Reeves is the new Director of National Intelligence over there," Bill said. "I'll call ahead and make sure he's expecting you."

Akil got up off the couch. "They're not going to be happy with me dropping in on them like this," he said, knowing that despite all the progress that had been made in the past decade concerning intelligence gathering, information sharing was still a work in progress. Every agency held on to its own precious bits and pieces—their secrets—for a reason. It wasn't a conspiracy, like some liked to think. It was just human nature. And, as with all information, it was leverage.

"So? Ingratiate yourself," Bill said. "Bite your tongue off if you have to, but make nice."

"No problem. You know me."

"That's what I'm worried about."

22

FOR OVER A year now Jalal had worked in the shipping and receiving department at Macy's. He had only applied for the job at the behest of the sheikh, and not without protest. What he really wanted to do was work alongside his Muslim brothers in the community. When he told the sheikh this, he'd been admonished and told not to question the will of God. All would be revealed in time.

The sheikh had always been true to his word, and because of this, Jalal agreed to take the job. This morning Sayyid had finally explained why he had been asked to work at the department store.

The irony of it made him smile.

Exiting the subway at 79th street, Jalal proceeded on foot to the staging grounds near 77th. On the way, he checked the time. It was almost 8:15. He was running late. He could see that security had been beefed up around the staging grounds. That was to be expected, but now that he had something to hide it unnerved him to see so many police officers. As an official Macy's employee and parade volunteer, he'd been given an official pass, which he hung around his neck to deflect suspicion. Under different circumstances, the pass would allow him to enter the cordoned off staging area. But passing through one of the many security checkpoints, with explosives strapped to his chest, was too risky. Fortunately, Sayyid had arranged another way in, a way that would avoid any possible search or pat-down.

Twenty feet ahead he noticed a police officer watching him with prying eyes. Jalal tried to ignore the officer and kept moving, but he felt as if the police officer could see right through his clothes, could tell what he was thinking, and wearing, just by looking at him. It wasn't actually possible—he knew that. It was just his fear speaking.

Sayyid had warned him and the others about this feeling. Ninety-nine percent of it is in your head, he'd told them. Jalal reminded himself to relax. I've never been stopped and searched before. Why should today be any different?

But today was different.

Tensions always peaked around the holidays, and he had Arab features. From experience, he knew his ethnicity was more than enough to arouse suspicion. He had often caught people staring at him on the subway. It was most noticeable after the Rome bombings—the looks ranging from fear, to distrust, to hatred. He took a deep breath and thought about what Sayyid had told him just before he left the house: *You belong in this city. It's your secret weapon. Use it.*

Sayyid was right. Jalal had lived his entire life in New York. He was different from the others. Unlike a Saudi or an Egyptian—or even a Brit—he belonged. He was an American. Better yet, he was a native New Yorker. It's one of the reasons he'd been chosen.

Jalal elected not to cross the street. Instead, he passed within a few feet of the officer. He had to will his legs forward, one step at a time, forcing himself not to avert his eyes. Growing up a New Yorker, his body language was distinctive. The police officer may not have consciously registered it, but it was Jalal's body language, more than anything else, that pegged him as a native. A friendly. He would have to do something else before the police officer would stop and question him. Being accused of racial profiling was not a good way to get yourself promoted in the ranks of the NYPD these days. And it wasn't yet a crime for an Arab-American to walk the street, minding his own business, especially one who looked more hip-hop wannabe than Arab extremist.

The police officer eventually turned and concentrated on someone else.

A short distance later Jalal ducked into an alleyway. It smelled of cat piss and compost. Amid the dumpsters was a fence blocking the entrance to a small courtyard. Jalal knelt down in front of it to tie his shoe, and to look for the man he was told would be waiting for him.

There was nobody there.

He untied and then re-tied his other shoe, wondering what to do. Then, out of the shadows, he heard an angry whisper: "You're late."

"*Ana asif*," Jalal replied. I'm sorry.

"We need to hurry. I have to get back," the man said as he removed a pair of wire cutters from his jacket. He nervously looked down the alley as he knelt down and began severing the metal links. He moved quickly from one to the next, cutting every second tie, the fence slowly curling away from itself.

Jalal saw now that half the links had already been cut before he'd arrived. It had been impossible to tell from a distance, and it meant less time being exposed in the alley.

After cutting the last tie, the man stood up and took another look down the alley. "C'mon, squeeze through," he said. "Hurry."

Jalal crawled through on his hands and knees. Three-quarters of the way through, he felt his jacket snag on the fencing. The man with the wire cutters cursed in Arabic, then leaned down and unhooked the fabric. "C'mon," he said.

Jalal made it through and brushed himself off while his accomplice patched the fence with several pieces of aluminum wire. "They won't notice anything unless they come up the alley and get nosy."

Jalal nodded as the man turned and hurried across the small courtyard and down a set of crumbling concrete steps.

Jalal followed.

The two of them entered a dusty basement that had cardboard boxes stacked up to the rafters. In the middle of the basement was a single box separated from the rest, its lid hanging open.

"Your costume is in there," the man said. "Get it on and get to your rally point before someone starts asking why you're late. Once you're dressed, go up these stairs." The man pointed to the end of the room. "The door up top opens onto the staging area. Good luck."

The man left before Jalal could thank him.

Walking over to the cardboard box, he peeled open the lid and peered inside. On top was an oversized green head made of foam. As he pulled it out the pointed crown of Lady Liberty sprang out in all directions.

23

MICHAEL HELD ONTO his mother's hand as they walked along Broadway, headed toward 72nd street. It was his birthday today and he'd asked to come see the Macy's Thanksgiving Day Parade. His mom had tried hard to talk him out of it at first, but Michael had insisted, knowing she wouldn't refuse him—not on his birthday. Now that they were finally here, he was awed by everything he saw around him. The parade hadn't even started yet, but he was completely absorbed, marveling at the buildings that reached up so high he could barely see their tops. If only he could find a way onto their roofs, he thought. With his head tilted back at an almost ninety-degree angle, he kept bumping into people's legs. He'd never seen so many people before. There were zillions of them—everywhere—moving in all directions.

Hannah kept her eyes open, looking for a spot they could watch the parade. The crowds had already formed though. She didn't mind. Manhattan was as beautiful as ever today—the air cold and crisp—and all around a festive mood. Thankfully, the storm clouds had cleared and the sun had come out.

She felt Michael's tiny fingers squeeze her hand. Looking down, she smiled at him. Still anxious about being in the city, she was determined to get through the day for Michael's sake. She owed it to him. She owed it to herself too.

Michael was just an infant when his father had died. She had avoided coming downtown after that, abandoning the city she had loved so much. The skyscrapers were just too much to bear. She had experienced the tragedy of that day from a distance, watching the drama unfold on television instead of in person. A frightened neighbor had called to tell her what was happening. Turning on the television she had watched in shock as the North Tower burned, a dark plume of smoke carrying across Manhattan. Her husband was an accountant, and though he didn't work in Manhattan, he often conducted business there. She was not an anxious person by nature, and she told herself that Gamal's office was nowhere near what was happening on television, but she called him anyway, just to put her mind at ease.

Calling Gamal's cell, she got no answer. She let the phone ring until the voice mail kicked in. Her breathing quickened along with her pulse. She left a message, then hung up and dialed again, her fingers trembling now.

Why isn't he answering?

She eventually called his work and was told that he was out of the office all morning seeing clients. Her imagination seized on the information and she felt weak, barely managing to thank the receptionist before hanging up the phone.

It was later that afternoon that her husband's boss showed up at their front door. He arrived with his wife and asked if Hannah had heard from Gamal.

No...no...please God!

She hadn't heard from her husband, she told them, her voice unsteady. They all sat down in the living room as her husband's boss explained that Gamal had rescheduled a meeting at the First National Bank of America for that morning. He explained that First National was located on the 96th floor of the North Tower in Manhattan—that everyone at the firm had been accounted for except Gamal.

Hannah had broken down in tears.

From that day on everything had changed, including her. She had never felt as secure or as confident as she had before the terrorists had struck. In the days that followed, pictures of Gamal had been posted and people from his accounting firm had trolled the streets hoping to hear news that he was still alive. But there was no news. No miracle.

Eventually, platitudes were offered along with condolences and flowers.

Gamal's brother, Akil, had returned from his job overseas shortly after. He'd been supportive in his own way, staying with them on and off for the first two months, helping take care of Michael, allowing Hannah time to grieve. He was restless most of the time though, and she often wondered if it had something to do with his work—the work he would never talk about. In the end, she wasn't surprised when he went back overseas. He couldn't get out of it, he'd told her. No one believed that. Still, he wrote often and sent money every month, even though she told him the insurance covered all their expenses. But Akil insisted and the checks kept arriving on a steady schedule.

Years passed.

During that time she'd made only a handful of trips into the city, avoiding crowds and never staying long. Today was the first time she had brought Michael. Akil—for whatever reason—had come back into their lives and stayed this time. It had been a blessing. Michael was growing up so quickly, and he needed a father figure in his life. She didn't ask Akil when he would leave again, but she knew he would, eventually. He seemed unfulfilled in his new job at the university. But let come what may, she thought. Some things were simply out of her control.

As Hannah searched for a place to watch the parade, cutting a path through the throng of people that flowed both ways along the crowded sidewalk, she felt Michael break free and start running away from her. A surge of panic erupted inside her as she rushed to catch up, trying not to lose sight of him in the crowd.

"Mom! Mom!"

A tiny gap had opened up by the barricade along Central Park West and Michael was rushing to go stake his claim to the spot. She almost stumbled and fell as she ran after him, the adrenaline making her legs unsteady. Catching up to him, she grabbed him forcefully by the shoulders, spinning him around. "Don't ever run away from me like that again," she told him.

She wasn't angry, she was scared, but when she saw Michael's face begin to quiver, she immediately regretted her outburst. Michael didn't understand what he'd done that was so wrong. Tears welled up in his eyes. Hannah got a hold of her emotions and knelt down on one knee. She gave him a kiss on the forehead and a big hug. "It's alright, honey," she said, soothing him with her voice. "You did great. We'll be able to see the entire parade from here!"

"I'm sorry," he said sheepishly, still shaken by his mother's reaction.

"Sweetie." She gave him a forgiving smile. "Just don't run away on me like that again, okay? You understand?"

"Okay," he said, nodding.

Michael's tears vanished as quickly as they had appeared. Soon the incident was forgotten and they settled in, waiting for the parade to reach them.

24

SOPHIE MARTIN PUNCHED her security code into the cipher-lock and entered NCTC's secure conference room. She had been inside the room more than a dozen times since being posted to the agency, and still she was fascinated by it. It was like something out of a Hollywood movie, all polished glitz and hi-tech wizardry. A dozen wireless mice sat on the conference room table waiting for computer screens to rise up from their hidden compartments. LED displays on the wall offered the time in cities all over the world while recessed lighting crowned the room, and overhead, projectors sat ready to deliver hi-def video feeds from the battlefield or the White House. It was the nation's intelligence nerve center, and it had been constructed to look and act the part.

The room was empty at the moment. Sophie took a seat next to the media screens that covered the far wall and reviewed her hastily written notes. Fully aware she was about to deliver the most important briefing of her career, she couldn't stop her feet from bouncing up and down on the carpet as she read over what she was going to say.

A few minutes later the door to the conference room swung open and Sophie turned quickly to see who it was, but it was only a tech checking that everything was set up for the meeting.

Glancing back at her notes, she took a drink of water and waited for the others to arrive. *Just stick to your analysis,* she told herself, *and everything will be fine. Don't tell them what they want to hear, tell them what you know and what you think it means.*

The invited guests and heads of department eventually filed in and took their seats, culminating with the Director of National Intelligence: David Reeves. Sophie's job was to brief him on this latest threat against America, a threat that appeared to be imminent. Her interpretation would help determine how credible the threat was and what actions would be taken by various government agencies. Taking action was a serious proposition; it would mean hundreds of millions of dollars in associated costs. Thousands of police officers and military personnel would be called up, transportation routes would be shut down, commerce would be disrupted, all hinging on what she had to say. That didn't even take into account the emotional toll on the national psyche or the political fall-out that would ensue. Taking action, more than anything else, was politically risky. She knew she had to put that out of her mind. She had a specific job to do and she intended to do it.

The DNI sat down at the head of the table and the room fell silent. Under normal circumstances, the DNI did not chair NCTC meetings, though he frequently sat in on them. Today was different, which told Sophie just how seriously the threat was being taken. People at the highest levels wanted to know what NCTC had as far as intelligence went, and she was going to be held accountable—at least partially—for what they heard.

"Okay everybody, let's get started," Reeves said. "NSA, good morning. CIA, good morning. White House, good morning."

The large screens at Sophie's end of the table provided live feeds from the separate agencies and the White House, including the National Security Advisor to the President. With the acknowledgment that the various video feeds were up and running, the meeting began.

"You've all seen the intercepted email by now," Reeves said. "NYPD and additional law enforcement agencies have been alerted and made aware of the potential threat. The FBI has called in extra agents and is following up all possible leads in cooperation with JTTF. At this stage, all the preliminary safety measures have been taken. What we need to do now is determine if the threat is credible enough to take additional action. To that end, we have FBI special agent Sophie Martin here. She's going to brief us on the contents of the email and explain what it is we're dealing with. Sophie."

Individual video screens—hidden inside the conference table—rose without a sound. Sophie stood and approached a much larger screen set against the wall. Displayed on the screens was the text of what had quickly become known as The Damascus Letter.

From: Dhul Fiqar
Sent: Tuesday, November 24, 8:29 PM
To: 863175297
Subject: Good News

It is in your hands now.

Our cousins have made everything possible. They wish you the best in your endeavors.

Have a Happy Thanksgiving. Spread the word of Allah.
Your gifts will arrive soon.

AA

"Thank you, Director Reeves," Sophie said. "Through my own analysis and in conjunction with—"

Before Sophie had a chance to finish her first sentence an aide entered the room, walked over to Reeves, and whispered in his ear. The DNI stood. "Excuse the interruption, Ms. Martin. This will just take a second," he said.

Reeves approached the conference room door and exited.

Sophie didn't like to be interrupted and wondered who or what could be important enough to disrupt a meeting like this. Were they already too late? She didn't want to think about that. Like others in this room, she had witnessed first hand what terrorists had done at home and abroad. In Madrid, she had sifted her way through the toppled concrete, much of it spattered with blood, collecting the personal effects of victims. The items, scattered throughout the blast zone, had been cataloged as evidence: a wallet, a cell phone, a make-up compact. Years afterward, what she remembered most—what haunted her—was not the blood or the minutiae, but the wailing of mourners held back beyond the barricade as their husbands and wives and children were put into body bags.

Reeves re-entered the room accompanied by a man Sophie didn't recognize.

"Everybody, this is Akil Hassan, Central Intelligence," Reeves said. "He'll be sitting in. Sophie, please continue." The Director sat back down while Akil took a seat on a bench along the room's periphery.

"As I was saying," Sophie continued, "through my own study, and in conjunction with NSA and NCTC analysts, we have come to a consensus on what we're dealing with here. I will go through the text from top to bottom and explain."

Sophie stole a glance at the man who had interrupted her by arriving late. He was tall and handsome and had a casual elegance about him. Was it genuine or merely an affectation? she wondered. And what was he doing here anyway? Typical CIA, she decided, sticking its nose where it didn't belong. Besides, NCTC was already feeding everything to the Central Intelligence Agency across the secure network.

Almost everything.

"The email, encrypted and composed in Arabic, was sent two days ago from Damascus," Sophie said, making eye contact around the conference room table as she spoke. "The letter was intercepted by satellite and collected at Menwith Hill. It was then forwarded to NSA headquarters where it was flagged and brought to our attention."

She picked up a laser pointer sitting on the desk in front of her and used it to focus attention on the opening words of the email.

"The recipient of the email is currently unknown," she said. "The sender's name is recorded as *Dhul Fiqar*. We are almost positive this is an alias, but we're running the name through our databases just to be sure. The name itself is significant in that it means *The Prophet's Sword*. The first line of the email states: *It is in your hands*. Being given the Sword of the Prophet, metaphorically speaking, is tantamount to receiving permission to fight on behalf of the Prophet and the Nation of Islam. In this case, we believe whoever sent the message is giving permission for the recipient to carry out an attack.

"The email is composed in such a way that many interpretations are possible," Sophie explained. "This is not an accident. It was constructed to deliver a message, a message that would be clear to the recipient and deliberately vague for anyone else who might get their hands on it. But we can still determine a great deal from the letter's contents."

Sophie pointed to words further down on the screen.

Our cousins have made everything possible.

"We think that someone, most likely the terrorist network in question, has made possible the attack by acquiring materials or by gaining authorization to conduct the operation on American soil. As you know, these organizations are often strengthened by bonds of kinship. That used to mean blood relations. These days, more often than not, that means like-minded terrorist organizations operating under a loose coalition such as al-Qaeda or ISIS. *Cousins* could refer to the network's leadership or some of its affiliate organizations. There's no way to tell for sure.

"It is the three sentences that follow that are most significant," Sophie said, pointing once again at the words on the screen.

They wish you the best in your endeavors.
Have a Happy Thanksgiving. Spread the word of Allah.

"We all agree that *endeavors* refers to a forthcoming attempt to carry out an attack. The specific reference to *Thanksgiving* denotes the day the attack will be carried out. Significantly, these two lines are followed by the order to *Spread the word of Allah*. Terrorists often refer to attacks against their non-Muslim enemies as spreading the word of Allah.

"The next line: *Your gifts will arrive soon.* We think this alludes to the promise of Paradise for the martyrs who will die in the process of carrying out these attacks."

Sophie paused to take a sip of water before carrying on.

"Finally, the letter is signed with the initials *AA*. This could be the actual initials of the sender, someone such as Abd Al Aziz Awda of Palestinian Islamic Jihad or another such known enemy. We are compiling a list of all known subjects with those initials and cross-referencing information we have on their known whereabouts.

"However, the second, and I believe the more likely scenario, is that the letters represent a common phrase among Muslims. *Allahu Akbar*. The phrase can be used in a multitude of situations from expressing happiness or approval to use in Islamic prayer. It is also a common battle cry: God is Great."

Sophie took a second to look straight into the camera that fed her image to NSA and the White House. "There are no absolutes, I'm afraid," she said. "The summary I've just given you constitutes the best educated guess of analysts from three different intelligence agencies, all with years of experience. There is no specific part of the letter we can point to and say: this is definitive—this is authorizing a terrorist cell in America to carry out an attack. Taken as a whole, however, all indicators point to exactly that—a thinly veiled message supporting an attack against America on Thanksgiving Day. Today."

Sophie turned toward DNI Reeves. She was about to put her career on the line because she believed in her training and in what her gut was telling her. Her instinct for self-preservation told her to tone down her message, but she brushed the impulse aside. "In my opinion, sir," Sophie said, "this letter indicates that we are under imminent threat of attack. Further action should be taken immediately. If we wait, it could be too late. It may already be too late."

25

Akil's first impressions of Sophie Martin were positive. She was smart, articulate and well schooled in her area of expertise. A pro, from what he could see so far. She was also disarmingly attractive. The latter wasn't the kind of thing you missed in a room full of suits.

When the DNI had introduced him to the room, Akil had made eye contact with her. Her eyes, ocean green and full of piercing intensity, were intimidating on first glance. Fortunately, the government had spent a great deal of money training him to hide such reactions from people. Maybe she'd received some of that training herself, he thought, but just a taste of it. Not enough. The look of indifference she gave him was a solid effort, but he could see she was annoyed at him for interrupting her briefing. She was also wondering who he was, gauging whether or not she had to worry about him, politically. It wasn't her fault. People were hard-wired to give away far too much through their facial expressions and body language. It took a serious amount of discipline and effort to conceal the truth that was aching to get out of your every pore. Poker players knew all about that, the good ones anyway.

It couldn't have been easy working her way up the ladder, with looks like hers, he thought. She obviously had the smarts, but some men still had a problem with women in positions of authority. The dynamic just wasn't compatible. It was that buried DNA from millennia ago that tripped some men up. You had to fight it, but most didn't bother, and that made life for a woman like Sophie Martin harder than it should be. The question was: had it made her bitter and hard to work with?

Whatever the case, she had done a good job interpreting the letter, at least as he saw it. As for thinking the attack was going to be perpetrated on American soil, it was an educated guess, he supposed, and one that was hard to argue with. His opinion differed from hers on one or two small details, but the core of her analysis seemed spot on. The country was in serious peril.

She had guts too. Telling DNI Reeves to take immediate action was not the politically shrewd play here. He couldn't help admiring her for that. He tried to imagine what it must be like to stand in a room like this and speak your mind, the DNI and the NSC advisor hanging on your every word. Under that much pressure, she had gone and told them exactly what they didn't want to hear—that there was an imminent threat of attack against the United States and they needed to do something about it right now.

Waking a nation to the very real possibility that another large-scale terrorist attack was imminent presented the worst kind of Catch-22. If the attack didn't happen, then you were the one who cried wolf, scared a nation, and cost it hundreds of millions of dollars. And if it did happen? Well, shit, why didn't you do more?

It was a potential career killer.

"I don't think we should overreact here," said Calvin Bennett, the President's National Security Advisor. "The letter is inconclusive, at best. If we start mobilizing our infrastructure and we're wrong—"

"With all due respect, sir," Sophie interrupted. "The language in this letter has been intentionally designed to appear ambiguous. The enemy wants us to hesitate, but the inherent message is clear. As I tried to explain—"

"That's all fine and good to say, Ms. Martin, but we're talking about hundreds of millions of dollars in associated costs. We're talking about the American people's sense of security being shattered the moment we start shutting down transportation networks, bridges—ordering the National Guard into the streets armed with assault rifles. If we cry wolf now and we're wrong, there'll be a backlash. Are you prepared to risk your career on a hunch?"

Akil watched as Sophie Martin looked over at DNI Reeves. The Director remained tight-lipped.

She was on her own.

Sophie stared back into the camera. "You're right, Mr. Bennett. Our analysis is based on an educated guess. If it were definitive, we wouldn't be having this conversation at all. But erring on the side of caution is the most prudent course of action considering the number of indicators pointing to an imminent threat of attack. Not tomorrow. Not next week. But today. If we wait and do nothing, as you seem to be suggesting, and we're wrong, what will *that* do to the people's sense of security? What then? The answer to your question is yes, I'm willing to take the risk if it means saving hundreds, if not thousands, of lives."

26

WHEN HANNAH WAS a little girl her mother and father had made the Macy's Thanksgiving Day Parade an annual event. After marrying Gamal she had made a point of introducing him to the time-honored tradition. Seeing the parade for the first time, Gamal had told her that what he liked most was its grandeur. It was like nothing he'd ever seen—the huge balloons, the sheer number of people. But since his death, Hannah had not been back. Couldn't go back.

Now, seeing Michael mesmerized by all the colorful characters, it brought tears to her eyes. Michael had missed out on so much because of her. In a lot of ways, it was the return of Akil that had given her renewed hope. With his help, she had gained the confidence to begin rebuilding her old life. Progress had been slow, but steady. The fact that she was standing with her son in a massive crowd of people—in the heart of the city—was testament to that. She was beginning to trust the world again. Finally.

Hannah watched Michael's eyes light up at the sight of a fifty-foot Snoopy floating above their heads. He craned his head back to take in the spectacle. He was having so much fun he hadn't even mentioned his birthday party. With Akil's help, everything had been organized, right down to the balloons and chocolate cake. For months Michael had been asking for a new hockey stick, and Akil had promised to see what he could do. He had phoned yesterday to tell her that he'd gotten the stick, a Nike-Bauer composite. He'd even managed to get a couple of the Washington Capitals to sign it.

How had he managed that?

It didn't matter. Michael would be so excited. She could already see the look on his face.

Michael pulled at her coat, pointing down the parade route. "Mom! Look!"

"What is it, honey?" she asked. She put her hand on Michael's shoulder and looked to see what he was so excited about.

"Liberty statue!"

About seventy yards down the parade route she could see a costumed figure dressed as the Statue of Liberty. She smiled at Michael's reaction. Akil had taken Michael to go see the Statue of Liberty in September. It was all Michael could talk about for a week, the Liberty Statue and the hot dogs he and Akil had shared on the ferry ride over.

"You'll have to tell your uncle Akil," Hannah said.

Michael looked up and gave her a large, toothy grin.

27

SOPHIE MARTIN'S ADVICE to take immediate action had been approved by a narrow margin. Now DNI Reeves and other agency heads would convene and decide on exactly what to do. Their task was to try and prevent the attack from happening or, at the very least, mitigate any damage that might result. But without knowing who was involved or when or where the attack was planned, their job was all but impossible.

DNI Reeves and Sophie Martin walked over to Akil. He stood and shook Reeves' hand. "Sir."

"This is Sophie Martin," Reeves said.

Akil looked her in the eyes and gave her a firm handshake. "Nice work on the analysis."

"Thanks."

Her response was faintly dismissive.

"Sophie is going to lead the investigation on behalf of NCTC. I've told her that Bill Graham personally asked for you to be involved and that I have no objections," Reeves said. "In fact, I think it's a great idea. We're all on the same side, it's about time we started working more closely together. I'll let her fill you in on where we're at. Right now I have to go brief the President."

"Thank you, sir," Akil said.

"Good luck," Reeves told the two of them as he turned and hurried away.

Sophie kept her eyes squarely on Akil. "This is a domestic matter at the moment," she told him bluntly.

"For now."

"You have any relevant information that might help aid the investigation?"

Akil gave an amused laugh.

"What? I'm serious."

He didn't doubt that for a minute. "You're a real charmer, you know that," he said, wondering if he should tell her about Nasir Khan, the al-Qaeda go-between the Jordanians had picked up trying to enter into Syria. They already had the intercepted email though; Khan at this point was incidental.

"I want us to be clear," Sophie said.

"About what?"

"About our roles here."

"Okay," he said, his tone sharpening. "Let's talk about roles. If this threat turns out to be real, we both know where it's going to lead. It's going to lead overseas. And that, Miss Martin, is where the CIA operates." Akil paused, then continued in a more congenial tone. "Until then, I'm just here to stay up-to-date. And to help. As you see fit, of course."

She gave him an icy stare. "I don't like people looking over my shoulder while I do my job."

He smiled at that. "You don't have much choice, do you?"

"No. I don't. Just remember who's in charge."

"I think you've made yourself quite clear on that point."

"Good."

"Look," Akil said, taking a quick look around the room. It was almost empty now. "I'm not here to step on your toes. My boss just wants to be prepared. It's as simple as that."

"It's never as simple as that and you know it."

"Maybe," he said, shrugging his shoulders, "but we both have a job to do, and no amount of bickering over turf is going to change that."

She began to say something, then thought better of it.

"Why don't you show me around," Akil suggested.

Sophie headed for the exit and he followed. On the other side of the conference room door was NCTC's operations center—better known as the bullpen—an open area where analysts and agency liaisons did their work. It was a generous space with high ceilings and glass-partitioned offices lining the perimeter. It felt a bit like an overcrowded newsroom with desks and computers crammed together, agents collecting and following up various leads. At the CIA they didn't have the luxury of open spaces like this. It was more institutional: thousands of rooms with locked doors. In many ways, the Agency's infrastructure was a remnant of the cold war, while this place had been conceived and constructed with a 21st Century mindset. To Akil, it looked and felt the way an intelligence center should—integrated, energetic, and adaptable. Unfortunately, it was just one more in a long succession of intelligence gathering agencies with limited power. NCTC was touted as being different, of course. It didn't run operations like the CIA. Instead, it had been designed so that each of the sixteen agencies that made up the nation's intelligence community could share their information with one another. NCTC was meant to be the cog at the center of the intelligence wheel. But that's how good operations got blown. That's how intelligence leaked out. You could share—had to share, sure—but only up to a point.

Sophie stopped at an outcropping of desks and turned to confront him. She had fire in her eyes again. She obviously wasn't done marking her territory.

"I want whatever information comes in, from whatever sources the Agency has. We work together or we don't work at all."

"Fair enough," he said.

She stared at him for a long beat, judging his response. "Everything," she insisted.

There was no point splitting hairs at this point.

"Agreed," he said.

28

JALAL MARCHED DOWN the middle of Central Park West dressed as Lady Liberty. He was sandwiched between the McPherson High School Buccaneers Marching Band and the Miss USA Float.

The band was giving him a headache. He was tired of listening to the same three tunes played over and over. Despite this, he continued to wave to the crowd, going so far as to smile as he did so, though no one could see him.

There were cops all over the place, more than in the morning. The suit had been an inspired touch, he had to admit, but it was proving cumbersome. He was having difficulty seeing out of the rectangular mesh opening that was built into the costume's head. Sweat was trickling down into his eyes—stinging them—and there was nothing he could do about it; taking off the costume's oversized head wasn't an option.

It must be close to nine-thirty, he thought. He looked around, trying to figure out where he was. He felt the bombs strapped to his chest shift beneath the costume. Then someone in the crowd, no more than five feet to his left, toggled an air horn in his ear. He winced, his head feeling as if it were going to crack open.

Staggering forward to get away from a second blast, he noticed the big white balloon he'd been using as a marker slowly begin to turn.

Just in time, he thought.

Columbus Circle.

The cameras would be filming here, and both sides of the street were packed seven or eight deep with people watching the parade. Through the nylon mesh of his costume, they seemed hazy and distant. Still, he could make out children and their parents crammed together, clapping and smiling, enjoying themselves. It made him think of his own parents. He wondered where they were right now. His father had taken them on picnics every summer when he'd been in primary school. The parks had always been full of people in the summer, and he suddenly felt sorry for all the people watching the parade along the side of the road. Not because he was going to kill them, but because they were *kafir*. Non-believers. They were damned no matter what he did. It was the statement their deaths would make that would give their lives meaning. Today was a declaration that the Islamic world was strong and that it would no longer stand by and be denigrated by Israel and the West.

Gripping the detonator in his hand, he placed his thumb over the trigger, then quickened his pace, hoping to get as close as possible to the marching band before he detonated the bombs.

Sayyid had told them to maximize casualties if possible, and that's what he intended to do. His heartbeat hammered away in his ears as he prayed under his breath. Death is life, he repeated to himself, tears filling his eyes. Barely able to see, he kept moving forward, waving at the crowd as he went.

What happened next took him by surprise. He had bumped into something or someone.

Stumbling backwards, he heard one of the band members yell at him: "Watch where you're going." He wanted to do it now, right now, but the detonator had slipped from his hand in the commotion. It was dangling inside the suit. He cursed himself for being so careless.

Stopping in the middle of the street, he shook his arm in the air, frantically trying to grab hold of the detonator. He needed to get hold of it and push the button. Three times, Jalal reminded himself. Three times quickly and he would see his place in Paradise.

As his left arm thrashed about, there was no longer any noise. The crowd. The band. They had disappeared. He was alone with Allah now.

Finally, he got hold of the detonator.

29

MICHAEL YELLED OVER the noise of the marching band, asking Hannah to take a picture of the Liberty Statue.

Hannah grabbed her camera and turned it on. The screen on the back lit up with a sing-song she could barely detect. She lifted the camera and pointed it down the street, aiming past the last of the marching band. She focused on the Statue of Liberty and snapped a photo.

"Let's see, let's see." Michael's arm was outstretched. Hannah looked at the picture first. It wasn't very good, she thought. Too far away. She would take another one when the costumed figure got closer to them. For now, she bent down and showed the picture to Michael.

"We'll take another one, okay?" she suggested.

Michael liked the idea and said so.

Hannah stood up and prepared to take another photo. The parade was moving ahead at a steady pace and the street was packed on both sides with eager spectators. They were lucky to have found the spot they did.

She held the camera above her head and used the display screen to center the image. Just when she had it perfect the costumed figure suddenly lurched forward and bumped into one of the band members. A tuba player. The crowd roared with laughter and Hannah wondered if it had been done on purpose or if it was an honest mistake.

She followed the commotion from behind the camera's tiny digital display and waited. Finally, the person inside the costume stood still. He was close enough now that she could get a full frame picture if she zoomed in.

She took the shot, then knelt down again and showed it to Michael.

"One more," Michael said excitedly.

Hannah stood up and prepared to take another photo, but never got the chance.

30

THE EXPLOSION CAME without warning, the blast echoing down Central Park West all the way to Columbus Circle and the Time Warner Center. Those closest to the blast were eviscerated by the sheer force of it. Others were hammered unconscious by the concussion wave driving outward from the point of detonation, knocking them to the ground like bowling pins. Others were struck by shrapnel, their screams mingling with the sound of shattered glass falling onto the pavement from above.

People stampeded in every direction. Dozens, who had survived the blast, were trampled under foot. Those who were able, moved away from the epicenter, leaving only the dead and wounded behind. Television cameras recorded the aftermath, most of the images too graphic to broadcast. Above, helicopters circled like vultures.

A small crater was visible now, blood pooling at its edges.

31

INSIDE NCTC'S BULLPEN, Akil focused on the dozen different plasma screens that lined its two-story facade. The televisions were of varying size, displaying everything from air traffic control grids to various news outlets to live feeds from Iraq and Afghanistan. Dead center was a large projection screen. At the moment it was showing black and white video from a Predator drone over Afghanistan. The drone was tracking Taliban militants walking down a country road. They were using innocent women and children as human shields against a possible drone strike. An old tactic, Akil thought, but effective.

He shifted his gaze to one of the small screens in the bottom right corner that was tuned to the Arab Al Jazeera. The feed came out of Doha, Qatar, and the channel was much better than most American journalists liked to admit. It also had more integrity than at least one domestic news network Akil could no longer bring himself to watch.

Sophie walked over and stood beside him. "At the moment we're tracing the email addresses linked to the intercept," she said. "We're talking to the ISP providers in New York and Damascus. Unfortunately, we don't have much to go on at the moment. The Syrian government—"

Sophie stopped abruptly.

The large projection screen had been switched to CNN. The news channel had gone live to New York and was showing a wide angled shot of the crater that had been blown into the middle of Central Park West. The scene was chaotic. There looked to be forty or fifty bodies strewn around the crater. A camera zoomed in on a twisted brass tuba hanging precariously from a nearby streetlamp, its owner nowhere to be seen. The image was held for several seconds as the commentators reiterated what had happened only moments ago.

"We're too late," Sophie said.

Akil didn't respond. His mind was already racing. Where had Hannah and Michael been watching the parade? Had they said where they'd be? More than a million people attended the parade each year. The chances of Hannah and Michael being at that precise location when the bomb went off was incredibly small. Still, he felt a knot forming in his stomach.

Out of the corner of his eye, Akil spotted someone hurrying toward them. He motioned for Sophie to turn around.

"What do you have, Jim?" Sophie asked.

"We're getting reports that a suicide bomber just blew himself up at the El Al check-in counter at JFK," he told her. "The Parade has been hit as well. Looks like heavy casualties at both locations."

"I want the subway shut down, buses, everything," Sophie said. "Now!"

"Already done," Jim said.

Akil stared at the dozen different news channels on display. "They're not done. There's more of them out there," he said.

"We don't know that for sure," Sophie replied.

But another agent stood up, as if on cue, and reported that an NYPD officer had just shot two males at Grand Central. "Still waiting for more information," he said. "No word on whether the men were armed with explosives or not."

Then someone else stood up. "We've got a report of a bomb going off at an Army recruiting center out in Jersey City."

Something about the recruiting station had caught Sophie's attention. Akil could see it on her face. "What is it?"

Sophie looked at Jim. "This morning, in the SITREP. There was a report of Arab men entering a vacant house in Jersey. Didn't look like anything at the time."

"Yeah, I remember," Jim said.

"Find out if one of our agents made it out there. If not, I want that place secured. Maybe we'll catch a break."

32

To win the war they were going to need as many holy warriors as they could find. The martyr videos were an important part of that effort. It's why Sayyid had insisted on having them made.

Still photos would be extracted from the videos and posters would be printed up showing the faces of the young men who had sacrificed themselves today. To help bolster recruitment, the faces would be surrounded by the words of the Prophet, extolling the virtues of jihad. They would then be distributed all over the Arab world, and perhaps more importantly, in the West. It would be done in minutes and hours, not days or weeks or months. The most powerful tool—the most powerful weapon at their disposal—was the internet. It alone had transformed the Muslim struggle into a global jihad.

For Sayyid, the effort to recruit warriors throughout the Islamic world, and in the heart of the West itself, was not dissimilar to America's own recruitment efforts. The Americans' lurid commercials for the Army and Air Force depicted the soldier's life made glamorous and heroic. The low-budget videos and posters produced in Gaza and Islamabad were similar. Both were tailored for results. But the American message was a lie. Become a martyr to Islam? Everyone understood what that meant. The Americans still promised adventure, as if war were some kind of summer camp for grown-ups with hi-tech gadgets. A video game. A movie. The American soldiers dying at the hands of his Muslim brothers in Afghanistan and the

Middle East knew different. War was about sacrifice. It always had been and it always would be.

By now, the young men Sayyid had sent into battle had either completed their missions or failed in their attempts. He was confident that at least three of the young men—and with the will of God, all of them—had succeeded. The final tally rested in God's hands though, not his.

Sayyid checked the time on his watch. He had left the house in Jersey more than an hour ago and returned to the rented apartment in Queens to focus on the next stage of his plan. A few suicide attacks in the heart of New York would rattle the cages of the American public and inspire the Mujahideen, but it wouldn't significantly change the status quo. The Americans were a stubborn people who didn't admit to their errors easily. More had to be done before that would happen, and it would begin here, in this apartment.

Sayyid put on a pair of latex gloves and flipped open his laptop. As the computer booted up, he went to the bedroom closet and grabbed a large duffel bag and hauled it into the living room.

Digging inside the bag he removed a book on the Holland Tunnel that he'd purchased at a used book store in the Village. Its pages were well worn and dog-eared. Inside were some photos of the Holland Tunnel that he'd taken himself.

He placed the book, along with the photos, behind the tattered couch that had been pushed up against the far wall. Next, he took a series of rolled up maps and placed them back in the bedroom closet behind a panel he'd cut into the drywall. The rest of the items he placed around the apartment in select locations, pausing when he was done to inventory his progress.

Satisfied, he sat down in front of his computer and logged onto one of the more radical Islamic websites that proliferated the web. He entered the site's chat room using the handle ALI599. He had been posting on the site for the past day and a half, inciting others to join the global jihad.

It was the duty of all Muslim men to fight the enemies of Islam. Especially America, he wrote. Many who replied to his posts vehemently agreed with his views. Others argued for moderation. The idea had been to get noticed and he was pleased to see how fast the thread of comments had grown. There were over three hundred now. This would be his final post, and it would send shockwaves through the Muslim online community. It would also capture the attention of those outside of it, those who were not necessarily Muslim or radical, but who watched with particular interest. This was his true audience. He was sending them an invitation.

Sayyid typed the message, reviewed it, then hit enter. After today there would be no more ALI599.

My brothers. Praise be to Allah for the attacks of today. I bring good news. You have not seen the last of these attacks. As long as the United States supports Israel's domination of the Palestinian people, the citizens of New York will continue to suffer by my hand and those of my Mujahideen. May God's blessing be upon you. AA.

He left the website without delay, then logged into his Gmail account. Once in, he created a new email and attached a video clip he'd prepared with the help of Jalal. Because no one wanted to listen to a masked man preach, Jalal had agreed to deliver Sayyid's message to the American people himself. In doing so, Jalal would provide a human face for Sayyid's message and preserve the Palestinian's anonymity at the same time. In the days to come Sayyid would be just another ostracized Muslim suffering the predictable backlash of a nation under siege.

Having addressed the email to fifteen preselected media outlets and internet portals, Sayyid's message would be posted online within the hour. Al-Jazeera and al-Arabiya would broadcast the tape throughout the Arab world. An edited version would air on the major networks in the US and Europe. The internet would do the rest.

Sayyid closed the laptop and left it on the kitchen table.

Returning to the duffel bag, he pulled out five small explosive devices he'd purchased through a contact outside of Toronto. The number of Muslim brothers who wanted to participate in the jihad was growing, yet some still insisted on making a profit. That could not be avoided; not everyone was as committed to the cause as he was. He had initially asked Asad to build the bombs himself, but his friend claimed he didn't have the expertise required for what Sayyid wanted. His artistry was crude and efficient, but it lacked subtlety.

In the end, they had contracted the job out. Asad acted as the go-between. During the negotiations, it was agreed that the explosive devices would be delivered to a specific location inside the U.S. for an additional fee. This additional fee had proved higher than the original cost of the explosives—much higher, in fact—but Sayyid had not hesitated in accepting the terms. Avoiding the risk of being caught crossing the border with explosives was worth ten times what he'd paid. His mission was too important to allow that to happen. He knew that once the devices were in the U.S. he would have no problems transporting them across state lines.

The explosive devices were phosphorus-based and had been designed to kill, not necessarily destroy. That was important, and he hoped that the money he had paid had not been wasted.

One at a time, he placed the modified explosives around the room and began linking them together. As he did this he checked the clock, wondering how much time he had before his guests arrived.

33

"It's Rome all over again," Sophie said as she logged into her computer.

"The email that alerted us, that's a new twist. I don't like it," Akil replied. "At this point, we don't know if the bombers themselves were domestic or foreign, but we know where the email originated from, and it wasn't some misguided kid in Brooklyn who sent it."

"No, it wasn't," Sophie agreed.

They sat across from one another in the middle of NCTC's bullpen. At the moment they didn't have much to go on, but that would hopefully change soon. It was in the hours immediately following an attack, when the energies of a dozen agencies were powered up and focused on a solitary objective, that the most valuable intelligence was collected and brought to light. If they were lucky a picture would begin to form and those responsible would be identified quickly. No matter how much someone tried to cover their tracks or attempted to commit the perfect crime, there was always a trail. The Damascus Letter was the first clue. They just had to keep digging in order to uncover the rest.

To keep abreast of the information pouring into NCTC, Sophie concentrated on dual monitors, switching from one screen to the next, looking for any fragment of information that would begin to connect the dots and tell them who exactly they were looking for.

Her wrists were getting sore from working the keyboard and mouse when she spotted something from the FBI's Carnivore system. Carnivore monitored internet traffic inside the U.S. and around the world. Analogous to the old-world wiretapping that had netted countless fugitives in the FBI's heyday, Carnivore tapped directly into the internet by accessing the hardware used by internet service providers. Using proprietary software and a pre-determined set of criteria, agents could sniff out whatever internet traffic they were interested in while their colleagues monitored web-posts in real-time. Only moments ago an agent attached to the program had posted a security alert regarding a radical Islamist website: *www.divinerevelation. net.*

Sophie immediately opened the file and read the report. Its connection to The Damascus Letter appeared obvious.

Was it the break they were hoping for?

She looked up from her screen and saw that Akil was plowing through his own mountain of data. Could she trust him? she wondered. She was no longer the young naïf who had first entered the FBI straight out of university. Back then she'd been eager to please and ignorant of the political machinations that played out around her. People had zeroed in on that inexperience and exploited it. Men mostly. A few senior agents had taken credit for the work she'd done without her knowing. Others simply ignored her altogether, making her job that much harder. The lessons learned had been hard to take at the time, but no one pushed her around anymore. It had been a long and lonely road to NCTC. Many of her female colleagues had ended up quitting or acquiescing to more modest roles inside the agency. She'd made a vow early on to never let that happen. Now she was being asked to trust someone she didn't even know on the biggest case of her career.

Keep your friends close, but your enemies closer, she thought, unsure of what category Akil fit into.

It was a cynical impulse and she admonished herself for even thinking it. She'd have to trust Akil until he gave her a reason not to. Working as a team was the best way to catch these bastards.

"Hey," she said, "take a look at this."

Akil walked around to Sophie's side of the desk.

"One of our Carnivore team has been monitoring radical websites," she told him. "Someone posted this declaration on a site called divine revelation dot net shortly after the attacks."

Akil read the two-page report in under a minute. "You think this guy is connected to the attacks?" he asked.

"Hard to say for sure, but whoever it was signed it with the initials AA. And that part about the good news…"

"It'd be a hell of a coincidence otherwise," he agreed.

Akil walked back to his chair and sat down. "The question I have, is why would the leader of a terrorist cell post to a website right after the attacks? It's an unnecessary risk."

"I don't know, but this ALI599 has been posting on that website for the past day and a half," Sophie said.

Jim Neville came rushing down from the second floor with a piece of paper flapping in his hand and a cat-like grin on his face. "Just got off the phone with Agent Sanchez at the house out in Jersey. Sanchez thinks there's a definite connection to this morning's attacks."

"So those men coming and going in the SITREP, they could be our guys?" Sophie asked.

"Could be. No one was home when Sanchez and his men arrived, but they found a number of videos. Usual bullshit, holy war and jihad for all. The house was pretty empty otherwise. Looks like they weren't there very long."

"Did they come across anything definitive?" Sophie asked. "Something that we can connect to the bombings directly."

"Dogs from the bomb squad picked up traces of explosive. The forensics team just arrived. We'll know more once they get to work."

"Okay, make sure forensics goes over the place from top to bottom. And see if you can find out what kind of explosives the dogs hit on."

"Sure thing. They also found this address on the kitchen fridge," Jim said, handing Sophie the piece of paper he was carrying.

"The fridge?"

"It was just sitting there. These guys can make some pretty monumental mistakes," Jim said. "But don't look a gift horse in the mouth, right?"

Akil couldn't help thinking of the 1993 bombing of the World Trade Center. The conspirators had rented a Ryder rental truck and filled it with a huge amount of explosive material. On February 26th, they drove the truck into the basement of the World Trade Center and set it off. A key conspirator—Mohammad Salameh—reported the truck stolen following the attack. In what became a benchmark act of stupidity, Salameh then returned to the rental agency six days later to collect his deposit on the truck. What he didn't realize was that the FBI had been able to recover the VIN number off a piece of the rear axle buried in the rubble. When Salameh entered the rental agency, FBI agents were waiting to arrest him. But for every bumbling terrorist, there was another who was well trained and disciplined enough to be considered a true professional. Unfortunately, it was still too early to know which kind of terrorist they were dealing with.

"So, where exactly is this?" Sophie asked, referring to the address in her hand.

"It's an apartment in Queens," Jim said, "and it's definitely the lead we've been searching for."

"What do you mean *definitely*?" asked Akil.

"I ran a search on a web posting flagged by Carnivore."

"We were just looking at that," Sophie said.

"It originated from a domestic ISP in New York. With a little digging I came up with an address," Jim said. "It just happens to be identical to the one found on the fridge in Jersey. The post was sent less than an hour ago. Whoever sent it might still be there."

"We get a name from the ISP provider?" Akil asked.

"Mohammad Ali," Jim said, shaking his head. "I know, it's the Arab equivalent of John Smith. It was on the credit card he used to pay for the internet hook-up. Most likely an alias. I ran the name through the

TIDE database and got forty-seven separate hits. Lots of Mohammad Ali's on the watch list. Haven't come up with anything substantial yet. We're still checking."

"Okay Jim, good work," Sophie said. "Get NYPD's Emergency Services Unit over to that address right away. And make sure you contact them on a secure channel. Tell them they need to lock-down the building, but they're not to enter. Got that? They're to hold the perimeter until FBI agents get there."

"Yeah. Roger that."

"And get FBI SWAT en route, ASAP."

Jim turned and headed for the stairs.

"Alert JTTF too," Sophie yelled after him.

Grabbing her cell phone off the desk, Sophie hit the star key plus four digits. She crossed her legs, her feet bobbing nervously on the carpet as she waited for someone to pick up.

"Hi, Carey?......yeah, it's Sophie Martin here......good, look, we have a lead on a suspect and I need immediate transport to New York City......uh-huh, that's right......closest available location to 6405 Shepard Avenue......right......can you make that happen?"

Akil looked over the Carnivore report once more as he listened in on Sophie's end of the conversation.

"You can?" Sophie asked. "Great...no, we're on our way." She ended the call and pocketed her phone, then reached down and pulled a holstered 9mm semi-automatic from the top drawer of her desk. She placed the gun on her hip.

Akil watched her slip on a leather coat, then flip her hair out from under the collar.

"You coming?" she asked.

Before Akil could answer she turned and started walking away. Several people in the bullpen were watching and Akil supposed the mini-theatrics were deliberately intended to serve notice to more than just himself that Sophie Martin was in charge.

"Where we going?" Akil called after her, rising to his feet.

"New York. Helicopter is waiting on the roof," she told him, not turning or slowing down.

She was more than half-way across the bullpen now and picking up speed. Akil smiled as he grabbed his own coat and put it on. He was beginning to like this woman, despite himself.

34

Sayyid knew that the FBI and NYPD would be coming for him. In fact, he was counting on it. The question was, how soon would they arrive?

Inside the apartment, he finished linking the explosives and stepped back to take a look. The bombs were properly spaced and not too obvious. Now he removed the last item from the duffel bag: a digital clock with a preset timer holding at seven seconds. The back of the clock had been removed and two wire leads were soldered to the inside circuit board along with a loop of filament wire.

Unscrewing the faceplate surrounding the doorknob, he took the loop of filament wire that was connected to the alarm clock and delicately wrapped it around the locking mechanism. Reattaching the face plate, he closed the door and made sure the deadbolt was secure.

The looped filament wire, not much stronger than a strand of human hair, would break as soon as the door was opened. This would trigger the clock and begin its countdown. All he had to do now was connect the wire leads from the digital clock to the bombs, then place the batteries back in the clock, which he'd left out as a safety precaution.

His fingers felt sweaty inside the latex gloves, but his hands remained steady. There was no room for error at this point. Slow and steady, he reminded himself.

Binding the wires tight, he gently placed the clock down against the wall next to the door. The explosives were now armed and ready to go off.

With the bombs in place and the timer set, he needed to make sure his handiwork was completely out of sight. He went to the bedroom and returned with two plastic bags filled with garbage and some dirty clothes. He placed the garbage bags by the front door with an empty pizza box on top, then made several adjustments until he felt confident no one would be able to detect the clock or the wires.

The bombs inside the apartment were more difficult to conceal. They had to be out in the open, which meant he'd have to camouflage them and hope for the best. There would be seven seconds from the moment the timer was triggered until the bombs detonated, barely enough time to get into the living room, let alone spot the bombs and react.

35

LIEUTENANT DOYLE O'CALLAHAN'S SWAT Element had just been ordered to an address in Queens. He had a strong feeling that their deployment was connected with this morning's terrorist attacks. The information he'd been given by his commanding officer was sparse, but explicit. They were deploying at the request of the FBI. His men were to secure the target location but remain outside on the perimeter.

Do not go in, he'd been told, unless absolutely necessary. The FBI's own SWAT team would conduct the assault themselves.

This is bullshit! he thought. Doyle hadn't said what was on his mind, of course, but he didn't like the idea of playing bridesmaid to an FBI SWAT team. He wanted to be the one to nab the bastards responsible for this morning's attacks.

So did his men.

36

THE ESU TRUCK came to a stop a block from the target. Doyle jumped down and ordered his men to form up. His element, or team, consisted of ten men in total. His scout, always the first man in, would enter the apartment building and evaluate the situation from close range, then report back. A rear guard, armed with a twelve gauge automatic shotgun, would provide cover. If necessary, three assaulters would initiate a forced entry into the apartment on his command, while two snipers positioned nearby would identify possible suspects and report any movement. If the situation called for it, the snipers would be given a green light to down any hostiles at their own discretion. Two spotters would accompany the snipers and aid in identifying targets.

That left Doyle, the team leader, to give the orders.

"Danny," Doyle said, addressing his scout, "get inside and confirm the apartment location. Let's make sure we got it right."

"Yes, sir."

"Kyle, you go with him."

37

AKIL FOLLOWED SOPHIE onto the roof of NCTC and headed for the waiting helicopter. The rotors were already turning at full speed, and they both ducked as they climbed aboard.

For the first time all morning Akil had a chance to collect his thoughts. He felt overwhelmed by the sudden stream of events. Less than forty-eight hours ago he'd been teaching a freshman class at Georgetown University. Now he was back working for the Agency and responding to a terrorist attack on American soil. On top of everything else, he couldn't stop thinking about Hannah and Michael, wondering if they were okay.

At the moment all they had was a muddle of conflicting information, possible red herrings, and best guesses. It wasn't a domestic operation. The Damascus Letter had made that clear. What bothered him was why the terrorists had posted inflammatory comments to a website immediately following the attacks? And why had they made the mistake of paying with a credit card that could be traced? None of it made any sense. Maybe Jim Neville was right, they were dealing with amateurs, deadly as they'd proven to be.

To get to the truth and track down those responsible, Akil needed Sophie Martin's expertise, and more importantly, her access to information. He was not a trained detective in the classic sense, but he shared many of the same skills. Most people didn't realize that spies spent an inordinate amount of time sifting through data, looking for fragments of information and clues they could exploit. Information, after all, was leverage, and leverage meant getting more information. Better information. With enough connections, they'd eventually find a lead they could follow, one that would help them locate those responsible. The information could come from a seized laptop in Birmingham or a scrap of paper left behind in a Tangiers hotel room, or from an NSA intercept. It could come from almost anywhere. The key was finding it and recognizing it for what it was.

"We're nearly there," Sophie said over the headset.

Akil nodded and looked out the window at the vastness of the Manhattan skyline. The city, set against a pearl blue backdrop, looked stunning. The audacity and grandeur of it had no equal in Akil's eyes. More than anything else the nation had to offer, New York City represented the country's spirit. Manhattan in particular. Surrounded by water, it was an island unto itself, a powerful symbol of wealth and unbridled potential. For that reason, more than any other, it was a target and always would be.

Seeing the city from the air made the attacks feel far away. Like so many others who had come to New York, Akil had grown up in a much smaller city. Seeing Manhattan for the first time he had been fascinated by its sheer size, but it was New York's unpredictable character and her off-color charms that he'd fallen in love with. Right away he knew this is where he'd go to university. Registering at Brown, he had enthusiastically become one of the city's eighteen million denizens, if only temporarily, and during—

Akil's thoughts were interrupted by the sound of Sophie's voice in his headset. "What?" he asked.

"I said a car will be waiting for us when we land. It'll be about a ten-minute drive to the target."

"Okay, good."

38

SAYYID TOOK ONE last look around and made sure all the window shades in the apartment were down before he crawled out onto the fire escape. Closing the window behind him, he removed the latex gloves from his hands and placed them inside his pants pocket.

The air outside was freezing, but he barely noticed. He felt charged up. Invincible.

Standing on the fire escape, the sounds and smells of the city came to life with remarkable clarity. Traffic noise peeling off the Van Wyck Expressway hung in the air like wallpaper. A bakery down the street was pumping out the smell of freshly baked bread. A child was crying somewhere in the near distance, while two stories above him, the sound of a television filtered through an open window, delivering news of the attacks.

He looked around and saw that the alley was empty. He made his way down the fire escape as descriptions of what he had wrought continued to drift out the open window above.

I'm just getting started, he thought. It's just the beginning.

39

DOYLE LISTENED AS Danny gave his report. They were dealing with a corner apartment on the fourth floor. Looked like a standard one bedroom. Two windows faced the front of the building with two more along the alley where the fire escape was located.

"Listen up," Doyle said. The team moved into a loose huddle. "FBI SWAT is on their way. Our job is to secure the site and hold tight for their arrival. If the suspects get spooked or start shooting, we move. Otherwise, you wait for my command."

The men grumbled but agreed. None of them liked the idea of babysitting a target so that someone else could go in and do the job for them.

Doyle scanned the surrounding buildings, gauging potential sniper positions and subsequent angles of fire. "Tom, you want to set up on the roof opposite the front entrance?"

"Looks good," Tom said. He grabbed his Remington 700 and took off with his spotter in tow.

"Dave, you and Carey use that roof over there," Doyle said, pointing. "You'll cover the alley side of the apartment and the fire escape."

"Roger that," Dave said.

"Danny, I want you to go back in and keep an eye on the entrance to the target apartment. The rest of us will move into position, then hold tight and wait."

"Got it chief," Danny said.

Doyle hated having to wait around for the feds. He had good men who trained hard and there was no reason why they shouldn't be allowed to do their jobs. But he had his orders. Set up a perimeter, and under no circumstances enter the apartment and engage.

God forbid ESU stole the feds thunder.

As each member of the team got into position they radioed in over an encrypted channel. Both snipers indicated that the shades were drawn on the apartment windows. They couldn't see inside.

Doyle told them to stay sharp and look for any kind of movement. They were to report in if they saw anything. *Anything* at all.

"Understood," came the reply.

Once the entire element had reported in, Doyle allowed himself the luxury of a cigarette. He tapped the Lucky Strike against the hood of the ESU truck, then lit it. By the time he was finished smoking, he'd made a decision. He would give the feds ten minutes to arrive and not a second more. If they weren't here by then, his team would breach the apartment. In the end, who would care as long as they got the terrorists?

Yeah, right, he thought.

Maybe that's the way it should be, but it was wishful thinking. The FBI would care plenty. He had no qualms about letting them take the credit—he wasn't worried about that—but he wanted his men to have the personal satisfaction of taking down these bastards. How many of them had lost colleagues and friends in 9/11? How many had lived with that trauma for years?

All he needed now was an excuse to go in.

40

As THE HELICOPTER began its descent, Akil leaned over and looked down. Thanks to some behind-the-scenes phone calls, a local baseball diamond had been cordoned off, allowing them to land in the heart of Queens. A dozen police cars formed a ring around the field, their lights flashing. As the helicopter touched down, Akil and Sophie jumped out and ran across the gravel infield, then got in the back of an unmarked car and proceeded to the apartment.

Akil stared out the window at the passing cars, thinking about what they might find. Who they might find. Where it might lead.

Sophie broke the silence. "Where did you grow up?" she asked him.

Akil kept looking out the window. "Near Tacoma."

"Were you born there?"

"No," he said, turning now. "No. I was born in Lebanon. My parents emigrated when I was nine. You?"

"D.C.," she said. "My father was in the diplomatic corps, so we moved around a lot. I spent my childhood in half a dozen different countries. Finally, my father moved us back to the States permanently. He said he was worried I wasn't getting a proper American education. He was really worried about that."

"My father was the same way," Akil said, chuckling. "He bought me and my brother season's tickets to the Seahawks. Insisted we go. We were Americans now."

Sophie laughed and he wondered if this was her way of making nice, by sharing past histories. He wasn't comfortable sharing anything about himself. The habit had been drummed out of him a long time ago. *Reveal nothing. Learn everything.* That was the mantra he had lived by for as long as he could remember. She already knew more about him than most people did.

"Why the FBI?" he asked, turning the tables.

"Why the CIA?"

"Answering a question with a question, that won't get us anywhere."

The instructors had pressed upon him, that given half a chance, people would talk about themselves at length. They were right. The hard part had been learning how to listen to what was actually being said, the true meaning hidden behind the words. That took patience and training.

"My father kept pushing me to follow in his footsteps, wanted me to become an attaché or, god forbid, work for the UN. I guess I wanted to do something that made a difference, that you could walk away from at the end of the day and know you'd done something tangible. The FBI seemed like the best choice."

"Dad couldn't have been happy."

"He didn't like the fact I carried a gun. I think he envisioned something more elegant, maybe with heels and a corner office," she said, snickering at the idea. "And the CIA?"

"I watched a lot of movies as a kid," Akil said. "Doesn't every boy dream of being a spy?"

"I don't know. Do they?"

41

EVERYTHING WAS READY to go.

Almost everything. Doyle had ordered the assaulters to quietly evacuate the other tenants from the apartment building. Now he pushed the PTT switch on his tactical radio: "Danny, get the optics out and lets have a look."

"Copy that, taking a look."

Danny and his rear guard Kyle were holding on the edge of the fourth floor with a line-of-sight to the target apartment. Danny removed the backpack from his shoulders and placed it in front of him, then grabbed his toolkit. He removed the wireless fiberscope along with the video headset he would need to see the images.

The fiberscope was an indispensable tool in situations like this and weighed a mere 1.4 pounds. It used a miniaturized camera chip on the end of a fiber optic wire that allowed him to peer into a room by feeding the flexible cable under a door or through a tiny hole in the wall. The image quality was remarkably good, considering the size of the camera. In situations like this size was important because it precluded all but the most attentive and paranoid suspects from becoming aware of its presence. If a suspect spotted the camera and started shooting or came charging at the door, it was Kyle's job to protect him. In such an event Danny would yell and hug the floorboards while Kyle opened up with his Super-90, 12-gauge automatic. The first shot would rip a gaping hole in the door and the second would drop anybody on the other side if they weren't already down and bleeding. The first and second shots would be separated by less than a second. They both hoped it didn't come to that today, but you could never tell.

Outside on the street, Doyle paced back and forth beside the command vehicle. He had to find a way to get his team into that apartment that wouldn't get them all suspended. He would be countermanding explicit orders, and while there was no love lost between the NYPD brass and the FBI, pressures would be exerted. Someone would be made to pay for the transgression, unless…unless there was a plausible explanation for why he and his team had gone in.

Inside the apartment building, on the fourth floor, Danny shimmied up to the door on his stomach and tested the camera. On his headset, he could see a clear image of Kyle standing just a few feet away. Satisfied, he fed the wire slowly underneath the door. The apartment was dark with low-levels of ambient light coming through the window shades in the living room. Thankfully, technology had kept advancing and the new fiberscope models had a light sensitivity switch that allowed the camera to cope with such extremes.

Danny dialed up the sensitivity until the image reached an acceptable resolution.

A short hallway led into the main living room. No one was visible. He moved the camera left, and immediately the image went dark. He adjusted the focus and moved the camera up and down. What he saw were garbage bags piled up next to the door with a pizza box stacked on top. He moved the camera to the right and found paint peeling off the wall and a broken door stop sitting up against the battered floorboards. He checked the hallway that led into the living room once again. There was still no sign of anybody inside.

Remaining flat on his stomach, Danny shimmied backwards until he was several feet from the door, then spoke in a whisper over the tac-radio: "Front entrance clear. No visual on the tangos."

Both the receiver and microphone Danny used had been incorporated into his earpiece. The device picked up the near sub-sonic vibrations from his jaw bone as he spoke. Although his voice remained barely audible inside the hallway, the rest of his team could hear him loud and clear.

"Keep watch. Let me know if you see any movement in that apartment," Doyle replied.

"Roger that," Danny said, moving back toward the door.

Doyle looked up at the apartment's fourth-floor windows. There had been no movement—nothing that would give them an excuse to go in. His window of opportunity was closing fast. The FBI would be here any minute.

Doyle looked around, thinking seriously about his next move.

Fuck it.

"Tom," Doyle said, addressing one of his snipers. "I thought I saw movement in the front right window. In fact, I'm sure of it. Can you confirm?"

Doyle was hoping that Tom understood the subtext of what he was asking him, because when they went over the audio later—and they *would* go over it—he wanted it on the record that they'd moved in for a reason. It didn't matter how good of a reason, as long as there had been one.

"Checking it now," Tom replied.

Doyle waited impatiently. He knew the entire team wanted to get these bastards as much as he did.

"Chief, confirm, I've got movement with the blinds," Tom said. "I think they know we're here."

That would do, Doyle thought. It was his call. It would be his head on the chopping block if things went bad.

Doyle addressed his entire team over the radio: "We've got movement inside the apartment. Prepare to breach the target." He took a deep breath, then motioned his three assaulters over. They huddled around him. "We don't know what we're dealing with in there. Could be civilians inside, so watch your triggers."

Doyle toggled his radio again. "Danny, stay on the camera until we get there."

"Copy that, chief."

"Okay, let's go."

42

THE CAR CARRYING Akil and Sophie stopped a block from the target building. A large truck was blocking the street in front of them. Big bold letters along the side of the truck read NYPD: ESU.

Sophie and Akil jumped out of the car. Several police vehicles were already on scene and officers had cordoned off the area. This far back, they remained invisible to the target.

Akil and Sophie presented their IDs to one of the officers and ducked underneath the yellow tape that marked off the outer perimeter. Akil scanned the rooftops as he walked, spotting the two ESU snipers positioned at ninety-degree angles to one another, their rifles trained on the building's fourth-floor windows. The FBI's SWAT Team was nowhere to be seen.

"We must have made good time," Akil said.

"Looks that way."

Two of New York's finest stood sentry, protecting the inner perimeter. Akil flashed his ID again, along with Sophie.

"Where's the ESU commander?" Akil asked.

"Just went inside," the officer replied.

"What do you mean he just went inside?" Sophie said, her voice strained.

"Went in with the assault team a minute ago."

"Son-of-bitch!"

Sophie pushed past the police officers and started running toward the target building's main entrance.

"What the hell are you doing?" Akil yelled at her.

Sophie ignored him and kept running.

"Dammit!"

43

THE ASSAULT TEAM climbed the stairs as quickly and as quietly as possible. Doyle knew the element of surprise was still intact and he had no intention of losing it now. One of the assaulters would handle the battering ram while the other two deployed flash-bang grenades. Then they would enter the apartment together and secure it in less than ten seconds.

Assembling just outside the door, Doyle signaled for Danny to move back so the battering ram could get into position. The other two members of the assault team pulled the pins on their flash-bangs and waited.

Doyle gave a silent prayer, then made eye contact with the man holding the battering ram. He nodded his head, sending the team into action.

He watched the heavy metal tube swing backwards, suspend itself in mid-air, then come crashing forward, hitting the door just below the deadbolt.

44

AKIL CHASED SOPHIE into the target building.

He saw that she was taking the stairs two at a time, headed for the fourth floor. *What the hell does she think she's doing?* Neither of them were equipped to take part in a raid like this, and rushing up to a potentially armed conflict without body armor—or a plan—was a bad idea.

They were almost at the floor landing before Akil caught up to her. That's when he heard the distinctive sound of a door being busted in. It was followed by the report of two flash-bang grenades. They were too late to prevent ESU from entering the apartment. He wondered if their suspect was still inside? Did ESU know that it was vital they take the suspect alive?

Akil darted past Sophie, stepping onto the fourth-floor landing ahead of her. The hallway in front of him led directly to the target apartment on his left. As he turned toward the entrance he could see the apartment door hanging awkwardly on its broken hinges. Then he caught sight of two ESU members running straight for him at full speed. The two men were still deep inside the apartment's front hall, their arms waving through the air frantically. The alarm painted on the men's faces felt familiar—Akil had seen the look before—but it took a fraction of a second before he understood exactly what they were telling him.

Then he wasn't thinking at all.

He was simply reacting.

His training kicked in and everything started to slow down. This is what the instructors at the special forces school promised would happen if he stuck with the long hours of training. Instinct and reflex would take over. They were lifesavers. But those skills could atrophy over time, the same as any other muscle in the body.

Akil didn't have time to worry about that now. Halting his forward momentum, he pivoted on the balls of his feet and turned around in one fluid motion. Sophie had stepped onto the fourth-floor landing behind him. She was staring at ESU members, confusion etched on her face. Akil bent his knees and lunged at her, bridging the three-foot gap in less than a second. As he made contact, he wrapped his arms around her torso, lifting her feet up off the floor, letting his forward momentum propel them away from the door.

A bright flash filled the stairwell an instant before the concussion wave struck. The force of it propelled them violently toward the far wall as flames shot out into the hallway.

Akil crashed hard onto the floor, Sophie landing on top of him. He felt his ribs compress and break under the impact. Pain lanced inwards toward his lungs as blood gushed from his nose.

He lay on the floor of the hallway. Stunned. Breathless.

The ringing in his ears was a raging storm.

When he finally opened his eyes, the darkness was already edging out what little light he could see. He blinked several times and lifted his head, but his vision continued to narrow rapidly, folding in at the edges. A heavy cloud of darkness was swallowing him up.

He couldn't breathe.

Couldn't feel his legs.

Still, he struggled to move, but it was no use; the darkness was everywhere now. With the last of his strength, Akil reached out for Sophie, finding only empty air.

Then he was gone.

Part II

IN THE WILDERNESS

OF MIRRORS

45

TEHRAN.

Ahmad Hashemian, the head of Iran's Ministry of Intelligence and Security, woke to the sound of knuckles rapping on wood.

Someone was at his door. The knocking came again. Louder this time. Adamant.

"*Ba'leh*," Hashemian shouted.

The oversized bedroom was dark and cold, an Iranian winter storm hammering at the windows. The small coal fire he'd lit earlier in the evening had vanished. For the first time in weeks, he had retired early, asking not to be disturbed. Why then was he being disturbed?

Throwing the heavy covers aside, he slipped out of bed, feeling the cold nip at his exposed skin. He fumbled for his housecoat, put it on, then walked to the door. On the other side he found his deputy, Reza, standing in the hallway, his face grim.

"What is it?" Hashemian asked.

"New York. There's been an attack."

Hashemian opened the door wide and let Reza enter the room.

"Suicide bombers. It's all over the news," Reza said.

"How many?"

"Three that were successful. Early reports indicate several hundred are dead and wounded."

Hashemian shut the door and went to his bureau to fetch his cigarettes. He lit one and blew a dense cloud of blue smoke toward the ceiling.

"These are dangerous days, Reza."

"Yes, sir."

Hashemian tapped the ash from his cigarette into a small metal bowl. "Our people are still keeping watch?"

"They are."

"And there's nothing new to report."

"Only the attacks on New York. The package is still in transit."

"Then we wait," Hashemian said, his voice full of resignation. "We wait and we see."

"It may still turn out okay," Reza offered optimistically.

"Yes. Let's pray that's the case."

46

SAYYID CRUISED TOWARD Washington, DC and the next stage of his operation. The martyrs he had dispatched to kill this morning had shocked New York City and the nation as expected. On the radio, reporters continued to describe the attacks in graphic detail. To Sayyid, it felt gratuitous. He didn't like it, even though it served his purpose. There was no pleasure in the things he had done or the things he still planned to do. They were, however, necessary.

A lot of hard work had gone into planning for New York and it had paid off. He regretted the need to sacrifice brave men like Jalal, a devout Muslim who had held the promise of youth. But what other options were there? War required sacrifice. They were in paradise now anyway, celebrating their victory. As for the innocent American civilians, were their lives more important than those Palestinians who continued to suffer and die every day? In the West Bank? Gaza? The refugee camps? Were American tears of grief stronger or more poignant to the rest of the world? And if so, why?

Israeli tanks and Israeli troops terrorized the Palestinian people with American weapons, American money, and American political support. Now the American people would have to deal with the consequences of those actions. Couldn't they see that cause and effect was at work here, that something needed to be done? He would explain it to them if they didn't already understand. Better, he would let one of their own tell them.

The Thanksgiving Day attacks were only the first step. He'd shaken the sleeping giant back to consciousness. Hopefully, he could bring it to its senses as well. After all, his people had been refused the same thing America claimed to champion: life, liberty, and the pursuit of happiness. For more than sixty years the Palestinian people had sought these basic rights, but the Israelis and Americans continued to refuse them.

Sayyid engaged the cruise control on the Ford Taurus and leaned back, leaving one hand to steady the wheel. The long day, full of stress, had taken its toll. He could feel the energy that had carried him through the morning begin to fade away now. Soon it would be replaced by fatigue, both mental and physical. With luck, he would be settled in Washington by early evening, able to relax and enjoy a long hot shower and a cup of tea. Then later, he would meet the others.

On the passenger seat beside him sat a vetted American passport and driver's license. He'd paid a premium for the added security the documents offered him. If run through the system, both documents would check out. For the moment his name was Michael Kahn and he was a native of Dearborn, Michigan on his way to Washington for a home renovation conference. He had business cards with his name on them if anyone was interested. He was counting on his excellent English to deflect any lingering mistrust that a police officer might have, were he to be stopped as a result of his untimely heritage and complexion. And should he be forced to use it, he had procured a Glock automatic as well, which was stowed under the driver's seat, just in case.

Racial profiling might be widely acknowledged as politically incorrect, but it was still an all-too-common occurrence. After what happened this morning, Sayyid could hardly blame the police for targeting Arabs. The irony was, such behavior only isolated Arab-Americans further. It made them feel as if they didn't belong in their own country. For some, the bitter feelings passed with time, while in others it festered like an open wound. A precious few held tight to their hatred until it calcified inside them. These were the ones that could be cultivated and recruited to the cause. Whenever the American people burned a mosque or beat a Muslim out of ignorance, the wedge between Muslims and non-Muslims was driven deeper. In a time of war, such events were a blessing. Hearts and minds had to be turned toward the cause, and today's events would aid that process.

Sayyid leaned forward and turned the dial on the car radio, switching back and forth until he found the local NPR station. He turned up the volume and listened to the breaking news. There had been an explosion at an apartment building in Queens, the announcer said. Witnesses claimed to have seen a large fireball shoot from a series of fourth-story windows in the sixty-four hundred block of Shepard Avenue just after one o'clock in the afternoon. Whether or not the explosion was linked to the terrorist attacks in Manhattan, authorities said, remained unclear.

Sayyid turned off the radio. Kamal was right, the American agencies had not been given enough time to stop the attacks. They had followed the breadcrumbs he had left for them with predictable efficiency though. Then they had rushed in like moths drawn to a flame, too eager to see the danger.

What would they cull from the ashes? What would they make of the clues he had left for them?

47

AKIL WAS BATTERED, but alive. He had suffered non-life-threatening injuries. Others had fared far worse.

Following the explosion, he'd been rushed to New York's Bellevue Hospital along with two ESU members. After he regained consciousness he tried to recall what had happened and found his memories shrouded in uncertainty. He had stepped onto the fourth-floor landing and seen two men exiting the apartment, running straight at him. That had been his first clue that something was wrong. He remembered turning and spotting Sophie, lunging at her without thinking, hoping to protect her from the blast he somehow knew was coming.

Everything after that was a blank.

Bill Graham had walked into his hospital room at some point later on, somber as a priest. He'd brought fresh clothes, telling Akil that he'd come to New York to make sure he was okay. Akil knew there was another reason. He could see it on Bill's face, and it was bad news.

Fighting the drugs that were forcing him back into unconsciousness, Akil asked the question that was plaguing him: "It's Hannah and Michael, isn't it?"

48

WHEN AKIL WOKE again, day had turned to night and Bill Graham was gone.

He wished seeing his boss had been nothing more than a bad dream, but their conversation was still playing over and over in his head, every sickening detail of it.

Climbing out of his hospital bed, Akil grabbed the sweatpants Bill had brought him, along with a New York Jets t-shirt. As he dressed, he noticed for the first time the overpowering smell of bleach and latex that permeated the room. It was an unpleasant odor that triggered memories he'd rather forget. He had always hated hospitals. Whether here or abroad, it was the sense of helplessness he got from being around them that bothered him most.

Entering the corridor he was forced to move through a sea of patients. Triage had overflowed and injured bodies, many of them still covered in blood, were strewn about in every direction. He noticed police officers milling around alongside doctors and nurses, interviewing the wounded. From what he could see, the violence inflicted by the suicide bombers had been indiscriminate: men and women, both young and old, had been struck and disfigured. Children too. Those who could wait for stitches or an X-ray were shuffled off to the side while others were given drugs and put in line to see the next available physician.

Muffled cries and moans filled the dead space between gurneys as he weaved his way toward the elevators. His mind kept going over what Bill had told him. The news had sounded too extraordinary to be real, but Bill's body language assured him it was no joke. Akil knew Michael had been looking forward to the Macy's Thanksgiving Day Parade for weeks. It was all he could talk about and Akil had planned on taking him before Bill had tracked him down and offered him his old job back. Michael had been disappointed that his uncle wouldn't be there, but Akil promised to make it up to him.

The wrong place at the wrong time. That's the way Bill had phrased it. Hannah had suffered severe head trauma, and though the doctors had put her on life support, they left no hope for her recovery.

Once she's off the machines, it'll only be a matter of minutes before....

Bill had let his words trail off into silence. Akil understood. Hannah was already dead.

And Michael?

Amazingly, the boy had survived with only a few scrapes and bruises, Bill told him. He'd been shielded from the blast by the adults in the crowd.

Akil was tied to the day's attacks in a very personal way now and he could feel his anger mounting. Like a deep-seated hunger, it demanded to be satiated in some way. The reflex emotion was common among victims of crime, but unlike so many others, he would not have to face a growing sense of helplessness. Instead, he would pursue the attackers relentlessly, and with the backing of the government. Those he passed in the hospital's corridors—their eyes downcast, their features marred by blood—wouldn't be so lucky.

Passing the nurses' station, Akil carried on to the end of the ICU. The door to Hannah's room had been propped open and he leaned against it for a moment, peering in. The lights were low, but he could see her motionless body, the respirator pumping air into her lungs with pneumatic precision. Like in the movies, he saw and heard the fixed hiccup of her heart rate, the illuminated wave of the respiratory rhythm, numbers jumbled together to indicate oxygen saturation, hemoglobin count, blood pressure. The machinery that was keeping her alive robbed the room of emotion and he thought again of what the doctors had told Bill: *Once she's off the machines, it'll only be a matter of minutes before....*

He crossed the threshold and immediately wanted to escape the room—pretend this day had never happened. Instead, he forced himself to the edge of her bed.

Hannah's features were awash in the glow of the monitors. He saw her for the first time as someone other than his brother's wife. It felt strange, but that's what death did to you, it stripped you of your associations. She was beautiful, someone Akil could have been attracted to under different circumstances. She had always reminded him of classmates he'd known at Brown—active and opinionated, but not confrontational. Who was she outside her role as sister-in-law? he wondered. He wished now he'd gotten to know her better.

He had begun to.

Now it was too late.

He pulled a chair close to the bed and sat down. Avoiding the I.V., he took her hand and held it firmly inside his. "I'm sorry," he whispered.

Emotion raged inside him. He wanted to scream at the top of his lungs, but focused instead on Michael. Akil was the boy's only living relative now, aside from his grandfather. This fact had been percolating into his consciousness ever since his conversation with Bill. Raising a child—his brother's child—seemed crazy. How could he take care of a child now that he'd finally been given the opportunity to resume his career? He wanted to go back overseas where he could make a real difference. He had dedicated himself to a career in covert operations, and now he was faced with having to give it up. Again.

Michael would have to come first, of course. Yes, that's how it would have to be. Wouldn't it? Maybe not right away. Eventually, though. In time he'd have to take on desk duties, work the diplomatic circles in DC perhaps, keeping his hand in the cookie jar as it were. Diplomats were as duplicitous as anyone else, and there was always the chance of recruiting an important asset.

Who was he kidding? DC was not an appealing thought. Was he even up to the task of raising a child? Maybe that's what worried him most. Afternoons spent in the city were one thing, but being responsible for raising another human being, that was something he'd never really thought about until now—right now—and it scared the hell out of him.

49

LOOKING UP, AKIL saw Sophie standing in the doorway. He quickly wiped his eyes, erasing the tears that had formed but not yet fallen. How long had she been watching him?

Walking over, he led her out into the hall. His initial irritation at her intrusion faded almost immediately. He was grateful for the company.

"How's Michael?" he asked.

"He's doing okay. Sweet kid," Sophie replied.

"Bill said you were keeping an eye on him. Thanks."

"Of course."

"It's his birthday today. He was supposed to have a party," Akil said, suddenly distracted by the thought.

"I didn't know."

He looked at her. "I wish I knew what to tell him about his mother."

"Just tell him the truth," she told him. "It's the best way."

He wished it were that easy. He thought of how Michael would take the awful news. There seemed no way to convey his mother's situation without traumatizing the child. His father had died in a terrorist attack, and now his mother was the victim of another one. How did you explain that to a kid? How did you explain that to anyone?

"And you? How are you doing?" Sophie asked.

She looked concerned.

"I'm fine. A couple broken ribs. Doctor says I'll be okay."

"No. I meant—"

"I know," he said, "I'm fine."

"You sound exhausted. You need some rest," she told him.

"Trying to get rid of me?"

"That's right."

"A couple of broken ribs isn't going to keep me off this case. Not now."

"I'm serious."

"So am I."

Sophie paused. "You need to look after your family first."

"There's not much of a family left, is there?"

Sophie stared down the corridor without comment.

"I'm sorry," he said. "I just—"

"You don't need to apologize."

"If we're going to catch the people who did this we can't afford to waste time. Michael's grandfather is flying in tonight. Michael will be in good hands."

"And what about you?"

"Like I said, I'm fine."

But he wasn't. Shifting his weight he felt pain pierce his side. He grimaced and clutched at his rib cage. The painkillers were wearing off.

"Yeah, you're tip-top," Sophie chided him.

"The pain isn't that bad."

"You're full of shit."

He laughed and immediately regretted it. "Maybe," he said, wincing some more. "You get checked out?"

"Yeah. Just some bruises, that's it."

"Good."

"Look, if we're going to keep working together," she said, changing the subject, "you'll be following my lead still. Nothing's changed."

This was the Sophie Martin he'd met that morning: self-assured, willful, more than a little defensive. But she was wrong. Everything had changed. There would be thousands of agents on the case by now, and all the three-letter-agencies would be involved. That said, being the FBI's lead counterterrorism expert at NCTC had its privileges. Sophie had immediate access to the Center's intelligence database, and she had a level of autonomy most investigators would kill for. It meant she'd be able to follow her own leads and he intended to be right there when she did, especially since the Agency's powers on domestic soil were limited. At the moment she was his best hope of finding those responsible.

"It's your investigation," Akil told her, "but I want to know everything."

Sophie gave him a hard look. "As I said before, that's a two-way street."

"I know that."

"So whatever the Agency gets, and I'm talking about the stuff that never reaches NCTC, I want to see it."

In her eyes, he was an asset, same as she was to him. "Fair enough," he said. "But anything that comes from the Agency is for your eyes only, unless

I say otherwise. That means DNI Reeves too. No one hears anything about it. That's the deal. It's non-negotiable."

She made a show of thinking about it, then stuck out her hand. "Deal."

"Good," he said, shaking her hand, their eyes meeting and locking on one another.

Their hands remained clasped. Neither spoke. The moment—whatever this moment was—engulfed them equally. The day's events became background noise for a few precious seconds before Sophie broke the spell.

"I never thanked you for earlier today, for doing what you did," she said.

They let go of each other's hands.

"I didn't do anything," he said.

"Don't be modest. You know exactly what you did and if it weren't for you—"

"Thank my instructors at Fort Bragg. They're the ones that—"

"I'm thanking you," she said, forcefully. "Didn't anyone ever teach you how to take a compliment?"

"No, not really," he said, surprised that she wasn't treating him with kid gloves despite everything that had happened. Instead of bothering him, her demeanor only fueled his attraction to her.

"You're welcome," he said.

"Much better. When you finish with Michael, come by the field office downtown. I've got something you're going to want to look at."

"Alright. I'll be there as soon as I can."

50

Justin Travers was born into a family of privilege whose patrician blood ran deep, and like the princely royalty of old, he was offered every opportunity for success. The right tutors. The right connections. But Justin Travers never felt comfortable having everything handed to him on a silver platter. He wanted to succeed on his own merits and on his own terms.

He started modestly by earning an athletic scholarship to Yale the old-fashioned way, through grit and hard work. With flowing blond hair and sky blue eyes, he exuded a quiet confidence and authority that people naturally gravitated toward. And like his father and grandfather before him, he quickly gained legendary status off the field, as well as on it. Professors celebrated him. Coaches praised him. Students, both men and women, were drawn to him. He wasn't just popular, he was admired, and others took notice.

His family's money and their connections to industry prompted political scouts to make overtures toward him. More than once, attending formal gatherings, Travers heard that he was a shoo-in for Congress or maybe even the Senate. Being president was possible too, one day, further down the road, if he played his cards right.

His star was shooting skyward and it seemed everyone wanted to catch a ride. On the surface, it seemed like the beginning of a perfect life, the kind people wrote about in books and magazines. And if you believed in fairy tales, Justin Travers was destined to be what others imagined him to be: a "great man."

He didn't want that life though.

Never had.

After graduation, Travers left school and disappeared without a trace. The social universe he had held sway over for so long could only speculate about where he'd gone and why he'd left. When he resurfaced a few years later, it was not to pursue politics or big business, as many believed. It was to go to war.

Travers had decided to join the Central Intelligence Agency. His first few years out of The Farm were spent in Prague and Berlin. During those early years, his expectations were tamed and hard lessons were learned. He became a pragmatist and an effective case officer, garnering several commendations in the process. His blue-blooded background made him a natural fit for old Europe, so it came as a shock to many when he requested a transfer to the Middle East.

He told his station chief that he wanted to be where the action was. If you asked him now, he couldn't tell you what it was he expected to find, only that what he found wasn't what he expected. The Middle East was like a fever that kept rising and falling, then rising again. It was relentless. And just when you thought the fever had finally broken for good, it came back with a vengeance. For a privileged kid from New England, the toll was growing heavy. His friends at Yale wouldn't have recognized him in his current state. He smoked cigarettes with an unusual intensity and drank with a tolerance that only came with repeated abuse. Despite this, he never once faltered in performing his duty. It was something he took a great deal of pride in.

Standing six one, his uniform consisted of loose jeans and a white golf shirt with a tan colored photo vest. His dirty blond hair was cropped short these days and hidden underneath a Patriots baseball cap. A scruffy half-beard, bleached from the sun, inched up either side of his face, and under his eyes, deep trenches formed half moons that never seemed to go away.

When he first arrived, Iraq was little more than a killing field. He'd worked hard to quell the insurgency by recruiting agents, establishing relationships with influential imams, and successfully delivering information on the militias—information that netted several key players.

Some form of stability eventually descended on the country itself, but not the region as a whole.

He knew the calm wouldn't last.

And it didn't.

ISIS had risen from the ashes of Saddam's rule and the aftermath of the invasion. The Syrian civil war only accelerated the extremist's ambitions. They wanted to create a modern-day Caliphate: a hardline Sunni Islamic state within the Levant. To that end, they leveraged the centuries-old conflict between the Shias and Sunnis. The brutal sectarian violence between the two religious groups that had become a gruesome hallmark of the Iraqi conflict was once again rearing its head. That morning alone a suicide car-bomb had killed thirty-seven at a market in Al-Doura. Sitting on the roof of his barracks he'd heard the sound of the explosion as it rippled beneath the cloud-covered sky like rolling thunder. He no longer bothered to get up and look, just waited for the telltale sound of claxons and rising smoke to pinpoint the location.

The bombings had long been part of the landscape, and though they had ceased for a while, they'd become an almost daily occurrence again. Nowhere was safe, except maybe the military base Travers called home. But that too could change. One never knew. And if you had to go outside the fence to conduct a sanctioned operation—a rare occasion these days—you were required to take along a security escort. Travers had not been outside the fence in months. His days were spent filing reports, surfing the internet and smoking cigarettes. But it had only been a matter of time before he was called upon.

Rummaging through his desk, Travers grabbed the camera he was looking for and headed for the stairs. He needed the camera because he was being sent back out into the Red Zone—named on account of all the bloodshed. The details of the operation were sketchy. It seemed that an intelligence officer attached to Task Force 67—a special operations group still operating inside the country—had been contacted by a local Sunni sheik. The Iraqi claimed to know where several high ranking Sunni militia members were holed up. The problem was, they were all dead—likely targeted by a Shi'ite death squad.

In situations like these, it was standard operating procedure to investigate and collect any intelligence that might exist. TF-67 had its own complement of intelligence personnel who dealt with these kinds of situations. They were trained soldiers themselves and protected by a contingent of special forces, some of the last combat troops still inside Iraq. Unfortunately for Travers, TF-67 was tied up in the north on something more important and were unable to respond. CENTCOM wanted a look, so they rang the station chief in Balad who phoned the duty officer in Baghdad who finally got hold of Travers.

Everyone knew these sort of bullshit assignments were the ones that got you killed. Less than a month ago another case officer had been eviscerated by an EFP device that shot a slug of molten copper through the beefed-up armor of his escort vehicle.

Travers tried not to think about the danger.

What was the point?

With his digital SLR in hand, he headed downstairs. Beyond the air-conditioned lobby doors, the mercury was rising and the low angle of the sun made it difficult to see. Throwing on his Oakleys, Travers made his way over to the trio of Chevy Suburbans parked in the courtyard. A man in battle fatigues turned to face him.

"You Travers?"

"Yeah."

"Name's Price, mate. We're your escort. Here's your vest."

The guy spoke in a strong Aussie accent as he handed Travers the body armor. The vest was mandatory on outings like this and he didn't need to be prompted to put it on.

"Ready to move out when you are," the Aussie added.

Private security contractors—Red Sky something-or-other. Travers had been out with them once before. The military had been stretched thin for years, unable or unwilling to provide this type of secondary security. Instead, the military paid private contractors five times as much to do the job for them. But these guys knew their shit, and that's all Travers cared about. It would be a quick trip anyway. Pop down, take a look at the carnage, and be back in time for afternoon beers on the patio.

Or so he hoped.

51

THE YELLOW CAB dropped Akil off at 26 Federal Plaza in lower Manhattan.

The building in front of him towered forty-one stories above the street, a model of late sixties high-rise architecture whose façade formed a zig-zag pattern of glass intersected by slabs of concrete. From the street, it looked like a giant checkerboard. The FBI's New York field office was located inside, six blocks from the World Trade Center Memorial.

Akil checked in with the security desk, then took the elevator up. He found Sophie waiting for him on the twenty-third floor. She greeted him and handed over a laminated security badge. "How did Michael take the news about his mother?" she asked.

"Not well," he said. "He's angry and confused. I can understand. I feel the same way."

"Poor kid. I wish there was something I could do."

"He just wants to be left alone right now."

Sophie looked pained. She seemed to genuinely care. He told her how he had left Michael with some friends until his father could pick him up and take him back to Akil's house.

"At least he'll be with family."

"Yeah, my father will take good care of him," he said, checking his watch. It was just past midnight. "You said you had something to show me?"

"C'mon."

He followed Sophie through the front lobby and into the core of the FBI's New York operation.

"We've been going over the video the terrorists distributed to the media," Sophie said. "We don't know exactly who it's from, and there's been no official claim of responsibility. You mind taking a look at it and telling me what you think?"

"Sure."

They moved past a sea of cubicles and workstations, each buzzing with activity. The entire force was working overtime, hundreds upon hundreds of agents called away from turkey dinners and family gatherings to help run down leads. The low rumble of so many people hard at work gave Akil renewed energy. New York City had the largest FBI field office in the country, for obvious reasons. Spread out over three floors, it employed in excess of 2000 full-time special agents, all of whom were looking for the people who had orchestrated this morning's attacks.

Sophie showed him into one of the meeting rooms situated along the north wall. The room was set up with a media screen, conference table, chairs, and a pot of hot coffee. The beige paint, cream-colored blinds and chocolate-brown furniture were from another era, and under the green tint of fluorescent lighting, the room felt depressing.

Akil poured himself a cup of coffee and added several cubes of sugar, took a sip, then spooned in some powdered milk. He still felt groggy from the meds the hospital had given him when he was first admitted and he was hoping the caffeine would help clear his head.

He felt a sharp stab of pain as he lowered himself into a chair. His ribs were wrapped tightly with tensor bandages. They were still extremely tender. The doctor had given him some medication to take home, but he hadn't used it. He would rather deal with the discomfort than lose his mental edge.

Sipping his coffee, Akil studied the image of a young man frozen on the media screen. "One of the bombers?" he asked.

"Yeah."

"We have an ID?"

"Name is Jalal Mahmoud. His friends knew him better as Jordan," Sophie said. "He was the one chosen to deliver our terrorist's message."

"American?"

"Born and bred in Brooklyn."

The kid looked nineteen or twenty years old and was clearly of Arab extraction. He held a Qur'an in one hand and an AK-100 series in the other. The assault rifle was the modern version of a Russian classic that still held great symbolic value for terrorists and westerners alike.

"What do we know about him?" Akil asked.

Sophie closed the door to the meeting room. It was just the two of them. "We were able to get a hold of his parents. They told us that, as a teenager, the boy suddenly renounced the anglicized version of his name and began speaking out against American foreign policy. His religious studies became more spirited as well. Apparently, he memorized large sections of the Qur'an. Never missed prayers."

"Friends?" Akil asked.

"Not really. Everyone we talked to in the neighborhood had lost touch with him over the years."

"Which attack did he carry out?"

Sophie stood facing the screen, a file folder in her hands. "Forensics places him at the parade this morning."

Akil looked up at the six by four screen on which Jalal's frozen image was projected. The young man had an air of innocence to him, and yet he had brutally killed dozens of men, women, and children, including Hannah. Zeroing in on the face, Akil saw a young man not unlike himself at twenty years of age. Not a terrorist, but an American Muslim whose parents had immigrated from the Middle East for the chance at a better life—someone who had grown up an American, but by the provenance of his heritage and faith had found himself caught between two worlds. In Akil's case, this is what separated him from the pack and made him an extremely valuable covert officer. He could blend in and adapt more easily than most. He'd spent his entire life doing just that. He had come to America and embraced his new country with enthusiasm and passion. But for Jalal, America was the only country he had ever known, yet he had turned against it, embracing radical Islam instead. Where had their two experiences diverged so fundamentally? How was it that Jalal had chosen to sacrifice his life in order to kill in the name of a fascist ideology while Akil had sworn an oath to fight against it?

Sophie sat down across from Akil with the growing file on Jalal Mahmoud spread out in front of her. "At first the parents thought his dedication to their religion was a blessing," she said. "As the prayer and fasting became more pronounced, they convinced themselves it was nothing more than youthful exuberance. But things got worse."

"And the family's history?"

"No history of terrorist links or associations." Sophie sifted through the file. "Father owns and operates a licensed cab in Manhattan," she said. "There's no evidence that the parents were involved or knew anything about the boy's activities. We're still checking."

"Don't bother," Akil said. "The parents didn't see it coming the same way most parents don't see what their children are capable of until it's too late."

"We think he was cultivated by a local, someone inside the Muslim community who had regular contact with him. Someone his parents may have known."

"I'd bet anything someone engineered this kid. Taught him to hate. Encouraged the persecution fantasies so common amongst radicals. How about the mosque he attended?"

Sheikhs, as with priests, wielded an immense amount of influence over young followers. It wouldn't be the first time a radical sheikh or imam had turned a young child into a human bomb for God's army.

"The parents sent him to the local mosque after school from the age of six, but he suddenly stopped going when he turned fifteen," Sophie said.

"Do we know why?"

"No. His parents asked him, but he refused to discuss it. They didn't want to pressure him, so that was it."

"That's why he never showed up as a person of interest in your files," Akil said.

"Whoever was running him wanted to protect their investment. You think he was a sleeper?"

"That's exactly what I'm thinking." Akil had heard the arguments many times: America wasn't like Britain—the great melting pot wouldn't produce home-grown terrorists.

They were wrong.

"Dig and we'll find the person who did this to Jalal," Akil said. "Start with the sheikh at the mosque he attended up until he was fifteen."

"He's already been ordered into custody. Forensics has identified three of the bombers so far. The other two were international students studying in New York. Both were British with Pakistani heritage. We think they were recruited at home and sent here to help carry out the attacks. MI5 has sent us some background information on them."

"Can we take a look at the video?" Akil asked.

"Of course." Sophie got up and turned the lights off, then pressed play on the handheld remote. The frozen image came to life and Jalal began to recite a scripted statement in English:

In the name of God the merciful and his prophet Muhammad, blessings and peace be upon him.

New York is no longer safe. The bombings which have taken place today are a response to the continued occupation of Muslim lands by the Jews. Israel's military and political backer, the United States of America, must end their support for the Zionists' occupation of Palestine. If not, there will be more attacks. America can not involve itself in a war and expect to remain beyond reproach.

Keep in mind that we are not hostile to the Jews because they are Jews. We are hostile to them because they have occupied our land and expelled our people. Even today they continue to do so. For every Jew who is killed by the resistance, ten Palestinians are killed by the Jewish war machine. There is no justice in this.

Our lands were occupied and our people were driven out more than sixty years ago. Today we continue to be forced to live our lives without dignity, prisoners to the Zionists and their supporters. I call on all Muslims to fight the enemies of Islam in the name of Allah and free Palestine from occupation. We seek justice for our people. No more than this.

To the citizens of America, we have attacked you because of

your government's support of Israel. Over three billion dollars a year is sent in aid, most of it for the purchase of weapons. These weapons are used against the Palestinian people who seek only to return to the lands that were stolen from them. Convince your government to change its policy or be prepared for more attacks on the city of New York. You have been warned.

Our Lord! Give us good in this world and good in the Hereafter and save us from the torment of the Fire! Praise be to Almighty God.

The screen turned black as the video ended.

Sophie got up and turned the lights back on. "What do you think?" she asked.

"A little preachy."

"Very funny. Anything else?"

"It's propaganda. Directed at us as much as the Muslims back home. We know a few things right away. It's not al-Qaeda, at least not directly. They're fighting in the name of Palestine, which is unusual because the Palestinians have never sought to attack us on our own soil. That's the provenance of al-Qaeda and ISIS and domestic terrorists like Timothy McVeigh. Hamas is the obvious choice, but the telltale signs are missing. No visual representation for starters. You'd expect Jalal to be wearing the customary green headband, and there's no flag or marker in the background."

"I agree. But then who are we dealing with?"

"Hezbollah? Maybe? But again, no consistent visual or textual evidence," Akil said.

"They probably fear reprisals from us," Sophie offered. "Better to attack and not claim responsibility as an organization. Hamas, Hezbollah, Abu Nidal—none of them want to claim responsibility and be hunted into extinction."

"Whoever wrote this was educated in the United States or Canada. Listen to the language. Your analysts have already told you this, I'm sure."

"That's right."

"They need to check university and college records. Start making lists and pare them down. He's not calling for the destruction of Israel and he's not calling for jihad against the West." Akil stood up and stretched his legs. "The message is specific, which means those responsible are most likely Palestinian."

"*We are not hostile to Jews because they are Jews,*" Sophie repeated. "*We are hostile to them because they occupied our land.*"

"Uh-huh."

"That's the language of Hamas."

"But the rest of the language, it doesn't fit their profile."

"They refer to Palestine as *our land.*"

"We could be dealing with a splinter group," Akil said, walking the length of the room.

"Or worse," Sophie said. "It could be someone operating under the umbrella of more than one organization."

"It's possible," he conceded. "After Iraq and Syria, the proliferation of small, well-trained terrorist organizations has become ubiquitous. With the right connections—"

Akil stopped pacing. He thought about what Bill had told him that morning—about Nasir Khan. "The Agency has spent millions training the Jordanian Intelligence Service in exchange for information," he continued. "Six days ago they informed us that they'd captured a man trying to slip across the border into Syria. His name was Nasir Khan, an al-Qaeda go-between. Under interrogation, he revealed that he'd been sent to give al-Qaeda's blessing for an operation. Unfortunately, Khan had not been given any of the operational details. Wasn't even aware of who he was meeting with. We can assume that whoever it was, they were responsible for the email we intercepted."

"You're just telling me this now?"

"We had no idea where or when the possible attack was going to take place. Was it going to take place in the Middle East? Europe? We didn't know the scale of it or the people involved. It was possible Khan was supplying us with disinformation. The Intel was unsubstantiated."

"Still," Sophie said, shaking her head in frustration.

Akil didn't respond.

"You think New York is still a target?" she asked.

"The threat is there on the tape. It's mentioned twice, but it's hard to say. How can we know for sure?"

"Nobody was inside the apartment when the ESU team entered. They recovered a laptop that was badly burned, but forensics was still able to access its memory. They found traces of the emails we intercepted and the video we just watched. Other than that, it was clean."

"Whoever we're dealing with is clever enough to know our capabilities," Akil said. "He probably bought the computer with cash, as a one-off, just to send the email and distribute the video. Trace the serial number, see if anyone remembers who they sold the computer to. We might get lucky."

"We traced The Damascus Letter back to a user account in Syria. Looks like whoever sent the original email created a generic account, then piggy-backed another user's internet access and sent the email that way," Sophie said. "No way of tracking down the sender."

"That figures."

"They're still combing the apartment in Queens for clues," she said.

"Then we should get over there and take a look."

Sophie gathered Jalal's file off the table. "I was already planning on heading over there. I can fill you in later if you want to get some rest."

"No, I want to see the apartment for myself," Akil said.

52

THE ESCORT VEHICLE carrying Justin Travers raced down a Baghdad boulevard at high speed.

Beyond the bulletproof glass, Travers counted the burned-out cars and trucks that littered the side of the road. Each one had fallen victim to violent forces, their insides consumed by fire, their tires reduced to black stains on an ashen road. For Travers, the charred and twisted frames conjured up images of surrealist art, like those made by Dali or Picasso. How long had these products of a mad bomber been sitting here, he wondered. The odds of being killed by a car bomb were relatively small if you crunched the numbers, yet he couldn't shake his anxiety. The fact was, people in and around Baghdad were still dying from targeted attacks. Life was cheap, and outside the security of the base, his was no different. Suicide bombers and

IED's were the great equalizer, and the convoy they were traveling in was a ripe target.

"Hold on," one of the soldiers yelled from the front seat.

Travers instantly reached for the handle above his head and grabbed hold as the SUV jerked left and hopped the center divide at high speed. Instinct told him to anticipate the worst as the Chevy bucked hard, its wheels hitting the concrete curb, then jumping into the air. As the front of the SUV slammed back down on the other side of the median, it gained traction and accelerated hard into a forty-five-degree turn, moving down an unmarked street, headed north.

One of the soldiers in the back seat turned to him. "Intersections are too dangerous, sir. You're a sitting duck if you aren't constantly moving out here. Gets a bit bumpy sometimes, but stopping for anything is bad mojo."

The kid was in his mid-twenties and seemed too young for this kind of outfit. Travers nodded at him and settled back into his seat. He was against bad mojo as much as the next guy.

The driving skills employed by the private contracting firms was impressive. They rarely slowed down and never stopped outside the fence, not until they'd reached their destination. The idea was to get where you were going as quickly as possible, and with a measure of randomness that left the enemy guessing. Each driver had two-way communication with the other vehicles in the convoy, and they spoke constantly with one another. Traveling at high speeds, only feet apart, the lead driver indicated to the rest of the convoy exactly when he was going to speed up or turn or brake. The result was a harrowing ride at high speeds with unpredictable turns and frequent off-road detours that seemed choreographed. The vehicles always stayed in a tight formation, buffering the center vehicle—and hence the client—from attack. The main objective when going from point A to point B was to remain highly adaptable to the moment and your environment without sacrificing the integrity of the convoy itself. It was a marvel to see in action. Travers only hoped it would be another month or two before he had to go through it again.

Haaaaaaaangh!

The lead truck in the convoy was sounding its horn and it brought everyone to attention. Travers leaned forward to get a better look at what was going on and saw that a yellow sedan was getting too close to the escort vehicles. He knew these guys were more than willing to shoot out the tires or an engine block if their warnings were not immediately heeded. In the summer he had witnessed a contractor shoot and kill a female driver who got too close. *Stupid bitch wouldn't back off,* the contractor explained later. Maybe she didn't understand or maybe she was a legitimate threat; no one knew for sure because the escort vehicles didn't stick around long enough to find out. Such actions were always meant to be a last resort, and they usually were, but it was the wild west out here, and the rules of engagement for private contractors remained deliberately vague, even now. The contractors knew this and counted on it. If and when the time came to use deadly force, Travers had no doubt the Red Sky team would not hesitate to pull the trigger. The politicians back in Washington criticized the way these men conducted their business, but he felt safer knowing they had such a wide latitude within which to operate. After all, his life was in their hands.

53

THEY ARRIVED AT the kill site in a cloud of dust.

Jumping out of the SUV, Travers was greeted by the sound of gunfire and high-pitched car horns off in the distance. Two Red Sky contractors flanked him, their hands resting on their holstered sidearms as Travers took a cursory look around, then approached the building.

The address Travers had been given turned out to be a two-story concrete structure just off one of the main roads.

A domestic residence.

The front door was shut and he could see no one on the property. He knocked, but there was no reply. After several seconds he knocked again using the bottom of his fist to make sure he was heard. The wooden door shook on its hinges, but again, no one answered.

Giving up, Travers turned and headed toward the mosque that occupied the next lot over. Perhaps someone knew where the owner of the two-story was or where they could find the bodies.

During his time in Iraq, Travers had seen more than a hundred mosques of varying size and consequence. Without much effort, he had learned a great deal about them. This particular mosque looked to be no more than three hundred years old: relatively new, at least in this part of the world, and too young to be a holy site for either the Sunni or Shi'a. This was a small blessing considering Muslims of either sect were uncomfortable with armed foreigners in close proximity to their holy sites. Just being close to a mosque was bad enough.

Travers stopped at the main entrance to the mosque and spoke stunted Arabic to an Iraqi sitting just inside the door. The man listened to him with a blank stare as though he were deaf and dumb. When Travers finished asking where the imam was, the man got up and disappeared inside. Travers hoped the man understood the question he'd asked, but it was possible the man had just wandered off, tired of listening to the American butcher his language. It wouldn't be the first time.

Since non-Muslims were forbidden from entering the mosque, Travers waited outside with the others. Several minutes later he spotted the imam approaching at a leisurely pace followed by a different man. The man Travers had spoken to was nowhere to be seen.

"Salaam alaikum," Travers said to the imam, his closed hand moving to his chest and away in the standard greeting.

"Alaikum salaam," the imam said. The reply was reflexive and not particularly gracious.

"Do you know the man who owns that building?" Travers asked in Arabic, motioning to the building that stood next to the mosque. "We need to speak with him."

The imam nodded, then turned and walked back into the mosque's entrance hall. He addressed the Iraqi who had accompanied him. The imam was clearly agitated, but he spoke in a whisper so that Travers couldn't hear what he was saying.

Travers wondered if either man knew who had perpetrated the killings. Was the imam actively involved with one of the Sunni militias? There was no point asking him these questions—his inquiries would only be met by stern denials. Most likely, offense would be taken, then he would be asked to leave, and in the end, they'd garner no intelligence at all.

When the imam finished speaking with the Iraqi, he disappeared into the shadows of the mosque's interior without looking back. The Iraqi the imam had spoken with stepped forward. "I am the owner of the building," the Iraqi said, speaking plainly so that Travers had no problems following his words. "I will show you where the bodies are."

"*Shukran.*"

Travers thanked the man and debated if he should question him before or after he had looked at the kill site.

Afterwards, he decided.

The Iraqi led them away from the mosque and back to his two-story home. Along the way Travers lit a cigarette and smoked it feverishly, keeping an eye on his surroundings.

On the opposite side of the home, the Iraqi stopped beside a series of concrete steps that led down to a basement. Travers took a last drag of his cigarette and flicked it away, noting that the narrow passage between the two-story building and the one next door was sheltered from view on three sides. The basement door was further concealed due to the fact it was below ground.

Without being prompted, the Iraqi wandered down to the bottom of the stairs and removed the old padlock that secured the solid wooden door that led to the kill site. When he came back up, he motioned for Travers to go have a look.

At the bottom of the stairs, Travers faced the closed door, hesitated a moment, then pushed it open.

The stench of rotting flesh hit him head-on like a tidal wave and he felt the muscles in his throat contract. He stepped back from the door and removed a handkerchief from his pocket.

Placing it over his nose and mouth, he stepped forward again.

The stench inside the room cut through the handkerchief with a vengeance, but there was nothing he could do about it except work as fast as possible. With the spill of daylight coming in through the open door, he could just make out the horror waiting for him at the far end of the room. The dead bodies were nothing more than dark silhouettes: four, maybe five of them, lined up against the wall.

Removing a small flashlight from his pocket, he ran its beam around the room hoping to locate a light switch. Finding one, he flipped it. A naked light bulb hanging from the ceiling brought the horrific scene to life.

Four bodies were slumped over in chairs against the back wall, arms hanging slack at their sides, legs splayed open. Their dead weight had pulled the bodies down and away from the back of the chairs, making them look like over-sized rag dolls. A couple of the victim's heads were bowed forward as if in prayer. Travers could see that blood had pooled around their legs and begun to flow toward the center of the room. Coagulation had stopped the flow mid-way. The fifth victim, at the end of the line, had fallen to the floor and was lying face down.

The room, approximately fifteen feet wide by twenty feet long, appeared nondescript. Bare concrete walls ran along the outside with a compacted dirt floor underneath. A lone table sat in the middle of the room now bereft of chairs.

Travers took some establishing shots of the scene with his camera. Coiled wire, a plastic bucket, and a pile of old bricks were stacked in a nearby corner. The presence of the table indicated the possibility this place had been used as a meeting room. Was this a regular occurrence? Was it for social gatherings or was this where Sunni militia members congregated after evening prayers to discuss their operations?

On top of the table there were sheets of paper strewn about. Travers collected the documents and stuffed them in his pants pocket without analyzing them. That would come later, back at the base. He wanted to minimize his time on site any way he could.

"Bloody hell, mate."

Startled, Travers swung around. One of the Red Sky Security team stood just inside the door, a hand cupped over his nose and mouth.

"Pretty grim, huh?"

"Jesus! The smell."

"What's your name?" Travers asked.

"Duane."

"Justin. Don't touch anything, alright?"

"Yeah, no problem."

Travers looked at the neat line of chairs, each claiming a cadaver except for one. Using the camera, he took several wide angle shots of the bodies.

Once that was done, he approached the first victim. He needed to take facial identification shots. It was a grisly task he'd rather avoid, but it was important.

The first victim was tall with a medium build. His head hung over the lip of the backrest, causing his Adam's apple to project up and out in a grotesque fashion. Spread unevenly on the wall behind him was dark blood spatter with bone fragments and bits of hair. Leaning over top of the victim he saw a neat hole in the man's forehead, which explained the blood spatter. Luckily, he could still get a good picture of the face for identification purposes. The techs would run the pictures through their facial recognition software and hope for a match. If they were lucky, one of these guys would already be in the database.

Once the first victim had his picture taken, Travers searched for his identification papers. Finding the ID, he removed it.

Jabbar Kathem Nasser
Sunni
27 years old
Truck driver

Travers pocketed the papers and moved to the next victim. This one was not as tall as the first and wore an old Liverpool football jersey. It was a cheap knockoff popular among the youth. Across the front was the team's former sponsor—*Carsburg*—without the "l" in place. It had three gunshot holes in the center of it. The man's head hung forward, his chin resting on the top edge of his chest. Travers tried gently tilting the man's head back so he could get a good shot of his face with the camera. Rigor mortis had set in though, stiffening the muscles and ligaments in the neck, making the head impossible to budge. He took the picture as best he could by getting down on his hands and knees and shooting the face from a low angle. It wasn't perfect, but it would do.

He located the second victim's identification papers and took a look.

Omar Adnan
Sunni
24 years old
Clerk

As Travers approached the third victim, Duane interrupted his work again: "Shi'a militia do this?"

"Hard to say for sure," Travers said, not turning. "Looks that way."

"These guys are Sunni then?"

"Yeah," Travers said. He wished this guy would just leave him alone and let him finish his work. He wasn't in the mood to chat.

"Hell of a murder scene."

No, thought Travers, a gang-style execution back home might have a similar feel, maybe, but this was different. This was genocide and it had been going on all over central Iraq ever since the war. No one used that word, of course. Sectarian violence sounded much less ghastly, but it didn't change the facts. The Shi'a had been repressed and brutalized by the Sunni minority during the rule of Saddam Hussein. They'd taken the opportunity that the war presented to exact a bloody revenge on the entire Sunni populace. The Sunni, in turn, struck back at the Shi'a. And so the cycle went, year after year after year. It had all but disappeared for a while, but it was ramping up again.

The fever was back and it was rising.

Travers gathered some empty shell casings off the floor. The perpetrators who had busted into this basement had probably used suppressed weapons and attacked late at night. Most likely they'd come and gone before anyone knew what had happened. The victims' hands weren't tied, and there didn't seem to be any signs of torture, which meant the killers had worked fast.

They had busted in, lined up their prey against the wall and shot them, one by one, in quick succession. The victims were lucky. This kind of attack often happened in isolated environments where they were tortured before being killed. Eyes were often gouged out, body parts chopped off, flesh burned to the bone. It was the product of an abhorrent bloodlust that still seemed far from satisfied.

"How much longer?" Duane asked.

"I'm almost done," Travers said. "Five...ten minutes."

"Good, place gives me the creeps."

Travers was happy to hear Duane's boots on the concrete steps outside.

He took head shots of the next two victims and grabbed their ID papers. They were both Sunni and both in their late twenties.

No surprise.

The final victim had fallen off his chair and was laying face down on the floor. Travers knelt down beside the body and placed his camera off to the side. With both hands, he went to roll the man over so he could get a good shot of the face. As soon as he laid his hands on the body though, he recoiled—instinctively—staggering backwards in shock.

"Jesus Christ!"

The body was still warm.

He took a deep breath—letting the shock dissipate—then leaned forward and grabbed hold of the man's shoulder and hip again. He rolled the body all the way over this time and checked for a pulse.

It was there. Faint, but steady.

The man was still alive.

54

AKIL AND SOPHIE arrived at the apartment in Queens around 2 AM. As they started up the stairs to the fourth floor, they passed two members of the FBI's Forensic Services Team carrying samples headed for the laboratory at Quantico. Akil let them pass, then carried on to the scene of the crime, retracing his footsteps from earlier in the day. As he stepped onto the fourth-floor landing, Akil turned toward the burned-out apartment and saw one of the ESU members running toward him.

What the...?

Sophie came up behind him and put her hand on his forearm. Akil flinched at her touch. "You okay?" she asked.

The image of the ESU man had vanished. At the entrance to the apartment was a bored NYPD officer standing watch.

"Yeah," Akil said, looking at Sophie. "Yeah...fine."

"You seemed lost there for a moment."

"Remembering this morning, that's all," he said. "Let's take a look inside."

Akil showed his ID to the officer posted at the door and went inside. The front hall was about eight feet in length and narrow. This is where the explosive power of the blast had been funneled out onto the landing. The lingering odor from the explosives brought back memories of holidays Akil had shared with his brother and father in Seattle.

"Smells like—"

"Fireworks," Akil said.

"Yeah," Sophie replied.

Akil carried on into the apartment and began looking around. What struck him first was how little damage there was. Fire had scorched the inside of the apartment, but it had not gutted the place the way he'd expected. The windows had blown out and there was widespread surface scarring, but that was it.

A couple of FBI agents were still inside the apartment. The forensics team had packed up and left already, which was good news because Akil wanted to snoop around without stepping on anyone's toes. The feds tended to be extremely territorial in these kinds of situations and they didn't like strangers looking over their shoulders, especially someone from the CIA.

One of the agents who was still inside the apartment sauntered over. He was in his mid-forties with a medicine ball gut and a shaved head.

"Can I help you?" the agent asked.

Akil turned to face him.

"Special agent Martin," Sophie said, coming to his rescue. She presented her ID. "We talked on the phone I believe. Special agent Cain, isn't it?"

"That's right. You the one attached to NCTC?"

"That's me. Thanks for waiting around. This is Akil Hassan. He's assisting me with the investigation."

"Civilian?" Cain asked.

"I'm with the Agency."

Cain did little to hide his disdain, but Akil didn't care, he just wanted access. He wasn't here to make friends.

"You're a little late to the party, agent Martin," Cain said, "we're just wrapping things up here."

"We won't keep you long. Can you go over the forensics for us?" Her voice was firm, yet conciliatory. It was late and everyone was tired, including her.

"Sure. Not much to tell. Lab rats couldn't find a single fingerprint.

Lots of smoke and fire damage, as you can see," he said, looking around the apartment as he spoke, "but whoever did this wiped the place clean before they left. The forensics team managed to recover some DNA evidence, but it won't do much good if there's no match on file."

"At least we'll have something to prosecute with when we catch them," Sophie added.

"True."

"What else?" Akil asked.

"Laptop was recovered over there," Cain said, pointing toward the kitchen. "We managed to get some stuff off the hard drive, but she was beat up pretty good."

"We've already reviewed the report on its contents," Sophie interrupted. "You can skip that."

"Okay. Well…there was a book on the Holland Tunnel tucked in behind the couch. Fire didn't get to it. We found pictures inside, snapshots of the tunnel from both ends. Timestamps on the photos tell us they were taken two weeks ago. Again, no fingerprints."

"And the photos themselves?" Sophie asked.

"They weren't your standard tourist shots if that's what you're asking. Whoever took them wasn't concerned about aesthetics. They were shooting the structure itself. Different angles, access doors, that kind of thing. Wouldn't be the first time these bastards went after her."

The "her" Cain was referring to was the Holland Tunnel itself. The FBI had busted an al-Qaeda plot to bomb it in 1993. The terrorist cell responsible wanted to carry out a "Day of Terror" in New York City. They were stopped. In 2006 the FBI foiled another attempted bombing of the tunnel, this time in the early stages of planning. But if there was one thing the World Trade Center proved, it was that terrorists were persistent. They wouldn't quit. There had been eight years between the two Trade Center attacks, and the terrorists succeeded the second time around. Maybe it would be the same with the Holland Tunnel.

"The photos have been scanned and are already on the network," Cain said. "You can see them for yourself."

"Anything in the bedroom?" Akil asked.

"They found several maps of the New York subway system. They were hidden at the back of the closet in a hole that had been cut into the wall. Five stations were circled in red on each map. Same stations. Transport authority was notified immediately. We also found several printouts from a variety of websites and chat rooms. The fire destroyed whatever else was lying around."

Akil struggled to make sense of the information he was being given. The subway maps. The Holland Tunnel book. The photos. The laptop. Why were they in the apartment? Whoever had planned this had not left in a rush. They'd taken the time to set up the explosives, rigged a delay and slipped away before ESU arrived. So why had they left stuff behind?

Cain was getting ready to leave. He threw his coat on and turned to Sophie. "Almost forgot," he said, "they found a Qur'an as well. Fire got to it, but the stamp on the inside was still legible. Came from the Al-Hidayah Mosque in Brooklyn, the one on Atlantic Avenue. They raised millions for al-Qaeda before Homeland started clamping down. A search warrant should be in someone's hand by now."

Akil could picture it already; a dozen armed FBI agents entering a mosque was going to create a storm of protest. A lot of people were going to be upset, not all of them Muslims. Recriminations would fly in both directions—from Muslim and non-Muslim alike—with little thought to weigh them down.

"And the explosives. What about those?" Akil asked.

"What do you want to know?"

"Everything."

"Well, the bastards were clever," Cain said. "They wrapped strands of filament wire inside the doorknob and rigged them to a timer. As soon as the door was smashed in, the wire broke and the timer automatically started counting down. Six to eight seconds later the bombs went off. ESU didn't have a chance."

"The bombs weren't made with high explosives though," Akil said, using his hands to gesture at the walls.

"No, it was some sort of incendiary device according to the lab coats. They seemed pretty excited. Said the work was exceptional. You believe that? Exceptional? Like they admired the bastard who made it."

"They identify the signature?" Sophie asked.

"Not yet," Cain said. "They'll take what's left and pick it apart, put it back together. May take some time."

Like any artist, bomb makers left subtle but distinctive identifying marks during the construction of their masterworks. The way a device was wired, tool marks left behind during assembly, the configuration of the detonator—any combination of these provided the bomb maker's signature.

"Do we know the kind of explosive that was used?" Sophie asked.

"They were magnesium based, mixed with something or other," Cain said. "Not really sure about the details, but they say it sucked all the oxygen out of the room. Fire burned itself out, for the most part. Fire department did the rest. It'll all be in the forensic report.

"Look, if there's nothing else, it's late and I still have a lot to do back at the office."

Sophie nodded. "No, that's it, thanks for sticking around."

"Sure."

Sophie watched the agent leave, then turned to Akil. "Two more potential targets," she said. "The tunnel and the subway. Confirms what was on the tape."

"Seems that way."

Akil walked over to where the book on the Holland Tunnel had been found. The front of the couch was soaked and charred black. Cream colored wadding had been ripped from the seat cushions by the fire department. He pulled the couch away from the wall, finding no fire damage at all on the backside.

"What are you doing?" Sophie asked.

He looked at her. "Something's not right."

"What do you mean?"

Akil spoke as he continued his inspection of the apartment. "Put yourself in the terrorist's shoes," he said. "You're planning to attack key locations in New York City and you're using this apartment in Queens as your base of operations…or one of them, at least. Why leave evidence behind? Laptop? Maps? Photos?"

"The place was rigged with multiple incendiary devices. I'm sure they expected it to burn to the ground," Sophie said, playing devil's advocate. "We got lucky."

"Why wipe the place down then? Fingerprints wouldn't survive a fire," Akil said.

"Better safe than sorry?"

"No. If you're going to go to that much trouble you wouldn't take the chance of leaving anything behind. And why not use gasoline or some kind of accelerant? The techs said the work on the bombs was exceptional. We have to assume they didn't malfunction."

"We're not dealing with amateurs, I agree," Sophie said, abandoning her role as Akil's foil. "What bothers me is why they would access the internet from this location. They must have known we would trace the chat room postings. They didn't even try and cover their tracks. It was a straight line from the user account to here."

"And the address we found on the fridge in Jersey? It doesn't seem like such a lucky break anymore, does it?" Akil added.

"But what does it all mean? They didn't go to this much trouble just to kill a few members of the ESU," Sophie said.

"Misdirection maybe. A message?"

"We have to assume these targets are in play. The tunnel. The subway stations."

"I doubt that. But whatever the case, we're no closer to the people who did this than we were this morning," Akil said. "We need a fresh lead."

55

JUSTIN TRAVERS YELLED for help. A second later he looked up and saw three men from his security escort rush into the dimly lit basement, weapons drawn.

"Get a medical team down here right away," he said, "one of these guys is still alive."

Price, the man in charge of the escort team, was staring at the dead bodies slumped in their chairs at the back of the room. Travers could see that he was struggling to reconcile what he'd just been told with what he was seeing.

"Price!" Travers shouted.

Price snapped to.

"Call CENTCOM, get a medical team down here now. Tell them we've got a high priority target."

"Right," Price said, running outside to radio for help.

The wounded man at Travers' feet had lost a lot of blood and desperately needed medical attention if he was going to live. He wore a bullet-proof vest underneath his loose-fitting tunic. It was unusual, but not unheard of for a militia member. Two shots had been fired into his chest at close range. Luckily the force of the bullets had been dispersed by the reinforced Kevlar. Despite this, the sand-colored vest was partially saturated with blood, meaning the bullets had pierced the man's chest cavity to some degree. How far, he couldn't know for sure, but he didn't want to remove the vest and check right now. Better to keep pressure on the wounds and prevent the man from bleeding out.

On closer examination of the body, he discovered a third wound. A final bullet had skirted the edge of the vest and entered the upper left shoulder. Again, there was no telling how much damage the bullet had done. It could have struck the shoulder blade and corkscrewed down into the chest cavity causing internal bleeding, or it could have lodged harmlessly in some muscle tissue.

"Medical team is on its way," Price said, entering the room again. "Ten minutes."

"Thanks."

"Here's the medical kit from the truck." Price handed it to Travers. "Need any help?"

"No. Just make sure the area is secure. We're going to move him as soon as the medics get here."

"Understood," Price said, heading back outside.

Travers dug through the medical kit looking for a trauma pad and some bandages. Finding them, he dressed the shoulder wound, applying pressure with an elasticized bandage. Once he was finished, he sat back on his heels and tried to picture how events had transpired.

The evidence suggested that the Sunni were meeting when Shi'a militia members stormed the room and lined them up against the back wall. One or more shooters had gone down the line, killing each man in turn. They shot the last man three times but got sloppy. The third shot had struck high, missing the vest. It had entered the shoulder and spun the victim off his chair, causing the man to end up on the ground, face down, blood pooling near his head. As far as Travers could tell, it's what saved his life. Assuming the man was dead and unaware of the Kevlar vest, the Shi'a had fled the scene, their work done.

If the Shi'a had been more thorough, the man would have had a fourth bullet in him. These kinds of incidents were precisely the reason professional assassins always put an extra bullet into the head of their victims when given the chance, even when they thought the target was already dead.

Having dressed the man's shoulder, Travers searched the body for an ID. What he found were two bundles of cash hidden under the victim's tunic—American hundred dollar bills stained with blood. He estimated there was at least ten thousand dollars in cold hard cash and checked to see if the money was counterfeit.

It wasn't.

Why was this guy carrying that kind of money?

Continuing his search, he eventually located the man's ID. It was also hidden away, tucked up under his blood-soaked Kevlar vest. An odd place to keep your identification papers, Travers thought as he examined them.

He quickly realized why the papers had been concealed.

The fifth man was a Shi'ite.

Each new revelation heightened his curiosity and confusion. What the hell was a Shi'ite doing in a basement filled with Sunni militia members? And why was he carrying ten thousand American dollars?

Travers checked the man's pocket litter for anything that would help explain who he was and why he was in this basement. What he found next shocked him. The whole time he'd been in Iraq he had never been this excited or this afraid. The small vial he had plucked from the man's pocket had a small hazardous materials symbol stenciled along its side. The vessel was the size of a standard D battery, round, and made of polished aluminum. He put the vial on the ground and hastily retrieved the documents he had collected earlier from the table. In light of the vial he'd just found on the Shi'ite, the papers could prove a vital piece of the puzzle.

He scanned the papers quickly. They were photocopies of official government documents. The technical jargon, in its original Arabic, was difficult to decipher. He recognized what looked like a spec-analysis and data summary for some kind of chemical compound. The numbers stated the compound's boiling point, vapor density, molecular weight, and volatility. Switching from one page to next he kept searching for the name of the chemical but found no indication of what he had on his hands. On the fourth piece of paper, he noticed a section on *Administration Routes*. The information here detailed the methods and lethality of various modes of dispersal.

He lowered the pages in disbelief. He was holding the breakdown analysis for a WMD. The stamp on the bottom right corner of the last page confirmed it. The stamp indicated that the documents were the property of the al-Muthanna facility at Samarra, 70km northwest of Baghdad. Al-Muthanna was well known as Iraq's primary chemical weapons research, development and production facility during the eighties under Saddam. Travers folded the papers back up and put them in his pocket. He grabbed the vial from the ground and held it at arm's length, staring at it. Did it contain a WMD? He tested the cap to make sure it was sealed tight and placed it inside a zippered pocket on his vest jacket, then stood up.

The medical team would be here any minute. He quickly began searching the other bodies. The pocket litter of the first three cadavers produced nothing of note. On the fourth, however, Travers found a sealed envelope with no address or name on it. The envelope was made from a thick bonded paper and had been sealed with tape.

There was paper folded inside. A letter? He tried using his flashlight to see if he could make out any of the writing, but the envelope's security lining left him guessing. He briefly debated opening the letter and looking at it, figuring it might help explain the bizarre situation he'd stumbled upon. Unfortunately, that wasn't the way things worked—the letter needed to be opened and analyzed by a trained forensic technician. So did the contents of the vial.

He quickly formed a mental to-do list in his head. He'd need to brief his station chief right away, then detail everything in a report and upload the pictures he'd taken. As for the vial and the letter, he would hand deliver them. They were vital to unlocking this mystery. The man clinging to life at his feet was the only one who could explain them though. He was the key.

In a sudden fit of panic, Akil knelt down and checked the Shi'ite's pulse again, afraid he might die before the medics got to him. His survival was suddenly paramount.

56

BILL GRAHAM ENTERED Anthony Marchetti's outer office through a set of double glass doors.

"Good afternoon, Bill," his secretary said.

"Dorothy."

Dorothy was in her mid-fifties and elegantly dressed. Many mistook her for just another career secretary at Langley, but Bill knew better. He understood the power she wielded as a gatekeeper and respected it. "He's expecting me," he told her.

"He's on the phone with the President at the moment. He asked me to show you in."

Dorothy led Bill into Marchetti's corner office with its mahogany desk and ornately framed degrees, various commendations and group photos plastered throughout. The ephemera had been arranged for effect. Each time Bill entered the office he felt like he was stepping onto a film set, one designed to bestow a sense of gravitas with its well placed American flag, eagle sculpture, side bar, and twin leather chairs. Appearances were important to Marchetti. Bill hoped he understood that it was the individual and their actions that mattered most, because the decisions that were delivered in this office could easily alter the course of a nation.

"Yes, Mr. President, we've got every possible resource working on this." Anthony Marchetti motioned with his free hand, urging Bill to take a seat in one of the leather chairs.

Bill sat down and pretended to review his notes while he listened carefully to Marchetti's half of the conversation. It was a technique mastered by covert agents and little old ladies worldwide and it worked remarkably well.

He was always surprised at the things people would say when they forgot you were in the room. And how easily people forgot.

It sounded like the President was putting the screws to Marchetti and that meant Bill was going to get the same treatment as soon as Marchetti got off the phone. He'd known this was coming. The officers under his command were working every possible lead to uncover those responsible for the attacks, but were getting nowhere. Bill wasn't going to start micro-managing them though. They were professionals who had been given strong direction and told to go to work. He would wait and see what surfaced. Sooner or later they'd find the thread that would unravel the case.

Bill eventually abandoned the phone conversation and walked over to the Director's glory wall. A law degree was framed in gilded wood alongside a group photo of Senators from 1992, the first year Marchetti had been elected to office. He was a southern gentleman by self-proclamation, though there were more colorful names on offer around Washington. The President had made Marchetti a political appointee a little more than two years ago. Political appointees to the office came and went depending on the prevailing winds and Bill had seen his share of them over the years. Most had little or no experience in the intelligence gathering business. The ones who succeeded listened to the veterans who had a lifetime of experience. Those that failed, did not.

The man in charge of Operations before Bill took over had spoken out against Marchetti's politically motivated policies and had been forced to resign as a result. Mitch Wallace was a legendary case officer with decades of experience. Bill had worked with him briefly in Moscow during the eighties. The day before Wallace had "retired," Bill had been named his successor. Before leaving, Mitch pulled Bill aside and gave him some words of advice: *Tread carefully,* he told him. *Let Marchetti think he's running the show, then do whatever it takes to get the job done.*

Those words had sent a chill through Bill. *Do whatever it takes to get the job done.* What exactly did that mean? Anyone who knew him knew he respected the chain of command, even if he didn't always agree with it. He'd only been Head of Operations for six months and was still settling in, learning to navigate the political landscape that permeated the seventh floor. But already he could empathize with Wallace; the Director's obsession with appearance over substance was making his job more difficult than it needed to be. Bill told himself he wouldn't bow to political pressure from Marchetti or the President or anyone else, not when it really mattered, and certainly not for political reasons.

That resolve was about to be tested though. He had a worst case scenario to contend with now: a major terrorist attack on American soil. And there were no easy answers to the questions he faced, like how the CIA had missed the planned attack. How the entire intelligence apparatus had missed it.

It was possible there'd been a breakdown somewhere in the intelligence pipeline. Or maybe it was just bad luck. It certainly didn't help that the case officer ranks had been depleted in the not-so-distant past. That human assets—essential to any intelligence operation—had been sacrificed for more SIGINT. Machines were easier to control than humans and they didn't betray you or embarrass you. Because of that, the Agency's HUMINT networks on the ground had slowly been dismantled or left to atrophy. Today, things were changing for the better. Had been for a while. There was more money, a new attitude, but the damage done had been widespread and it would take decades to repair. You couldn't create entire networks in only a few years, especially in hostile territory. Networks had to be built from the ground up over time. Assets had to be recruited and trust established. Continuity needed to be maintained. It all required experienced case officers with years of experience. It was a major reason Akil had been given a second chance at the Agency. To Marchetti's credit, he was in favor of the renewed effort. He wanted to do the right thing. But he was a politician first. Because of that, he would always be risk-adverse. And now wasn't time to play it safe. Not if they were going to stop the next attack.

57

"I UNDERSTAND, MR. President. Thank you."

Anthony Marchetti hung up the phone and walked over to where Bill was standing. "The President's pushing hard," he said. "I need some answers for the old man, Bill. What have you got for me?"

"I'm afraid we don't have much."

"I was worried you might say that."

"Every asset at our disposal, both domestic and foreign, is digging for answers. We just don't have anything solid we can act on yet. We need time."

"We need more than a good team effort here, Bill. We can't afford to fail on this one."

"The Cousins are pitching in," Bill said. "Their networks in the Middle East are much better than ours at the moment. I've asked them to shake the bushes, see what they can dig up."

"By all means, use them, but the responsibility lies here with us, not the Brits."

Bill was about to respond, but the Director kept going.

"American civilians are dead or dying, attacked on their own soil. The President wants to send a message. And quick."

"What's he have in mind?" Bill asked.

"I'm not sure, but he wants to know who's responsible. We need to tell him something."

Bill nodded his understanding. "On the surface it looks like the Palestinians are involved. Maybe Hezbollah as well," Bill said. "The email we intercepted, the one that alerted us to the attacks, originated in Syria. Unfortunately, the trail went cold."

"They covered their tracks, I know, I looked at the briefing," Marchetti said. "Do we think al-Qaeda is behind this?"

"There's still too many intangibles to be sure of anything right now," Bill said. "We can't rule anyone out at the moment. But no, we don't think al-Qaeda is the main sponsor."

Marchetti turned and headed for the leather chairs in the middle of the room. Bill followed a step behind.

"I need something concrete I can tell the President, something I can stand behind, Bill. Telling him we don't know a god-damn-thing isn't going to be good enough in a few days."

"I know that," Bill said.

"These attacks couldn't have come at a worse time. With the election tightening the President needs to reassure the nation. He needs to gain their confidence before everyone goes to the polls."

Bill's Scottish blood was beginning to boil. God forbid the President's poll numbers dipped. "The FBI is heading the investigation," he said. "Technically, it's out of our hands."

"Don't give me that bullshit," Marchetti responded, his voice rising. "If we can solve the riddle, I want it solved. We tell the DNI and the President who's responsible and we kill two birds with one stone. We get the bastards and the Agency gets rewarded."

You get rewarded, Bill thought.

"Who do we have working with the FBI right now?" Marchetti asked.

"The Deputy Director of Counterterrorism at the Bureau is one of ours: Sam Coupland. In exchange, a federal agent is acting deputy at the CIA's Counterterrorism Center. It's a reciprocal agreement that's been in place for years."

"We both know the FBI hold tight to their secrets, same as us, no matter what Homeland Security proclaims. Coupland isn't one of them and he sure the hell isn't all the way inside. You know it and I know it. I want to know what you're doing to secure the latest information being generated outside our sphere."

Marchetti may have undermined the Agency's work at times by putting politics first, but he wasn't stupid.

"I've assigned Akil Hassan to NCTC already. He's working with the FBI's lead investigator over there: Sophie Martin. They're following up on the apartment we found in Queens," Bill said. "He's reporting directly to me."

"Akil Hassan?"

"One of our best," Bill said. "Served in the Middle East for years. We reinstated him a couple of weeks back."

"Slick Willy?"

"Excuse me?"

"The one who got himself involved with that Iranian asset in Lebanon."

"Yes, sir."

"Jesus Christ, Bill! You can't put him on a high profile case like this."

Bill had prepared for this moment, knowing it would come eventually. "This kid is one of the best officers I've ever worked with," Bill argued. "He's intuitive, he has unparalleled experience, and it doesn't hurt that he's Arab. If we need him to, he can work both sides of the street for us."

"Look, I don't care how many languages the boy speaks. I said you could bring him back, ease him in, not put him on something like this. Shit, you know what kind of exposure this leaves us open to?"

Marchetti just didn't get it. "It's all hands on deck right now, Tony."

"Replace him."

"It's not that easy."

"I don't care. Find a way. I want him out of there."

"He's been shadowing agent Martin since we first got word of the threat. I'm already stretched thin as it is. If we pull him out now we lose NCTC altogether. We can't afford that."

"Goddammit."

Marchetti took a deep breath.

Bill hoped the Director could see reason in what he was saying. This wasn't the time to keep experienced officers on the sidelines. They had to learn from their mistakes.

"I don't need another Aldrich Ames on my hands, Bill. Especially an Arab."

"With all due respect, sir—"

Marchetti raised his hand. "Fine. You trust him, use him. But he's your responsibility."

"Yes, sir."

"You just make sure to keep him on a short leash. He steps out of line, even a little—"

"He won't."

"And I'll hold you personally responsible. You'll be the one to answer for it."

"Understood."

"You better be god-damn sure about this."

Bill stood up. "I'm sure."

"Fine, then go find me something I can give to the President."

58

As SOON AS Bill left the office, Marchetti picked up his phone and dialed an internal extension. A phone situated in a distant corner of Langley rang six times before someone finally answered.

"Office of Security," said the raspy voice on the other end of the line.

"Get me Peters."

There was a short delay as Marchetti waited for the head of internal security to pick up.

"Peters here."

"It's Marchetti. Listen. I want surveillance set up on an officer. Akil Hassan. It's closed book. I don't want Bill Graham or anyone else to know about this. Round the clock until I say otherwise and don't get too close. He can't know we're watching him."

"Yes, sir."

"You'll report directly to me. No one else."

"Understood."

Marchetti hung up the phone. If Akil Hassan crossed any lines, he wanted to be the first to know about it.

59

CURTIS STONE WALKED down H Street, past Lafayette Park. Off to his right the White House stood resolute and he paused a moment to take in its majesty. As a rule, he didn't succumb easily to patriotic sentiment. Today was different. Twenty-four hours ago New York City had been attacked. Again. And like everyone else, certain emotions inevitably rushed to the surface.

Having just filed another story with his editor at the Washington Post—his third in less than thirty-six hours—Stone was looking forward to a well earned double Martini and a porterhouse at Marlow's.

It wasn't easy getting a table at the venerable steakhouse on short notice. You needed to book well in advance because Marlow's didn't pander to politicians or their rich friends like other places. A name alone wouldn't guarantee you entry. But Stone had known the manager when he was still earning his stripes as a waiter, and a phone call was usually all it took to get a table, if not in the dining room itself, then in the lounge at least.

The thing Stone liked about Marlow's was that it bore little resemblance to the pretentious private clubs that were so popular in DC, the ones where you needed to be invited to join by an existing member and paid a small fortune for the privilege. Stone knew these places well. It's where certain Senators and Congressmen wasted away their afternoons on double scotches and rumor. He'd been inside and seen them surrounded by sycophants and lobbyists of different stripes. He'd spent untold evenings alongside them—eating, drinking, but most of all, listening—hoping to ferret out a big story or confirm information he'd received elsewhere. They were the places in which he did some of his best work, but it didn't mean he liked the atmosphere and what they stood for.

Entering Marlow's, Stone headed straight for the lounge. He wore a navy blue sweater with dark slacks and oxfords. His hair, which had abandoned him up front and gone fallow along the back forty, was cropped short. His wire-rim glasses gave him a bookish quality, and he hadn't been to a gym in years, but whatever Stone lacked cosmetically and physically, he made up for with a fierce intellect and tenacity for the truth. His steely reputation as one of the country's top investigative reporters and editorialists was hard earned. The Peabody and Pulitzer were among a variety of honors he had earned over the years. Refusing to meet with Curtis Stone was an invitation for scrutiny, and politicians didn't like to be scrutinized, especially by someone with his credentials. In an ironic twist, this gave Stone unprecedented access despite his refusal to toe the political line. Congressmen, senators, lobbyists, they all sought out information from Stone on a regular basis. In turn, they gave him whatever they knew concerning the goings on in DC—that which did not involve themselves, of course. Curtis Stone was far more powerful than he looked, and those in Washington knew it.

So did Sayyid.

60

SAYYID ENTERED MARLOW'S and took a seat at the bar. He wore an Armani suit and was clean shaven. Just another Washington lobbyist to anyone who was paying attention.

No one was, of course. They were all looking for bearded men with dark skin and thick accents. Sayyid had neither of those traits. While attending university in California he had worked hard to rid himself of his Palestinian accent. Even after returning to the territories and living amongst his countrymen for years, his American accent remained remarkably authentic. And his light-colored skin was finally a blessing this far from the scorching Mid-East sun.

The attacks on New York had created an impressive amount of panic in New York City and around the country. People were talking. They were paying attention again and Sayyid was pleased to see it. Now it was time to take it a step further.

Ordering a tonic with a wedge of lime from the bartender, he watched his quarry with calculated interest. He had been following Curtis Stone for the past three hours and the information he had received was proving accurate. Curtis Stone was a creature of habit, which would make the next part of his plan that much easier. Specific patterns of behavior equaled predictability. Predictability meant you could plan your actions with greater attention to detail and thereby increase your chances of success. Sayyid knew they would only have one shot at Stone, and they needed that shot to be perfect.

It was strange seeing the journalist in the flesh. Sayyid had only ever read Stone's articles in print and on the internet. The man was not what he'd imagined. He had always thought of him as being taller, more virile. A lion in print, Stone looked pedestrian in person. The name alone evoked a different image. Maybe that was his advantage, the same way Sayyid took advantage of people's preconceptions of what a terrorist looked like.

Sipping his drink slowly, Sayyid watched Stone down two Martinis in quick succession, then turned his attention to the television above the bar, watching as the news cycled from yesterday's footage of smoke and ruin to the camcorder image of Jalal Mahmoud delivering his ultimatum to the American people.

Everything had gone beautifully so far. He had been right in his assessment—three of the suicide bombers had succeeded. It was a good number, and the news outlets were still showing wall-to-wall coverage of the attacks. This was not the first time he had seen Jalal's taped declaration on television. Even the apartment in Queens had gotten plenty of coverage showing emergency crews buzzing around the exterior of the building like angry wasps, the commentators explaining that the fire, which had resulted from a bomb blast, had been quickly brought under control, but not before several ESU members had lost their lives.

A few stools down from him, a man in a tweed jacket raised his voice. "You won't get away with this," he said. He was watching the television, his face reacting to the images of burned bodies covered with dark sheets of plastic. The man was clearly intoxicated and Sayyid couldn't tell who he was speaking to, if anyone. What he could see for certain was that the man wasn't addressing him, the one responsible for it all.

Looking back over at Curtis Stone, Sayyid wondered if he had chosen the right man. The journalist's reputation was well known: he was committed to the truth. Sayyid only hoped the man's reputation had not been exaggerated.

Pulling a ten dollar bill from his jacket pocket, Sayyid laid it on the bar, then got up and walked out. A black town car was waiting for him on the street. Issam, one of his most trusted mujahideen, was behind the wheel.

Sayyid got in the passenger side and closed the door.

"We proceed tomorrow," he said.

61

THE MAN WAS tall and dressed in a military uniform. He walked briskly down the wide hallway, his loafers tapping steadily against the hard marble floor.

Clack, clack.

Clack, clack.

Clack, clack.

He was in a hurry, holding in his hand a communiqué marked top secret.

At the end of the corridor, he stopped at a set of double doors painted green. Off to the right a brass plaque was bolted to the wall at eye level.

VEVAK

كشور امنیت و اطلاعات وزارت

Vezarat-e Ettela'at va Amniat-e Keshvar
Iranian Ministry of Intelligence and Security
TEHRAN

He knocked on the door and waited. A moment passed before one of the doors swung open. An armed guard stuck his head out. Recognizing the man, the guard let him in at once.

The man proceeded down another long hallway toward the offices of the Lead Minister, his loafers brushing against carpet now, making almost no noise. When he reached the end of the second hallway he stopped. The double doors here were painted red.

He knocked.

"Come," said a gruff voice from inside.

The messenger opened the door and entered the room. The warmth inside provided a stark contrast to the outer reaches of the office. He headed straight for the Minister who stood beside a stone hearth alight with coal. The Minister was reading a file and did not acknowledge the man's presence right away.

The messenger waited patiently. The Minister's name was Ahmad Hashemian, and he was in charge of Iran's Intelligence and Security Service—VEVAK—the equivalent of America's CIA or Russia's FSB, and the counterpoint to Iran's Revolutionary Guard.

Hashemian took the communiqué and scanned it. His brow furrowed as he read the piece of paper.

"Shakran," Hashemian said finally.

The messenger, taking his cue, left the office and closed the door behind him.

As soon as the messenger was gone Hashemian walked over to his desk and opened the top drawer. He removed a blue plastic bottle and tilted it up to his lips, letting the chalky-white liquid pour into his mouth. He swallowed several times to get rid of the unpleasant taste, then picked up his phone and dialed.

He made several calls, each one short and to the point, confirming that what he had just read was true. It was a dangerous time to be in the intelligence business. Enemies were everywhere. Those who claimed allegiance were often the most dangerous of all. Power struggles were nothing new, of course. With the Iranian military and the Revolutionary Guard both vying for increased power in the country, Hashemian knew VEVAK was a target of opportunity. The Revolutionary Guard was particularly dangerous. With a burgeoning intelligence service of its own, many in her ranks wanted to get rid of VEVAK altogether. Hashemian had no intention of letting that happen.

Sitting down in his leather chair, he read the communiqué again, then grabbed the blue bottle and gulped more of the chalky liquid. The news was not good, and the communiqué had been confirmed by several sources. He already had plenty to deal with without this. America, reacting to Iran's growing sphere of influence and it's nuclear ambitions, had for years been ramping up its intelligence operations inside the country. He had to admit that Iraq had turned out better than he could have hoped. No longer having to deal with Saddam Hussein was a plus, and the Shi'a majority in Iraq had been set free and allowed to express its political will, albeit violently. The Americans had not understood the Pandora's box they were opening back then. The invasion had been a tactical error from the very beginning. Backers of the Shi'a militia, Iran was ideally positioned to become the region's dominant power broker while America further isolated itself. However, too much of a good thing was always dangerous. Hashemian knew this because he had studied his history. The Greeks. The Romans. Lawless lands meant room for lawless men, and such men could be as dangerous, or more so, than your enemy. The communiqué was proof of that.

Hashemian put the blue bottle back in its drawer and pressed the intercom. A second later his deputy came into the room. He was impeccably dressed in a charcoal grey suit made of Italian wool. His hair was slicked back and he had a dark beard that was well groomed.

"Sir," the deputy said as he approached the Minister's desk.

"Read this, Reza," Hashemian said. He handed the communiqué over. "We have a serious problem."

His deputy read the paper. The look of alarm on the man's face did nothing to settle his stomach.

"Bashir Khalini? Have we confirmed this?" Reza asked.

"Yes. No one knows where he is," Hashemian said.

"Three? Four days now?"

"Yes. He's been missing far too long. This complicates matters."

"And the militias?"

"They don't know anything," Hashemian said. "None of the Shi'a militias in Iraq know where he is."

"Then he's either dead or—"

"Or?"

Reza hesitated. "Or he's been captured."

Hashemian reached for his cigarettes. "Better he's dead. If he were not an important member of the Revolutionary Guard I would have buried him in the woods surrounding Sari a long time ago," Hashemian said.

"If he has been captured, we need to know."

"I want everyone looking for him. Scour the entire Crescent if you have to."

"Yes, sir."

"We have accomplished so much these past years. It would be a shame to lose everything on the account of one man."

62

THE OLD ECONOLINE van moved slowly through the suburban neighborhood of Still Creek just outside Fairfax, Virginia. Stylized letters were painted on its side. *Capital Cleaning.* There were no cleaning supplies inside the van, however, only three armed men and some rope.

Still Creek was a quiet and affluent neighborhood, the lawns framed by white picket fences and hemmed in by manicured hedges of forest green. All the way down the street oversized sport utility vehicles rested on concrete pads. The place felt like a post-modern pastiche of a Norman Rockwell painting come to life. Is this the American Dream? Sayyid wondered. The sight alone made him angry. His people survived on so little while these Americans lived like spoiled kings.

It was almost 11 PM and the streets were empty. As the van rolled past the cookie-cutter houses, old-style lamps cast small pools of light on the sidewalk. A car from a private security firm had patrolled the area five minutes ago and wouldn't return for another half hour unless summoned. Sayyid's men had been watching the target's house for three nights and had discovered that the patrol cars operated on a strict schedule. There was no guarantee the pattern wouldn't change tonight, but they had no choice but to proceed.

As the van came to the end of the street, Sayyid slowed to a stop, then turned left onto Birch Avenue. The avenue bordered a large park with a swing set and monkey bars. Sayyid pulled over to the side of the curb and put the van in park. It was nearly pitch black at this particular spot. The two street lamps, which normally illuminated the edge of the playground, were not working, his men having disabled them the previous evening. Turning off the van's headlights, he let the engine idle while he swung around to face his companions in the back.

Sayyid checked his watch by pressing a small button on the side. Black numbers became visible on an illuminated green background. 11:03 PM.

"Okay, just like back home," he said. "We move fast and make sure we are done and gone before anyone sees a thing. Remember, we need to take him by surprise."

In the back of the van Issam was dressed for jogging. He wore tight leggings along with a pair of New Balance runners, a baseball cap, a Gore-Tex shell with reflective trim, and a cheap digital watch on his right wrist.

Asad, the third member of the team, quietly slid open the van's side door.

"We take him right here, Issam," Sayyid said, looking the young engineer in the eye.

"Okay."

"Get going."

Issam exited the van and took off at a leisurely jog while Asad pulled the door shut, making sure to leave a small gap. Once Issam was out of view, Sayyid turned the headlights back on, put the van in drive, and pulled away from the curb.

Their target, Curtis Stone, went for a walk every night after the eleven o'clock news. For three nights in a row, Issam had watched him take the exact same route without the slightest deviation. Twenty minutes, two cigarettes, and back to the house. Stone was a creature of habit and Sayyid hoped he stuck to his routine. For an operation like this, it would have been better to observe the target for longer than three days, to find out where he was most vulnerable, to see when or if he changed his routine. Knowing every detail was the key to success, but they didn't have that luxury. Three days was all the time they could afford.

Sayyid drove slowly around the block and stopped a few hundred yards from the playground. He checked his watch again. It was 11:14. His heart was beating fast against his chest and his hands were becoming clammy. Having one of America's preeminent journalists as his hostage was a heady prospect. His fear at the moment was the possibility of fumbling the snatch. That's where the real danger lay, at the moment of confrontation. People were inherently unpredictable when confronted by dangerous situations. The timing had to be perfect. If they failed, there would not be another opportunity. The cops would be alerted, routines would inevitably change, questions would start to be asked.

At 11:28 Sayyid began to get worried. The previous three nights the journalist had appeared at approximately 11:15, with a variance of less than two minutes each night. Had Curtis Stone decided to forego his evening walk?

"Where is he?" asked Asad from the back of the van.

Sayyid muttered in Arabic for Asad to be patient, but he was having a difficult time following his own advice. His fingers drummed loudly against the steering wheel. Noticing this, he placed them in his lap.

A few seconds later, the orange glow of a cigarette blossomed in the darkness beyond one of the street lamps, then faded. Sayyid leaned forward, his hands gripping the steering wheel. He waited for the person to emerge from the darkness, hoping it was Stone.

He gave an audible sigh of relief when he finally saw Stone's features illuminated by the street lamp. "Welcome my friend," he said, easing himself down in the driver's seat as Stone approached the intersection next to the park. The van was half a block away and in the dark. He doubted Stone would even be able to see him, but there was no reason to take unnecessary risks.

Peering over the dash, he watched as Stone turned onto the avenue that ran past the playground. With the target's back facing the van, Sayyid quickly sat up and put the van in gear, then crept forward with the headlights off. In the distance he could see Issam jogging toward them from the other end of the park.

Stone was pig in the middle.

As the van continued inching forward, Issam picked up his pace gradually, avoiding any sudden bursts of speed. He was just another member of the community out for a late night jog. Nothing to be alarmed about in this neighborhood.

Sayyid checked both sides of the street as he drove. They had made provisions in the event that there were other people around. If the van didn't stop Issam was to keep jogging and ignore Stone completely, then rendezvous later at a prearranged location. But tonight there were no witnesses. Only the target.

Thirty feet from the journalist Sayyid stepped hard on the accelerator while Issam broke into a sprint. They were on a collision course with Stone now. The next fifteen seconds would determine their success or failure.

63

CURTIS STONE WAS lost in thought. He'd filed another column late that afternoon, reworking an editorial that responded to the terrorist's taped declaration. In the end, he had rewritten a large portion of it, expanding his point of view to include the intelligence community's response to the crisis. Then, on the way out of the office, his boss had stopped him. He wanted something for tomorrow's edition as well. *We need to capitalize on the hottest news story of the year,* he told him. Stone protested half-heartedly, then acquiesced, his mind distracted by news that his sister had just been diagnosed with breast cancer.

Taking a drag off his cigarette, Stone crossed the street and turned north on Birch Avenue. He walked past the playground, failing to register the burned out street lamps. His sister was putting on a brave face, but he could tell she was scared. He had promised to take her to the doctor tomorrow morning, and that meant being in the office by 5 AM to make sure his column got written. All he needed now was a decent idea on which to hang his story. So far, he hadn't come up with one.

Throwing the tail end of his cigarette to the sidewalk, he spotted a jogger headed toward him. At first glance, the man looked like any other jogger you might see in the park. Half past eleven seemed late to be out for a run, but to each his own, Stone thought, walking on, still trying to formulate tomorrow's column in his head.

A few seconds later Stone's concentration was broken again by the sound of an engine being revved behind him. He stopped this time and turned, looking to see what was going on. A blue Econoline van was speeding up the street, angling itself toward the curb. It was headed straight for him. Having taken one of those combat preparation courses tailored for journalists heading into war zones, Stone had been taught to react instinctively and to move fast when confronted with a potential threat to his safety. Here…now….he froze, trying to make sense of the situation. And what he saw made no sense at all.

Not right away.

Then he realized that he'd reported on situations like this before, in Baghdad, and Beirut back in the eighties.

The jogger was sprinting at him full stride now. Fifteen feet…five feet.

Stone's knees bent in preparation to get away, but it was too late. As the jogger's shoulder slammed into his chest, the air exploded from his lungs.

64

TIMING IT PERFECTLY, Asad threw the sliding door open as Issam tackled the journalist. The two men careened into the back of the van, crashing awkwardly onto the padded flooring. Asad slammed the sliding door shut and immediately set to work on Stone as the van pulled back into the street. The entire snatch and grab had taken less than ten seconds.

Placing a wadded up rag in Stone's mouth, Asad duct taped it in place, then slid a black hood over the journalist's head and tied his hands with rope.

"Make sure he can breathe," Sayyid said. "We need him alive."

The street—receding behind them—held no visible signs of a struggle. Thanks to the speed with which the operation had been carried out, there had been no confrontation or screams of protest.

65

AKIL LEFT NEW York and flew back to CIA headquarters at the request of Bill Graham. Even over the secure phone, Bill remained cryptic about what was going on. *There's been a new development*, he'd told him. Whatever Bill had found, it sounded important, and Akil had no problems leaving New York. He and Sophie were stalled out on the case anyway and the pressure to garner a new lead was wearing them both down.

He had been going over the ins and outs of the New York attacks every waking minute, trying to make sense of what little evidence they had. Every possible lead had been investigated and bled dry. The FBI had served their warrant on the Al-Hidayah Mosque in Brooklyn, uncovering indications of money laundering and some financing schemes, but nothing that would lead them to the whereabouts or identity of the terrorists at large.

The sheikh from Jalal's neighborhood mosque had been arrested too and was still being questioned by the feds. He would remain in detention indefinitely, possibly for years, but he wasn't talking. Chances were he had never met the men in charge of planning the attacks. These terrorists were not the usual suspects. They were smarter than that, having compartmentalized their operation from all appearances, recruiting from within the country as well as from without, using intermediaries whenever possible.

The Immigration and Naturalization Service was tracking down and accounting for every person with a suspicious passport who had entered the country in the last six months. The process consumed vast resources and vast amounts of time, but all they'd managed to learn was that two of the bombers had come from England—Birmingham to be exact, through Glasgow International. Beyond that, the evidence was sparse at best.

An aide met Akil at the airport and took him straight to Langley. Ten minutes later he found himself in *The Vault*. It was one of the Agency's in-house shooting ranges. An unusual place to conduct a meeting, Akil thought, but Bill insisted on getting out of his office.

Once they were on the range, Bill asked: "The apartment? Is it a dead end?"

"Mostly. There was nothing that told us who ordered the attacks or where the perpetrators might be."

"And the forensics?"

"Nothing definitive."

They had two dozen suspects in custody now, but none of them matched the DNA samples they'd collected from the apartment. They were also unable to tie any of the suspects to the planning and execution of the attacks. Many of the suspects had already been cleared. The rest were still being detained and scrutinized with a few being held on unrelated charges or awaiting deportation.

They were grasping at straws.

"I read Sophie Martin's report," Bill said.

"And?"

Bill placed a hand-crafted gun box on the shelf in front of him and opened it. "She says New York is in imminent danger of another attack."

"Well, you saw the tapes. The terrorists admitted as much."

"Lot of people are making noise. Resources are being pumped into the city from all over the east coast. FBI Director Wright and DNI Reeves are convinced."

"Of course they are," Akil said. "The feebs found maps to the New York subway system with specific stations marked off in red felt. Pictures of the Holland Tunnel. Identifiable targets."

"But you disagree."

"On paper, absolutely."

Bill had read Akil's report. It was an internal memo and therefore beyond the purview of NCTC or any other agency. His conclusions were quite different from Sophie's for one major reason: he could afford to speculate where Sophie could not. If Sophie ignored the obvious circumstantial evidence that was found in the apartment and the terrorists struck New York again, her career would be over. That the evidence was inconclusive—that the facts didn't add up—made no difference. Sophie had to play by the rules. Akil, because he wasn't directly involved, had the luxury of speaking his mind.

Akil removed the gun he had started carrying after Bill reinstated him and checked it. "Nothing says the terrorists won't attack New York again," he said. "What we found in that apartment, though, that was just window dressing. Sophie knows it too, she just can't take that position. Not officially."

Bill mulled the idea over. "How can you be so sure?" he asked.

"Because it's too perfect. The series of leads that led us to that apartment in Queens were orchestrated. At the time we thought the terrorists were being careless. With the dead and wounded still bleeding in the streets and everything pointing to that apartment, we moved in. Looking back with some perspective, you can see we were led there on purpose."

"A trap?" Bill asked.

"I think so."

Bill removed his gun from its box and slid out the magazine. "What's your theory?"

"Of all the evidence we found in the apartment, none of it has led us to any potential suspects. No fingerprints, no incriminating literature, nothing. Is that just a coincidence?"

Bill looked him in the eye and raised his eyebrows.

"No such thing...exactly," Akil said. "Whoever we're dealing with is smarter than that. We can see they're skilled and organized. We weren't able to trace The Damascus Letter because they were smart enough to cover their tracks, right?"

"Right."

"Yet we found the address for the apartment on the fridge in Jersey. The address was then confirmed when we did an ISP trace off that web posting which was signed with the initials AA, same as in The Damascus Letter. Naturally, we thought we'd hit the jackpot. It no longer feels like sloppy tradecraft. It feels deliberate."

Bill was methodically loading one bullet at a time into the empty magazine of his gun. "Keep going," he said.

"It was the bombs the terrorists planted in the apartment that really got me thinking. Why didn't they use an accelerant to fuel the fire or high explosives to obliterate the place? Who cares about collateral damage? Instead, the bombs they planted were incendiary based and did little more than scorch the surface of the apartment. The lab coats tell us they were designed that way. It's the only reason we were able to recover the evidence we did."

"Assuming they wanted us to find this stuff...why?"

"A diversionary tactic. They want us to focus our attention and resources on New York, which is exactly what we're doing. My bet is they're going to hit us somewhere else and we're not going to see it coming."

Bill slowly slipped the last bullet into his gun's magazine. "The theory has legs," he said. "I'll admit that. Marchetti is convinced New York is still the primary target though."

"But that's what I'm trying to say, Bill. These guys are professionals. The attacks all happened within ten minutes of each other. They left us no time to respond once the first bomb went off. No evacuations. Nothing. We got lucky at Penn Station, that's all. They're not going to announce their targets in advance. Misdirection is the only explanation."

"For the record, I think you're onto something, but we can't sell it without some hard evidence."

"For Christ's sake."

"We need to know who's responsible for this. Who trained these guys," Bill said. "Where the next attack is coming."

"The entire fertile crescent is a combat zone these days. These guys could have got their training from any one of a dozen different terrorist organizations or intelligence services."

Bill slid the fully loaded magazine into his Walther PPK, then racked the slide. With a fresh round loaded in the chamber, he turned and aimed down range, squeezing off all seven shots. Akil hadn't been on the range for months and he knew he should get off a few rounds himself. He turned and fired at his own target. The recoil of the gun felt good in his hands, but he could feel his busted ribs every time he pressed the trigger.

"Feels good, doesn't it," Bill said.

"Not really."

Akil noticed that Bill's grouping of shots was exceedingly tight. "You've been practicing."

Bill pressed the release on the side of the gun. The now empty magazine dropped from the grip. "Coming down here helps me relieve stress. I've been down here a lot the past six months." He put the gun on the shelf in front of him and carefully began loading fresh rounds into the empty magazine.

"That bad?"

"Some days are better, some worse," Bill confided. "I called you down here because we may have found a connection to the bombers."

Akil's face lit up. "Really? Great."

"We're still trying to determine what exactly we have. Only a handful of people even know about this," Bill said.

Akil nodded, acknowledging that he was about to become part of a select group.

"One of our men stationed in Baghdad—Justin Travers—arrived at a kill site two days ago. Sunni dominated neighborhood. What he found was a room full of Sunni militia executed in cold blood."

"And?"

"There was a Shi'ite in the room among the dead Sunni and he somehow managed to stay alive. He was shot three times, just like the others, except he was wearing a Kevlar vest. He caught a bullet in the shoulder. The other two barely managed to pierce the torso."

"What the hell was a Shi'ite doing in a room full of Sunni militia?"

"That's a good question."

"I still don't see the relevance."

"We identified the survivor as a member of the Iranian Revolutionary Guard," Bill said. "Name's Bashir Khalini. We have a dossier on him. He's been operating out of the north, working with the Shi'a militias."

"Pasdaran? You're sure?"

"We're sure."

Bill slid the reloaded magazine into his PPK. "With all the chaos in the Middle East, the Pasdaran have become more and more emboldened," he said, resting the gun on the shelf in front of him. "They're still funding and training Hezbollah, making overtures to Hamas, fortifying the Shi'a militias in Iraq."

"Iraq's their golden goose."

"And it's still up for grabs."

Akil removed the empty magazine from his own pistol. "I still don't see the connection to the New York attacks."

"You haven't heard the best part," Bill said. He turned, took aim, and fired a second volley of bullets down range. When all seven shots were spent, Bill laid his weapon down and turned back to Akil. "Travers found more at the kill site than just bodies. Khalini was carrying a small vial. We ran some tests and found VX."

"Nerve agent?" Akil asked, stunned.

"Weapons-grade. Serious stuff."

VX was one of the deadliest weapons ever created, a synthetic nerve agent that could kill within seconds if used effectively. Aside from a nuclear bomb, it didn't get much worse.

"The vial contained nothing more than a sample," Bill said, "but Travers was able to recover some documents at the location."

"What kind of documents?"

"Spec sheets detailing the manufacture of the VX at al-Muthanna."

"Saddam's chemical weapons facility?"

"We've verified their authenticity," Bill said.

Akil couldn't believe what he was hearing. Speculation persisted that Iraq had dropped three bombs filled with VX on Iran in 1988, but there was no evidence to back it up. Even today the facts remained shrouded in secrecy. In 2003, a United Nations Special Commission determined that

Iraq had indeed successfully weaponized VX, but after the first Gulf War Saddam claimed to have destroyed all existing chemical and biological stockpiles.

"I thought we didn't find any WMD's in Iraq," Akil said. "Or is there something I don't know?"

"I wish," Bill said. "Three years we scoured the countryside for something that would validate the government's decision to go to war. Nothing. Until yesterday."

"A little late."

"No shit."

"Is there a link between al-Muthanna and the vial found on Khalini?"

"The signatures match. The VX in that vial was produced at al-Muthanna sometime during the late eighties. Unfortunately, that's all we know."

"So we have no idea how much there is or who controls it?" Akil asked.

"What we know is that an Iranian agent meeting with a group of Sunni militia with al-Qaeda connections had a sample of this stuff on him at the time of his attempted murder."

"Jesus."

"It gets worse," Bill said. "One of the militia was carrying a letter from Abdul Saqr, a fixer for Hezbollah."

"I'm familiar with him," Akil said. "He was becoming a serious player when I was there."

"Still lives in Lebanon. He smuggles weapons in from Syria. Rockets, explosives, you name it. Very connected."

"What did the letter say?" Akil asked.

"It was addressed to Khalini. Abdul Saqr was telling him that he had received the gifts from his friends in Syria. He was thanking Khalini and signed the letter personally."

"What friends in Syria?"

"We don't know yet. Al-Qaeda? Palestinian Islamic Jihad? Your guess is as good as mine."

"And he used the word *gifts*?"

"Just like in The Damascus Letter. Yes."

"Could be a coincidence," Akil offered, though his instincts told him that it was far more than that.

"We believe Saqr sent the letter to Khalini as proof he'd received the VX."

"Makes sense."

"Travers found ten thousand dollars in American cash on Khalini at the kill site. We think it was the final payment for the Sunni militia's part in delivering the package to Saqr's contacts in Syria."

Akil ran his hand through his hair as he tried to absorb the new information.

"In the letter, Saqr tells Khalini that he'll deliver the gifts—the VX—as promised," Bill said. "They should arrive in two weeks."

"Arrive? Where?" Akil asked.

Bill shrugged his shoulders. "If it's going to take two weeks, all we can assume is it wasn't meant for Hezbollah."

"Maybe they're planning to smuggle it into Israel," Akil said.

"Maybe. Or the UK. Or here. After the attacks on New York, we have to assume the worst."

"And we don't know how much lead time these guys have had?" Akil asked.

"No, and there's no use speculating. We need facts. Khalini was taken to our base hospital and patched up. Doctors tell me he lost a lot of blood, but his injuries were not that serious. Once he regained consciousness, we questioned him. He was uncooperative, so I had him rendered," Bill said.

Akil loaded his gun and aimed it down range again. He didn't know what to say, so he started shooting. He knew extraordinary renditions still happened, though he'd never been involved in one. The CIA had used the technique for years until there was a public outcry against human rights violations, then a policy shift. The rendering of terror suspects was rare these days. Technically, the procedure was no longer sanctioned, which made it a black book operation. Khalini would have been transferred from the military base at Balad to a secret location inside a co-operative third-party country. Once on the ground, he could be questioned without legal restriction. Tortured if necessary.

"He's at one of our facilities outside Cairo," Bill said. "I want to you to go and find out what he knows."

"Me?" Akil asked.

"Is there a problem?"

Akil hesitated.

"No."

"Good."

Bill put his gun back in its case before he addressed Akil again. "If the planners of the New York attacks are still out there, and if they're as smart as you say, they could be planning on using this VX."

"You think this guy knows who's responsible for the attacks on New York?"

"I think he can tell us things we don't know, like where the VX is headed. That means we need to know everything he knows and fast. If that means crossing boundaries," Bill said, pausing for effect, "so be it."

"Including torture?"

"Not necessarily. But whatever it takes, yeah."

"Right," Akil said. He had never contemplated the idea of torturing someone to get information. There were other ways, more reliable ways, but they took time.

"I need to know you can do this," Bill said, putting his hand on Akil's shoulder.

"What exactly are you asking me?"

"Our people are working on Khalini now, softening him up, trying to get him to talk. But we have days, not weeks to get the information and act on it. I'm sending you to Cairo to make sure we get what we're after. Oversee the interrogation. Put the pressure on. That's all I'm asking. Make sure we get the intelligence we need before it's too late."

"Okay," Akil said, picturing Hannah lying in her hospital bed at Bellevue, hooked up to the machines. And Michael. How far would he go to protect Michael?

"I'll make sure we get the information."

"That's it then. Travers will meet you at the airport in Cairo."

"And Sophie Martin?"

"What about her?"

"We need to bring her in on this."

"No way," Bill said. "This doesn't go outside the Agency."

"Who knows where this is going to lead us. We may still need her."

"It's too dangerous."

"If we want everything NCTC and the feds have, or will have, we need to offer her something in return. You'd want the same."

"I have faith in your ability to smooth out any ruffled feathers. You're good at that."

"Not this time. We'll lose our access. There'll be consequences," Akil argued.

Bill stood with his hands resting on top of his gun box, weighing the argument, deciding what to do.

Akil waited, wondering which way the penny would drop. He didn't want to lose his connection to NCTC or Sophie Martin, but he knew whatever Bill asked of him, he'd do it.

"Alright," Bill said, placing his gun box underneath his arm. "Get her to sign an NDA and don't tell her a god-damn thing until you have her signature on that piece of paper."

"Done."

"So you know, Khalini doesn't exist. The trail is already in the process of being scrubbed. If she tries to blow the whistle on us she'll be throwing away her career. Make sure she knows that."

"I'll tell her."

Bill put his free arm around Akil and led him toward the exit. It was a casual gesture, but there was nothing casual about what they'd just discussed. "We need to know what Khalini knows, kid. He may be our only hope of stopping another attack."

Akil nodded, noting the urgency in Bill's voice, feeling the weight of the mission on his shoulders already.

66

Sayyid stopped at the entrance to the industrial complex just long enough for Issam to open the gate and let them in.

The complex was scheduled for demolition, the buildings already stripped bare of anything valuable, which meant there were no longer any security guards, only a chain link fence to keep out vagrants.

As they drove through the dark maze of buildings, Sayyid spotted the meat-packing plant up ahead, recognizing its hulking silhouette and the gaping hole that had been cut into its side by one of the salvage companies.

He drove through the hole and into the building's interior. As the van slowed, Issam jumped out and placed two large sheets of corrugated metal across the opening to conceal the van's presence.

Looking around, Sayyid noticed the heavy chains and large metal hooks that still hung down from the ceiling. They were parked inside the killing room where the cattle had been electrocuted and bled out before being processed.

"Take him downstairs," Sayyid ordered.

Sayyid's men grabbed the journalist from the back of the van. His hands were still tied and his head was covered. They nudged him along, the chipped concrete crunching noisily underfoot as they made their way through what had once been the processing area. Here the meat had been sectioned, trimmed and conveyed to the packers downstairs where the huge walk-in fridges and freezers were located. The heavy insulated doors had been removed, leaving large metal lined rooms. For Sayyid, the seclusion of these rooms provided the perfect setting in which to confront his guest.

When they got to the basement, Issam walked to the far end and removed a blanket that covered a gas-powered generator. He yanked on the machine's rip-cord, bringing it to life. The noise was obnoxious in the tightly confined space and fumes from the motor had to be vented with a fan.

"Take him into the first cooler and sit him down," Sayyid ordered Asad. "Remove the gag, but keep the hood in place for now."

Asad led Stone into one of the larger rooms and sat him down on a fold-out metal chair. The chair sat next to a small card table on which was placed a pad of paper, a pen, and a digital voice recorder. The noise of the generator was reduced to a muscular hum inside the room, and a halogen lamp in the corner, connected to an extension cord, provided plenty of light.

Sayyid entered the room and addressed his captive.

The journalist instinctively moved his covered head toward the sound of Sayyid's voice.

"You will not be harmed if you cooperate with us. If you try and scream or fight, I cannot be held responsible for the actions of my associates," he explained in a calm and professional voice. "You understand?"

"Who are you?"

"Do you understand," Sayyid said, his voice suddenly tinged with the threat of violence.

"Yes, I understand. Who are you? What do you want with me?"

"Be patient Mr. Stone. Try and relax. I will explain everything in a few minutes."

Outside the room, Sayyid set up a mirror on a section of exposed concrete. He placed a plastic bag beside it. From a glass jar he applied prosthetic adhesive to his jaw-line, then removed a fake beard from the plastic bag and gently applied it to his face. He shifted the beard around until he was satisfied with its positioning, then repeated the process, applying a mustache to his upper lip, gazing into the mirror to see its effect.

The look would not pass muster at a customs booth, but it masked his natural features and that was enough for today. Next, he removed a contact lens case. Inside were a pair of contacts suspended in a mild cleansing solution. Using his forefinger, he picked up one of the contacts and inserted it. When both contacts were comfortably in place he looked at himself in the mirror again. His eyes were dark blue now and he was pleased with how completely his appearance had changed. Lastly, he put on a pair of heavy rimmed spectacles, the plain glass lenses having no effect on his vision.

With the transformation complete, he could now talk with the infamous Curtis Stone without wearing a balaclava to protect his identity. That would have sent the wrong message. He needed the reporter to see that he was more than just another cliché. He was not a madman or a fundamentalist. True, he had learned to work with both, but he was a human being, as unique and as vulnerable as the next. He was capable of love and of reason. Murder too, but not without cause. He was not brainwashed or a zealot as people would assume. He had been born of a mother and raised by a father who cared deeply for him, a father who had suffered a lifetime of indignity at the hands of the Jews and the West.

Sayyid put the mirror back into the plastic bag and took a deep breath. The reporter was going to tell Sayyid's story to the American people. But first, he had to be convinced.

67

SAYYID ENTERED THE cooler.

Stone sat quietly in front of the small fold-out table, the hood still over his head.

"Put your masks on," Sayyid told his associates. "Then untie him and remove the hood."

With his hands free and the hood removed, Curtis Stone struggled to adjust his eyes to the bright light while he rubbed his wrists where the rope had chaffed his skin raw.

Sayyid stood in front of the reporter, taking stock of him. "You may call me Ali," he told Stone, handing him a bottle of water. "I apologize for having abducted you, but it was necessary under the circumstances. You must be wondering who I am."

"Yes."

"I am the man responsible for ordering the suicide attacks against New York City," he said, maintaining eye contact with the journalist.

Stone stared back at him in shock.

Sayyid wondered if the reporter believed him.

"You're a murderer!"

"Reserve your judgments for later, Mr. Stone," Sayyid said. "Many people from many nations have blood on their hands. Americans more than most. You killed almost four million people in South-East Asia during the Vietnam conflict. Women and children. Innocent farmers. US casualties totaled fifty-eight thousand during the same period. How can you justify that discrepancy?"

"That was different," Stone said, reacting from his gut. "That was war."

"War justifies many things, doesn't it? Almost half a million Iraqi children died from repeated US bombing during the Nineties, and from sanctions imposed by the U.N.'s Security Council. Was that war too?"

"Your point?"

"Recriminations are easy, but they don't help either of us. You say I'm a murderer, Mr. Stone. Okay, I'm a murderer. A soldier even. Fine distinctions either way, I'm sure you'd agree. America is guilty of murder too, far worse than what was dealt to the people in New York two days ago."

Stone was trembling. From anger or fear, Sayyid couldn't know for sure. Maybe both.

"What do you want from me?" Stone asked.

"I don't want to get into a debate with you. You're a reporter. I have read your articles and your books. You're passionate. You are, in my estimation, fair. I want to give you something. I want to give you a scoop, Mr. Stone."

"You want me to interview you?" Stone asked, sounding surprised.

"Yes. An exclusive."

Sayyid tried to gauge the journalist's body language. He knew Stone would be disgusted with what he had done in New York. He could understand that emotion perfectly. He had felt the same way about many Israelis following attacks in places like Ramallah, Tulkarem, and Jenin. The catch here was that Sayyid was making Stone an offer no journalist could refuse—the opportunity to interview a terrorist behind an attack on American soil, and to report it only days later. It was a once in a lifetime opportunity. He was sure Stone would not pass it up.

"You can't justify your actions to me," Stone said brusquely. "There's no justification for what you did."

Sayyid was impressed by the journalist's boldness, but not deterred. "You can ask me any question you wish and I will try and answer you as honestly as I can," he said. "In turn, I will give you my side of the story. The story of my people. All I ask is that you keep an open mind. That you listen. Then report without prejudice. Can you do this, Mr. Stone?"

"I doubt it."

Sayyid sat down in the fold-out metal chair opposite his captive. "Of course you can," he said. "This is a great opportunity for you, Mr. Stone."

"How can I be impartial when you're holding me as a hostage?"

Sayyid ignored the question. Stone would write the story. And why not. But first they had to establish a basic trust with one another. "You are not going to be harmed," Sayyid said. "Feel free to take notes, record the interview if you wish." He motioned to the pad of paper and the voice recorder sitting on the table.

"Why did you murder those people?" Stone shouted, rising up out of his chair.

Issam, who stood behind the journalist, reacted quickly. Grabbing Stone by the shoulders, he shoved him back down into the chair.

Stone shrugged away Issam's hand. "Those were innocent women and children you killed. The U.S. government won't stop supporting Israel. You must know that."

Sayyid could hear the contempt in the Stone's voice. "I acted out of desperation," he said.

"Desperation?"

"Our people are dying, Mr. Stone. They have suffered for more than sixty years, made to live like caged animals by the Israelis. Our movements are restricted, our right to self-determination constrained. Your government speaks of freedom. You want to be a beacon to the world, and yet you support Israel, a country responsible for countless human rights violations. Documented violations. You give them billions of dollars a year in military aid, but more than that, you give them license."

"You can't expect sympathy. Not now. Not after what you did."

"Innocent Palestinians and Muslims die every day because of American foreign policy. Because of the Jews," he said, spitting the last word out like venom. "The American people must force their government to change. Until they do, they are complicit and they will suffer the consequences."

"You're mad. Democracy doesn't work that way. Violence only begets more violence."

"Politics and violence are blood brothers. One does not function without the other."

"The civilians you killed were not responsible for your people's suffering," Stone said, shifting his weight on the small metal chair.

"That's not true. They are responsible. And they have the power to affect change," Sayyid said. "Indifference is not an excuse. The politicians won't listen, but the people will. If not to reason, then they will listen to their fear and act from it. It will be different when the bombs start exploding in the restaurants and shopping malls of Nebraska and Iowa. In Los Angeles. Instead of Tel Aviv and Haifa. Then we'll see what support Israel gets."

"You're wrong. It'll only strengthen the American resolve to stand behind Israel."

"We'll see."

"And diplomacy? The peace accords? What about them?"

"Don't be naïve, Mr. Stone. You know we have nothing to trade, nothing to bargain with except our lives. If there was another way we would have chosen it."

Stone sat silent as Sayyid stood up and started pacing around the room.

"Questions. Give me more questions," Sayyid urged his captive.

Stone reached for the digital recorder and pressed the red button on its side. The small machine made no noise, but he could see the numbers on the tiny display moving. "Who do you represent? Hamas? Al-Qaeda?"

"That's not important."

"It is."

"Many people wish to see America destroyed. All of them have a vested interest in the success of my mission. But to be clear, I don't want Islam to rule the world any more than I want American foreign policy to rule the world. I want Palestine given back to her people. That's all."

"You know that'll never happen. I mean…you realize that it's too late for that. Don't you? Some of your land may be returned, sure, but—"

"Our land was stolen from us! We will fight for another hundred years if we have to."

Sayyid sat back down at the table and looked Curtis Stone in the eyes. "I'm going to tell you a story, Mr. Stone. My father's story. In many ways his story is the story of the Palestinian people. Maybe then you'll see why more American men, women, and children will have to die before the people of Palestine can be free."

68

THE GULFSTREAM 550 was waiting for him on the tarmac. The private jet had flown up from South Carolina that morning and was fueled and ready to go. Glistening in the late afternoon sunlight, it looked as if it had just rolled off the assembly line. From what Akil had been told the jet had a remarkably long range and approached Mach 1 when taken to its limit. That meant tonight's flight to Cairo would be direct. No stopovers. No crowds.

The jet was owned and operated by the CIA's aviation wing, which functioned as a private contracting firm called Arrow Contractors Ltd. It was an evolution of the old Air America outfit the Agency operated during the Vietnam War. For obvious reasons the Agency couldn't rely on commercial airlines for covert operations and Arrow was their saving grace.

Akil handed his bag to the waiting steward and looked around for Sophie. She had agreed to meet him at the airport. He had given her specific directions along with the gate number and a plausible cover story. He would tell her the truth when she arrived and they were both onboard the plane. For now, Sophie was under the impression they were following a lead SIS had uncovered in their efforts to assist the investigation. He told her that whatever the Brits had, it was significant because they'd requested a face to face. When he asked if she wanted to go, she'd jumped at the opportunity. He suggested they'd be back in less than twenty-four hours, but cautioned her to pack for a longer trip in case something came up.

Growing impatient, Akil checked his watch again, then he caught sight of her coming through the gate with her carry-on bag in tow. Spotting him standing alongside the aircraft, she waved, then quickened her pace. He waved back and watched her walk toward him with her hair blowing in the breeze. Despite himself, he felt the now familiar pang of attraction. It was those green eyes that had commanded his attention that first day at NCTC. They were intense and hard to read. He'd found himself drawn to them. To her. He'd wanted to know the woman behind those eyes—partly because the situation demanded it, but also because he was genuinely curious. Then he'd listened to her briefing. It had been clear, concise, and aggressive. In front of the DNI, the White House, NSA, it had proved quite impressive. Of course, their first introduction had not gone the way he would have liked, but since then they'd worked well together. At the hospital, she'd even taken the time to comfort him.

"Hey, sorry I'm late," Sophie said, stepping around the plane's wing, smiling.

"No problem," he said. "Here, let me get your bag."

He noticed she was wearing make-up. Not much, just some eyeliner and a light shade of lipstick. He had never seen her wear make-up before.

Sayyid handed Sophie's bag to the steward, then turned back to her. "After you," he said.

"Thanks."

She climbed up the short set of stairs, her hips swaying gently back and forth. Akil couldn't help noticing that she kept herself in great shape and that she chose her clothes with particular care. They emphasized the natural curves of her body and amplified her femininity while still managing to stay suitably conservative. Most women he had met from the FBI were less than fashionable. Many renounced their femininity altogether, adopting a more androgynous persona. Not Sophie.

He followed her into the plane's cabin, noting the hint of perfume that was left in her wake.

"I feel a little out of my league," she said, looking around the cabin.

"Me too. Beats flying economy though."

The interior of the plane was nothing like a commercial airliner. Plush leather seats and a small sofa filled the rear portion of the cabin. Thick carpeting ran throughout. Rosewood cabinets with nickel trim provided an accent to the cream-colored upholstery. It felt like a swank hotel suite. A plasma television sat atop a well-outfitted media center, the screen adjustable for optimal viewing throughout the cabin.

Akil gestured toward the sofa.

Sophie sat down.

He sat beside her.

The steward had already closed the cabin door and they soon felt the aircraft taxiing toward the runway.

"Is it okay to talk freely?" she asked, looking back at the steward.

"Yes. The crew have all been vetted."

"Of course they have," she said. She had a mischievous grin on her face. "You love your toys, don't you?"

"Me?"

"The CIA."

"I guess," he conceded. "They come in handy sometimes. Wouldn't you agree?"

She leaned back into the cushions and ran her hands over the soft leather. "No complaints," she said.

"I'm glad you approve."

The steward came by and introduced himself. He asked them if they wanted anything to drink. Akil told him they were fine for now.

"How's Michael?" Sophie asked once the steward had left.

"He's angry and confused."

"I suppose you have to expect that."

"I spent some time with him today," Akil said. "We went for pizza, but he didn't want to talk about what happened. It's hard. Hard for my father, especially. I feel bad putting him in this position, having to take care of Michael."

"That's what families are for."

"I guess."

Akil got up and walked to the front of the plane. He returned a few seconds later with two bottles of water. He handed one to Sophie. "About the latest developments in Britain."

"What has SIS found out?" she asked.

"That's what we need to discuss." He changed his position on the couch so he was facing Sophie directly.

"Alright," she said, her tone shifting slightly.

"Bill Graham didn't want you to come on this trip," he told her. "I told him that wasn't an option. That we'd made a deal to cooperate with each other."

"I appreciate that."

Akil noted the skepticism in her voice. "It's the truth. We had an agreement, right?"

"Enough with the soft sell. What's going on?"

Her eyes had grown cold, and her body language was suddenly very businesslike.

"We're not going to London," he said.

"What do you mean we're not going to London?"

"We're going to Cairo instead."

"Egypt? What are you talking about? I thought SIS—"

"I lied. I'm sorry."

Akil removed the eight page non-disclosure agreement from inside his jacket. "I couldn't go into the details on the phone. Where we're going and what we might learn is highly classified. Once you sign this paper I can explain everything in more detail."

He handed her the NDA. She took the paper from him and began to read it.

"What is this?"

She knew exactly what it was.

"A standard NDA," he said.

"A non-disclosure agreement? You're serious?"

"Afraid so."

"What for?"

"Bill Graham's orders." He could see she was upset. "It's the only way he'd agree to let you go. It's standard procedure, really."

"Standard? For who?"

"It prevents you from disclosing or sharing anything you may learn or see while we're in Cairo."

"I work for the FBI. I work out of NCTC. Have you forgotten that? This is ridiculous," she said, tossing the paper back into his lap. "I won't sign it."

Akil picked up the NDA and held it in his hand. "It's your choice. We have what could be a major break in the case. This NDA is the only way I can read you in on it."

"What kind of break?"

"I can't tell you that until you sign the paper," he said.

"You and your bloody secrets." Her voice was edging toward anger now. "That's what this is about. Not working together, not pooling our resources. It's a one-way street with you people?"

"You people?"

"Always has been. The CIA doesn't want to share information with anyone. You arrogant bastards still don't get it, do you?"

She was up and off the couch now, staring at him with venom in her eyes. He should have anticipated her reaction and wondered if his feelings for her were clouding his judgment.

"We had a deal," he said, his own frustration mounting. "Remember? We agreed I would share information with you, but that information would go no further unless I said so. This NDA is just an extension of that."

"No, it means you don't trust me. So how am I supposed to trust you?"

"I have no choice in this particular matter."

"Of course you do."

"I don't," he said, getting up off the couch. "You want to stay here in DC. Fine. I'll follow the lead myself. I'm going to Cairo with or without you, Sophie."

"I won't sign it."

"I fought for you. I convinced my boss that we needed to cooperate and work together." He hesitated. "There's a good reason you need to sign this piece of paper, but I can't explain that until I have your signature."

"What possible reason could you have to make me sign an NDA?"

He took a deep breath and let it out slowly. He knew he should tell the pilot to turn around right now so they could drop her off. So why wasn't he?

"The Agency doesn't always operate within the law and the FBI is bound by it," he told her. "You understand?"

Sophie uncrossed her arms and stared at him. He couldn't tell her any more than that, not until she signed the paper. He had gone too far already. "This isn't about keeping the FBI out of the loop. This is about preventing another attack on American soil," he told her. "Our best hope of doing that lies in Egypt."

"You've got someone in custody, haven't you?" she asked, still staring at him. There was a sparkle in her eye that made him uneasy.

"Just sign the paper," he said. "Please."

"My god, that's it. You've captured someone and you've rendered them to Egypt. Why else would I have to sign an NDA?" She wanted him to tell her she was right.

"Sophie, just sign the paper and I'll explain everything," he said, his voice softening perceptibly. "Otherwise I have to leave you behind."

"It's about torture?"

He gave her a blank stare.

"Deny it. Tell me I'm wrong."

Still, he said nothing. She wasn't part of the Agency. She was FBI. Without a signature on the NDA, she couldn't be allowed behind the curtain.

"Rendering prisoners without due process...it makes us no better than them, Akil," she said plaintively.

"You think you understand, but you don't," he said.

"I understand perfectly. You can't treat suspects like this, with contempt for the law. American law."

"And what about the terrorists?" he countered. "You think they play by the rules and obey our laws." He was tired of listening to those who thought the world was black and white. "The terrorists manipulate our laws and our freedoms in order to attack us. I won't defend their rights," he said. "They forfeited their rights when they declared war on us."

He should stop right now. He was letting himself get dragged into an argument he knew he couldn't win, not against Sophie Martin. It was in her blood to uphold the constitution and follow the rule of law. It was her training. The feds were okay with bending the law here and there, but not breaking it. That's why the Agency would always be the country's first line of defense. It operated overseas under a different set of rules. The CIA could go places and do things no other agency could. That's what made it unique and indispensable. The public might only see the failures, but there were countless success stories, most of them filed away in the Agency's vaults. That was the nature of the organization. It was also its Achilles heel in the modern media age.

"The law is what separates us from the fascists," Sophie said, her voice steady. "If we go against our principles, what are we fighting for? Freedom? Liberty? It's just empty rhetoric."

"Sometimes there needs to be an exception to the rule for the good of the people," he argued. "You know that as well as I do." How could you fight an enemy with one hand tied behind your back? This wasn't a war with fixed rules of engagement, it was a back alley brawl and you had to come prepared to fight dirty if you wanted to win. "I wish the rules didn't have to be broken," he told her. "But sometimes there's no other way."

Sophie's shoulders were hunched up, her face full of tension. She seemed to have nothing more to say.

"Even if you don't agree with me you can still help me stop them before it's too late." He held out the NDA, hoping she would take it. After a long interval, she finally did, dropping it on the table in front of her.

He waited as she stared at it.

"Say something," he said.

"I work hard to defend the law, to maintain the integrity of it," she said, her eyes moistening. "If I sign this...I'll be turning my back on that."

"No," he countered. "If you sign that paper—or if you don't—it makes no difference. The reality doesn't change. With or without you, the process will go on. But if you sign that paper, we can work together to stop the people who killed Hannah and the hundreds of others in New York. We can stop them from killing again. You can either choose to help with that or hold fast to your principles, but you can't do both."

There wasn't anything more to say. It was up to Sophie to decide for herself now.

The pilot came on over the intercom. They were in line to takeoff and would be wheels up in approximately five minutes.

69

THE PRISON CELL was pitch black, but the lights wouldn't stop flashing. They were ghosts dancing on the back of his eyelids.

Finally, he opened his eyes. The strobe lights had been shut off. For how long?

Laying down on his mattress, the smell of his own urine no longer perceptible, he wondered what day of the week it was. What month? What time of day? Or night? There were no answers in here, only questions left unanswered. He was a prisoner—he knew that much—but where? Held by whom?

Shaking uncontrollably from the cold, he tried to remember what they had taught him during his training outside Esfahan. *Tell them only what they already know, nothing else.* He turned his head, sensing a presence in the room. A voice, perhaps. Unable to see in the dark, he listened, hearing only the sound of his own breathing. Exhaustion and hunger were probably up to their old tricks, he thought.

A few minutes later he heard it again. It was faint, but he was sure of it this time, recognizing the cadence of the language. It was Arabic. A man? No! Men and women speaking together. Yes. More than one. He could not understand what they were saying at first, but the voices were gradually getting louder.

Lifting himself up off the mattress, he stumbled to his feet, trying to remember where the door to the room was. Keeping his hands out in front of him, zombie-like, he moved toward the voices. When his fingers struck concrete, he groped the wall, feeling for the door, then moved to his left until he found it.

Just beyond the door, the people's voices began to mimic the roar of traffic on a busy street. He could feel the vibrations of their movements in his chest. "Help!" he shouted, banging his fists against the metal plating until he could no longer lift his arms.

But there was no response.

As the sound of the people began to fade, he yelled again in desperation. "Help me!"

The voices disappeared altogether and he stood alone next to the door, shrouded in silence. His training had not prepared him for this. Why was this happening to him?

A torturous scream shattered the silence. It was so close and so loud that he recoiled from the door, staggering back into the middle of the room. He stood in the darkness. Shaking. Weeping. Be strong, he admonished himself, you can get through this. But he wasn't sure anymore.

The sound of a distant train whistle entered the room. He had grown up near a train station outside Tabriz in the northwest. Were there train tracks nearby? A station maybe? A way out? Then the train whistle was replaced by the roar of a jet engine overhead, dogs barking, metal clanging against metal, a muezzin delivering the call to prayer. He tried to concentrate on the words of the muezzin, but the words kept changing. Then the strobe lights came back on, illuminating the room in frantic bursts of light. He started turning, searching for a way out, then fell to the ground, his head spinning.

The strobe lights stopped once again, plunging him back into darkness. He crawled forward on his hands and knees to the edge of the wall and turned to his left. When he reached his mattress, he laid down and closed his eyes.

There was no escape.

70

INSIDE THE CONTROL room, the technician watched Bashir Khalini on several LCD monitors. He consciously manipulated the prisoner's environment and recorded his reactions at each step of the process. With a final flick of a switch, he turned off the strobe lights and leaned back in his chair.

Taking a sip of his Diet Coke, he watched the Iranian crawl on his hands and knees toward a random wall, then turn left. The technician had noticed that the prisoner always went left in these sort of situations. Using the infrared camera, he followed the detainee as he felt his way around the perimeter of the room and back onto the soiled mattress that had become his refuge. When he finished recording the prisoner's actions in the log book, he swung his chair around.

"He's all yours, sir," the technician said with a thick Louisiana accent.

The Interrogator sat at the back of the control room going over a backlog of paperwork. "How is he?"

"He's a fucking mess, sir. Severe disorientation. Emotional distress. He's been in there three days, but it might as well have been three months as far as he's concerned."

"Good."

71

SAYYID TOOK AN old sepia-toned photo from his jacket pocket and handed it to Curtis Stone.

Stone took the photo and studied it. He could find no identifiable landmarks in the photo, but the geography suggested it had been taken somewhere in the Middle East.

"That's a picture of my father, Mr. Stone. It was taken before the Jews forced him to leave the town where he grew up, the town where his father grew up, and where his grandfather and great-grandfather raised their families before him."

"What was his name?" Stone asked.

"His name was Muhammad."

Stone took another look at the picture. The young boy, maybe nine or ten years old, was smiling. He was missing his two front teeth and stood along the side of a road, his hair upended by a strong wind.

"My father was only a child when the first Arab-Israeli war began in nineteen-forty-eight. Jewish families had begun emigrating to Palestine during the second world war, encouraged by the British and American governments. The Jews needed somewhere to go, but no one wanted them. Finally, they were offered Palestine."

Stone sat up straight. "It was a controversial decision, even then," he said. "But it was the Jews ancestral homeland, they had lived there for centuries."

"The Western powers had no right to play God," Sayyid said, raising his voice. He stared at the picture of his father and felt his eyes warming with tears. He pushed them back as he had so many times before. "The Western powers conquered the Ottoman empire, then drew their arbitrary lines without caring about the consequences. The people of Palestine were ignored. We should have fought to have our voices heard. But we didn't."

Stone leaned forward, pen in hand, and recorded Sayyid's words and his own editorial comments with a practiced shorthand. He had developed the skill over three decades, interviewing everyone from bell-hops to heads of state. But this interview was unlike any he had ever conducted before.

"We learned our lesson," Sayyid said, adjusting the glasses he was wearing. "We are making our voices heard now. Back then we believed we would be treated with dignity, but we were wrong. Quotas were set limiting the number of Jews to be allowed into Palestine. We had lived with the Jews for thousands of years, we could live with a few more. When those quotas were met, however, the Jews kept coming, tens of thousands of them. The quotas were not real. They were a lie meant to pacify us.

"The Jews—I give them credit—were prepared," Sayyid continued. "They were determined to stake a claim to the land they had been promised. Hardened by the atrocities in Europe, they terrorized the British with bombs and used tactics similar to the ones we use now. The ones you condemn. Because of this, they got their land."

Unable to contain himself, Sayyid stood up and circled the room. "When the Arab-Israeli war broke out in forty-eight, the Palestinian people were forced from their homes," he said. "The Israeli Forces, counter-attacking against the Arab armies, terrorized the Palestinians caught in the middle. The Palestinians fled, fearing for their lives. Most believed it would only be a matter of weeks before they would be allowed to return home, but the Arab armies failed, and, flush with victory, the Jews refused to let the Palestinians return to their land.

Stone listened without interrupting.

"My father was nine years old at the time. The Jews told them that their land—their homes—belonged to the Jews now. A quarter of a million people saw their lives devastated. For what? For the Jews? Who are the Jews to claim this right over us?"

Stone was growing uncomfortable with the lengthy diatribe and responded: "They had been herded into the gas chambers by the Nazis and exterminated like vermin," Stone said. "They had nowhere to go. No one wanted them. They were desperate, the same way you claim to be desperate, Ali."

"So the abused became the abusers. Are we supposed to forgive them for that?"

Sayyid put the picture of his father back in his pocket. He felt the old anger rising like a tide inside him. How could this journalist question his right to fight against such injustice?

"The division of Palestine," Stone offered, "was handled wrong. I agree. Most people agree about that now. But the Arab countries should never have attacked Israel."

"Do not blame the Arabs! Don't! It has been sixty years. Are the Palestinian people no more than a footnote to history?"

"You can't erase the past."

"You can change the future, though. But you have to use force. It's the only way to get back what is rightfully ours."

"Not by terrorizing people. Not by killing innocent civilians," Stone argued.

"We call that time, when we were forced from our homes by the Jews, *al-Nakba*. The Catastrophe. My father never saw his village again. If you asked where he came from he would say Safad. If there were small children around, they would protest. That's in Israel, they would say, laughing, thinking he was joking or mistaken.

"That hurt my father and he worried that the children would forget their past—forget what had once been theirs. So he sat us down and told us his story. Others did the same in refugee camps from Gaza to Amman."

"What did he tell you and your friends?" Stone asked, his pen resting on the page.

"He told us a familiar story—about how the conquering Jews had driven the Palestinian people into exile."

Sayyid could see the doubt painted on Stone's face, but continued. "My father's story began in May 1948, when a group of Palmach fighters stormed the Arab positions at Safad. More than ten thousand Palestinians were forced to flee by these Jews. In one afternoon, people who had lived on the land for centuries lost everything. They became refugees for life. At the time there were only about a thousand Jews living in Safad. A tenth of the town's population. Now, who knows. It's part of Israel."

"I'm sorry," Stone said.

Sayyid felt the journalist was being sincere, but would he write the story he needed him to tell. The Americans were obsessed with their consumer goods and their petty amusements. The world beyond their borders seemed to have little or no impact on them. New York had shaken the populace and focused their attention for the moment. But for how long?

"At the age of nine my father became a refugee, and so I too became a refugee when I was born," Sayyid said.

"Where?" Stone asked.

"At al-Amari, outside Ramallah. Generation after generation continue to be born into the camps. There are millions of people whose entire lives have been spent in the camps. Refugees from birth."

"But you escaped?"

"Yes, because of a relative, after my father died."

"Tell me about that. How old were you?"

"No. This is my father's story," Sayyid said defiantly. "Life in the camps was harder than you can imagine, Mr. Stone. Overcrowded, the narrow streets flanked with open sewers. Shortages everywhere. Houses barely fit to live in."

"I've been to the camps," Stone said.

"Then you have the faintest suggestion of what it is really like. The conditions keep getting worse. My mother died giving birth to me because there was no medicine, no facilities to help her with the complications that I brought. With the right medicine, she would have lived. Instead, she died like so many others. For nothing."

"And your father raised you?"

"Yes. He walked seven kilometers every day to go find work. He would come back in the evenings, exhausted, his hands raw from physical labor. He made just enough money to feed us. Can you imagine what that's like, to go down the street and see a television...to see people living an entirely different kind of life in Tel Aviv and Beirut? In Cairo? At that moment you realize how trapped you are. It's like drinking a slow-acting poison. It eats away at you gradually until one day you find you can't take it anymore."

"And then what? You turn to terrorizing innocent people?"

"Yes. Or you give up."

"Your people have suffered. There is no debating that. But your actions only make a lasting peace more difficult."

"There are seven million Palestinian refugees, Mr. Stone. More every year. For decades they have been humiliated, deprived, forced to live in fear without a home to call their own. Imagine what it's like to live your whole life without a home of your own? Or a country?"

"I can't pretend to understand. But—"

"No, you can't. It leaves you with a feeling worse than death," he said. "My father died ashamed he could not do more for his sons. And still, a quarter century later, my people's right of return continues to be denied by the Jews. By the Americans."

"They'll never allow the right of return. There are too many of you. The Jewish state would disappear. You know that. You must."

"Must!" Sayyid leaned in toward Stone, his voice seething with anger. "They stole our land. Our homes. Our lives. We want them back!"

Sayyid backed away, letting his anger dissipate. "Don't we have the right to fight for that?"

"This cycle of violence needs to be broken, Ali."

These Americans, Sayyid thought, they were so far from the suffering. For them, it was all academic.

"Fighting back is the only option we have."

"I don't believe that."

"Maybe you don't want to believe it. When you have nothing, Mr. Stone, death is not a curse, it's an opportunity."

Sayyid waited for a response, but Stone made no reply. Had he convinced the American in some way that his cause was just? There was no way of knowing, but they had debated long enough.

"Tell the American people that they have a choice in this. Tell them that I am giving them a choice."

"You promised more attacks," Stone said. "If I write my story—*your* story—will you stop this madness?"

"Without immediate action from the government or from the American people, the next attack will go ahead and it will be far more devastating than what happened in New York. You tell your readers that our war is just. Or don't. That's up to you now. The American people can decide for themselves if they want to remain the enemy of the Palestinian people or not."

72

THE GULFSTREAM LANDED at Abdel Nasser Airport outside Cairo.

For Akil, it was a homecoming of sorts, the place where he had gotten his start with the Agency. So much had happened since that first day driving through the outskirts of Cairo with Bill Graham at the wheel of his beat-up sedan. He could still picture the man's face he'd been brought to see: his body lying half-buried in a pile of refuse and discarded plastic bags, limbs twisted haphazardly—the Egyptian police officers nearby, smoking their cigarettes with indifference as the smell of rotting flesh and garbage ripened under the mid-day heat. It had been his initiation into a shadow war most people only thought existed in movies.

Stepping off the plane, Akil grabbed his bags. And Sophie's.

After speaking with the pilot before takeoff, he'd made his way back into the main cabin and found Sophie in one of the jump seats. Her head was back, eyes closed, shoes off. He'd picked up the NDA that was sitting on the edge of the couch and flipped to the back page, finding her signature at the bottom. At the time he'd felt a small stab of guilt, but it didn't last. She was coming. That's what mattered.

Sophie joined Akil on the tarmac, and together they set off to go find Justin Travers. On the plane ride over Akil had told Sophie about Bashir Khalini and the VX and the letter from Saqr that pointed to WMD's being on the move in the Middle East, possibly headed for America. This was the reason Khalini had been rendered. They had to know if the shipment was going to be used by the terrorists they were hunting.

Once he'd explained the situation, Sophie had softened her stance. She was still opposed to the use of such methods—she had made that clear once more. But the fact VX was involved altered her point of view, if only slightly. She agreed that Khalini needed to be questioned. It was how that questioning would be conducted that remained a contentious issue.

Justin Travers, who had been watching the plane's approach from the dark recesses of the hangar, finally stepped out into the bright sunlight. Akil and Sophie spotted him at a distance. When they got close, Travers introduced himself.

"Mr. and Mrs. Black. My name's Justin," he said. "Welcome to Cairo."

"Thanks for meeting us," Akil said, shaking hands.

Bill had arranged for a pair of false passports, or shoes as they were called, under the name Black.

"How was the trip?" Travers asked.

"Good."

Akil couldn't help noticing that Travers—who had found Khalini in a Baghdad basement a few days prior—looked haggard and worn down.

"If you'll follow me," Travers said. "I've made the necessary arrangements already."

Akil and Sophie followed him through an unmarked door which led to an air-conditioned room with no windows. Akil could smell the alcohol oozing from Travers' pores. The heat had given him away, and Akil wondered if Baghdad was to blame. A lot of officers were fond of the bottle—it was one of the hazards that came with the job.

Once they were inside and the door was closed, Akil handed over their passports. There was no need to go through regular customs, Travers explained. The Egyptians had been made aware of their arrival.

Disappearing for a few minutes, Travers returned and handed the passports back to Akil. "Okay, tourist visas are inside. We're all set to go," he said.

"Great. Where's the car?" Akil asked.

"This way."

They headed outside to a waiting Mercedes. Travers got in the front seat beside the driver while Akil held the back door open for Sophie. She accepted his gesture and stepped into the back seat without a word. Maybe she'd decided not to take the NDA personally after all, Akil thought. He hoped that was the case, otherwise it was going to be a long and uncomfortable few days.

They drove an hour outside the city on a busy highway while Travers told them everything he knew about Khalini and the VX. They were still unsure if Khalini was operating in an official capacity as a member of the Revolutionary Guard. What they did know was that Khalini had passed VX to Sunni militia members in Baghdad who had arranged safe passage of the material to a man named Saqr—a Hezbollah fixer—in Syria. Besides that, facial recognition software had identified one of the dead from the basement in Baghdad as a suspected al-Qaeda operative. The other men's identity, and the details surrounding any planned operation, remained uncertain.

"With any luck, Khalini can fill in the blanks," Travers said.

"Let's hope so," Akil offered. "Right now all we can do is speculate."

"The Revolutionary Guard, Hezbollah, al-Qaeda…they all seem to be working in unison on this," Sophie said. "Or members of those groups, at least."

"The Revolutionary Guard and Hezbollah are tied at the hip," Travers said. "They're both Shi'a." He was turned sideways in the front seat looking back. "You'd expect them to collaborate. But al-Qaeda?"

"Sunnis working directly with Shi'as would be unprecedented. You're right," Akil said. He paused a moment. "That said, we know Hamas is being supported to an extent, albeit indirectly, by the Iranians. Have been for a while. It's possible this is a new paradigm when it comes to conducting terror attacks against Israel and the West."

"We represent a common enemy," Sophie added. "As much as they hate each other, they hate us more."

"The lack of unity among the fractious terror networks—amplified by the Sunni-Shi'a split—has always limited their potential and worked in our favor," Travers said. "If what you're implying is true, if Shi'a and Sunni networks are actually cooperating—"

"Then we're in serious trouble," Sophie said, finishing the thought.

The conversation ended there. It was a scary proposition and one that had been speculated over by those in the intelligence community. Now there was growing evidence that it was no longer just a theory.

The Mercedes turned off the highway and took a series of looping turns that led to a parallel service road. In the distance, a large sign read: IPCRESS PLASTICS & MANUFACTURING LTD. The name was repeated below in Arabic. The facility was well outside the city, far from any populated areas, and was surrounded by two chain-link fences with razor wire. In-between the fences Egyptian security guards patrolled on foot with dogs. As they drove by, Akil watched a Doberman Pinscher strain at his leash, teeth bared.

A hundred yards further down the road, they entered the compound through a well-fortified security gate that suggested Ipcress Plastics was more than your run-of-the-mill manufacturing plant. Inside there were a myriad of buildings, each of varying size and purpose. They drove amongst them for a while before stopping at the foot of a small white cube with two glass doors. The doors were tinted black so you couldn't see inside. Looking out the window of the Mercedes, Akil saw no indication of the building's function. It appeared commonplace in every way except for the security camera bolted to the wall above its doors. The camera was slowly tracking from left to right.

Someone was watching them.

"This it?" Akil asked.

"This is it," Travers said, leaning across the front seat. "You'll need this to get in." He passed Akil a security fob. "Someone will meet you on the inside."

"You're not coming?" Sophie asked.

"No. I have other business."

"Thanks again," Akil said, shaking Travers' hand. "Bill Graham wanted me to send a message. Says your transfer to Washington is in the works. A commendation too."

"If you see him before I do, tell him I appreciate it."

"I will."

Akil opened his door and stepped out of the car. He hoped the transfer hadn't come too late for Travers. If he was lucky, he could still clean up and turn himself around.

Collecting the bags, Akil watched the Mercedes drive away. He took a look around. There was no one coming or going from any of the other buildings. They seemed completely alone, but Akil knew better.

He walked over and swiped the security fob across a grey box bolted to the wall beside the double doors. An electronic lock gave way and they entered. Inside was a traditional American-style waiting room with a couch and chairs, a coffee table scattered with magazines, and a water cooler off in the corner. The rattle and hum from an air conditioning vent filled the room.

Akil dropped their bags on the floor and looked around to see if there was a phone or a buzzer or something to signal their presence, but there was nothing. He tried opening the only other door in the room and found it locked.

"Travers said someone would meet us," Sophie said.

"Well, they know we're here," Akil said, looking up at another surveillance camera in the corner of the room. "I guess we wait."

"Guess so," Sophie said, sitting down on the couch. She picked up a copy of *Vanity Fair* and noticed that it was two years out of date. She leisurely flipped through its pages.

Opposite the couch, Akil noticed a large map hanging on the wall. He stepped over to take a closer look while they waited for someone to come meet them. One of his professors at Brown had been fond of saying that maps were windows onto the past. The map he was looking at now certainly proved the theory.

He read the date off the small legend in the lower left-hand corner: The Middle East, circa. 1920. The map appeared old and fragile behind its glass veneer. Akil wondered if it was an original. In 1920 the British and

French were dividing up the spoils of the Ottoman Empire after the Great War. The British and French Mandates—Palestine, Lebanon, Syria, Jordan, Iraq—they were all marked off with angled borders, a testament to their arbitrary nature. Israel was nowhere to be seen. It would be another quarter century before its creation. Saudi Arabia, he noticed, was still a collection of tribal regions whose borders were organic in nature. Many of the names here had been lost to history: Nejd, Hejaz, Aden. Ten years earlier and the map would have been awash in red—the great Ottoman Empire had controlled all of it. The Middle East was shifting, had been for a long time now.

Akil stepped closer and used his index finger to trace the bold lines that divided the topography into nations. The lines, ever-shifting, were evidence to the aftermath of wars and forced treaties, the meteoric rise and calamitous fall of empires and ideologies. The shock waves from these great tectonic shifts in history, Akil mused, traveled unimpeded through time, often striking decades on with unforeseen consequences. History was fluid; cause and effect were not always immediate. That's what made it such a fascinating subject.

The locked door Akil had tried earlier swung open. A young man in his mid-twenties poked his head into the room. His hair was cropped short and he wore camouflage pants and a tan shirt. He took a long studious look at Sophie, then turned to Akil.

"Mr. Hassan?"

"Yes."

"Name's Flynn. We've been expecting you. Sorry for making you wait," he said, speaking in short declarative bursts. "If you'll follow me."

Akil turned to grab the bags he had dropped just inside the door.

"You can leave those there. Someone will take care of them," Flynn said.

"Okay."

The three of them walked down a whitewashed corridor, then through a series of locked doors before descending two flights of stairs. They emerged into a huge underground bunker. A series of doors were evenly spaced on either side of a long corridor.

"The detainees are kept down here," Flynn said. "Completely isolated. We control their environment, their diet, sleep patterns, everything. They hear and see what we want them to. Nothing more."

By his tone and demeanor, Akil could tell that Flynn took enormous pride in what they did here.

"How big is this place?" Sophie asked.

"We can hold up to eight persons in the interrogation ward. Aside from that, I've been instructed not to discuss any other aspects of the facility."

"More secrets."

"Excuse me, ma'am?" Flynn asked, pretending he hadn't heard Sophie's comment.

"Nothing," Sophie said.

Flynn led them to a cell door at the end of the corridor and opened it with a fob that was attached to a keychain on his belt. They stepped through the door and entered an antechamber, a small rectangle of unfinished concrete. The walls were bare. Flynn closed the door behind them.

Akil, who had been the first through, faced an identical door straight ahead. "What's this?" he asked.

"The detainee is on the other side of that door, sir. We keep the prisoner isolated at all times. The antechamber allows us to enter the cell without exposing the detainee to the outside in any way, even if only to a passing guard. It breaks the illusion we've created for them."

Akil looked around the small rectangular room.

"On your left there's a one-way mirror," Flynn said, pointing. "If you want, you can observe the prisoner without him seeing you."

Both Akil and Sophie moved over to take a look.

"The walls are soundproof as well," Flynn added.

"It's pitch black," Sophie said.

"Yes. We keep the cells completely dark sometimes. Never for too long. It varies. Those goggles beside you? You can put them on to see."

Akil grabbed the night vision goggles beside him and put them on. What he saw took him by surprise. Inside the room was a man—Afghani by the looks of it—moving back and forth erratically, his hands clasped over his ears with his head bobbing up and down.

"He looks like he's gone mad," Akil said.

"No, not mad." Flynn stepped alongside Akil and hit a switch. Loud music poured out of speakers positioned above their heads.

"Rap music?" Sophie asked.

"Yes, ma'am. Cypress Hill to be exact. A favorite around here. The detainees don't understand the words, and the music is extremely foreign to them. Drives them ape shit. We've had good outcomes," Flynn said.

"Who's the prisoner?" Akil asked.

"Came in from Kandahar Province two weeks ago. US special forces took him in a firefight. Taliban. High level. Very tough nut."

Akil removed the goggles he was wearing and hung them back on the wall. "We want to see Bashir Khalini. That's the reason we're here."

"Of course." Flynn hit the switch again, cutting the music. "Jiri would like to see you first."

73

JIRI HAD BEEN trained by the CIA to get information out of hardened warriors who would rather die than reveal their secrets. He did this not by using torture per se, but through the application of science. He'd been chosen for the job after an exhaustive evaluation back at Langley. For weeks he'd been placed under the microscope—personality analysis, in-depth interviews, psychological work-ups, aptitude evaluations, lie-detector tests. Eventually, the Directorate of Science and Technology had decided he fit the profile they were looking for. Then his training began in earnest.

He'd been at it for years now.

A native New Yorker, Jiri had a thick head of hair, narrow eyes, and a sharp jawline. He had been born with the Slavic features of his grandparents and had inherited their proletarian demeanor. With no tattoos or visible scars, Jiri appeared commonplace. Then again, looks could be deceptive. Akil knew it took a certain kind of individual to carry out this sort of work full time. The individual could neither enjoy the process or find it distasteful. One in a thousand, maybe more, had the right psychological matrix and cognitive skill set to be a CIA interrogator. Jiri represented a rare breed.

After Flynn had introduced them, Jiri agreed to cooperate in any way he could. At the moment Bashir Khalini remained nothing more than a name on a piece of paper and Akil told Jiri he wanted to see the Iranian first hand. There was no objection.

As Jiri led them to Khalini's holding cell, he seemed to sense Sophie's disapproval of what they were doing here. "Have you been to a facility like this before?" he asked her.

"No," Sophie replied.

"You may think this place is nothing more than a series of torture chambers, but you'd be wrong. This place is a science facility more than anything else."

"That seems a bit rich," Sophie said.

Jiri laughed, an honest smile spreading across his face. "Perhaps, but we're very precise in what we do here."

"It's still torture though, isn't it?"

Jiri didn't laugh this time. "No, it's not torture, not the way you imagine it."

"That's right. Enhanced interrogation is the term these days. The German Gestapo had a similar name for it. *Verscharfte Vernehmung*. It meant—"

"Sharpened interrogation techniques. Yes, I know. Not that long ago we used to turn people like Khalini over to our friends," Jiri said, placing air quotes around the word *friends*. "The Jordanians. The Moroccans. The Syrians, sometimes. We let them do whatever they wanted, turning a blind eye to it all. That was torture. Real torture. Fingernails pulled out with pliers, blowtorches used on the skin until the victims passed out or died. Electrocution of the genitals. Even sodomy. Crude techniques...and vicious. But they didn't work. The information we received was often unreliable. The process was more about retribution than intelligence gathering. Those being tortured would say anything to make the pain stop, and we were left to sort through a pile of conflicting lies. It was a waste of time and resources."

"And what you do here? It's really that different?"

"You're a skeptic," Jiri said, smiling again. "That's good, we should all be skeptics. But what we do here is far more sophisticated than pulling fingernails. We utilize a combination of drug therapy, sensory distortion, and mild physical contact in order to coax out information. Actionable intelligence."

"Mild physical contact? What does that mean?" Sophie asked.

"Everyone has their breaking point, Miss Martin. If they have the information, they give it to us eventually. It's inevitable. Call it torture if you like, but I've seen what real torture is, and this is not it."

Akil had chosen to stay out of the argument altogether. He'd been down this road already and he didn't want to do it again. Yet, what he had seen at the prison so far had disturbed him more than he wanted to admit. The ordered efficiency of it all, the ease with which detainees were stripped of their humanity and thrown into bedlam, near madness even, shocked him. And the screaming. The screams were too human. It was one thing to understand the necessity for a place like this, and quite another to be involved in it. It seemed such a slippery slope. What was permissible when hundreds of lives were at stake? Thousands? Hundreds of thousands? He had to constantly remind himself of who these prisoners were and what they were capable of. You couldn't forget that. That was the key. These were mass murderers—destroyers of not only life, but a way of life.

As distasteful as it was, this place represented a necessary evil. He had resigned himself to the logic. Sophie would not or could not. For him, the alternatives were far worse. Places like this saved untold lives from being destroyed. With luck, the information they got from Khalini would prevent another attack on innocent Americans. Who could argue against that?

They stopped in front of a cell with a blue door, then entered the ante-chamber. Akil looked through the one-way. The speakers had been turned on so they could hear what Khalini was hearing.

Verses from the Qur'an were being recited in Arabic over and over again. The voice was authoritative. Male. The verses were specific—each surah addressing the subjects of repentance and the sanctity of life. The words—the words of God—told Khalini that Islam was a religion of peace; God would be displeased with the killing of innocent men, women, and children. *Atone* for what you have done, the voice suggested.

Akil noted that Khalini's hands were cuffed behind his back and that he stood on a stool with one leg tied up behind him. An Egyptian guard stood nearby to make sure Khalini maintained the stance. He would be forced to stay like this for fifteen minutes or half an hour. Maybe longer. It was different each time.

As Akil watched Khalini wavering on the stool, his body tilting slightly to one side, struggling to stay upright, Jiri explained that there was method to the madness. At this point in the process physical and mental exhaustion would be tearing at every fiber of Khalini's being and he would continue to be given no respite. Hour after hour, day after day, the regimen would continue to break down Khalini's ability to defend himself mentally. It was only a matter of time before he talked.

"How long has he been on the regimen?" Akil asked.

"Going on four days."

"And what have we learned?"

"Not much as of yet. But that's not unusual."

"Specifics?"

"We know he's Iranian, part of the Revolutionary Guard stationed in northern Iraq. He's been funding the Shi'a militias, smuggling weapons. He gave us some names."

"We know most of that already. Is that all you've gotten from him?" Akil asked, not masking his disappointment.

"So far," Jiri admitted. "We know he's been trained in counter-interrogation techniques because he readily agrees to those things he suspects we already know—that he's a member of the Pasdaran, for instance. But he denies everything else. His training is making it harder to break him. The process takes time."

"The one thing we don't have is time," Akil said. He was being direct so that there were no misunderstandings later on. "New York has been attacked. More attacks are in the offing. We have to know if the VX is in play. If it's headed for the United States."

"I understand," Jiri said.

"What did he say when you asked him what he was doing in that Baghdad basement?"

"He doesn't remember being there. It's a lie, of course, but his training is slowly failing him. It's only a matter of days until we know everything."

"You have twenty-four hours, Jiri," Akil said. "We need the answers now, before it's too late. Do whatever it takes, I don't care. But get the information."

Jiri nodded. "Twenty-four hours. Got it."

74

SAYYID SAT IN the passenger seat of the van as it sped along the Interstate outside Washington, D.C. His fake mustache and beard were gone now, as were the colored contacts and eyeglasses.

He felt better having told Stone his reasons for attacking New York City and was already looking forward to reading the article. All he hoped was that Stone would be fair and deliver his message in plain words. The people of America would not escape another attack. That was unavoidable. They could, however, prevent themselves from becoming a target for years to come.

Sayyid spotted the sign indicating a rest stop up ahead. He tapped Issam on the arm and told him to pull in.

Issam slowed down as he entered the rest stop.

"Don't park," Sayyid instructed. "Everyone stays in the vehicle. There could be cameras."

It was raining, and as they drove through the rest area Sayyid looked to see if there were any cars or people present. Thankfully, it was completely empty.

"Stop by that garbage container up ahead," he said.

The van stopped with the sliding door facing a pair of dumpsters. Asad undid the rope that held Curtis Stone's hands behind his back. The black hood, which had been secured with duct tape, remained in place. Sayyid grabbed one of the journalist's hands and placed a disposable cell phone and several twenty dollar bills in the palm. Then he closed Stone's fingers around the items so they wouldn't fall.

"The phone works. Call a cab or a friend. I expect to see the story in the paper tomorrow morning, Mr. Stone. Again, I'm sorry for having to do this, but there was no other way."

Sayyid signaled Asad who opened the sliding door and pushed Stone out, tossing the digital voice recorder and notepad out after him.

75

STONE FELL HARD to the ground, his head knocking up against the metal dumpster as the van sped off into the distance.

He rushed to remove the duct tape that secured the hood over his head. He had to hurry if he wanted to catch a glimpse of the license plate. Something. Anything. But by the time he had freed himself, it was too late. The van had vanished back onto the Interstate.

Stone took in his surroundings quickly, then collected the recorder and notepad. Next, he unlocked the phone and dialed his editor at the Washington Post.

76

AHMAD HASHEMIAN FACED Mecca and completed the last of his afternoon prayers. When he was finished he remained kneeling on his prayer rug. He breathed deeply, slowly letting the air out through his nose. He repeated the process several times, allowing the tension to flow from his body.

This time of day offered a welcome respite from the rigors of his job as head of Iran's Intelligence and Security Service. He would not admit it, but he was feeling the stress more than ever these days. They still didn't know where Bashir Khalini was. With each passing hour they failed to locate the Pasdaran agent, he imagined increasingly disastrous outcomes for his country. The VX, from what his own people told him, was on the move. Trying to contain the situation was proving difficult. Quietly, he offered up a short prayer asking for God's help in the matter, then got up off his knees and rolled the small prayer rug in his hands. As he was placing the rug in the corner behind his desk there was a knock at the door.

"Come," he barked.

His deputy, Reza, entered the room and walked over to the edge of the desk. He held a thick file in his hands. "Sir. We've located Bashir Khalini."

Hashemian turned to his deputy in surprise, but the look on Reza's face told him it was not good news.

"Where is he?" Hashemian asked, not sure he wanted to hear the answer.

"He's been captured by the Americans and taken to Egypt. Our sources in Cairo say an Iranian is being held at a CIA black site outside the city. The prisoner in question arrived four days ago. The description we've gotten matches Khalini."

Hashemian slumped down into his desk chair. He could not have received worse news. The death of Khalini would have been a blessing. But this? "If they learn what he was up to. If they find out about the VX..."

Hashemian let the unfinished thought occupy the room. The tension between the United States and his country kept rising to dangerous levels. But this latest development could mean all-out war.

"Where is the VX now? Do we know anything new?"

He needed something to work with.

"We've been trying to trace it," Reza said. "It left Beirut almost two weeks ago. After Khalini handed it off to Saqr, his role was over. The operational details were kept secret. Compartmentalized."

"I'm afraid we're in very serious trouble, my friend. We need to know exactly where the VX is headed."

"There's something else," Reza said.

"What?"

"One of our men in Cairo managed to take some photographs of three Americans arriving at Abdel Nasser. The airport has a much smaller capacity than Cairo International. The CIA are fond of using it. We monitor it sometimes," Reza said, removing a selection of 8x10 photos from a file. He handed them to his boss. "The shots are long range. Telephoto. A bit grainy, but you can see the faces well enough."

"Do we know who these people are?"

"We know the one on the left."

Reza leaned over the desk and pointed out one of the men in a group shot. "His name is Justin Travers. CIA. Baghdad. We've known about him for more than two years. The man and woman he met at the airport were initially unknown."

"Initially?"

"Yes. We ran their faces through our database and got a hit on the second male."

"Get to the point, Reza."

Reza walked around the desk and flipped through the stack of photos and plucked out a second 8x10. "Take a look at this photo," he said.

Hashemian studied the picture. The photograph was not like the others—it had been taken somewhere else under different conditions. The face took up almost the entire frame and was clear, the lighting more balanced. But still, he was looking at a man's face he did not recognize.

"This photograph," Reza said, pointing to the headshot, "was taken almost three years ago in Lebanon."

"So?"

"Compare it with the photos taken at the Cairo airport yesterday."

Hashemian flipped back to the picture of the three Americans at the airport outside Cairo and studied it for several seconds, then flipped back to the older, but much clearer, headshot. A moment later he held the two photos next to one another and compared them again, shifting his eyes back and forth.

"They're the same man," Reza said

"Who is he?" Hashemian asked.

Reza straightened his posture. "We don't have a name yet. The photo popped up when we cross-referenced our files. The man in the photo was linked to a member of our Beirut Embassy staff several years ago. We apparently vetted him at the time and he came up clean."

"But he's CIA."

"Looks that way. We should have identified him in Beirut. Now that we have a face, and we know he's CIA, we'll have a name very soon."

"And the woman he was involved with?"

"Her name is Tara Markosi. She resigned from the Foreign Ministry about a year and a half ago. She teaches at the university in Tehran now."

"Was she passing information to this man?" Hashemian asked.

"We've gone back over the files. We suspect so, but there's no hard evidence. The man she became involved with had posed as a journalist. Ms. Markosi saw him socially and reported her activities as required. There was no reason to be overly suspicious of the liaison, especially since she had not tried to hide it. The man left Lebanon abruptly about a year after they started seeing each other. There was no further contact that we know of."

"And the woman he is with in these pictures?" Hashemian was poking a finger at the lower quality 8x10.

"We have no idea who she is."

Hashemian opened the top drawer of his desk and removed the blue plastic bottle. He placed it in front of him and stared at it while he assessed the situation. "It's only a matter of time before the Americans learn about the VX."

Reza walked over and warmed himself by the fire. "I agree."

"They'll link it back to us. To Iran."

"Almost certainly, sir."

Hashemian shook his head. Why had the Americans taken Khalini in the first place, he wondered. Khalini was a scoundrel, but he was also a skilled operative not prone to taking unnecessary risks. It made no sense. But that no longer mattered. He had to deal with the here and now.

"God help us if the next attack on American soil utilizes the VX," Hashemian said. "We must find a way to handle this crisis quickly and quietly."

"Just tell me what to do."

Hashemian didn't respond right away. He had an idea that might work and he mulled it over silently, tapping his fingers on the top of his desk as Reza waited dutifully for his orders.

It didn't take long. By process of elimination, Hashemian concluded that his idea was the best option—maybe the only option—he had. If it worked, they might be able to salvage the situation before it spiraled completely out of control. But there was still so much that could go wrong.

One step at a time, he told himself.

"I want you to find Tara Markosi for me and arrest her," Hashemian said. "She's going to help us get out of this mess."

"Tara Markosi?"

"Yes. And find out where the VX is headed. Make whatever deals you have to, with whomever you have to, but we must know everything."

"Yes, sir."

Reza headed for the door while Hashemian grabbed the blue bottle off his desk.

"And Reza, make sure they put the fear of God into her."

77

THE SUN WAS setting on the Middle East as Bill Graham poured his morning coffee at Langley. It was 4 AM EST, and on top of the President's Daily Brief was an inflammatory article from the Washington Post. The editor-in-chief had sent Bill an advance copy late last night, telling him it would run on the front page the following morning. He had done this as a courtesy, he said, and Bill's efforts in persuading him to kill the article had proved futile.

Bill was not overly surprised at the development. The FBI had already opened an investigation into the kidnapping of Curtis Stone. So far the initial leads were sparse. The terrorist had used an alias—Ali—and had worn a disguise. He had also spoken English with a broad American accent. By Stone's own admission, the man was surprisingly articulate. For Bill, that meant the target had likely attended an American university at some point. The problem was, hundreds of thousands of foreign nationals with Arab backgrounds had attended universities in the United States going back more than two decades, and with no name or picture to go on, the lead was useless. The only valuable piece of information they had was forty-seven minutes of digital audio from a voice recorder that had been left on after Stone's interview had ended.

The recording device had been damaged at some point, probably when Curtis Stone had been dumped along the Interstate. The audio was mostly background noise intermingled with small fragments of dialogue, most of which was too garbled to understand.

The recording had been run through proprietary software at the FBI's forensics lab, significantly enhancing the audio, but all they were left with was a series of one and two-word non-sequiturs that felt like a code of some kind. The mention of *Philadelphia* and a reference to *my contact* were intriguing, but ultimately inconclusive pieces of a much larger puzzle. That's because the conversation surrounding the recovered fragments were missing. And therefore, so was the context.

Were the terrorists headed to Philadelphia? Was Philadelphia the next target? There was no way to tell. It was possible the reference to Philadelphia was altogether unrelated to the next attack. And who was this contact? Where was he?

Bill picked up the early edition of the Washington Post that had just arrived by courier. The fifty-point headline—TERRORIST CONFESSES ALL—was sensational stuff. The interview Stone had conducted with the mastermind behind the New York bombings was inside. No one was going to question its authenticity either, not with Stone's name attached to it.

In a couple of hours, more than a million people would be reading the article for themselves. Every national and international wire service in the country would pick it up and run with it. It was going to be a media frenzy: cable news, the major networks, radio talk shows, the internet. For the next 24 to 48 hours everyone would be focused on the interview and the editorial that accompanied it.

There was no denying that the article was a gripping read. The terrorist who had orchestrated this stunt was going to get more publicity than he could have hoped for, but if he thought the American public was going to be sympathetic after he'd killed their own brothers and sisters, their husbands and wives—their children?—he was mistaken.

The phone on Bill's desk rang. He picked it up and was told that Anthony Marchetti had just arrived. Bill thanked Dorothy, then grabbed his copy of the Washington Post and headed down the hall to Marchetti's office. He was going to be angry as hell. Not only did the article make the President look bad, it made the Agency and the FBI look bad. And it made Marchetti look bad.

"America doesn't negotiate with terrorists," Marchetti said as he read the article, his voice a gathering storm. "We need to catch this son-of-a-bitch."

Bill made no comment. He had slept maybe a dozen hours in the past six days. Every officer he had was working around the clock.

"Goddammit, Bill! What are we doing about this guy?"

"Everything humanly possible, sir."

"The President has made it clear that when this is over there's going to be an intelligence review. How are we going to look?"

"Like we did everything humanly possible to stop the attacks."

"No. It's going to look like we didn't do our jobs. That's what it's going to look like."

Bill's frustration level was reaching an all-time high. Engaged in a fight to save American lives, all the politicians could offer was criticism and provocation.

Bill took a seat, hoping to defuse the situation. "The head of SIS assures me they're pushing as hard as they can in the Crescent. There are several leads that could still pan out."

"What leads?" Marchetti asked.

"The Brits are looking at former Hamas members. Hezbollah. But at the moment it's difficult to get good information."

"Offer more cash, use the Israelis."

Marchetti looked flustered and he sounded desperate. You could tell a lot about a person from the way they responded to pressure. "The Brits are our best shot," Bill said. "They're on the ground and they're in contact with Hamas' leadership, but the Palestinians aren't cooperating. All we're getting is static and official denials of involvement."

"Then turn the screws on them."

"How Tony? We've already cut off aid to Hamas. You can't expect much cooperation after that."

"We don't deal with terrorists, Bill. We can't go around making exceptions just because we feel like it."

But we do it all the time. "I wasn't suggesting otherwise," Bill said.

"What about Fatah?"

"What about them?"

"What are they saying?"

"That Hamas is capable of anything, but they don't know any more than we do right now. Besides, they're busy playing to the home crowd. The men responsible for New York are living martyrs over there."

Marchetti got up and walked out from behind his desk. "And the Iranian? Khalini?"

"I'll know more in a few hours," Bill said, getting up out of his seat. "I'll keep you posted."

"Alright. Let me know right away."

78

Bill knew better than to tell Marchetti that Akil was the one overseeing Khalini's interrogation. There was no point fanning the flames. He'd wait and see what Akil learned first.

Back in his office, Bill sat down and started making calls, applying pressure where he could, reminding his station chiefs that time was running out. If they had anything in the works, now was the time to pull the trigger. Then, with a fresh cup of coffee, he scanned Stone's article one last time.

They weren't dealing with a Wahhabi, the kind of radical Islamist who constituted the majority of what was traditionally known as al-Qaeda, the kind of radicals who wanted to turn the clock back to the Ninth Century. They were dealing with a far less fanatical opposition, but one, that by all indications, was just as deadly. Whoever this Palestinian was, he was acting out of desperation and an ill-conceived notion that America would respond to threats and violence. America was never going to ditch Israel, and although no one could question that there were injustices in the Middle East, politics made the point largely immaterial. What mattered to Bill right now was that this madman was still out there and that he was being supported by powerful organizations—al-Qaeda among them. Perhaps even the Iranian government.

Bill picked up the phone on his desk. None of the leads they were chasing looked promising except for Khalini. If Stone's article was correct, another attack was imminent. He needed Akil to understand that Khalini was their only hope.

79

The Ipcress Plastics and Manufacturing Facility had its own well-appointed sleeping quarters, which is where Akil went after he'd finished meeting with Jiri.

Entering his private room, Akil dumped his bag on the floor and took a much-needed shower. Afterward, he sat on the edge of his bed and started going over Khalini's file. He had already decided to let Jiri do his job—

without interference—and see where that got them. But he wanted to be prepared in case they needed a plan B.

Flipping back and forth amongst the pages of the file, he began looking for the prisoner's weakness and his own point of attack, were it needed. After more than two hours of searching, he found what he was looking for. It was all in the file—snippets of information culled from dozens of different sources. He pieced the bits of information together, one by one, until he had a picture of Khalini's life.

A part of it at least.

The man loved his wife and his family—not just a little, but passionately and noticeably. When Khalini was at home, he doted on his wife as if she were still a new bride. And yet they'd been married for almost a decade. And when he was away from home he would often send his children small gifts, sometimes three or four parcels a month.

It was endearing.

It was also risky behavior for a man in his position. The information could be used against him, would be used against him should the time come when Akil was forced to use it.

He closed the file and threw it on the bed, then got dressed and headed up onto the roof for some fresh air. Along the way he managed to scrounge a bottle of wine and some paper cups, inviting Sophie to join him for a drink. A peace offering of sorts.

He was first on the roof. The heat outside had dissipated, leaving a cool evening breeze that was refreshing, and though the sky was still bright, it was no longer onerous. There was a pair of plastic chairs and an old wooden crate already on the roof. He placed the wine and the cups on top of the crate, using it as a makeshift table, then sat down and waited for Sophie to join him.

Low on the horizon, a giant sphere of orange rippled behind a wall of radiating heat. The distraction was pleasant enough, but he couldn't stop thinking about Khalini. How much did he know? Could he tell them where the VX was headed? Could he tell them when and where the next attack was going to take place?

Or were they wasting their time?

He heard Sophie step out onto the roof and looked over, motioning for her to join him.

"The sunset is gorgeous," she said, settling into the chair beside him.

"I always loved the sunsets here," he told her, thinking back to his early days in Cairo. "Something about the desert sands, the colors are more intense."

She had just taken a shower and her hair was still damp. Loose strands clung to the edges of her cheek and neckline. The white dress she wore flowed past the knees and was meant for the fall weather in London more than the heat of Cairo. That was his fault. Too many secrets.

"Glass of wine?" he asked.

"Please."

He poured her a cup and passed it over. As he did this he couldn't help associating her presence—here, now—with memories of Tara. How many times had he and Tara spent their evenings just like this, at the beach cafes near Tripoli or in Beirut, watching the sun go down over the Med? Tonight the sea had been replaced by an ocean of sand. Tara by Sophie. The café by whatever this place was.

He tried to dismiss the impulse. He wanted to forget the past, not dwell on it, but being back in the Middle East made that impossible.

Sitting back in her chair, Sophie took a sip of her wine. "This place is completely insane," she said. "These people too. You know that, right?"

He knew exactly what she meant, but didn't want to get into another debate. "No politics tonight, okay?"

"I guess I can lay off for one night."

"Good. We'll just enjoy ourselves. Relax."

She held up her cup. "To a ceasefire."

"To peace," he said, raising his cup to hers.

They both laughed.

"I have a confession to make," she said. "I've done some digging, trying to find out more about you."

"Really?"

"Yeah, I have a few contacts at the Agency. I asked around."

"And why were you asking people about me?"

"I wanted to know who I was working with. I'm sure you did the same," she said, her eyes daring him to deny it.

He'd made a few calls, of course. Sophie was considered a top talent. A common theme, however, was her *strong* personality. Someone had described her as pig-headed. It depended on who you talked to.

"So? What did you find out?" he asked.

She took another sip of wine and looked at him with mischievous eyes. "Lots."

Was she flirting with him?

"I doubt that," he said.

"According to my sources you were very good at recruiting and running agents."

"What sources exactly?"

"Good try," she said, enjoying herself. "There was one thing that surprised me though. I was told you'd been fired from the Agency. Yet—"

"Here I am? Sounds like your sources aren't very reliable."

"What happened?"

Akil rotated the paper cup in his hand, taking his time before answering her question. "It's a long story," he said finally, hoping she'd get the hint and drop the subject.

"I don't mind long stories. And we've got all evening," she countered, smiling sweetly as she did so.

Tenacious as ever, he thought.

"I was told there was a woman involved."

Akil didn't respond this time, just stared at the sun as it dipped below the horizon, wondering again if he'd done the right thing bringing her along, knowing it was too late to do anything about it now.

Sophie tried to wait him out, hoping he'd divulge a little more about his past—about himself—knowing too that her curiosity was getting the better of her. She decided to give in, not wanting to spoil the evening. "Look, I was just curious," she said.

"Can't help yourself, huh?"

"I'm an investigator, what can I say."

"I made a mistake and I paid for it. It's ancient history."

Sophie grabbed the bottle of wine and filled her cup, then held the bottle out for Akil. "Have some more wine and we'll forget I brought it up."

He looked over at her, letting her top off his cup. "I'm sorry too," he said.

"We all have secrets. I get it."

"It's just...it's not something I like discussing."

The tension between them faded quickly as they sipped their wine and talked about everyday things.

After a while, Akil swung the subject back to work. "About tomorrow," he said.

"Forget about tomorrow," Sophie told him. She put her hand on his arm and squeezed it gently. "We still have half a bottle of wine and nowhere to go. So, like you said, let's just enjoy it."

He gave her a smile and they clinked cups again, but the moment was interrupted by the pinging of a cell phone.

"It's mine," Akil said, fishing in his pocket. He grabbed the phone and checked the caller ID. There was no name, but he recognized the number. It was Bill Graham.

80

THE TOWN CAR pulled to a stop in front of Tehran's central police station. From the back seat, behind tinted glass, Ahmad Hashemian watched Tara Markosi being escorted from the building.

With the eyes of an appraiser, Hashemian focused his attention on her. She was beautiful, a Persian princess with long black hair that flowed past her shoulders. The closer she got the more he liked what he saw—the hazel eyes, the delicate hands, the lovely olive skin, the well-defined cheekbones that caught the afternoon sunlight. She didn't look forty, despite what her file said.

She should have been working for me, Hashemian thought, trapping American spies instead of working for one.

The car door opened and Tara was pushed into the back seat by one of Hashemian's men. As soon as she was inside the door slammed shut. From the front seat, someone engaged the automatic locks. A loud *ka-chunk* resonated in the back seat of the car as they pulled away from the curb and accelerated into traffic.

He could see a bruise had already formed above her left eye, likely the result of an overzealous police officer. She had been taken into custody and held overnight at his request. In the morning an interviewer from the VEVAK offices had been dispatched to ask a series of questions. On the surface, the questions appeared wide-ranging and non-specific. The impression they were meant to leave, however, was quite precise. By now Tara would have no doubt that she was being held on suspicion of treason.

"Miss Markosi?"

"Yes."

"My name is Ahmad Hashemian. I'm—"

"I know who you are," she said, her eyes locked on his.

"Good," he said, giving her the short end of a smile. "That will save us time."

The car turned off the main boulevard and sped toward a nearby suburb where a VEVAK safe house was located. "You know why you're here?"

"No. I don't."

Feigning innocence. That was to be expected.

"If you tell me the truth now, it will be less unpleasant later," he told her.

"I don't know what you want me to say."

"This is a difficult situation, I understand. At the moment you still have options. If you tell me the truth, I can ensure that you don't get hurt. If not?" He could see the fear entrenched in her eyes. "You worked for the Ministry of Foreign Affairs up until two years ago, didn't you?"

"That's right."

"Why did you quit?"

"I wanted to be closer to my mother. She's sick. I needed to take care of her."

"Yes, I'm sorry about your mother," he said, his voice sympathetic. "It's a shame. Horrible disease. She lives with you in Dardasht, doesn't she?"

"What do you want, Mr. Hashemian?"

"The truth."

He handed her an envelope containing an 8x10 photo in black and white. The photo had been taken almost three years ago in Lebanon, out-side the port city of Tripoli. His deputy, Reza, had managed to acquire a name to go with the photo. Not without some difficulty.

Tara took the envelope and opened it. He watched her closely, waiting for her reaction. As she pulled the photo from the envelope and turned it over, her face told him everything he needed to know: the faint blushing of the cheeks, the unconscious furrowing of the brow, the visible swelling of the carotid artery as her heart reflexively quickened its pace.

"Who is he?"

Tara paused, still staring at the photo. "This was a long time ago," she said, placing the picture face down in her lap. She turned and looked out the window.

"Not so long ago," Hashemian said.

"Long enough."

Hashemian thought he detected sadness in her voice. A touch of mel-ancholy. "Who is he?"

"Someone I met in Beirut. His name was David. He was a journalist."

"A journalist?"

"Yes. I knew him for about eight months. I never saw him again after that." She handed the photo back.

Hashemian carefully placed the photo back in its envelope. He could see that Tara still held a glimmer of hope that she could escape her past. She couldn't. "You were friends? You and this...David?"

"More than friends. I reported it, of course," she said. "Is that what this is about?"

"Where did you say he was from?"

"I didn't."

His eyes bore down on her.

"Jordan," she said.

"And you were intimate?"

"What is this about?" she demanded.

"Answer the question."

"Yes, we were intimate. Why does it matter?" she asked, allowing her anger to overpower the fear that was surging inside her.

Hashemian decided to let her have her moment of indignation. Taking a silver cigarette case from his jacket pocket, he opened it with both hands. Then, with care, he removed one of the yellow cigarettes from inside and lit it with a wooden match.

"This David of yours," Hashemian continued, "we've discovered some very interesting information about him."

"Is that so?"

"Yes."

He waited for her to respond, curious to see how she would react.

"Well," she said, "our relationship, if you can call it that, was a long time ago. Whatever the information, I'm sure it doesn't concern me."

"On the contrary, my dear, it does concern you. Very much."

"Like I said, I only knew him for a short while."

He gave her a hard look. "The man you knew in Lebanon, Tara. We know he wasn't a journalist. He was a member of the American Central Intelligence Agency. A spy. His real name is Akil Hassan."

81

THEY ARRIVED AT a gated estate with tall hedges that blocked the view from the street. Hashemian led Tara inside and made her wait in one of the lavish sitting rooms.

The curtains were drawn, making the room dark and gloomy. She was perspiring. Her heart was pounding. More than two years had gone by since she had last seen David. Or was it Akil? Was that his real name?

He had left one day without warning. Weeks later she'd found the hastily written note balled up and hidden at one of their dead drops. He said he was sorry, that he'd been ordered back to the States unexpectedly. That was the last she had heard from him. For a long time she held out hope that he would come back to her, but he never did.

She had been intoxicated those first few months by the fear and exhilaration of breaking the rules. Surreptitious meetings in hotel rooms. Car trips up north on weekends. In David's arms, she felt she could say whatever she wanted. Her country and her colleagues were not so accommodating. But when he left without warning, a hole had opened up inside her. Six months later she had left the Foreign Ministry and returned home to take care of her ailing mother. In turn, her mother had taken care of her. Now, here she was, her past having finally caught up to her.

Hashemian lumbered into the room. "What documents did you give the American?" he demanded.

"I didn't know he was an American spy. I never—"

"Don't lie!" Hashemian shouted. He was short and fat and his voice was much angrier now. His eyes tracked her constantly as he paced back and forth in front of her. "You betrayed your country. Why? Tell me that much at least."

"Please," she pleaded with him, fighting back the hot tears that ran down her face.

"The penalty for treason against the Islamic Republic is death."

"I didn't do anything wrong."

"Stop lying!"

She held her hands over her face, a mixture of fear and shame taking hold of her.

"If you die, who will take care of your mother, Tara? You need to think of her."

When Tara had returned home from Beirut she had watched her country grow more and more repressive. New restrictions on music, literature and dress were imposed. It made her feel justified in having helped the Americans.

"You see over in the corner there," Hashemian said, pointing.

Tara didn't look right away. Then she felt his meaty fingers wrapping themselves around her jaw, turning her head forcefully.

His nicotine-stained fingers were hurting her.

"Look!" he ordered, his voice so loud it made her cringe.

She looked at the machine in the corner, its tangled wires coiled on top.

"That's a lie detector," he told her. "It will confirm what we already know, that you betrayed your country by passing state secrets to the enemy. The evidence will be used at your trial. What do you think your mother will say?"

"No. Please." She was sobbing now.

"She will be shamed into an early grave."

"Please."

"Admit the truth," he told her.

"You…you already know the truth," she cried.

"But I want to hear it from you," he said, his face only inches from hers now.

"Yes. I'm guilty. I did it."

There, she had said it. She felt as if a dam had broken inside her.

Hashemian took a step back.

There was a long silence.

"That wasn't so hard, was it?" He handed her a handkerchief. "C'mon, no more crying," he said, "the hard part is over."

He walked over to a side table and poured a glass of water for her.

"What now?" Tara asked, still wiping the tears from her face.

"An opportunity to redeem yourself," he said.

Tara looked up into the cold, colorless eyes of her interrogator. What would she have to do? she wondered. She watched as he took out another cigarette and lit it. The action was deliberate and precise, the same as in the car.

"I have a mission specially tailored for you, my dear," he said.

She stared at him in disbelief. His tone and manner had changed completely. "I'm not a spy," she told him.

"That's not entirely true, now is it."

"I did clerical work. I have no training."

"Shhhh. Let me finish. If you agree with what I propose, you will be allowed to take care of your mother after it's over. As for the future, we can discuss that later. The alternative, I'm afraid, is a public trial." Hashemian stabbed his cigarette out in the porcelain ashtray that sat atop the mantle. "The outcome, I believe, has already been determined."

She didn't know what to say. What did he expect of her?

"So? Will you help me, Tara?"

"Yes," she said. What other choice did she have?

"Excellent."

82

Bashir Khalini sat handcuffed to a chair in the middle of the interrogation room. He had not slept or eaten in more than thirty-two hours and his exhaustion was threatening to overwhelm him.

He could feel himself drifting off again, his eyes slowly closing.

A fist slammed down onto the metal table, shocking him back to consciousness.

Akil watched the scene from the control room, on HD monitors. Jiri had been working Khalini for six hours straight, circling his prisoner like a wolf stalking its prey. Methodical. Disciplined.

There was no question who was in control. Everything Jiri did had a reason. Pointed questions followed allegations. Then more questions. Over and over he asserted Khalini's guilt, not letting the Iranian answer the charges hurled against him. The clear implication was that these were facts, not suppositions.

Despite being asked more than once, Jiri never mentioned who he worked for. He spoke impeccable Farsi and reverted to English or Russian only periodically, in an effort to heighten the prisoner's sense of dislocation. Several times Khalini appeared to break down emotionally, but the information he gave at these moments was pure fabrication. Jiri immediately dismissed the outbursts, telling Khalini they knew all about the VX and his ties to the Sunni militia. They knew everything. They only wanted confirmation. A confession of guilt.

"There's no use lying," Jiri said sympathetically. "We know what you were doing in Iraq. The only way out of this madness is to admit it."

Khalini remained defiant.

Inside the control room, Akil stood up. He knew what was coming next. The endless hours of interrogation combined with five days of physical and mental manipulation were driving Khalini toward an inflection point—the moment where his will to resist would fail him. How close they were to that point—exactly—was impossible to know. Every person had a different threshold. There were ways to tip the balance though, to force a person over the edge.

Jiri continued circling the table, tracking his prey under the bright lights that rained down from above, his eyes focused on his target, not saying a word. Then he stopped suddenly, next to the prisoner. Stared down at him, waiting a moment before leaning in, slowly, not wanting to alarm Khalini with any sudden movements.

Without warning, he slammed his fist into the Iranian's face, striking the bridge of his nose.

Blood gushed onto the table.

Jiri stepped back and kicked Khalini to the floor.

Hands still cuffed, the Iranian had no way to cushion his fall. He landed hard on the bare concrete, a guttural sound sling-shotting from somewhere deep inside him.

Jiri stepped around the chair and stood over his prisoner again. This time he swung his steel-toed boot into the Iranian's ribs with full force.

The Pasdaran agent had to be wondering what the hell had just happened. Why this sudden violence? Let him wonder, Akil thought, as he watched the monitors.

The prisoner was balled up in the fetal position on the floor, moaning in pain. Jiri glanced up at the camera as he left the interrogation room. Akil checked his watch. Twenty-seven hours had elapsed since he'd first spoken to Jiri, and so far the Iranian had not given them the information they needed. He'd wanted to give Jiri every opportunity to finish the job, but Bill had not minced words on the phone the previous evening. *We need to know everything he knows, no matter what it takes, and we need to know it now.*

The pressure back home was intensifying. The words, and the tension in Bill's voice, were an unpleasant reminder of what was at stake. How far would he have to go to save American lives? Akil wondered. Jiri was supposed to have finished the job by now, but he hadn't.

As a worst case scenario, Akil had formulated a plan of his own and discussed it with Jiri that morning. They had both agreed it should remain a last resort. It was risky. An all-or-nothing stratagem that might not pay off, and worse, could set them even further back.

Now it appeared it was their only option.

As Jiri entered the control room there was no sign of the anger Akil and Sophie had witnessed only moments ago. Jiri grabbed a bottle of water and unscrewed the cap and took a drink. "He's teetering on the edge," Jiri said. "Now's the time if you still want to try your plan."

"I don't think we have a choice," Akil said. "We've run out of time. Plus, his condition gives us a unique advantage."

"Alright, he's primed, just like we discussed. Let's hope all he needs is one last push."

"Good. Go back in, keep roughing him up," Akil said, "but leave him in one piece. I'll be right in."

Jiri nodded, downed the rest of his water, then left. Seconds later he entered the interrogation room and screamed for Khalini to get up off the floor. When the Iranian moved too slowly, he punched him in the side of the face and forced him back down onto the concrete, continuing his verbal assault from above.

Sophie turned away from the monitors. "What are you going to do?" she asked.

There was apprehension in her voice.

"I'm going to get some answers," Akil said. He could tell she wanted to say more, but she didn't and he was grateful for it.

Akil walked from the control room to the antechamber. Watching through the one-way as Jiri finished his work, he pondered how he had arrived at this precise moment. How he'd ended up in this place. Part of this craziness. Then forced the thought from his mind. This was not the time or place for introspection. He needed to focus on what had to be done.

Picking up a small red toolbox, Akil entered the room. "You!" he yelled at Jiri. The single word, spoken in Arabic, was full of fury and accusation. "Enough!"

Jiri dropped Khalini to the floor and stood at attention.

"Get out," Akil ordered. "I'll deal with you later."

Jiri left the room as Akil placed the toolbox on the metal table that was bolted to the floor. The toolbox had been painted fire-engine red at Akil's request.

Next, he went over to Khalini and tried to help the Iranian to his feet. Khalini recoiled in fear.

"It's okay," Akil said in Farsi. "I apologize for the way you've been treated. Sometimes they get carried away." He grabbed Khalini by the arm and helped him up, then walked him back to the table and sat him down in his chair.

"Guard," Akil said, turning. "Remove the cuffs on this prisoner immediately."

Khalini watched Akil suspiciously.

"Are you hungry?" Akil asked.

Khalini made no indication he had heard the question.

Akil repeated it.

This time Khalini nodded his head slightly. "Bring us some tea and some food," Akil ordered. "And a blanket," he said as an afterthought. When the guard hesitated, Akil looked at Khalini and smiled warmly. "The prisoner won't be a problem. Go."

The guard left the room, leaving the two of them alone. Akil was dressed in a sport coat with a plain collared shirt and no tie. He wore only gray, a mirror of the room itself. Even the metal table was gray. The only color that existed within the four walls was the red toolbox.

"I'm sorry you've been put through this," Akil said.

Khalini remained guarded.

With one hand resting on top of the toolbox, Akil stared at Khalini. "It's okay, you don't need to say anything. We'll wait for the tea to arrive."

83

A FEW YEARS after Akil had graduated from The Farm, he'd undergone specialized training in counter-interrogation techniques at the John F. Kennedy Special Warfare Center in North Carolina. It had been a harrowing experience, one that had pushed him to his breaking point. He had been so physically and mentally abused by the end that the line between what was real and imagined left him questioning if it was a training exercise at all. It was because of this that Akil had some idea of what Khalini was going through. How he felt. It was knowledge he intended to use to his advantage now.

The guard returned and entered with a tray of tea and some sweets, along with a blanket. The guard placed the tea down on the table and handed the blanket to Akil, who in turn handed it to Khalini.

Khalini wrapped the blanket around his shoulders while Akil poured two glasses of hot tea. The Iranian seemed to be acquiescing to the sudden change in treatment.

"*Mamnoon*," he said, thanking Akil in Farsi as he took the tea.

The Iranian's hands were still shaking from the cold and some of the hot liquid spilled onto the table.

Akil removed a popular brand of Iranian cigarette from his pocket. "You smoke?" he asked.

Khalini shook his head no.

Akil placed the cigarettes on the table in front of him and returned his free hand to the top of the red toolbox. They sat in silence for nearly five minutes, drinking their tea. In the tiny room, five minutes felt like an eternity. Akil leaned back in his chair and watched Khalini patiently, noting how the Iranian's eyes kept shifting their gaze to the red toolbox.

Finally, Akil broke the silence. "So much suffering, and for what?" he asked in a conversational tone. "We know everything, Bashir. You'll confirm it sooner or later. We both know it's inevitable."

"I don't know what you want," Khalini said. "There has been some kind of mistake. I'm Pasdaran. I have no idea why I'm here."

"You've been playing with fire, that's why," Akil said, sipping his tea. It was sweet, in the Arab tradition, and hot enough that he had to blow on it before each new sip. "You shouldn't play with fire. You can get burned. Didn't your mother ever tell you that?"

"I don't know what you're talking about."

"The old rules no longer apply, Bashir. Keep that in mind. I suggest you not lie to me again."

Khalini seemed ready to say something, then hesitated.

"How is your a wife, Bashir?" Akil could see Khalini's brow furrow. "Your children? Do you miss them?"

Khalini was looking at him with hatred in his eyes.

"Who are you?" he asked.

"Does that matter? What matters is what I'm capable of. No one is safe anymore, Bashir. We know everything about you. How hard do you think it would be to get to your family."

"You're crazy."

"Accidents happen all the time. The world is made up of unfortunate tragedies."

"I don't know anything."

Akil leaned forward and put his tea down on the table. Khalini instinctively retreated. Reaching into his jacket pocket, Akil removed a small aluminum vial, the same one they'd found on Khalini in Baghdad. He had saved it for just this moment. "I want to know about this," he said, placing the vial on the table. "Then you can go back home to your family and you'll never hear from me again."

Khalini stared at the vial for a long time without saying a word, his feet shifting uncomfortably underneath the table.

"I've never seen that before."

Without warning, Akil lunged across the table and swatted the tea from Khalini's hand. The glass shattered against the nearby wall. "Don't lie to me!" Akil yelled.

Khalini's eyes swelled with shock.

Akil calmly sat back down in his chair and returned his right hand to the top of the red toolbox, drumming his fingers on its metal lid in a slow, deliberate rhythm.

"Let's start again," he said, his tone composed and relaxed. "Who ordered you to deliver the VX?"

Tears began to run down Khalini's face.

"Where's it headed?" Akil asked, showing Khalini the letter Saqr had sent him, the one Travers had found.

Akil laid the letter on the table beside the vial. "Saqr sent this to you. The VX arrived safe. I want to know where it's headed."

"I don't know."

Khalini's head was bowed down, his eyes clutched tight. He was lying.

Akil slammed his fist down onto the metal table and launched to his feet. He was running on instinct now. He opened the lid of the toolbox and removed an oversized wrench. Khalini stared at the wrench as Akil walked around to the other side of the table and stood next to him.

Akil spoke in a gentle voice, his lips at the edge of Khalini's ear. "Who ordered you to do this?"

He'd already started thinking of Hannah back in New York, letting the thought drive his anger. Khalini was no different than the terrorist he was chasing back home. This man, and others like him, had facilitated the murder of his sister-in-law. They had nearly killed Michael.

"Tell me where the VX is going."

Khalini was sobbing now. Emotionally, he was a wreck. He was primed to break. He had to break.

Akil raised his voice. "Who? Where?"

"I don't know," the Iranian cried, but the words were spoken without conviction.

Akil grabbed Khalini's right forearm and held his hand down on the table. There was almost no strength left in the arm and it gave easily. Without warning, Akil swung the wrench down onto the hand. The sound of shattered bone was drowned out by screams of agony.

Akil let go of Khalini's forearm and placed the wrench on top of the toolbox, then waited for the screaming to stop. "No more games, Bashir. I'll find your family and I'll kill them, and when I'm done I'll come back here and tell you all about it. But I won't kill *you*. There's no escape for you until you tell me what I want to know."

"Please," Khalini moaned. He loved his family—that was his weakness—and in his current state it was obvious he believed Akil would carry through with his threat.

"Who told you to deliver the VX?"

Khalini's words were indecipherable. Akil grabbed the Iranian's hair and pulled back hard so that he was looking straight up into the light.

"Who?" Akil repeated.

"Please."

Akil twisted his hand, jerking the hair on Khalini's head. "Who?"

"My superiors," Khalini said, his breathing labored.

That's it. Let it all out.

"What superiors?"

Khalini's words came only one or two at a time now.

"They ordered it."

"The Supreme Leader? The President? Who?"

"No...no. I don't know."

"Who?!"

"I don't know who planned it."

"Where's the VX headed?"

"To Saqr. Then...Beirut."

"And then where?"

"I don't know."

Akil pressed down on Khalini's broken hand.

"Aaaaahhhhhh!"

He waited a moment for the screaming to stop, then asked the question again: "Where is the VX headed?"

"America! To America," Khalini said.

"Where exactly?"

"I... I don't know. My family."

"What port?"

"East coast. I don't know the port. They never told me."

"You're lying!"

"No...please."

Don't pass out on me you son-of-a-bitch.

"What port?"

"It's arriving by container ship."

"When?"

"Soon."

"Tell me!" Akil shouted.

"Soon. Very soon. Everything's been prepared."

"Where exactly?"

84

PIER 82.

Sayyid held the high powered scope to his face and scanned the facility from across the river. Despite the late hour, the port was abuzz with activity.

Arclight flooded the asphalt and spilled over onto the surface of the river as people and trucks hastened back and forth.

Philadelphia was one of the country's busiest ports. Three thousand ships a year loaded and unloaded their cargo on the Delaware River. Strategically located at the center of the Northeast corridor, the port was directly accessible to a huge number of North American cities using rail and truck routes. No other port in the country could boast the same. That distinction meant it was also one of the most heavily protected in the country.

Sayyid had not chosen Philadelphia without good reason. It was ideally suited to his purposes. Miami was too far from his intended target and New York/New Jersey was too dangerous, logistically speaking.

No, it had to be Philly, despite the difficulties and the heightened risk it presented. As more money from Homeland Security trickled down the pipe, ports had become increasingly well defended. Major ports like Philadelphia, among others, spent tens of millions of dollars upgrading their security, significantly altering the playing field. CCTV cameras were the cheapest and most ubiquitous form of defense the ports had, and they now covered every square foot and angled recess of most facilities.

Sayyid had tracked these changes tenaciously over the years. There were sophisticated machines operating amidst the cranes and storage facilities, machines that could see through steel containers and spot weapons or explosives hidden inside. But what security experts feared most was WMDs. And for that, the ports had acquired radiological, biological and chemical sensor systems. Advanced sensors were constantly seeking out trace amounts of radiation or chemical residue given off by such deadly substances as Sarin and Hydrogen Cyanide. Despite the wildly optimistic scenarios of pop-novelists and security pundits, terrorists knew that it was virtually impossible to get a sufficient amount of radiological material into a port without being detected, never mind the difficulty of extricating it. The renewed emphasis on cargo-tracking technologies and the posting of US customs agents overseas only exacerbated the situation.

From the outside looking in, it appeared to be a fool's errand to bring in a WMD by ship. Unless, of course, you had a plan that could circumvent all this security. Sayyid had worked the details out over several months, fine-tuning his plan, relishing the challenge it presented. Once he had his solution down on paper, he'd spent two months camped on the edge of the Red Sea, finding out if it would work. Training every day was exhaustive, but if it paid off in the end, it would be worth it.

For all the money the Americans had spent on upgrading their security, they had failed to think in three dimensions. It would, he hoped, prove to be a fatal miscalculation.

Looking through the scope, Sayyid could see that the attacks in New York had resulted in more security guards being added to the port. The entry and exit gates were manned by two guards now, at all times, instead of just one. The perimeter fence surrounding the facility, with razor wire spooled along its upper edge, was being patrolled by armed guards as well.

None of this mattered to Sayyid's plan, of course, but it raised questions. Was this increase in security attributable solely to the suicide attacks on New York, or had his mission been compromised in some way? Had the Americans learned something?

He dismissed the thought, knowing it was unlikely. Nerves were making him question himself, question what he already knew—that the increase in security was a natural response. It was to be expected. The Americans didn't know anything. How could they?

Lying flat on his stomach, he adjusted the scope and turned his shoulders to look downriver. A container ship was plowing the water with the aid of a tugboat. He scanned the ship's hull until he could see the name painted on its bow.

ACHILLES.

White on black.

The ship was registered out of Athens and had left Lebanon more than two weeks ago, stopping in Algiers on its way to Philadelphia. It carried a mixed cargo, including dates, olives, and citrus fruits. Sayyid had arranged for an associate to get work onboard the ship. The man had worked on freighters before and knew them well. That was important because he was a vital link in the chain of events that would ultimately put the VX in Sayyid's hands.

Sayyid checked his watch.

The Achilles would be in position within the hour.

85

"THE EAST COAST?" Bill Graham asked. "You're sure?"

"Absolutely sure," Akil said. He was on the secure line from the CIA's Cairo station. He'd finished the interrogation of Bashir Khalini and was about to head home.

"Alright, I'll talk to Marchetti," Bill said. "Good work."

Bill hung up the phone and sat on the edge of his desk. The kid had come through for him. Khalini had been broken and now they knew for sure the VX was on its way to the United States. Where precisely remained a mystery, but Philadelphia seemed a likely prospect considering what they'd recovered off the digital voice recorder Curtis Stone had given them. His worst fears were slowly being realized. WMD's were headed to a terrorist on American soil, one who had promised to attack innocent civilians a second time.

Had the VX already made it into the country? Bill wondered.

He had no way of knowing for sure. For now, the best they could do was maximize security at the ports along the eastern seaboard and alert the coast guard. The Port of Philadelphia would be his first priority.

Bill got up and started searching the binders stacked on a shelf beside his desk. Pulling a three-ring binder off the shelf, he started flipping pages. He tried to remember what he'd read years ago. He knew VX was one of the most lethal nerve agents ever produced. The British had discovered it, but it was the Americans who had perfected it during the fifties and sixties. Far more toxic than Sarin, it could kill in extremely small doses through inhalation or by contact with the skin.

Bill found the insert detailing the chemical weapon and read down the page.

$$C_{11}H_{26}NO_2PS$$

Characterized by its high viscosity and low volatility, VX has the texture and feel of motor oil. It is also odorless, tasteless, and virtually impossible to detect, which makes it easy to transport—undetected—over long distances.

Bill skipped over the scientific accountings and stopped when he got to the section detailing exposure. Contact with VX seemed a particularly cruel way to die.

Immediately following exposure, a victim's central nervous system would be attacked. Neurotransmitters that controlled the body's various functions would begin to deteriorate and the body would start to shut down in seconds. Blindness, respiratory distress, muscle spasms, and vomiting would lead to debilitating tremors and loss of bodily control, including the bladder and bowels. Depending on the severity of exposure, the body would eventually go into convulsions. The time from exposure to death from asphyxiation could be as little as ten minutes, under the right conditions.

Bill threw the binder down in frustration. With radioactive material, sensors could at least detect its presence. Not so with VX, which is why it had the potential to be far deadlier than any dirty bomb.

New York-New Jersey. Miami. Philadelphia. Charleston.

These were the ports he would recommend shutting down, or at least restricting traffic in and out of. Philly in particular, for obvious reasons, but he knew the President wouldn't—couldn't—authorize such action. The monetary cost to the country would be enormous. The political fall-out would be much worse, both for the President, and his party.

Bill knew that the intelligence, as strong as it was, didn't constitute a slam dunk, and that left the President's hands tied. It was maddening because they were staring down the barrel of a loaded gun ready to go off and he couldn't do anything substantive about it.

Searching his desk for a fresh pack of cigarettes, Bill tried to figure out what he was going to tell Marchetti or the President if they asked who was behind the sudden appearance of Iraqi VX. Or how it had gotten into the hands of the terrorists. Was Khalini acting on orders from the Iranian President? The Ayatollah?

Bill shuddered to think where it could all lead. The evidence against Iran was strong, if inconclusive at the moment. But they had hard evidence that a Pasdaran agent had arranged for the VX to be passed to known terrorists. If those same terrorists managed to use it against American citizens on American soil, the President would have no choice but to retaliate against Iran. After that, there was no telling where it would lead. But with political instability mounting in the Islamic Republic, Bill had no way of knowing who had actually initiated, or at very least, facilitated the attacks.

With his head already throbbing, he threw his jacket on and prepared to go down the hall. He needed to tell Marchetti and the President exactly where they stood.

86

ON THE FLIGHT back to Washington Akil couldn't sleep. Every time he closed his eyes he saw the image of Khalini's hand being crushed. He could still hear the sound of bone shattering and the screams that followed. Had there been another way? The question was moot. The unsettled feelings, his questioning of events, they would fade with time. He knew this from experience. He'd done his job, for better or worse, and now he had to move on. If it bothered him so much he could always quit, but that thought had never crossed his mind.

He raised the shade on the airplane's oval window and looked out. They were still rocketing through the darkness somewhere over the Atlantic while VX was on its way into the U.S. Where exactly? To whom? They didn't know. Khalini had raised more questions than he had answered. One thing was certain, the threat was greater than first imagined.

Akil signaled the steward and ordered a drink. When the scotch arrived he straightened his seat and glanced over at Sophie. She was sound asleep across the aisle from him, her hair all scrunched up to one side. She looked like a child without a care in the world.

He knew different.

He thought briefly about waking her, feeling the urge to talk to someone. It didn't matter what they talked about as long as it didn't involve work. He needed some reassurance that the everyday still had a place in his life, that there was something beyond this apparent madness he found himself a part of again. Flying halfway around the world to coerce information from a man he'd never met may have been an occupational necessity—it may have even be the right thing to do—but it wasn't normal.

Instead, Akil turned and looked out at the passing darkness, letting her sleep. She wasn't interested in talking to him anyways. After finishing with Khalini, he'd returned to the control room expecting to find her there, but she'd gone. It was obvious she didn't want to see him. Then, on the drive to the airport, she hadn't said a word.

It had bothered him—was still bothering him now—more than it should have. He knew it and he hated himself for it.

87

THE PLANE TOUCHED down at Dulles around 4 AM. It was still dark out. Akil exited the plane first and waited for Sophie. When she finally appeared at the top of the jet's narrow set of stairs, her hair was no longer a mess.

"You sleep okay?" he asked.

"Yes. It's strange, I usually can't sleep on planes."

"I grabbed your bag."

"Thanks." She took the bag and they stood facing each other, the terminal lights casting long shadows.

"You okay?" he asked.

"I'm fine," she said.

He wasn't convinced.

Sophie lifted her bag onto her shoulder. "I have to tell my boss something when I see him," she said. "I can't tell him the truth—that I spent the last thirty-six hours at a secret CIA prison watching an Iranian national being tortured. Can I?"

There was no trace of irony in her voice.

"No, you can't," Akil said.

"That leaves me with a bit of a problem, doesn't it?"

He thought about it for a second. "Tell him things didn't pan out in London. Fill him in on the VX. Bill will have already alerted the FBI and NCTC by now."

"And if he asks where the information came from?"

"Tell him you were told it was classified. Usual Agency runaround. I'm sure you'll have no problem convincing him of that."

Sophie raised an eyebrow.

"If he has any problems he can talk to Bill Graham direct."

"And London? This is my career. I can't be caught lying to my boss."

He detected real concern in her voice. "Bill has London squared away," he told her. "Don't worry. Give him the names I wrote down for you. But only if he asks. SIS will corroborate everything."

"Got all the bases covered, huh?"

"Just remember, stick to the story. You and I were in London meeting with SIS the past forty-eight hours."

"Don't worry," she said. "I don't intend to lose my job over this." She turned toward the terminal. "I'll see you later."

"I'm sorry," he said. The words sounded more anxious than he wanted them to.

Sophie stopped and looked back over her shoulder. "Sorry for what?"

"For having to do what I did in Cairo. I'm sorry it came to that. I wish it hadn't."

Sophie nodded.

"I know how strongly you feel about it," he added.

She was thinking, measuring her response. "We got the information, didn't we?"

"That's right."

"I know you did what had to be done. Maybe you were right. I don't know. I just don't know anymore."

She sounded tired.

He was surprised by just how much he cared what she thought. "It wasn't me in that room with Khalini," he said. "Not the real me."

"Yes, it was. A part of you anyway."

With that, she turned and walked away toward the lights of the terminal building. He let her go, knowing it was as close as he was going to get to absolution this morning.

Akil re-boarded the plane and thanked the pilot and crew, then headed for the parking lot. If he hurried he could get home and grab a few hours' sleep, maybe have breakfast with his father and Michael before he had to return to Langley.

88

THE PAKISTANI HAD parked outside the terminal building at Dulles, the one used by private charter companies, corporate clients and those who were rich enough to operate their own private aircraft. The lightbox on top of his cab indicated it was off-duty, and on the passenger seat sat a photo of the man he'd been told to look for. The target appeared to be Arab, somewhere in his late thirties or early forties. He'd been told the target would be exiting—not entering—the terminal, but three hours had gone by with no sign of the man. Twice now the Pakistani had nearly fallen asleep, staring at the terminal entrance. Once again he could feel his eyelids growing heavy.

Suddenly the back door of his cab swung open, causing a wave of cold air to rush in.

The Pakistani turned.

"Jefferson Hotel. Make it quick," the passenger ordered as he got in.

He was Caucasian, late forties, dressed in a suit and tie.

"Sorry, off duty," the Pakistani said in a thick accent.

"Look buddy, there's no other cabs out here and I need to get to The Jefferson. I'll make it worth your while, alright?"

The man started to open his wallet. The driver quickly checked the terminal, then turned to the man in the back seat. "Get out," he said. "I can't take you anywhere. The light says off-duty, okay."

"C'mon. I'll throw in an extra twenty. Huh? Twenty bucks?"

The Pakistani turned back around. He could smell alcohol on the man's breath. As he decided what to do, he kept one eye on the terminal.

"Hey, buddy, just take me into D.C. I'll make it an even forty bucks on top of the fare, alright? Fuck."

The Pakistani got out of the cab, stepped to the back door, and ordered the man to get out. The man refused, so the Pakistani made a cursory check of his surroundings, then ducked into the back seat and seized one of the man's wrists. He violently bent the man's hand forward so that the tips of his fingers were almost touching the underside of his forearm. He could feel the wrist bones hovering at their breaking point and knew from personal experience just how much pain he was causing.

The move had been so fast and unexpected that the businessman in the backseat had not had time to defend himself. It would have been a futile effort regardless.

The Pakistani led the man out of the cab and pressed his face against the roof of the car. Using his forearm, he applied just enough pressure to the back of the man's neck to restrict the flow of blood. "I'm off-duty. Understand?"

"Yeah...yeah, sure."

"Find another cab," the Pakistani said as he released his grip. He stepped back a couple of feet, ready to react if the man tried to take a swing at him. Thankfully, he wasn't that stupid or that drunk.

At a safe distance, the man turned and hurled a series of racial slurs at the cabbie. The Pakistani ignored the comments and stepped back behind the wheel, praying he hadn't missed his target during the confrontation. Looking over at the terminal entrance, it appeared empty and he gave a sigh of relief. Then the Pakistani noticed a man in a dark sports coat walking through to the parking lot. He let out a curse in Urdu and reached for the binoculars lying on the seat beside the black and white photo of his target. He had only a few seconds before the man's face would be out of view. He centered the binoculars and focused as fast as he could. The man's face came into view for only a split-second before disappearing behind some shrubbery. He tried to get another look, just to be sure, but it was no use.

Putting down the binoculars the Pakistani picked up the photo, studied it, then reached for the cell phone wedged against the windshield atop the dash. He dialed the number for the Interests Section for the Islamic Republic of Iran in the United States. Iran, who didn't have an official embassy in the U.S., operated out of offices located in the Pakistani Embassy.

"Yes," a voice said on the other end of the line.

"He just arrived."

There was no reply. Then the line went dead.

The Pakistani put the cell phone back against the windshield and started the cab. He left the off-duty light on and drove away, his work done for the night.

89

Sayyid exited Interstate 95 and made his way down toward the Delaware River. Finding the access road that led past a series of warehouses and factories, he drove until he came to the vacant lot he'd scouted from across the river earlier in the day. He had used two enormous gear wheels lying at the edge of the field as markers. The empty field itself was fenced off.

He drove halfway down the length of the field before stopping, then killed the engine and turned off the headlights. Reaching below the steering column, he removed the main electrical fuse and placed it in his pocket. Jumping out of the truck, he lifted the hood and propped it open. The vehicle wouldn't start without the fuse, and anyone who happened by would assume the truck had broken down. To buoy the impression, Sayyid placed a handwritten note on the driver's side dash explaining the unfortunate situation. The note apologized and said the truck would be removed first thing the following morning.

Issam was already at the back of the truck retrieving the extra wide duffel bag they had stored there. He slid it out onto the tailgate, then signaled for Sayyid to come give him a hand. Together they lowered the bag to the ground, then shut the tailgate and locked the canopy. One man on each end, they carried the bag down the fence line about forty yards. At this point, Issam went to work cutting a hole in the fence while Sayyid kept watch. Once the hole was cut, they slipped through, dragging the bag after them.

It was pitch black out in the open field. Sayyid could barely see two feet in front of him. The lot closest to them belonged to a manufacturing plant that was closed for the night. A halo of white light surrounded the store yard out back, but the light didn't seem to travel.

They were part of the landscape now.

Invisible.

Using a small Maglite, Issam guided their way down to the river's edge. It wasn't long before they could hear the sound of rushing water. Still hidden by darkness, Sayyid opened the duffel bag and pulled out the dry suit he'd packed inside. He started to put it on while Issam removed the rebreather and checked it over. The rebreather was a closed-circuit apparatus that recycled the air you breathed while underwater. By filtering the carbon dioxide out and retaining any unused oxygen, the system allowed for longer dive times. More importantly, it produced no air bubbles. Once underwater, there was no way for anyone to know you were there. That was the beauty of the system, and the main reason special forces units had been among the first to adopt the technology.

Once Sayyid had finished getting into his dry suit, Issam fit the rebreather onto his shoulders and secured the straps. They were almost set. For a few precious minutes they would be exposed along the shoreline. The key was to get into the water as quickly as possible, and without being seen.

Together they carried the duffel bag to the edge of the water, then removed the DPV—Driver Propulsion Vehicle—and placed it in the shallows. The torpedo-shaped device, equipped with a battery-powered propeller, weighed almost seventy pounds. In the water, the vehicle was neutrally buoyant and much easier to handle. It would speed Sayyid's travel time down river, then allow him to return upriver as he battled the Delaware's strong current.

Wasting no time, Sayyid waded into the river. Issam handed him a small hand-held sonar which he clipped onto his belt. Then he gripped the DPV with both hands and slipped beneath the surface.

Issam grabbed the duffel bag and hurried back into the dark of the field. Daybreak was only a few hours away.

Underwater, Sayyid throttled up the DPV, submerging to a depth of 15 feet. The river was silt-laden and visibility was poor, not unlike sections of the Red Sea where he'd trained for this exact moment. The underwater light he carried increased his line-of-sight a few feet, but to maintain direction he relied on the DPV's compass. It was just over a mile from the abandoned lot to Pier 82 and the Achilles. Maintaining a speed of approximately 3 mph, he calculated his travel time to be about twenty minutes.

The biggest hazard facing him now wasn't being discovered, it was getting entangled in old fishing nets or snagging himself on something protruding from the river bottom. He concentrated intently on the task at hand, ready to adjust course in an instant. It was exhausting work, but he didn't mind. The VX had made an impossible journey, passing through various hands and crossing several international borders on its way to America. Now it was here, and it was going to be his. His to use the way he wished.

The Americans had spent hundreds of millions of dollars trying to seal their ports, but all their sensors and cameras and armed guards were above ground. They searched the cargo as it came off the ship's deck and out of its hold, but the VX wouldn't be there. It was, with the will of God, already in the water. Waiting for him to retrieve it.

90

DRIVING HOME FROM the airport, Akil couldn't stop thinking about Sophie and Michael and the whereabouts of the VX. He would be happy when this whole affair was over and things returned to normal. What exactly *normal* was going to look like now, after New York, he wasn't sure.

Pulling into his driveway, he put the car in park and turned off the engine. Not wanting to wake his father or Michael, Akil got out and gently closed the driver's side door, then headed for the house. He was already dreaming of falling asleep in his own bed and getting some much-needed rest when he noticed his front door was ajar.

Smothering the noise from his keys, he quickly ducked to his right and threw his back up against the front of the house. Crouching down, he felt a stab of pain in his ribs. He ignored the discomfort and leaned to his right, confirming the breach, then made his way around the side of the house to the backyard. There was no point going in through the front door and losing any tactical advantage he might still have.

As he moved around the side of the house he took out his 9mm Heckler and Koch. The pistol was small and extremely accurate at close range.

The back door was locked and the house was dark. He looked through the small window built into the top half of the door. The curtains were thin enough to see into the kitchen.

It looked empty.

He used his key and slowly engaged the lock. If someone was in another part of the house, chances were they wouldn't hear the key turning. That's what he hoped anyway.

Gently swinging the door open, Akil leveled his gun and proceeded through the empty kitchen to the edge of the living room. His mind was racing now. Where were Michael and his father? Were they alright? Had one of them left the door open? Was he overreacting?

At the edge of the living room, he placed his back up against the kitchen wall and took a deep breath, then stepped gun first into the living room, tracking rapidly from left to right.

No one.

He checked the rest of the ground floor one room at a time, suddenly grateful for his recent trip to the firing range with Bill. From what he saw the house had not been burglarized.

Then who—if anyone—had broken in?

Once he was sure there was no one on the ground floor, he moved cat-like up the stairs. Halfway to the second floor one of the steps creaked loudly under his weight. Akil instantly crouched down, gun pointed up, prepared for an assaulted from above, but the assault never came.

He waited a few more seconds, listening for any telltale sounds that would signal the presence of an intruder.

The house was silent, apart from the odd groan coming from the old wooden joists and ductwork hidden behind the walls.

Adjusting the grip on his gun, he continued up to the top of the landing, his eyes scanning the hallway as he went. At the top of the landing, he moved left, wanting to check the spare bedroom first. The door was closed, but not shut tight. Pressing his foot flush against the door, he rotated his body into the room in one fluid motion, the muzzle of his gun searching for a target.

The room was empty except for his father and Michel asleep under the covers.

He immediately lowered the gun and swept it behind his back, then moved closer to check on the two of them. They were both sound asleep, unharmed and unaware of his presence. He gave a sigh of relief and tip-toed out of the room. His father must have failed to lock the front door, he decided, both upset and relieved by the fact. He would talk to his father about it in the morning. Right now, he needed to sleep.

After quickly checking his own bedroom, he went downstairs and secured the front door, then headed back upstairs and started to undress. Fatigue from the trip, and the sudden burst of adrenaline that was now ebbing away, made his limbs heavy and uncooperative. He was already shutting down. He hadn't looked this forward to sleep in a long time.

As he came around the other side of the bed, ready to pull back the covers, he spotted a folded piece of paper on his nightstand. A small seashell lay on top.

His heart skipped a beat. The paper had not been there when he'd left for Cairo, he was sure of that.

He picked it up, letting the seashell skitter to the floor.

David,
   Meet me at the Echo Nightclub.
Tonight. 11pm.
Come alone. Lives are at stake.
       TARA

91

Sayyid had been traveling downriver with the current for just over nineteen minutes. Now he slowed down and angled himself toward the shore, hoping his calculations were correct.

Almost immediately he spotted the massive concrete pilings that supported the docks and warehouse facilities that existed on the surface. There were four bays comprising seven separate berths at this point on the river. Piers 78, 80, 82 and 84. He was looking for the third bay and the fifth berthing. That's where the Achilles was and where he expected to find the VX waiting for him.

He edged along slowly, drifting past what he recognized as the underbelly of the SS United States, a 1000 foot passenger vessel that was the largest and fastest ever built in America. History had been unkind to the great ship, and now she sat rotting at one of the berths. Thanks to his earlier reconnaissance, he was able to use the ship as a geographical marker. The next berthing belonged to the Achilles.

As the enormous twin propellers of the Achilles came into view, Sayyid turned off the DPV. Above him was the port and its attendant security. They would have no idea he was down here. Even if someone was looking directly at the river, it would make no difference. There were no bubbles coming from his rebreather and the water was too murky to see his diving light. He was, for all intents and purposes, undetectable. All he had to do now was find the VX.

His associate aboard the Achilles had been given explicit instructions on what to do. First, he was to bundle the VX canisters with tape, then secure long plastic streamers to the package. Orange or pink, Sayyid had instructed, like the kind used on construction sites. He was to carry the VX onto the ship with him in Lebanon, hiding the canisters in his tote bag along with his dirty laundry. They would be safe there. Under no circumstances was he to leave the ship at any of the various ports-of-call. Instead, he was to keep to himself and safeguard the package whenever possible.

Once the ship had docked in Philadelphia he would need to find a way to cause a distraction of some kind. In this regard, the man had been given free rein. He would know the ship intimately by then and be better able to choose the best course of action. While the other crew members were preoccupied, the man was to find a place near the stern of the ship where he could drop the package overboard without being seen. It would take only a second. That was all that was required. But that second was critical. No one could see him do it. If he failed, all Sayyid's plans would be for nothing. Worse, they could be waiting for him now as he attempted to retrieve the VX.

Berthed in one of the bays jutting out into the river, the Achilles was protected from the full force of the Delaware's current, and as Sayyid swam around the ship's keel, he could feel it ease slightly. This was important because it was essential that the current not carry away the package, yet remain strong enough to aid in its retrieval. The bottom of the river, thick with sediment, would have buried the canisters soon after they entered the water and hit bottom. The streamers attached to the package, each several feet long, were therefore designed to flutter in the current and mark its location.

Sayyid began searching for the VX by going back and forth along the river bottom in a grid-like pattern. After about fifteen minutes of searching, he still hadn't found the VX. He started to imagine what might have gone wrong, knowing that a thousand quirks of fate could prevent him from achieving his goal. But there was little he could do about those things that were beyond his control. Having planned everything with exacting attention to detail, this was the one part of his plan that required someone else to be in charge, and with no way to communicate with the man onboard the Achilles, he felt powerless.

Had his associate been discovered or failed to execute the drop for some reason? Was he searching in vain for canisters that were not even there?

Moving farther from the stern, Sayyid put the idea of failure out of his mind. The VX was here. It had to be. It was just a matter of finding the canisters. Perhaps the streamers were not enough in the sediment-laden river, he thought. Reaching behind him, he took hold of the hand-held sonar he had brought with him. As he fidgeted with the dials, he thought he saw a flicker of color off to his left. He stared in that direction but saw no sign of the streamers. As he was about to turn his attention back to the sonar, he spotted another flash of color. Still holding the sonar, he swam over and found four tendrils of orange tape coming up off the river bottom like some kind of strange kelp. They were fluttering at a forty-five-degree angle, the current pushing them downriver.

Sayyid quickly grabbed hold of the streamers and pulled the canisters free of the mud. Once they were secured, he swam back to the stern of the ship and retrieved the DPV, letting the force of the current pull him downriver a few hundred meters. Once he was a safe distance from the Achilles, he restarted the DPV and headed back upriver to rendezvous with Issam.

The journey was a struggle and took about forty minutes. When Sayyid broke the surface, he oriented himself by searching out the bright lights of the manufacturing plant and the black hole that marked the empty lot next to it, enabling him to find his landing point.

He immediately ditched the sonar and the diving light in the middle of the river, watching them disappear into the murky depths before swimming to shore.

Beaching the DPV, Sayyid crouched down in the shallows and shrugged off the rebreather, then took hold of it and waded back out into deeper water. When he could feel the current pressing hard against his legs, he let go and watched the rebreather drift away and sink. Next, he went back and removed the battery casing on the DPV, then pushed the DPV out into the current. Making sure the battery compartment was sufficiently flooded, confident that the unit would sink, he let go of it and returned to shore.

Issam was waiting for him.

Sayyid handed him the canisters of VX, and together they hurried into the empty field. Masked by the darkness, the two men embraced in celebration. Sayyid quickly removed his dry suit and left it where it lay.

"You get rid of the duffle bag?" he asked Issam.

"Yes."

"Good. Let's go," he said, smiling.

They left the empty lot the same way they had entered it. Sayyid lowered the hood of the truck gently, pushing it down so that it locked in place, then went around to the driver's side and took the note from the dash and replaced the fuse he had removed earlier. Then the two men got in and drove away, the VX stashed in the back.

The riskiest part of the plan had been flawlessly executed. Nothing could stop him now. In a few days, he would unleash his gift on the American people and show them just how serious he was.

Part III

AGAINST ALL ODDS

92

AKIL CLIMBED OUT of the taxi near Dupont Circle, several miles from the Echo Nightclub. It was 9:30 PM. He was scheduled to meet Tara at 11 PM. That gave him ninety minutes to run an SDR and find out if he was being followed.

Choosing a circuitous route, he headed south towards Georgetown. As he walked, he thought about the note left on his nightstand. *Lives are at stake.*

It could mean a lot of things.

He knew Tara had not been the one to break into his home and leave the note on his nightstand. He suspected those responsible were operatives of the Iranian government. Or Pakistan. The question was, why? What was this all about? His first instinct had been to contact Bill Graham, tell him about the note. Marchetti too.

But what could he tell them? The mere mention of Tara's name would only dredge up the past, including the fears surrounding his loyalty and good judgment as a CIA officer. It was the last thing he needed right now. He decided it was better to find out what this was all about first, then report in.

He only hoped Tara would be waiting for him like the note said, so he could question her.

So he could see her again.

Turning left on P street, Akil picked up the pace. His field training had been conducted on the streets of DC and he knew them well, which was important because surveillance detection routes were all about drawing your pursuers out into the open. To be effective you needed to know the terrain you were operating in and how to use it to your advantage. A subway station, for example, offered a classic opportunity to force a surveillance team's hand. Having multiple entry and exit points would force anyone following you to move in close or risk losing you. At that critical moment, your chances of spotting a tail increased exponentially. But conditions had to be favorable. Not just any subway station would do. One isolated in an open area offered a greater chance of spotting movement. And the fewer people around the better.

There were dozens of tricks that could be used, and Akil planned on exploiting as many as possible.

Heading toward George Washington University, he turned the corner at 31ˢᵗ Street and ducked into a busy coffee shop. He wasn't thirsty; he wanted to watch the people behind him as they passed by the large window. He would sort them by archetype, keying in on signature items of clothing, accessories or identifying marks, storing the information so that later, as he continued his SDR, he could compare it with what he observed around him. Seeing a baseball cap with a distinctive logo, then spotting it again forty minutes later, three miles away, would raise alarm bells.

Leaving the coffee shop he continued on to the university. He had chosen to enter the campus for several reasons. First, it had lots of open courtyards intersected by narrow pathways. This kind of environment, like the subway station, increased his chances of spotting a tail. He was also looking for anyone who didn't blend in, and stepping onto a university campus was like entering an entirely different ecosystem—the demographics and the way people dressed were in stark contrast to downtown. The surveillance team that blended in out on the busy streets of metropolitan DC, should, in theory, stick out on a university campus.

But no one seemed out of place. A man in a double-breasted suit caught his attention for a few moments before a rambunctious freshman threw her arms around him and the two of them left quickly, headed in the opposite direction.

Akil kept moving, varying his pace. Wherever possible he took a last minute turn down one of the narrow pathways that he knew led to wide open spaces. Draw them out into the open, his instructors had urged.

But again, he spotted nothing overtly suspicious.

At 10:30 PM he left the campus, continuing his SDR, all the time getting closer and closer to F street and the Echo Nightclub. A couple times he thought he detected someone, but each time they moved off.

Was he clean? There was no way to be positive. If the team dispatched to surveil him was big enough and skilled enough, he may have been unable to detect them with an impromptu SDR like the one he'd just run. Still, it paid to be thorough, because the only thing he knew for sure was that Tara wasn't going to be alone. Someone had sent her to him. But who, and why, were questions he still needed answers to.

93

THE ECHO NIGHTCLUB's neon sign shined bright against the red brick out front. The popular DC hotspot had been open three years and continued to draw large crowds. Outside, the street overflowed with revelers and a group of smokers corralled behind a thick velvet rope.

Making his way up a flight of stairs, flanked on either side by faded playbills and old concert posters, Akil tried to remember the last time he'd been to a club like this. Three, four years maybe? In university, he would blow off steam by drinking and dancing with his friends, then go grab breakfast at some all-night diner as the sun came up. It felt like a long time ago and he was relieved to find he could still blend in—for the most part— thanks largely to a fitness regimen he hadn't yet abandoned.

Skirting the long line of waiting patrons, he headed straight for the bouncer who stood sentry at the main entrance. He had a beefy chest and a mouthful of metal teeth that reminded Akil of an old James Bond villain.

Introducing himself, Akil discretely flashed a C-note so that only the bouncer could see it, then leaned forward and said a few words into his ear as if they were old friends. As he did this, Akil slipped the money into the man's shirt pocket, shielding the move with his body. Those in the line-up would assume he and the bouncer knew one another, nothing more, nothing less. The point was to draw as little attention as possible without waiting to get in.

The bouncer stepped aside and unlatched the red velvet rope so that Akil could enter. It was a hundred dollars well spent.

Inside, the club was dark and crowded. Whoever had arranged this meeting had chosen this location for good reason. With so many people, both inside and out, there was lots of cover to conduct static surveillance. He was probably being watched right now and there was no way to tell. Once he found Tara—*if* he found her—the thumping techno beats and bass drums would render any listening devices all but useless. Their conversation would remain private, which he assumed was the point of meeting here instead of a quieter location.

After finding the note on his nightstand, he'd questioned whether or not he was being lured into a trap. The notion, at the time, seemed highly unlikely. After all, he had not been a CIA officer for over two years. In the dimly lit club, surrounded by strangers, he was no longer sure.

Letting the wall of noise wash over him, Akil pushed deeper into the fray.

At the far end of the room, a DJ was spinning records on a raised platform, back-lit by what Akil guessed were five 1000-watt lamps. On the dance floor, a couple hundred disciples moved to the beat of bass drums and the scratch of synthesizers recorded on vinyl. Strobes, synched to the music, offered flashes of the crowd as they lifted up off the spring-loaded dance floor in unison. It was like watching hundreds of human bottle rockets going off at once, their bodies captured and held at the apex of flight by the frosted glare of white light.

He continued pushing his way through the crowd.

Where would he find Tara amongst all these people?

The most logical choice would be the club's chill room. Having done his homework, he knew the room was on the second level, opposite the stage. It would be much quieter than downstairs, and if they were going to talk, it was the only place they wouldn't have to shout to be heard.

He made his way to the stairs, cutting through a sea of sweat-soaked bodies. Halfway across the dance floor though, the DJ hit the kill switch on his rig—reversed it—then came back with a new beat, faster and louder this time. Akil watched the bodies around him freeze in that split-second of darkness—descend in slow-motion—then erupt back into a frenzy of light as if it were some sort of editing trick. All he could think about was how much of a security nightmare this place was. He didn't like it. Too many bodies. Too much chaos.

Surveying the waves of people around him was pointless, he didn't even know who was he looking for.

Climbing the stairs to the second level, he wondered again if Tara was connected to Khalini in some way. To the VX. Is that why she was here? He had spent most of his day trying to solve the riddle, but to no avail.

At the top of the stairs, he entered the club's chill room. It was full of battered couches and low slung drink tables. The ambient music offered a nice change of pace from downstairs, but the room was still full of people crammed shoulder to shoulder. Looking around he didn't see Tara—not at first—then glimpsed her through a crowd of college kids doing shots of absinthe. She was sitting alone at the far end of the room with her back against the wall, next to an emergency exit.

I taught you well, he thought, making his way over.

She smiled as he got close, her strapless red dress and black stilettos accentuating her natural beauty. She hadn't changed much in the years they'd been apart—only her ebony hair, free from the constraints of the hijab, appeared longer now. Cascading past her shoulders, it brushed the top edge of her breasts. As he sat down he felt a wave of emotion wash over him. The memories of his last months in Lebanon—his last moments with her—came flooding back.

94

ANTHONY MARCHETTI HAD ordered the blanket surveillance seven days ago. As a result, Peters had dispatched his best surveillance team to track Akil Hassan. Everywhere Akil went, Peters' men were to follow like silent ghosts. The Director of the Agency had not offered an explanation as to why the order was given and Peters didn't ask. This wasn't the first time he'd been tasked with surveilling one of the Agency's own. Those suspected of passing information to the enemy or compromising it in other ways often found themselves under the microscope.

He no longer underestimated what people were capable of. He'd seen all manner of transgressions. Many of the officers who worked for the CIA had been trained to deceive and it wasn't surprising that boundaries were easily crossed. Some gambled too much or drank too often or moonlighted for corporate clients with undisclosed third-party interests. Foreign interests. Compared to a precious few, their crimes were relatively minor. It was men like Aldrich Ames that represented the ultimate threat: men who actively conspired with the enemy. But the target this time—Akil Hassan—appeared to be a dead end. Every move he'd made the past week, excluding his time overseas, appeared legitimate.

Until last night.

Peters' men, who had followed Akil Hassan home from the Airport, had witnessed him enter his residence through the back door with a deployed firearm. He had never done that before, and anything out of the norm was considered suspicious and immediately red flagged. Although Peters was willing to attribute the incident to a potential eccentricity on the part of the CIA officer—for the moment at least—his interest had been piqued. The next morning, as a precaution, he had assigned additional manpower to the watch team tracking Akil.

Peters, who was having a drink with an old friend, got the phone call around 10:20 PM. The target, he was told, had traveled into DC by cab, then proceeded to execute an aggressive SDR on foot. Peters knew you didn't run an SDR unless you suspected you were being followed or you were trying to hide something.

After receiving the phone call, Peters apologized to his friend and excused himself, then caught a ride downtown. Along the way, he accessed Akil's file and went over it again. Much of it had been redacted, even for his eyes, but what remained gave him a clear picture. Akil Hassan was an extremely resourceful operative with a wealth of field experience. Peters had no doubt he was capable of spotting a small or poorly trained watch team. Lucky for him those under his command were highly skilled and, as of this morning, had been deployed in large numbers. His people were also adept at altering their appearance and utilizing multiple surveillance techniques.

Waterfall surveillance, for instance, sent numerous members of a watch team at the subject head-on, staggered one after the other. They did this instead of following from behind, where the subject would be concentrating his or her attention. It took vast numbers of personnel and was costly, but extremely effective in key situations. The commander of the watch team following Akil was adamant on the phone that the target had not detected their presence. If that was the case, then Akil Hassan had no idea he was being followed.

Then why the SDR?

As he entered downtown, Peters received a second phone call. The target had just entered a nightclub called The Echo. 11:03 PM.

Peters knew Akil Hassan wasn't going to spend ninety minutes running an SDR just to go clubbing. So what was he doing? Was he meeting a contact? If so, who? And for what purpose?

Getting let off a few blocks from the club, Peters moved in on foot. He met with the commander he'd spoken to on the phone and told him that he was taking control of the operation.

An observation post had already been set up on the roof of an adjacent building that overlooked the alley at the back of the club. A camera was positioned near the edge of the roof. Peters walked over and looked through its high-powered telephoto lens—a 400mm f2/8 that had been tweaked by the people at the Directorate of Science and Technology. The camera was focused on the rear exit. At almost 200 yards, even with the low light conditions taken into consideration, Peters knew it was capable of capturing a clear image. Now all he needed was an opportunity to present itself. With a bit of luck, he'd soon have a good picture of why Akil had come here tonight.

Peters ordered two more officers with cameras to be placed out front of the club to make sure all the exits were covered, then radioed his man on the inside. Three static pulses came back over his earpiece. The pre-arranged signal confirmed that the target was still inside the club and was being monitored from a safe distance.

All he could do now was wait.

95

AKIL SAT DOWN and tried to reconcile the fact that Tara, his one-time agent, was here in D.C., sitting across from him.

Neither spoke, both absorbing the shock of the situation. Looking into her eyes, he noticed they were rimmed with black charcoal. The makeup was an affectation he hadn't seen her use before, but then, they hadn't seen or heard from one another in almost three years, not since he'd been forced to leave Beirut.

The decision had not been his and had come without warning. Langley had cabled, ordering him to leave Lebanon on the next available flight. It was only then that he knew for sure they'd discovered the truth of what he'd done. Ignoring the order to leave would have meant throwing away his career. Desperate, he had scrawled a note and left it at a dead drop he and Tara used regularly. Then he'd gotten on a plane, certain he would never see her again.

Now here she was, sitting across from him, more beautiful than ever.

Akil broke the silence. "I'm sorry," he said. How many times had he wished he could have told her that in person? But he had no way of contacting her. It would've been too risky even if he had.

She smiled, not-quite-tears forming at the edges of her eyes. She held out her hand and he took hold of it. Her skin, the color of sandalwood, was soft and cool. He didn't know what else to say, and for a while there seemed no need for words.

But too much had been left unsaid for them to stay in the moment. "Why did you leave without saying goodbye?" she asked.

"I tried."

She wasn't convinced. "I waited for you. For months, asking myself why you had abandoned me."

Akil leaned forward. "I never meant for it to end like that," he said. "I wanted—"

Tara held up her hand, stopping him. "I was in love with you. You knew that, of course. You took advantage of it."

The sadness in her voice pained him.

"They forced me out," he said.

"Who?"

"The Company."

He remembered what Bill had told him when he returned from Beirut. *She was an asset, kid. Remember that.* But she had been much more than just an asset. That was the whole problem.

Tara pulled a square of faded yellow paper from her small black purse and placed it on the table. "I got your letter," she said.

He looked at the worn piece of paper, but made no attempt to pick it up. He knew what it said. "They questioned me. Held me for weeks," he explained to her. "Then they fired me."

Her eyes widened at the news. "Fired you?"

"Yes."

"But why?"

"Because of you and me. Us."

This was the missing piece of the puzzle for her. He could see that now. He watched her as she pieced the events together afresh, her perceptions shifting with the new information.

"I told myself you wouldn't have left without..."

She faltered a moment.

"Without a reason," she finished.

Akil let his other hand touch hers across the table.

"I questioned everything we had together after you left," she confided. "The stolen afternoons we spent together in bed. The promises we made each other." Tears began spilling down her cheeks. "I felt as if I'd been used."

"We used each other," he told her. He had intended the words to be conciliatory, but they came out sounding defensive. That was the guilt, he supposed. He'd manipulated her—sure—but he'd only been doing his job. He had tried to keep their relationship separate from the work, but it was nothing more than wishful thinking.

She gave him a brave smile. "I didn't mind at the time, but after..."

He brushed a tear from her cheek. What could he say? Time and circumstance had altered their relationship forever. They were no longer tied together as lovers—they were what they had always been: agent and handler. For over a year he'd used her to gather intelligence, putting her life at risk. She was quite a coup for him, working as part of Iran's embassy staff in Beirut. He'd recruited her over several months, convincing her to secret out documents so he could make copies, then getting her to return them without anyone noticing. In the process, he had fallen in love with her, or something approximating love. But he knew then, as he knew now, you couldn't have it both ways.

"Why are you here, Tara?" he asked, his voice hardening slightly as he slipped back into the role of handler.

She stared at him without answering his question. He could see she was shaking.

"It's okay," he told her, adopting a softer tone. "Just tell me what this is about."

"After you left," she said, "I moved back to Tehran. To start over. I quit the Foreign Ministry and found work teaching at one of the universities. Then a few days ago…"

Tears were streaming down her face.

"What happened a few days ago?" he prompted her.

"I was arrested."

"The police?"

"VEVAK."

The muscles in Akil's face tensed.

"They took me to a police station and held me overnight."

"Did they hurt you?" he asked, the old feelings rushing to the surface.

"They roughed me up a little. I think they wanted to scare me. In the morning I was interrogated by a VEVAK officer. He asked about my time in Lebanon. My associations."

"Did he ask about us?"

"Not at first. I thought maybe they were testing me. I kept asking myself why they were doing this. Why now?"

"You stuck to your cover story?"

"Yes. I told them nothing at first."

"And then?"

"The head of VEVAK, a man named Ahmad Hashemian, began interrogating me. Asking me questions about—"

"About what?"

Tara toyed with the silver bracelet on her wrist. "About you," she said.

"Me?"

"About the two of us."

Akil sat back and took a deep breath. He felt as if he'd been punched in the gut. "It was Ahmad Hashemian? You're sure?" he asked, trying to restrain his emotions.

"Yes. I'm sure."

Ahmad Hashemian was a legendary Iranian soldier turned spymaster. According to CIA files, he had risen quickly through the ranks to become a powerful force inside the country's political structure. He'd attended Qom's Haqqani School—a religious center—where he became a full-fledged cleric. It was the only way to attain the leadership of VEVAK. If he was meeting with Tara there was no doubt he knew exactly what she was guilty of and, so it appeared, with whom she had perpetrated the crime.

"What did you tell Hashemian?" Akil asked, not sure he wanted to hear the answer.

"He had pictures of us together in Tripoli. Pictures of you as well... more recent. He knew your real name," she said.

Akil could hear the sadness in her voice—the sense of betrayal. He shut it out. "My real name?"

"Akil," she said. "Is that your real name?"

He turned his head toward the crowded bar, ignoring the question. The Iranians knew he was CIA. They had his name, his address, his picture. But how had they found out? His relationship with Tara was a matter of record with the Iranians, but its true nature had been kept secret all these years. Until now.

Had she betrayed him? he wondered. He banished the thought almost immediately. It wasn't important. Not right now. "So they know about you and me," he said, looking back at her, his voice gathering momentum. "But that doesn't explain why you're here."

"Hashemian asked me to deliver a message."

"To me?"

She nodded. Dark veils of eyeliner had formed beneath her eyes from the tears. He couldn't help feeling bad for her—she'd been reeled in and used once again, this time by the Iranians. But he didn't have time to worry about her feelings, he needed to know what message Hashemian wanted her to deliver and why.

"You said in your note that lives were at stake."

"Lives *are* at stake," she said.

"Whose lives?"

"American lives. Iranian lives too."

He looked around to see if anyone had moved close enough to listen in on their conversation. The action was nothing more than reflex—the music, as loud as it was, provided ample cover.

"What do you mean American lives?"

"I was instructed to tell you that VX nerve agent has been delivered to al-Qaeda linked fighters in Iraq," Tara said. "Hashemian says you'll know this already. Is that true?"

Akil had to decide right now how much he was willing to disclose. You never gave away information if you could avoid it. What would he gain and what would he lose by telling her the truth?

She continued on before he could answer. "Bashir Khalini. You recognize the name?"

There was urgency and fear in her voice. She waited for his answer this time.

"Yes," he said.

How the hell did Hashemian know that the Agency had Khalini?

"You moved him out of Iraq almost a week ago," she told him. "He was interrogated in Egypt, outside Cairo. You were there."

"Jesus!" Akil exclaimed. "He knows?"

Tara nodded again.

"How?" he asked.

"I don't know how, but they had pictures of you and two others at an airport."

Akil tried to wrap his head around the new information. They had identified him as CIA by linking him to Khalini, and from there, had discovered Tara's guilt by association.

"Hashemian wants you to know that this action was not sanctioned by him or any member of the Iranian government," Tara said. "A rogue faction inside the Revolutionary Guard is responsible. They're the ones who recruited Khalini to hand over the VX to the al-Qaeda linked fighters in Iraq. They thought it could never be traced back to them."

Akil looked at her and wondered where the truth ended and the lies began. He doubted even she knew the answer. Iran had been aiding terrorists for decades, and if Hashemian knew the Americans had captured Khalini, he could be trying to cover his tracks by blaming the entire incident on some fictitious group of Revolutionary Guard. The plan to get the VX to the terrorists had been well thought out. If Travers hadn't found Khalini alive in that Baghdad basement they never would have traced the VX back to Iran. After all, the VX had once belonged to Saddam. How it had resurfaced would have remained a mystery forever.

"Where's the VX headed?" Akil asked.

"The east coast."

"Where exactly?"

"I don't know."

"Does Hashemian know?"

"I think so. But the VX may already be inside the U.S."

Akil had already accepted this possibility and yet the words, spoken anew, gave him a sick feeling in the pit of his stomach.

"Hashemian wants to meet with you," she said. "He knows you will have broken Khalini by now. That means you know the Pasdaran were involved. You probably think the highest levels of the Iranian government are involved too."

"What else am I supposed to think?"

"It's madness."

Akil had no way of knowing the truth. Even Tara, he had to admit, was not beyond reproach. How long had she worked for Hashemian? Maybe she had gone to VEVAK after he'd left Beirut and she was lying to him now. Either way, Hashemian was in quite a predicament. The Iranian government couldn't call up the President of the United States and apologize for passing WMD's to al-Qaeda or Hezbollah, even if it were the result of a rogue group of Revolutionary Guards. Nothing like that could be allowed to enter the official record. And besides, Hashemian still had a couple of outs. The VX might be intercepted or the terrorists could be captured before anyone got hurt. Hashemian could only pray that one of these scenarios gave him the escape he so desperately needed. In the meantime, he had decided to use a back channel to warn the Americans. Off the record, of course. This way he could try and gain a level of trust with which he might avert a catastrophe for both countries. And if not, maybe it would mitigate the damage that would be done later on, when the United States sought its retribution. Akil's connection to Tara, it seemed, had proved an auspicious avenue from which to initiate that contact.

"Where does Hashemian want to meet?" Akil asked.

"He wants you to agree to some conditions first."

"Conditions?"

If Akil had any tangible lead on the whereabouts of the VX, he'd refuse to meet Hashemian on principle alone. But he didn't. And he was desperate too.

"You must come alone," Tara continued. "If he detects any surveillance he won't make contact."

"Fine. What else?"

"He has your picture. He expects to meet with you. No on else."

"Understood. And?"

"That's it."

Tara stood, ready to leave. She handed him a piece of paper. "These are the locations and times where contact may be initiated. Whether or not contact is made will be at Hashemian's discretion," she said.

He took the paper and put it in his pocket. "I'll walk you out."

"I don't think that's a good idea."

He smiled at her. She was still thinking the way he'd taught her back in Beirut. "Don't worry," he told her, "we're not in Lebanon anymore. Plus, your side already has my name, what I look like, everything. It can't get any worse."

96

AKIL AND TARA headed back downstairs, then forged their way through the crowd to the rear of the club. Tara had been told to exit the club by way of the alley. Akil found a flight of stairs that did just that.

The stairwell was dark and smelled of beer and day-old trash. They descended slowly. At the bottom it was so dark Akil had to feel for the latch on the door. Once he found it, he told Tara to wait inside as he stepped out into the alley alone.

Akil spotted Tara's minders right away. At one end of the alley was a Pakistani woman. Standing beside her was an Iranian man with broad shoulders, smoking a cigarette. At the other end was a lean athletic type talking on a cell phone. Akil could see that the conversation was just for show. He made eye contact with the man for an instant before turning and motioning for Tara to join him.

"Tell Hashemian I need to know who was responsible for the attacks against New York and where I can find the VX," he said quickly.

"I will."

"If we don't stop the VX from being used, it won't matter who did what or why," he reminded her. "Understand?"

She nodded, acknowledging his point.

Akil gave a curt nod in return. He felt exhausted by the flood of conflicting emotions their meeting had stirred inside him. Looking at her now, standing in the alley—inches apart—he knew this was goodbye. It was the one they'd lost out on in Beirut, and this time, it was forever.

97

FROM THE ROOF across the alleyway, Peters reduced the camera's zoom so that both Akil and the woman were in frame.

He hoped that what he was witnessing was more innocent than it appeared. But the minders at either end of the alley, no doubt the woman's protection, presented a smoking gun he couldn't ignore.

Then he watched as the woman leaned in and gave Akil Hassan a kiss.

98

AFTER ARRIVING HOME from the club, Akil had sat in his living room and thought about what Tara had told him. He went back and forth over their conversation a couple dozen times.

By morning Hashemian's story remained as problematic as it had the night before. The description of a rogue group of Pasdaran who had taken it upon themselves to pass VX to al-Qaeda linked mujahideen was plausible. Frighteningly so, in fact, considering the autonomy the Pasdaran had created for itself inside the Islamic Republic. And yet, just as plausible was the idea that Hashemian had been running a false flag operation. That the Iranian Intelligence chief knew about the plan to move the VX all along— had masterminded it—and only now, his hand caught in the cookie jar, had come looking for a way out. Ironically, they shared the same goal now— preventing the VX from being used on American soil. In Hashemian's case, those reasons were self-serving. But at the moment that didn't matter. What mattered was stopping the terrorists.

First thing Akil had to do was report his contact with Tara to Bill Graham, then fill him in on the latest developments. On his way into Langley, he had called Bill and left a brief message on his voicemail. He'd told him that he had critical information concerning the case, but avoided any mention of Tara or Hashemian. Truth was, he was still trying to figure out how to explain the situation. His relationship with Tara had gotten him fired from the Agency once, and he didn't want it to happen again. He had done nothing wrong this time. Tara had approached him, not the other way around. But sometimes the facts weren't always enough. His ace in the hole was Hashemian, the only person with information on the whereabouts of the VX. And when he delivered the information on the whereabouts of the VX to Bill Graham and Director Marchetti, he hoped it would be enough to erase the specter of past wrongs and give him a clean slate.

Parking his car, Akil walked to the front entrance of the old headquarters building. The brisk November air invigorated him, if only momentarily. With little or no sleep the past thirty-six hours, he still felt exhausted. He wasn't used to being operational like this.

At the security kiosk, he unclipped his ID badge and scanned it. An ominous bleating erupted from a hidden speaker. A security officer, sitting behind his desk, shot to his feet. Dressed in a black blazer and white collared shirt, he referenced his monitor with a quick glance and asked Akil to step over.

Akil complied.

What now? The ID badge was new but he'd used it several times already. "Something wrong?" he asked the security guard.

"Routine check, sir. Just be a minute."

He didn't like the sound of that.

Eventually, the officer came out from behind his desk. "I need you to put your hands on your head, sir."

Out of the corner of his eye, Akil could see three additional security officers approaching the front entrance. Two were coming from the nearby elevators and another was descending the stairs. They weren't running, but they weren't walking either.

"What's going on?"

"Hands on your head," the guard said forcefully.

It was early, but several staff were already transiting the lobby. They stopped and stared as Akil raised his hands and placed them on his head. There had to be a simple explanation. A clerical error. Something.

As the other security guards arrived they formed a loose cordon around him. What information had the monitor given them? Did they think he was dangerous? He could be, if necessary. Not here though. Not now.

The officer who had taken his ID badge stepped forward and grabbed his left wrist, pulling his arm down behind his back. Akil felt the cold steel of the handcuffs strike his wrist, the half-moon of metal looping around and locking itself tight.

Is this is really happening? The officer had just finished cuffing his other hand when he heard a deep timbered voice coming from behind him.

"Take those off."

Bill? Thank god.

Akil turned to see his boss advancing on the small congregation. He was dressed in a blue Armani suit with a pin-striped dress shirt underneath and looked more like a banker than an operations director.

"Mr. Graham," announced one of the security officers, his voice acknowledging Bill's rank. "We have orders to—"

"That won't be necessary," Bill interrupted, "I'll make sure he gets where he's going."

The guard removed the handcuffs as Bill watched. Once free, Akil asked for his ID badge. The guard looked at Bill who gave his consent with a small nod of the head, then praised the guards for their due diligence.

Walking away, Bill kept one hand wrapped tightly around Akil's arm.

99

ON THE SECOND floor, Bill stopped in front of an empty conference room and opened the door. Akil entered first and Bill followed, locking the door behind them.

"What the hell is going on?" Akil asked.

"You tell me."

"They were going to place me under arrest for Christ's sake."

Bill's jaw was clamped shut. His back molars were grinding hard against one another. He walked over to the window and looked out at the mass of trees in the distance. "I don't know what you did, kid, but it's over."

"What the hell are you talking about?"

Bill turned and stared him straight in the eye: "The Office of Security has two men upstairs in Marchetti's office right now, waiting for you. The FBI and an Agency lawyer are in transit."

Akil suddenly felt nauseous. It all sounded so familiar. When he'd been ordered back from Lebanon two years ago he had walked into a room not dissimilar to the one Bill had just described. He had been questioned for days, then terminated shortly afterward.

"This is crazy," he said. "I've done nothing wrong!"

"Then you have nothing to worry about," Bill said.

But he *had* done something. Something extraordinary.

Then it clicked. He'd been right to run the SDR before meeting Tara, but it wasn't her Iranian friends he should have been looking for. It was Marchetti's people. The Director had placed him under surveillance and he'd somehow failed to spot the spotters. When had they started the surveillance? he wondered. Not that it mattered now.

By a fluke of circumstance, they'd caught him meeting with Tara Markosi. They probably had pictures. He had to assume so. And the pictures, taken out of context, were damning. But he had a surprise of his own. No one knew about Hashemian.

"This whole thing is an unfortunate misunderstanding. That's all. I tried contacting you this morning but got your voicemail." He took a deep breath. "I found someone who may know the whereabouts of the VX."

He watched Bill's eyes steel themselves. "Who?"

"Ahmad Hashemian," Akil said.

Bill scoffed at the mention of the name. "The head of Iran's Intelligence Ministry?"

"That's right."

"You think anyone is going to believe that?"

"Do you?"

Bill didn't respond right away.

"I've never lied to you about an operation, Bill. I'm not lying now."

"But Hashemian? It doesn't make any sense." Bill moved away from the window, back toward the middle of the room. "How did you get in contact with him?"

"I'll explain everything to you and Marchetti upstairs," Akil said. "Just give me five minutes to grab something from my office."

He was stalling for time. He needed to think how best to tell his side of the story now that Marchetti had sandbagged by.

Almost half a minute passed as Bill considered the request.

The fluorescent lighting hummed overhead.

"Hashemian?" Bill asked again. He sounded even more incredulous than before. "Jesus."

"I swear to god," Akil said.

"Why has Marchetti called the Office of Security in on this?"

"I was meeting with one of Hashemian's people. Marchetti must have put me under surveillance," Akil said, wondering how Bill would react when he discovered that he'd met with Tara.

Bill made a slow pivot back toward the window, absorbing the new information. "That would certainly explain it," he said. "Alright, you've got five minutes. No more. I'll try and settle the hounds before you get upstairs, but you better make sure you have your story straight, *whatever* it is. Marchetti smells blood. If he didn't, he wouldn't have set things in motion like this."

"Don't worry."

"Fat chance."

As Akil opened the door to leave, Bill called after him.

Akil turned, but Bill hesitated. "Forget it," he said.

Akil knew what Bill was thinking. "I'm clean," he said. "I haven't broken any rules."

Bill nodded. "Five minutes."

"I'll see you upstairs."

100

AKIL TOOK THE elevator to the basement where he had been assigned a temporary office his first day back. There wasn't much in the small room, mostly empty filing cabinets and a carload of books and assorted ephemera he'd dropped off in hopes of brightening up the room. Most of it was still packed away in boxes. He didn't actually need anything from his office. What he needed was a quiet place to gather his thoughts before he faced his accusers.

As the elevator doors opened, Akil could hear the sound of empty filing-drawers being opened and shut haphazardly, one after the other. The concrete corridor, off which his office was located, acted as an echo chamber, the noise reverberating loudly down its considerable length.

Akil immediately sensed something was wrong. Approaching his office with caution, he saw from a distance that the door was wide open. Staying close to the wall, he listened to the commotion coming from inside.

A clear rectangle of glass running alongside the door allowed him to peer in without being seen. Two men were going through his stuff. One of them concentrated on the boxes of books, taking one, flipping through its pages, then throwing it to the floor. The other man was rifling through his desk. They were wasting their time, but he wasn't going to stick his head in and tell them that.

Turning, he headed back the way he'd come. He had to assume his home was being searched as well. It looked like Marchetti was determined to prove his guilt. If it weren't for Bill, he would still be in handcuffs waiting to hear the charges mounted against him. Now, with Marchetti's men ransacking his office, he questioned whether or not he should even go meet with the Office of Security. The truth was, he had no evidence that could prove his side of the story, and if previous experiences were anything to go by, Marchetti would incarcerate him first and sort through the facts later.

Taking a deep breath, he wondered if he was overreacting. He didn't think so. He'd been through this once before. But what could he do? The options open to him were limited. He could stay and attempt to explain everything—take his chances—or he could run and make sure he met with Hashemian as planned. If he stayed and argued his case, they might believe him. They might not. Either way, it would mean taking the polygraph, then sweating it out in a small room until they were satisfied he'd done nothing wrong. That could take days and time was short. Lives were at stake.

But leaving? Leaving meant admitting guilt and he'd done nothing wrong. He would be placing himself out in the cold. There would be no going home. No explaining the situation to his father and Michael. He'd be a fugitive on the run with Marchetti and the CIA hunting him down. And his career? It would be over for good this time.

101

SOPHIE ARRIVED AT the FBI's Philadelphia field office first thing in the morning and spoke to the agent in charge.

"Where are they?" she asked.

"One's in holding. The other is being questioned," the agent told her.

Two men, possibly connected to the attacks on New York City, had been taken into custody the previous evening. Sophie had driven down to follow up on the lead in person.

"Who picked them up?" she asked.

"Local PD. The two men got into an argument with an Egyptian shop-keeper who accused them of stealing. A beat cop was passing by during the altercation and intervened."

"And he made the arrests?"

"He felt the men were acting suspicious so he booked them for shoplift-ing and disturbing the peace. Once they got to the station I was contacted. Considering the current state of affairs, I had them transferred over."

"Do they speak English?"

"Very little."

"They have any ID on them?"

"Yeah. Each one had a passport. High-end forgeries. That's when I knew these weren't your run-of-the-mill tourists or illegal aliens. You don't see that kind of quality very often. One of them had a New York subway ticket in his pocket as well. It was stamped for Thanksgiving Day."

"Sloppy. You run their prints and facials through the system?"

"Yep."

"And?"

"We got a hit on one of them through our CT database. Name's Asad Saleh, a known bomb maker working for Hamas. The other one? We don't know. Store clerk said he heard the name Issam, but that's not the name on his passport. Neither of them is very forthcoming at the moment."

"Alright. Mind if I sit in while you question them?"

"Be my guest. We've been at it all night, but we're not getting much. The younger one is our best shot. We're focusing our efforts on him at the moment. The older one, Asad, he's been at this a long time according to his file. A career terrorist. It's doubtful he's going to break."

Sophie followed the agent in charge down a long hallway and into a small room painted institutional green. They were questioning Issam next door, he explained. She could watch from here.

A small television sat atop an empty desk. The questions being asked were straightforward and non-confrontational. Name? Purpose for being in Philadelphia? Date of arrival in the U.S.? But Issam was evading even these basic questions, meeting them with repeated denials of any wrongdoing. Answering questions with questions.

"It's been like this all night," the agent explained.

The audio recovered from the digital voice recorder Curtis Stone had provided the FBI had mentioned Philadelphia. At the time there was no way to know its context, or whether or not the reference was meaningful. Now, with Issam and Asad showing up in the city, both with expertly forged passports, the significance of the recovered audio no longer appeared to be in question. These two men, more likely than not, were directly involved in the attacks on New York. They could possess information on the where-abouts of the ringleader too, a man calling himself Ali. It was the break they'd been looking for, but first, they needed one of them to start talking.

"Cup of coffee?" asked the agent in charge.

"Please," Sophie replied.

A minute later the agent returned and handed Sophie a paper cup. As she sipped the overcooked coffee, the questioning grew more antagonistic. The full weight of what was happening was being brought to bear on Issam. Not for the first time, either. They asked if he ever wanted to see his own country again? They told him that if he didn't start talking they would toss him in a cell and throw away the key, that he'd be lucky if he ever saw sun-light again.

"Just tell us what you know and we can work something out," the inter-rogator said. But it was no use, Issam wasn't budging.

Sophie wondered how long it would take before he finally broke down and gave them the information they needed? A few more hours? A few more days? Ever? Watching Issam shake his head in response to another question, she couldn't help thinking of Akil and what he'd told her on their way to Cairo: *I wish the rules didn't have to be broken, but sometimes there's no other way.* Now, more than ever, she wondered if he was right.

She thought back to that morning on the tarmac, returning from Cairo, finding herself awash in a sea of conflicting emotions. What had she gotten herself mixed up in? she'd asked herself then. Secret prisons. Torture. And yet, she'd found herself empathizing with Akil, this man who had, in front of her own eyes, used violence to pry information from a prisoner. What he'd done went against everything she believed in. So why hadn't she made it clear right then that she wanted nothing more to do with him?

The easy answer was that Akil might obtain vital information that could help her—help the FBI—solve the case. She wanted access to it. It was the same reason he had fought for her to go to Cairo. He didn't want to lose his access to NCTC. But if she was honest with herself, there was far more to it than that—for both of them.

Flipping open her cell phone, Sophie scrolled down to Akil's number and hit the call button. She wanted to fill him in on this latest development and see if he had any new information to share. They were getting closer to catching their quarry and neither of them could afford to let up now.

The call went straight to voicemail.

She flipped the phone shut without leaving a message. She'd try again later, she decided. Hopefully, by then, she would have something concrete to tell him.

102

THE SITUATION WITH Akil was an unwelcome distraction and Bill wanted to clear it up as quickly as possible. Entering Marchetti's office though, he knew it wasn't going to be easy. The air held a negative charge, like a major storm was about to make landfall and everyone had battened down the hatches, expecting the worst.

Marchetti sat behind his oak desk.

Off to the side was his assembled cast. Peters from the Office of Security sat with one of his subordinates. Both wore ill-fitting suits and had on skinny ties. A stenographer, her hair in a ponytail, was seated in the corner. Once Akil arrived she would record the proceedings. For now, she sat with her hands in her lap. To the right was an agent of the FBI. If a CIA officer was accused of a crime, the FBI were the ones who investigated. Obviously, Marchetti felt he had evidence that required the man's presence. And in the middle of the room, sitting alone with an attaché case at his heels was an Agency lawyer. He wasn't here to defend the accused—should Akil Hassan need counsel—but to represent The Company itself, in case any potential liabilities arose during questioning.

Bill ignored them and addressed Anthony Marchetti directly. "What's this about, Tony?"

Marchetti handed Bill a file folder. "See for yourself."

Bill opened the folder and began flipping through a series of photographs. At first, there was only Akil standing in an alley by himself, his hand outstretched behind him. It was clearly night-time and yet the images were remarkably sharp. Then he saw her. Tara Markosi. She was standing next to Akil. A couple pictures later she was giving him a kiss. Bill stared at the photos, unable or unwilling to believe what he was seeing. *I was meeting with one of Hashemian's people*, Akil had told him.

No wonder Marchetti was on the hunt.

Bill flipped ahead. There had to be thirty or forty photos in all. The last photo showed Tara walking away, the photographer having captured her in profile as she looked back at her one-time handler.

"You placed him under surveillance?" Bill asked Marchetti.

"He's dirty."

"Without telling me?"

"Yes," Marchetti said. "Without telling you."

Bill tossed the photos onto the Director's desk. "There's no way Akil is working for the Iranians. If that's the issue, you're way off base."

"We'll see, won't we?"

"I'm telling you that you're wrong."

"You should be careful where you place your loyalty, Bill," Marchetti warned him. "Look at the evidence. Put yourself in my shoes."

Bill didn't respond.

"Mr. Graham. A question."

Bill turned to the man who had addressed him.

"I'm Special agent Willis. FBI. Did you know about this meeting between Mr. Hassan and..." Willis stopped and flipped open a small notepad, referencing one of its pages. "Ms. Markosi?"

"No. Why?"

"Can you explain what Akil Hassan may have been doing, meeting with an agent of the Iranian Government?"

"She's not an agent of the Iranian Government," Bill protested.

Agent Willis pushed himself off the wall and assumed a more formal posture. "That's not the information we've been given, sir."

Bill turned back toward Marchetti. "She fed us vital intelligence for almost a year. What makes you so sure she's working for the Iranian Government?" he asked.

"She had an escort with her when she met your boy," Marchetti said. "Six, maybe seven people in total. All ISI. And she arrived at JFK two days ago on an Iranian diplomatic passport. It's not supposition. Those are facts."

Bill was stunned. This must have something to do with Hashemian and the whereabouts of the VX, he thought.

"I understand that Mr. Hassan and this Markosi woman have a history together," said Willis.

Bill ignored him. "This isn't what it seems, Tony. The kid can explain."

"He can try," Marchetti said, "but the evidence speaks for itself."

"It's circumstantial at best and you know it."

"It's enough to hold him indefinitely. Eventually, we'll know the truth. Until then we assume the worst and we protect ourselves as best we can."

Bill stifled his anger. "Akil has a source," he said, changing tack. "That's what this is about. This source may know where we can find the VX. This business with Tara Markosi is obviously connected in some way."

"How do you know about this source?" Marchetti demanded.

"I spoke with Akil downstairs. If what he says is true, and we have no reason to discount it, we may just be able to stop the next attack."

"What do you mean you spoke with him downstairs?" Marchetti's face was turning red. "I ordered security to place him under arrest as soon as he entered the building."

"I interceded."

"You what!"

Marchetti leaned across his desk and picked up his phone. He ordered his secretary to get the head of building security on the line.

"If he has information that could stop a WMD from being used on American soil, goddammit, we need to listen to him," Bill said. "Not treat him like a criminal."

But Marchetti was no longer paying attention. He was ordering a complete lockdown of headquarters, instructing security personnel to manually inspect all ID's for anyone trying to leave the building. Under no circumstances was Akil Hassan to be allowed off the premises.

As soon as Marchetti hung up the phone he stood, rage causing his pupils to contract. "You just made a huge mistake."

Bill didn't flinch. "I trained him. I know what he's capable of. Treason is out of the question."

Ten minutes passed as they waited for word on Akil's whereabouts. Then the phone on Marchetti's desk rang. The Director picked up the receiver.

"Marchetti," he barked.

Everyone in the room watched as the conversation played out in pantomime. Marchetti's eyes opened wide at first, then narrowed, his shoulders sagging as he grunted one last time into the receiver.

"They located a janitor in the south tunnel leading from the basement to the auditorium," Marchetti told them. "He's unconscious and his ID is missing, along with his uniform and keys. They found Akil's ID tag and his cell phone in a trash can nearby."

Bill ran a hand through his hair as he tried to absorb the news. *What the hell are you doing, kid?*

Marchetti directed his next comments at the two men from the Office of Security. "I want his home under constant surveillance. Seize his bank accounts. Isolate him. Do whatever it takes, but I want the son-of-a-bitch found and I want him locked up."

Bill was already headed for the door by the time Marchetti had finished giving his marching orders.

"Where are you going?" demanded Marchetti.

"Back to my office," Bill said, not bothering to turn around. "We still have a terrorist to catch."

103

SAYYID TRAVELED WEST, keeping to the slow lane along Interstate 80. He didn't want to give the police any excuse to pull him over. It was one of the reasons he had parted company with Asad and Issam in Philadelphia. Three Arab men traveling together would only attract unwanted attention.

He had given them money and thanked them for their efforts, but hadn't told them where he was going or what he was planning to do with the VX. They would find out soon enough.

Outside Pittsburgh, he switched vehicles, then again in Akron, Ohio on his way to Chicago. From the very beginning, he had planned on carrying out the final phase of his operation alone, relying on the help of only one vital contact.

When he reached Chicago, he navigated a dizzying number of viaducts, intersecting expressways and bridges on his way downtown. The reward was a neck-bending sea of high-rise architecture that rivaled New York City in both scope and beauty.

He had visited the "windy city" once during his university days. At the time he hadn't realized that Chicago was the third largest city in the United States or that the greater metropolitan area had a population of nearly 10 million people. At the time he'd not coveted such facts. It was different now.

Driving through downtown, he watched as thousands of office workers poured out onto the street, moving in waves along the sidewalks. It was the end of the day and they were headed home. In the morning they'd return, filling the downtown once again—the perfect spot to strike his next blow.

After scouting the downtown core, Sayyid drove to the city's West Side and ditched the stolen vehicle. He parked it in a rough neighborhood, left the keys in the ignition and the doors unlocked. Within hours the car would be gone, and with it, any link to him and the VX.

Next, he found a flower shop and bought a bouquet of yellow and white daisies before hailing a cab.

He exited the cab several blocks from his contact's home, then proceeded on foot. Dressed in slacks and a well-tailored sports coat—carrying the bouquet of flowers—he looked like the quintessential urban professional on his way home from work. This could have been my life, he thought. When he was a teenager his uncle had asked if he wanted to study abroad. He had jumped at the opportunity, eager to flee the hopelessness and suffering that surrounded him. Thanks to his uncle he'd gone to study at the London School of Economics where his life had taken on a dreamlike quality. After graduation, not ready to return home just yet, he chose to continue on and do his Masters in America. Like so many who had gone before him, he was determined to reinvent himself there.

During his time at Berkeley, Sayyid had dreamed of building a life for himself in America. Back then he'd pictured himself getting married and settling down with a high six-figure income, maybe working for a bank or investment firm in the city. He had seen himself living in a neighborhood not unlike this one, close to downtown, his two-story home outfitted with new carpet, new fixtures, a well-appointed bathroom...gas fireplace.

After graduation, however, he'd gone back home to the occupied territories to visit his uncle.

That decision had changed his life. Going back to the West Bank and Gaza brought him face to face with the suffering of the Palestinian people in a way he had not experienced since his childhood. He had been gone so long that the memory of those years—the lack of food, the indignities of daily life—had faded away. Or, more accurately, been repressed. Coming home, the memories—and the emotions tied to them—seized ahold of him with a power and intensity he could not easily explain.

Or resist.

At first, it was the profound disparity in living conditions that troubled him most. How long had he been abroad that he'd forgotten what it was like? Then there were the checkpoints, the endless waiting to move across arbitrary boundaries set by the Jews. Israeli soldiers were everywhere, with their guns and their disdain. The sense of despair among his people had grown more pervasive as well. His time abroad, studying and partying at school, suddenly felt shameful.

More and more the memories of his childhood came flooding back to haunt his dreams. His father began to occupy his thoughts daily, and without intending it, his homecoming became a clarion call to action.

A couple of months after returning, Sayyid decided he would use his education to help the Palestinian people. His people.

A cousin introduced him to some friends and he soon found himself working for Hamas' political wing. They were impressed with his education and put him to work managing some of their business affairs. He invested the money that was sent from overseas—from America—growing it slowly through a series of offshore investments. Then he went a step further and overhauled the way aid was distributed to the people, streamlining the process. Lavish expenditures were curtailed under his watch. The books were balanced. A budget was put in place.

Eventually, he branched out beyond his humanitarian work to help negotiate arms purchases for the mujahideen, and with their blessing, set up an accounting system and inventory controls. He was doing what he could to help fight the oppression that had robbed his father, not only of his land, but of his dignity too.

But it wasn't enough. He wanted to contribute in a more demonstrable way. Having earned the trust of those in charge, he asked to take an active role in the military side of operations and was not refused. It soon became evident that he was a natural tactician with a genuine aptitude for asymmetrical warfare. For many, it came as a surprise. His apprenticeship, an appeasement at first, was eventually broadened and accelerated. In the months that followed, he helped plan and orchestrate several highly successful suicide attacks.

His subsequent raids on Israeli checkpoints—brazen and cleverly executed—garnered him a burgeoning reputation within the organization and it wasn't long before he found himself being groomed for a leadership role. Sayyid embraced the idea and began advocating for Hamas to transform itself. He urged them to expand the scope of its attacks, even going so far as to suggest an alliance with al-Qaeda. Consolidate resources, he told them. Find a political consensus to work from. The next step in the evolution of the Palestinian struggle for freedom, he insisted, was to strike outside the Middle East, against those nations who supported Israel's oppression.

But Hamas wanted nothing to do with such revolutionary ideas. It was too risky. Too reckless, they told him. They wanted to foster their political power in Gaza. Take control of the West Bank. They wanted to fight Fatah and Israel, not America and Europe.

Sayyid was dismayed by their reaction. The Palestinian people needed someone to champion their cause on a global scale, not just inside their shrinking borders. Their Muslim brothers in Egypt and Jordan had already forsaken them, and the Gulf States preferred to spend their petrodollars on gilded palaces and state-of-the-art hotels, not freedom for the Palestinian people. The fact was, the Palestinians were alone and no match for Israel and their patron saint, the United States of America—not without bold action. Without that, nothing would ever change.

In the end, his ambition was too much for Hamas. But Sayyid wouldn't give up. Through his financial and logistical work he'd made valuable contacts throughout the Middle East: in Saudi Arabia, Syria, Iran. He turned to these contacts for support, irrespective of their political ideology or sect, hoping to secure the financial and logistical backing needed to carry out his plan.

It had been a struggle. Each individual he engaged was a maverick in his own right. Powerful and independent. But ambitious too. To unite all of them, he had to first convince each of them that they shared a common goal. A common enemy. And that he, Sayyid, would further their cause—that he would do it by attacking the United States on its own soil, and do it on an unprecedented scale.

In time, they had acquiesced to his logic and his ambition, setting the various gears in motion that had led him to this moment.

He was finally ready to reap the fruit of his labor.

104

AKIL'S DECISION TO run had not been easy, but he felt he needed to make sure his meeting with Hashemian went ahead, no matter the cost.

You must come alone. He will expect to see you. No one else. If he was locked up at some CIA safe house, answering questions, what then? How many people would die if they didn't get to the VX in time?

After his meeting with Hashemian, he would deliver the information on the whereabouts of the VX to Bill Graham and plead his case—ask for his forgiveness. Until then, he'd have to live with the consequences of his decision. He just hoped he'd made the right choice. Only time would tell.

Right now he was a fugitive, alone and on the run. Everything and everyone connected to him was dangerous. Watch teams would be looking for him everywhere. DC and the surrounding area had suddenly become hostile territory.

The first thing he had to do was find a bank. Using his ATM card, he withdrew his daily maximum of $500. It wasn't much money, but it would have to do. If he wanted more he'd have to go inside and deal with a teller. That was too risky. The banks may have already been alerted. Despite the looming terrorist threat, he was sure Marchetti would find the resources he needed to track him down. The good news, if you could call it that, was that the manhunt would not go public—no pictures in the paper or news coverage on television. It meant he could still move freely around the city as long as he avoided CCTV cameras and other potential pitfalls of a wired world.

Ditching his car in a parking garage, Akil spent most of the day lying low at a run-down diner outside the city limits. With a bottomless cup of coffee in front of him, he tried to formulate his next move. Hashemian was the key, not only to stopping the VX, but to his future—to getting his job back and staying out of jail. He had risked everything on the assumption that Tara Markosi and Ahmed Hashemian had actionable intelligence. If the Iranian was playing some sort of game, then he was already its first victim. No doubt there would be countless more in the days to come. No point dwelling on what could go wrong, he told himself, especially since there was nothing he could do about it now. Stay positive. Stay focused. Tomorrow, he would meet with Hashemian and know one way or the other. Before that, he just needed to take care of one more thing.

105

THE NAME OF Sayyid's contact in Chicago was Qasim Awad. His house was on a quiet residential street. Sayyid walked up to the front door and knocked, then waited patiently for someone to answer. Behind the frosted glass that flanked either side of the door, he could see a shadow moving slowly down the hallway. Whoever it was fumbled with the lock. Eventually, the deadbolt released and the door swung open. A young girl—no more than five years old—poked her head out. She stared at him, her hand still gripping the doorknob.

Sayyid had not expected to see children. He looked down at the girl and smiled. "Hello," he said in English.

At the sound of his voice, the little girl turned and ran down the hallway.

Sayyid could hear her yelling for her father in Arabic. Instead of standing on the stoop, he stepped into the house and closed the door.

Qasim hurried into the hall. *"Ahlan wa sahlan,"* he said.

"Ahlan bekum," Sayyid replied. He handed the flowers to Qasim. "For your wife."

"Shukran. Come."

Qasim gave the flowers to his daughter who had cautiously reappeared. He told her to take them to her mother. With the daughter gone, Qasim led Sayyid down the hall and out into the enclosed garage. Sayyid had never worked with Qasim before or met him in person. He knew only what others in the West Bank and Gaza had told him. They had praised Qasim, telling Sayyid that the Palestinian's loyalty was beyond reproach. With no other choice, he'd taken these men at their word, then done some digging of his own just to be sure.

Qasim had been born and raised in Gaza, moving to the United States at the age of twenty-six to help raise money for various Palestinian aid organizations. The money from these organizations and other charities Qasim had set up were laundered and sent back to Hamas and The Popular Front, among others. It had been a lucrative industry while it lasted. Nowadays the charities were under strict scrutiny by the FBI, the money tracked at every turn. A resourceful man, Qasim had worked hard to develop new revenue streams, not all of them legal, and money had once again begun flowing into Palestine, thanks in large part to his efforts.

Satisfied with what he had been able to find out, Sayyid contacted Qasim through a series of intermediaries. He asked him if he would help plan an attack on American soil, the specifics of which would be withheld until a later date. Qasim had agreed to do whatever he could.

Once inside the garage, Qasim's polite manner abruptly changed. His body language became unsettled as he confronted Sayyid in an angry whisper: "What happened in New York? Why wasn't I told about these attacks?"

"Very few people knew that was going to happen," Sayyid replied calmly. "I'm sorry you were unprepared."

"I should have been told," Qasim said. "Someone should have warned me."

"Security had to come first, my brother. Of all people you can understand that."

The anger Qasim had cultivated the past few days seemed to waver. "It was not wise to do what you did, Sayyid."

"But it was necessary."

"The authorities. They'll be watching now. Our chances of being caught have doubled."

"The authorities are concentrated on New York. They have no idea I'm here. Relax, my friend, everything is going according to plan."

"And this foolish interview in the paper?" Qasim asked, his frustrations rekindled. "Why?"

"The American people need to know this is not violence for the sake of violence. It's the reason I'm here. To send a message."

Qasim paced back and forth. "Bashir Khalini has gone missing," he exclaimed all-of-a-sudden. "Did you know that?"

"How do you know about Khalini?" Sayyid asked.

"I have my sources."

"What sources?"

"I have many powerful friends in Syria and Lebanon," Qasim said. "Same as you."

It was hardly a detailed accounting, Sayyid thought, but let it go. "And what have they told you about this man, Khalini?"

"They say the Pasdaran and VEVAK operatives in Beirut have been asking after him. They are desperate to know where he is."

"So?"

"He's involved in your plan, isn't he? How am I supposed to relax knowing this? Everything could be compromised."

Sayyid understood why Qasim was so nervous. He had never been involved in an operation quite like this. Funneling money from bogus charities to off-shore bank accounts had its risks, but Qasim had been doing it for a long time and he knew how to cover his tracks. What he was involved in now was something far more serious.

"The Iranian knows nothing," Sayyid said. "The operational details were not shared with the Pasdaran or anyone else. Not even your powerful friends, Qasim." He let his eyes wander about the garage before settling back on his new partner. "Everything has been compartmentalized for security reasons. For just this kind of situation. We proceed as planned."

Qasim nodded, but did not look satisfied.

"Have you made all the preparations I requested?" Sayyid asked.

"Yes. The truck has been arranged. In less than twenty-four hours the last of the materials will be here. Everything will be ready for assembly."

In the corner of the garage, a large orange tarp was draped over a wooden pallet. Qasim walked over and untied the ropes that held the tarp in place. "Come and take a look," he said. "I think you'll be quite pleased."

Sayyid watched as the tarp was peeled back. Underneath was the machine he had requested, along with an air compressor. They looked shiny and new and smelled of oil.

"Good work."

"It meets all the specifications you gave me. And I've taken care of the extra materials we discussed," Qasim said proudly.

Sayyid was impressed. "And there is no way the authorities know you have this?"

"It belongs to one of our dummy corporations. If the feds are tracking it, which I doubt they are, it would take them several days to nail down the shipment, then determine that it was sent to an address for a company that no longer exists."

Sayyid let a smile spread across his face.

"Now. Please. What are we are using this for?" Qasim asked.

Sayyid took the shoulder bag he had been carrying and removed an aluminum canister from inside. He handed it to Qasim.

"What is it?"

"VX. Weapons-grade."

Qasim whistled, holding the container at arm's length.

106

AKIL FOUND THE address he was looking for at an internet cafe in Falls Church, Virginia. He memorized it, then called a cab. When the cab arrived, he gave the driver the address and sank down into the back seat as they drove off.

It was dark out and he tried closing his eyes, hoping to doze off for a bit. It was no use; he was too strung-out to sleep. He'd been second-guessing himself all day. Had he made the right decision to rejoin the Agency? More importantly, had he been right to flee Langley and go on the run? Doubting yourself, he knew from experience, was a telltale symptom of fatigue. Still, he couldn't shake the uncertainty.

Twenty minutes later the cab turned onto a quiet suburban street lined with elm trees. Akil sat up and looked out the window, refocusing his attention. The homes on either side had been built in the late sixties and still had large front yards. He checked the house numbers, concentrating on the even-numbered houses to his right. He noticed that a paved lane ran in behind them. He told the cabbie to carry on to the end of the block and stop at the entrance to the lane.

The cabbie drove past the address Akil had given him without slowing down. Akil could see that there were lights on inside the house. The street itself looked clean. Sophie's house, it appeared, had not been placed under surveillance. Then again, why should it be? They barely knew each other. Still, he wanted to be sure because he needed her help and that meant he needed to talk with her face to face. The one thing he'd figured out sitting in the run-down diner was that he couldn't chase down the VX alone.

He just hoped he wasn't making a mistake by putting his trust in her.

107

SOPHIE MARTIN SAT on her couch eating cookie dough ice cream from a tub of Ben and Jerry's. Normally she would have felt guilty about the calories she was consuming, but ever since the attacks on Thanksgiving morning, she'd been working eighteen hour days. Finally getting a night off, she had decided to indulge herself.

That afternoon she'd flown back to DC, finding no good reason to stay in Philadelphia. So far, Issam had told them nothing they could act on. Either had Asad. Hours of intense questioning had only confirmed what they already suspected, that both men had participated in the attacks on New York City. Beyond that, they'd learned nothing new. Both men claimed they didn't know where the next attack was going to take place or who was going to carry it out. Were they lying? In all probability they were. But if so they understood how critical time was and that was all the motivation they needed to hold out. All her colleagues could do was keep pressing the two men for answers. She told them to call if they learned anything new, but honestly, she held out little hope there would be a break in the case.

Digging to the bottom of the container, Sophie loaded up another spoonful of ice cream and held it out for Teddy. Teddy was her six-year-old Springer Spaniel and the only male in her life these days. Her job at NCTC had made sure of that.

Seeing the spoonful of ice cream, Teddy scrambled to his feet, his paws fighting for traction on the hardwood floor. Once up he didn't waste any time licking the spoon clean, along with a good portion of Sophie's hand. Then he sat down on his haunches and waited for more.

He stared at Sophie, his tongue hanging from his mouth in eager anticipation.

Sophie looked into his sad, puppy-dog eyes. "One more spoon, that's it," she told him, unable to resist his obvious charms. Teddy barked in gratitude as Sophie loaded up another spoonful of ice cream and fed it to him.

"That's it. None left," she said, showing him the empty container.

Teddy barked again, but sensing there was no more ice cream in his immediate future, he laid down and started licking his paws.

Sophie reached over and picked up her cell phone, checking for any new messages, knowing she had none. She was still mulling over the call she'd received from the CIA's Office of Security earlier that evening. The man she spoke to—Peters—had wanted to know if she'd heard from Akil Hassan. It had been almost two days since she'd spoken to Akil, she told him, asking what this was about. The reply she got was purposely vague. Peters told her that Akil was wanted for questioning.

"Questioning for what?" she asked.

He said he couldn't divulge that information, just asked that she call him direct if she heard from Akil. To do otherwise, he explained, would be to obstruct an ongoing CIA investigation.

She couldn't believe what she was hearing: that Akil was a wanted man. Though it appeared the CIA were the only ones looking for him at the moment.

What had he done? she wondered.

She agreed to call, of course, taking down the number Peters gave her.

108

AKIL WALKED DOWN the lane, sheathed in darkness. He was careful to study his surroundings, still looking for any signs of concealed surveillance on the house, but saw nothing to worry about.

When he reached the backyard of Sophie's place, he quickly scaled the six-foot fence and landed on the other side with barely a sound. Not wanting to announce his presence prematurely, he made sure to skirt the motion detector attached to a large floodlight at the back of the home.

The effort proved to be in vain.

A dog started barking at the back door, no doubt sensing his presence. As any thief would tell you, dogs were much harder to fool than a ten-dollar piece of static hardware. From the sound of the bark, it wasn't a vicious animal, but that wasn't the point.

Rushing forward, Akil pushed himself flat against the house as the back door swung open. He watched the dog shoot out of the house and head straight for the back fence, triggering the motion detector along the way.

Blinded by the floodlight, Akil's eyes took a moment to adjust. When they had, he saw Sophie standing in the doorway, a gun in her hand.

The 9mm was pointed at his chest.

Akil gave her a nervous smile. "You're not going to shoot me, are you?"

"I haven't decided," she said, not lowering the gun.

"Just want to talk," he said.

She lowered the pistol, but not all the way. "People are looking for you."

"I figured they would be."

"You shouldn't be here."

"I know. Can I come in?"

She didn't answer right away. "I'd like to explain what's going on," he told her.

He didn't want to keep standing outside in the wash of a floodlight either, especially with a gun pointed at him. One of the neighbors could be calling the police right now and that was the last thing either of them needed.

By this time Teddy had doubled back and was jumping up on Akil, licking his hand. Akil bent down and started petting the dog, ignoring the gun that was still trained on him.

Sophie finally lowered the gun to her side. "Alright then, c'mon, you can explain inside," she said, holding the door open for Akil and Teddy.

Akil sat down on a stool in the kitchen and rested his forearm on Sophie's breakfast bar.

"So? Why is the CIA is looking for you?" she asked.

"I need your help."

"You didn't answer my question."

"You want the short version or the long version?"

"The truth would be nice," Sophie said. She walked over and reached up into a cupboard that served as her liquor cabinet. "You want something to drink?"

"Yeah. I could use one."

Sophie grabbed a bottle of Lagavulin and a couple glasses. She carried them over to the breakfast bar and took a seat opposite Akil, then poured two generous measures of the single malt.

"Here you go," she said, handing him a glass.

"Thanks."

"So?"

Akil took a large sip of the scotch. He knew he had nothing to lose by telling Sophie everything. He just didn't know where to start. "I've got a lead on the whereabouts of the VX," he said finally.

She stared at him the same way she would a suspect in custody, her eyes searching for signs of deception.

"I get it, I'd be skeptical too," he said. "Just hear me out. Getting this lead is how I got into this mess."

She must have spotted something in his eyes or in his tone of voice because she yielded slightly. "I'm listening."

Starting from the beginning he told her everything he'd avoided sharing on the rooftop outside Cairo. How he had spotted Tara his first month in Beirut. How he had orchestrated run-ins with her. How he had recruited her over the summer, convincing her to spy for the CIA. Then he explained their personal relationship and how it had developed, despite his better judgment.

"She was passing critical intelligence to you?" Sophie asked.

"Yes. But I broke a cardinal rule by getting involved with her. They tried to put another handler in my place, but Tara balked. We lost her."

Sophie poured more scotch into his glass, then into her own. "Were you in love with her?" she asked.

"I guess you could say that."

"What does that mean?"

He described his brother and how he'd died—confessed that he'd bottled up his emotions afterward, leaving them to fester, throwing himself into his work as a way to escape. He let the job consume him, building his reputation as a tireless officer, rising up through the ranks.

"And all that time I never took the opportunity to mourn him," he admitted. "With Tara...I don't know...I felt safe with her, trusted her— cared about her even though I was putting her life at risk. Then, one night, I found myself in her arms, crying like a child. For the first time in years, I'd let myself grieve for my brother, laying myself bare. Is that love?"

Sophie wasn't sure how to answer so she didn't. "And you were running her as an agent that whole time?"

"Yes," he said. "It was complicated. I made it complicated."

Akil finished off his scotch and poured some more. "The other night Ahmad Hashemian sent Tara to meet with me," he told Sophie. "He found out about us—found out that she'd been spying for the CIA."

"Who's Hashemian?" Sophie asked.

Akil explained who the man was and how he tied in with Tara and the VX. Then he explained how Marchetti had placed him under surveillance without his knowledge—that he'd been photographed meeting with Tara. The toughest part was explaining why he'd made the decision to run instead of facing his accusers back at Langley.

Sophie listened, interrupting only occasionally to ask a question. When Akil was finished telling his story, she sat silent for a long time.

"You did the right thing," she said finally. "Sounds like this Hashemian is our best hope of stopping the next attack. Maybe our only hope."

He was surprised—shocked really—to hear her say that. If Sophie felt he'd made the right decision, maybe he had. Maybe it was the only decision that made sense.

"Normally I'd say you were wrong to run," she conceded, "but Hashemian chose you. And if you were stuck in some room at Langley tomorrow, answering questions…? No, I think what you did was courageous. I don't know if I could have done the same thing."

"Don't sell yourself short."

"I'm being serious."

"I know you are. Thank you," he said. "This mean you're not going to turn me in?"

"Well, not tonight. I'm too tired."

He laughed at that, the stress of the last twenty-four hours ebbing away, if only slightly.

Sophie got up and gestured for him to follow her into the living room. The bottle of scotch they'd been drinking had dwindled significantly and they were both a little drunk.

"Have a seat," she said, stopping by the stereo.

Akil sat on the couch while Sophie put on some music. When she sat down next to him, she told him about the two men they'd picked up in Philadelphia, how the bastards weren't telling them anything they didn't already know.

"With any luck," he said, "Hashemian will lead us to Ali."

"I hope so."

Akil could feel the alcohol working on him, relaxing him. At any other time, the idea of telling Sophie—telling anyone—about his past, or about his work overseas, would have left him feeling unsettled. But he felt as if a great weight had been lifted off his shoulders.

Sophie leaned back and closed her eyes.

Melancholy notes full of longing filled the room. The music seemed to grow louder—the soft scratch of a snare drum building up unseen momentum. Watching her soak in the music, Akil noticed for the first time a faint ribbon of freckles running across the bridge of her nose. A holdover from childhood, he thought. Of innocence. Then he followed her lead, closing his eyes too, pushing away the day's events and the thoughts that surrounded them.

Sitting beside her, safe inside these four walls, he felt a stillness descend over him, something he knew would not survive the night. This place—this moment—was a temporary sanctuary. By morning it would be little more than a dream, and knowing that, he relished it all the more.

His reward was the first real sleep he'd had in days.

109

In the morning, Akil got up and went to meet Ahmad Hashemian.

The cab he called dropped him off near Lafayette Square next to the White House. From there he ran an extensive SDR on foot. Unlike the detection route he had conducted on the way to the nightclub two nights prior, this one was more nuanced and systematic. He had to be absolutely sure that no one was trailing him. The last thing he wanted was the CIA stumbling onto his meeting with the head of Iranian Intelligence.

Positive he wasn't being followed, he headed west across the Potomac River to Arlington National Cemetery. It was the first location Hashemian had chosen to meet. He arrived at the Memorial Amphitheater near the tomb of the unknown soldier just before 11 AM. The Amphitheater in November was eye-catching, the autumnal leaves forming a sea of yellow, orange, and red that popped against the memorial's white marble.

Entering the theater, Akil picked a spot with generous sight lines, then scanned the flow of visitors as they came and went. More than a hundred people passed through the theater. The Iranian Intelligence chief was not among them.

Forty-five minutes later he acquiesced to the fact that Hashemian wasn't going to show. He checked his watch. The next opportunity was at 4:30 PM in front of the National Gallery located at 4th Street and Constitution Avenue. The instructions were clear and quite specific. Front steps. East Building. Alone.

Akil arrived early and took up position outside the Gallery. He waited for over an hour this time, but again Hashemian failed to appear. Akil was beginning to get nervous, which didn't happen often. He had run a second SDR on his way to the Gallery, just to be safe. Again he detected no signs of surveillance whatsoever. So why was Hashemian not showing his face?

One opportunity remained. If Hashemian didn't show tonight, Akil would have sacrificed his career for nothing. Worse than that, the whereabouts of the VX and the identity of the terrorists would remain unknown.

By 10 PM Akil was in position at the final rendezvous point. He hid among a grouping of trees and observed the location from a distance.

At 10:15 he stepped out into plain view. The marble columns of the Jefferson Memorial, lit from below, sparkled in the frigid air. He took the steps of the monument two at a time, all the way to the top. Reaching the portico he found himself face-to-face with the 19-foot bronze statue of Thomas Jefferson. It was striking to see up close, its polished surface awash in a pool of light. He took a moment to appreciate its artistry, reading one of the quotations inscribed along the statue's base.

I have sworn upon the altar of God eternal hostility against every form of tyranny over the mind of man.

Akil laughed at the irony of Hashemian setting a meeting here, of all places, then turned and faced the tidal basin. The memorial was reflected in the shimmering water, an evening breeze sweeping across its dark surface. He wondered if Hashemian was going to show. He was late and this was the last rendezvous point on the list.

A handful of people had come and gone while he hid in the trees. Now there was no one.

Akil paced back and forth like a caged animal for ten minutes before he glimpsed a figure emerging from the shadows below. A rotund man had stopped at the base of the steps that led to the portico. The man wore a heavy wool overcoat with a black scarf and black leather gloves.

Akil wasn't sure if it was Hashemian or not. Regardless, he started down the steps. The desperation he felt was irritating. Everything hung on the word of this one man, a man potentially responsible for passing VX to those intent on harming the United States and her citizens.

As he got closer, the man looked up at him. Akil recognized the face. The eyes—distinctive for their lack of color—were small and deep set. They looked like dark crystals in the spill of light from the memorial.

"You're late," Akil said, letting his annoyance show. There was no point being timid.

"*Bebakhshid,*" Hashemian replied, apologizing in Farsi. "I had to make sure you came alone."

Akil looked around at the deserted memorial. "Satisfied?"

"Yes, quite satisfied."

"And this morning? This afternoon? Where were you?" Akil asked.

"I was certain your agency would have set up some sort of listening post or surveillance. We had to check. I can not be too cautious at the moment."

In Hashemian's place, Akil would have done the same, yet it bothered him that he'd been made to tramp all over the city for nothing. Lives were at stake and there was no time to waste.

"Let's walk," Akil said, moving away from the brightly lit memorial.

As they passed a small grouping of trees Hashemian stopped abruptly. "Are you wearing a wire, Mr. Hassan?" he asked.

"No."

"I'm afraid I must insist on checking. To be sure. You don't mind?"

It was a rhetorical question. Akil raised his arms. He understood that if what Hashemian had to say was genuine, there could be no record of their conversation.

The Iranian removed a small metal disc from his pocket. It was roughly the size of a hockey puck. An electronic sweeping device of some sort. Hidden by the trees, Hashemian passed the device over Akil's body. When he was finished, he apologized again for the impertinence of his request.

Akil ignored the apology. "I need to know where the VX is entering the country," he said.

"Through Philadelphia," Hashemian told him, moving down the path with his hands in his pockets.

Akil followed. "Philadelphia?"

"Yes."

"You're sure?"

"Quite sure."

"How's it being brought in?" Akil asked, trying to get a read on his adversary.

"By a crew member onboard a cargo ship, we think."

America's ports were still one of its weak points. There was a long list of things that were banned from airplanes, but you could smuggle almost anything onboard a cargo ship, especially in countries where the security controls were not as strict as they should be.

"And the name of the vessel?" Akil asked, still looking at Hashemian.

"I'm afraid that is no longer of any importance."

"What do you mean?"

"The VX is already in your country."

"With the terrorists?"

"I'm afraid we have to assume so. Yes."

"Is it or isn't it?" Akil demanded.

"Please," Hashemian said, stopping and turning. "I am not trying to hide anything from you. The information I have is limited. If your customs agents have not discovered the VX by now, we must assume it is in the hands of the terrorists."

"Then tell me who's responsible for the attacks on New York," Akil said. "Who are we looking for?"

Hashemian shook his head back and forth. "First I want to know what Khalini told you in Cairo."

Akil stared off into the dark water beyond the footpath. "Khalini told us plenty. But you know I can't discuss the details."

"Torture can make a man say almost anything. How can you be sure everything he told you was the truth?"

Akil chuckled and gave Hashemian a sideways glance. "With respect, you're not here because you think he lied to us."

Hashemian made no comment and betrayed no emotion.

"You're concerned," Akil said, staring intently at the Iranian Intelligence Chief now. "You should be."

Hashemian calmly shrugged his shoulders. "Things can appear one way and, in truth, be quite different. You know that as well as I do."

"They often are," Akil agreed. "But right now all we want to know is who was behind the attacks. Who is it we're looking for and where can we find them. Where can we find the VX?"

"I must reiterate that the Iranian Government did not sanction or know about this action until very recently, Mr. Hassan."

"Tara explained," Akil said, nodding his understanding. "A rogue group of Pasdaran operating outside the parameters of their authority."

"That's right. And I can assure you that actions have been taken to severely punish those responsible."

"That's good to hear," Akil said. "However, not everyone is convinced it's the truth."

Hashemian grunted and made a dismissive gesture with his hand.

"Can you offer any proof that your government was *not* involved?" Akil asked.

The silence suggested Hashemian had no proof. Or maybe he was just reluctant to discuss the matter in depth.

"Either way," Akil said, "it's a question for the politicians to debate. Not us."

"But I want you to tell your minders, Mr. Hassan, having heard it from me personally. We did not sanction this."

"You think they'll accept your word for it? The word of a spy?"

"The word of my government."

"The word of your government? If we don't stop the VX from being used, no one is going to listen to anybody. Both our governments will be too busy preparing for war. So tell me what I need to know so we can avoid that."

Akil's heart was racing and adrenaline was making his legs bouncy. The fact that the head of Iranian Intelligence was here, in person, illustrated just how desperate the situation had become.

"His name is Abu Sayyid al-Rashid Ibn Muhammad al-Filistini," Hashemian said, delivering the name with a lyrical cadence.

Akil understood why Hashemian had given the man's proper name in full. Arabic names were more edifying than their modern English equivalents. Each one told a story. The man's first name was Sayyid—his friends and family would call him by this name. In full, he was known as the firstborn son, the rightly guided one, son of Muhammad, the Palestinian.

"Sayyid grew up in the al-Amari refugee camp outside of Ramallah in the West Bank," Hashemian explained. "Horrible place. His mother died giving birth to him and his father was forced to raise him alone. A few weeks after Sayyid's eleventh birthday, his father died of a massive coronary. After that, everything changed for the boy."

"How so?"

"A wealthy uncle living in Hebron took him in. Helped him. Offered him an education."

"What's the uncle's name?" Akil asked.

Hashemian removed a cigarette case from his jacket pocket and opened it using both hands. "It's not relevant," he said, retrieving a yellow cigarette from inside.

"It is."

"The boy excelled at school," Hashemian continued as he lit his cigarette. "Later, his uncle paid for him to go abroad and study in England. After he graduated he received a scholarship from the University of California, at Berkeley, where he completed his MBA. Then he returned to the West Bank."

"And then?"

"He joined Hamas."

"Hamas?" Akil asked. "Why Hamas?"

"You've seen the camps, Mr. Hassan. Haven't you?"

Akil said nothing.

"Exactly. Eventually, Sayyid orchestrated a string of very successful attacks against Israel. But it wasn't enough for him. They say he wanted to change the way the war was being fought."

"Who is *they?*"

"The people he worked with."

"Is Hamas sponsoring him?" Akil asked.

"No," Hashemian said. "Not directly."

"But the Pasdaran arranged for the delivery of the VX."

"A rogue element in the Pasdaran, yes," Hashemian said. "It's an unfortunate situation."

"And you and your government had no knowledge of it? Had nothing to do with it?"

Hashemian reacted with impatience. "I told you already, we found out about this only very recently. There is no reason our two countries should go to war over this madness. That's why I'm here."

And the truth? What's the truth, Ahmad? Akil kicked a stone off into the grass. "From banker to bomber then," he said, referring to Sayyid.

"Doctors, engineers, religious scholars. All Muslims are the martyrs of God."

"Save the rhetoric. How do you know so much about Sayyid?"

Hashemian smiled. "You are surprised at how much I know."

"Suspicious is the word I'd use."

"You forget that my colleagues and I are Muslims. We have access where you have none. We have friends where you have only enemies. America, Britain, Israel…you think you understand Islam and its people, but you don't. Even you, a Muslim by birth, can infiltrate the fabric of our society only up to a point before you too become a stranger. So? You rely on others, like the Jordanians and the Egyptians. But everyone knows they are allied with the American regime. The truth is, as far as intelligence in the Middle East goes, you are blind and deaf, my friend. You are just too proud to admit it."

Akil didn't appreciate Hashemian's sermon, but the Iranian was right about the difficulties faced by the West. The Middle East and Islam were enigmas; it was a land and people as alien to the American sensibility as any imaginable.

Hashemian threw his cigarette away and reapplied his leather gloves with care. "We know of three potential contacts Sayyid may have inside the US," he said. "Men who have lived in your country for years, all of them actively working for Hamas." He handed Akil an envelope. "Here are the names of two of those men."

"And the third?"

"He is in one of your jails. The other lives in Kansas City, but we do not think he is involved. The last one lives in Chicago. His name is Qasim Awad. He raises money for Hamas, among other things. Sayyid will have had contact with him through his work with the charities or with those who know how to get in touch with him. Find him and we think you will find Sayyid. Find Sayyid and hopefully you will find the VX."

"Thank you," Akil said. He meant it.

"There's a photo of Sayyid as well. An older one, but it should help," Hashemian said. "Find Sayyid and the VX, Mr. Hassan. For the sake of both our countries. Whether you think I am guilty of subterfuge or not, neither of us wants to see this situation escalate."

They shook hands, then, without ceremony, the Iranian disappeared into the shadows the same way he had come.

110

BILL GRAHAM'S CELL phone vibrated loudly on the edge of his nightstand. He had just fallen asleep and the journey back to consciousness was a struggle. Opening his eyes, closing them, then opening them again, he reached for his cell.

The clock on his nightstand told him it was almost three in the morning.

"Graham here."

"Bill?"

The voice sounded muffled.

"Who is this?"

"It's Mick. You don't recognize my voice?"

Bill threw his legs over the side of the bed and was suddenly wide awake. The voice was being disguised. "What can I do for you, Mick? It's late," he said, making a show of being annoyed.

"Yeah, look, I'm sorry, but I want to meet up, discuss what we talked about before. I have new information on that South African you were inquiring about."

"Right," Bill said, the irritation in his voice magnifying. "I have a lot on my plate at the moment. It'll have to wait a few days."

"Sure, whatever works. As long as I get paid. Next week?"

"Yeah."

"The Bon Café?"

"Sure."

"Let's say Thursday, 10 AM?"

"Alright, fine. Goodnight."

Bill hung up and placed his cell back on the nightstand. A glass of water sat beside the clock radio. He grabbed it and took a drink as he replayed the conversation in his head.

Even assuming his phone had been tapped, there was nothing that would raise undue suspicion. True, the call had come in the middle of the night, but ever since he had taken over as head of Operations, such calls were not uncommon. What mattered was that Akil had contacted him. Bill's guess was he had met with Ahmad Hashemian. And although the conversation over the phone had been cryptic, Akil had clearly communicated when and where he wanted to meet up to discuss it. Not next Thursday, of course, but in a few hours time.

Working together in Cairo, Bill and his one-time protégé had established a very simple code for communicating over open phone lines. Any numerical date, address or time referred to during a conversation was to be reduced by three. If you said you'd meet at 10 AM, what you really meant was you'd meet at 7 AM. If you gave an address—1649 East 4th street—you really meant 1349, East 1st street. That way you established a safe separation between yourself and anyone who may have been listening in and wanted to join the party. This time, instead of using a numbered address, Akil had referred to a place name. The Bon Café. A quick search would reveal a dozen Le Bon, C'est Bon, Au Bon cafes in Washington, DC and the surrounding area. But Akil had not been referring to any of them. The place where he intended Bill to go was an old haunt of theirs. One Bill remembered well.

111

SAYYID AND QASIM had worked through the night preparing for the attack that would take place that afternoon.

The panel van had been stripped bare, then the air compressor and generator had been loaded in and bolted to the floor. They had insulated the machine as best they could in order to reduce the noise, then measured the flex-hosing and cut it to length. Next, the holding tanks for the VX solution were secured in place. Holes were cut in the roof for the nozzles, then welded into place by Qasim. At the same time, Sayyid clamped hoses to the generator, then connected them to the exterior nozzles. Finally, they both helped hook up the main shut-off valve that would go next to the driver's seat.

The work was technical rather than hard labor, and progress was steady. By mid-morning, all that was left to do was top up the compressor with oil and gas and prepare the VX. To optimize its delivery, Sayyid had to create a simple solution that would thin the VX without destroying its deadly effects. Under optimal conditions, 200 micrograms of VX was enough to kill an average sized man or woman. His associates had managed to secure nearly three kilos of the deadly substance. In a few short hours, depending on wind conditions and how many pedestrians were on the street, there was an excellent chance he would inflict massive casualties on the population of Chicago.

Bankers. Lawyers. Accountants. The deaths would affect not only the city's economy, but the entire country's. More significantly, it would destroy the average American's sense of isolation—the idea that the foreign conflicts perpetuated by their government were distant and largely irrelevant to their own pursuit of happiness back home.

Sayyid viewed the deaths he was about to inflict as abstractions. In his heart of hearts, he was not a killer. He was a soldier. But he knew that the bigger the attack, and the larger the number of casualties, the greater the fear imposed on a populace. If the American people wouldn't act on principle, he would make them act out of fear. His ultimate goal was peace, and whatever they would say about him afterwards, the irony was not lost on him. Countries fought wars for all sorts of reasons. Security? Influence?

Plunder? If he had to bloody his hands to give the Palestinian people a chance at regaining their dignity—their homeland—if that was the only option, he was prepared to go all the way. A handful of Israeli deaths every month was not going to sway the Jews or the world to seek an equitable peace with the Palestinian people. And the Palestinian people had no leverage to force the issue. If the world saw him as desperate—as having been driven to madness for what he was about to do—let them. In his mind, it was madness to stand by and watch his people suffer decade after decade while their fractious leadership did little to change the status quo.

"It's ready," Sayyid said, sealing the top of the holding tank containing the VX solution.

As Sayyid jumped down from the back of the truck, Qasim closed the roll-top door and secured it with a lock.

"Now let's go pray, brother," Qasim said, "for our success."

112

BILL LEFT HOME early and drove into the city, leaving enough time to make sure he wasn't followed.

He entered the small French-style brasserie around 7 AM and looked for a seat. He and Akil had discovered the place years ago. They'd fallen in love with it after discovering it carried close to sixty single malt scotches. As a result, many late nights had been spent cocooned in a corner of the brasserie, talking shop and debating the state of the world.

Bill took a seat that offered an excellent view of the street, as well as the interior. Although there were several tables in his section, only one was occupied. A woman in her late sixties, slightly overweight with thinning grey hair, sat off to his left.

The waiter arrived and took his order, then returned with a double espresso, placing it on the marble table-top in front of him. The aroma from the rich brew was exactly what he needed this early in the morning.

As he drank the espresso, Bill spotted a beautiful woman passing by the window outside. He followed her with his eyes, watching as she turned and entered the brasserie. Her blond hair was tied in a ponytail and she wore a tight fitting pair of jeans along with a silk blouse. She had a copy of the New York Times tucked under one arm and seemed to be searching for someone.

Bill wasn't the only person who had noticed her. Several men were staring in her direction for obvious reasons. The woman was striking, her tailored blouse offering evidence of a toned upper body while her jeans hugged the gentle curve of her hips and thighs. Bill stared for longer than was polite, but it had nothing to do with the woman's looks. There was something else about her that had caught his attention—something he couldn't put his finger on.

Was she part of a surveillance detail?

He dismissed the notion as unlikely. She was too striking for one. Looks like that drew attention. And second, he'd been very careful on his way to the brasserie, picking up no signs of surveillance whatsoever.

No, she didn't pose a threat, he decided. He was on edge, that's all.

Bill turned his thoughts back to Akil. He wanted to know what information Akil had obtained from his meeting with Hashemian. If there was actionable intelligence to be dealt with, he needed to find a way to get it to Marchetti without bringing up Akil's name. That was easier said than done, of course.

Preoccupied with these thoughts, Bill didn't notice the woman heading towards his table until she arrived.

Looking up, he surveyed her yet again, more closely this time. She was standing right in front of him, elevated on four-inch heels. No make-up. Piercing green eyes. She wasn't part of any surveillance effort, that was for sure. So, who was she? And what did she want?

Bill had his charms, but he doubted the woman was making advances.

"Hello," he said, waiting for whatever was coming next.

"Hello," she said, "may I sit here?"

"Of course."

She pulled back the chair and sat down.

The waiter appeared quickly. "*Bonjour,*" the woman said, looking up with a smile.

"*Bonjour madam,*" the waiter replied in French, visibly pleased.

"*Un café noir, s'il vous plait.*"

"*Merci.*"

The waiter left.

Bill had not taken his eyes off the woman, yet she seemed to be ignoring him. He watched as she unfolded her newspaper and laid it out on the table and began reading as she waited for her coffee.

What is this? Bill wondered. Then he noticed the words written in felt marker toward the top of the paper.

I'm Sophie
He's waiting for you at the Plaza Theater
Use the back door

Sophie's eyes flashed on him for an instant, just long enough to make sure he'd seen the message. Noting that he had, she unceremoniously began flipping pages until there was no sign of the note. She kept reading, acting as if she had no idea who the man across from her was or had any interest in speaking with him.

Her cloak and dagger routine felt overly cautious, Bill thought, but then you could never be too careful. He knew that from experience.

The waiter arrived and delivered her coffee. She thanked him politely.

How had Akil convinced Sophie Martin to help him? What had he told her? Did she know Akil was being sought by the Agency?

He wanted to ask her a dozen different questions but knew he couldn't. Not right now.

Drinking the last of his espresso, Bill gathered his coat and left without so much as glancing at her.

113

THE PLAZA THEATER was situated three blocks east of the brasserie on what used to be a bustling avenue. The theatre had been state-of-the-art once. Built in the late thirties, it had been an ultra-modern, two-screen movie house with flowing interior curves and an art-deco façade. The front doors were boarded up and locked now, its proud history nothing but a fading memory.

Bill crossed the street and headed around back. He found a solitary door with long strips of blue paint peeling from its surface. Scanning the length of the alley, spotting no one, he opened it and slipped inside.

Immediately locking the door behind him, Bill let his eyes adjust to the relative darkness before proceeding.

He was in a utility corridor that ran the length of the theatre. In front of him were two doors, each one leading to a different theater. One of the doors had a chalk mark on it.

He walked over to the marked door and stepped through.

The lights inside the theatre were up about halfway, making the soda-stained carpet and grubby seats clearly visible. He took a few steps toward the first row, then spotted Akil out of the corner of his eye, sitting on the edge of the stage.

Akil hopped down. "Thanks for coming," he said.

"I guess we can add breaking and entering to the list of charges."

Akil half-smiled, acknowledging the joke but not sharing in it.

"So? What've you got?" Bill asked.

"The VX is already here, inside the country."

"You met with Hashemian?"

"Yeah. Last night, right before I called you."

Bill pulled a pack of Marlboros from his coat pocket and lit up.

"Before I get into that, I'm sorry for hanging you out to dry with Marchetti," Akil said. "Hashemian made it clear he wouldn't meet with anyone but me. Said I had to come alone. When I went downstairs and security was already ransacking my office, I thought I had no other choice but—"

"Look," Bill said, interjecting, "you did what you thought you had to do. We can discuss the consequences of that decision later. Right now, what I want to know is: how does Tara Markosi fit into all this?"

It was a fair question. More than fair. Akil hadn't been sure how Bill was going to react after what he'd done—after learning he'd met with Tara—but Bill was debriefing him rather than admonishing him, and that was an encouraging start.

"Hashemian was using her as a cut-out," Akil explained. "The Iranians know we have Khalini. They're terrified of what could happen if the VX is used on American soil."

Bill leaned against the stage, processing the information. Hashemian's involvement suddenly made more sense.

"How did they find out we had Khalini?"

"Word must have leaked out of Cairo. From what Tara said, they had pictures of me and Sophie—along with Travers—arriving at the airport."

"You're sure about this?"

"That they know about Khalini? Positive."

"And the pictures?" Bill asked.

"It explains how they knew I was Agency. I assume Travers was a known commodity operating out of Baghdad. As for Tara, they must have cross-referenced their old files, traced me back to Lebanon."

"Or Tara has been working with them for longer than a few days."

"Could be," Akil said, resigned to the possibility.

"What else did you find out?"

Akil explained that the terrorist they were looking for was named Sayyid al-Rashid. He went through Sayyid's background as Hashemian had given it, then told Bill that Sayyid's contact in the US was a man named Qasim Awad.

"You think Hashemian is telling the truth?" Bill asked.

"He's desperate. Has to be to pull a stunt like this," Akil said. "Yeah, I think he's telling the truth. He knows what's at stake if the VX is unleashed."

Bill ran a hand through his salt and pepper hair.

"Okay, first thing we need to do is find an address for Qasim."

Akil handed Bill the envelope Hashemian had given him.

"What's this?"

"Qasim's address, along with a picture of Sayyid," Akil said. "Qasim is living in Chicago. Hashemian thinks that's where Sayyid is headed."

"Chicago, huh."

"Explains Sayyid's actions. He wanted us to think New York was going to be attacked again. He was trying to divert our attention and resources, masking the real target."

"Well, it worked," Bill said, his brow furrowing in frustration. "This information Hashemian gave you is a game changer, kid. But we still have a major problem."

"Marchetti is going to want to know where the information came from."

"Exactly. And he won't act on any of it if he thinks it came from you or Hashemian."

"He can't just ignore the intelligence."

"You wanna bet." Bill stubbed out his cigarette and lit a fresh one on its heels. "Without a reliable source for the intelligence, Marchetti won't pass it along to the FBI. He won't take that risk, and I'm not sure I blame him, not with the way things have played out up to this point."

"So what now?"

"Your conversation with Hashemian? You get any of it on tape?"

"What do you think?"

Bill took a long drag off his cigarette and let the smoke rush out through his nostrils in two violent streams. "I could try and backstop the information, create a trail for it," he suggested.

"We don't have time for that."

"No, we don't." He was grasping at straws and knew it.

"So? We have no choice but to cut Marchetti out of the equation," Akil said.

"Easier said than done. It's not like we can go to the FBI ourselves."

Akil thought about that—racked his brain, searching for a way they could act on the intelligence without involving Marchetti. Obviously, they couldn't take down Sayyid and Qasim alone, not without *some* help.

But who?

And how?

It's not like we can go to the FBI ourselves.

Bill wasn't wrong, but maybe there was still a way to engage the FBI. With some help. From a friend.

He was thinking about what Sophie had told him that morning, that she wanted to help. That she was willing to risk her career if necessary to stop the next attack. She'd meant what she said, he could see it in her eyes. And that was essential because she would be the key to making what he had in mind work, if it had any chance of working at all.

"I think I know how we can do this," Akil said.

Bill gave him a skeptical look but didn't interject, allowing him to explain.

"With Sophie Martin's help, we *can* go to the feds…in Chicago. We get them to do the heavy lifting for us. We're not asking for much, just that they take a person-of-interest into custody for questioning. It'll be a localized action coordinated through NCTC at the request of Sophie Martin, one of their own. It'll be off-book, of course, but they won't know that. And if we happen to stumble upon a stash of VX and Sayyid while we serve the warrant on Qasim, none of the particulars will matter."

Akil tried to measure Bill's reaction.

"We'll keep key details surrounding the op close to the vest until the very last moment. If everything goes smoothly, this whole thing could be over by tonight," he added.

Bill scratched his temple, smoke curling up past his hairline. "It's a creative workaround, I'll give you that. A bit of a Hail Mary though. A lot can go wrong."

"I know, but we don't know how close Sayyid is to unleashing the VX and Marchetti is a bridge too far. Time's running out and this is the only play I can think of. If you've got a better idea, I'm all ears."

Bill flicked the ash from the end of his cigarette and let it fall onto the soiled carpet. "You think Sophie's willing to put her career on the line to do this?" he asked. "Because if we're wrong and this goes sideways…"

"She's willing to do it if it means stopping more innocent people from dying."

"She said that?"

"Yes."

A grin slowly spread across Bill's face. "You're a real piece of work, you know that."

"It was her decision, Bill."

"Still."

"Look, if Sophie can convince the local feds in Chicago, we can be on the ground and ready to move by early afternoon."

"Alright then, I'll confirm Qasim's address and see what else I can find out," Bill said. He reached inside his jacket pocket and pulled out a small sat phone. He tossed it to Akil. "Take this. It's encrypted. I'll let you know when I have something."

"Thanks."

114

SOPHIE AND AKIL touched down at O'Hare just after one in the afternoon. Akil was traveling under an assumed name, yet he knew the airport's CCTV cameras would capture his image—may have already captured his image back in DC—and that his face would be fed into a recognition program back at CIA.

Eventually.

Not right away.

Nothing he could do about that. But he had one thing going for him: he was sure that Marchetti wouldn't want to air his dirty laundry out in the open, inviting unwanted criticism for losing his man. Not yet. Not until he had absolutely no choice but to go wide with the embarrassment. That meant that Akil was being tracked by CIA assets alone. Formidable as that was, it precluded other law enforcement agencies from being brought into the loop. If he was right, no one at the airport was going to be alerted to the fact he was a wanted man. That would buy him and Sophie a little time. He just hoped it was enough.

Bill had called earlier and confirmed Qasim's address and particulars. On paper, the Palestinian was a naturalized citizen of the United States and, therefore, no different than your average Joe. For that reason alone he was a valuable commodity to Hamas and Sayyid. But being legitimate made you transparent. Qasim's credit history, what he shopped for online, who he called on the phone—all that information was at Bill's fingertips. Not surprisingly, there was nothing overtly incriminating. Not under the name of Qasim Awad, anyway. Whatever illegal activities the Palestinian was involved in, and there was little doubt now that he was involved in something, he'd hidden it extremely well.

Outside the main terminal, a young FBI agent greeted Sophie, informing her that special agent Kieslowski was waiting for her by the car.

Akil turned to Sophie. "Kieslowski your man?"

"Yeah."

Kieslowski looked to be in his mid-fifties, but it was hard to be sure. He stood about 5'10 and was built like a rottweiler: bulky shoulders, thick neck, surly face. As soon as he set eyes on Sophie though, the FBI veteran adopted a childlike demeanor.

"Look at you," he bellowed. "You look great, love."

"Thanks, Skids," Sophie said, giving him a big hug. "You haven't changed a bit. How are you?"

"Yeah, me, I'm good," he said. "Looking forward to my retirement."

"You won't know what to do with yourself."

"You're probably right," Kieslowski said, turning to Akil.

Akil stepped forward and extended his hand. Kieslowski gave him a firm handshake and the once over, but didn't ask his name or who he worked for. Maybe Sophie had told him or maybe Kieslowski just didn't want to know.

"Skids and I worked in Portland together," Sophie explained as they piled into the waiting SUV and pulled away from the terminal.

"Taught her everything she knows," Skids said proudly. "SWAT is going to rendezvous with us several blocks from the house before we proceed to the target."

"Good," Sophie said. "Have they been briefed?"

"All they know is we're serving a warrant. That's it."

"I want a word with them before we go in then."

"Sure thing."

The call Sophie Martin had made to her old mentor Kieslowski—aka "Skids"—had been short and deliberate. New evidence appeared to tie a Palestinian by the name of Qasim Awad to the terrorist attacks in New York City and the suspect needed to be taken into custody for further questioning. She told Skids she was already on her way to Chicago and asked if he could arrange everything on his end.

Kieslowski and the Chicago field office were exceedingly cooperative. As Akil had hoped, the word of a senior FBI investigator working out of NCTC was enough to get bodies moving. This wasn't a major operation after all, they were just taking a secondary suspect into custody, or so the story went. Everyone assumed that senior FBI officials in New York were aware of what was going on.

They weren't.

By the time they found out, the raid would be over. Qasim, Sayyid, and the VX—with a bit of luck—would all be neutralized. That was the plan. And if everything worked out, Akil and Sophie would be heroes. They might even keep their jobs.

If the intelligence was wrong, however, they'd likely find themselves behind bars before the day was out.

115

SOPHIE, AKIL, AND Skids met up with the FBI SWAT team in the parking lot of a Seven-Eleven. Five minutes out from the target, Sophie could finally explain the full extent of who and what they were dealing with. She told the assembled SWAT members that they were going after a man named Sayyid al-Rashid and his American contact, Qasim Awad. Photos were distributed as Sophie explained who exactly these men were and what they were planning to do.

As Sophie spoke, the change in the team's energy was palpable. Engagements like this were few and far between.

Akil stepped in after Sophie was finished and explained that VX was potentially being stored on the premises. Nothing had been confirmed, but once the targets had been taken into custody, any potential chemical weapons inside the house needed to be found and secured.

Sophie jumped back in and explained that VX wasn't like a bomb that could be triggered at a moment's notice—it had to be prepared for distribution, then transported and deployed against its target using some kind of delivery system in order to be effective. If VX existed in the house, she said, it presented only a localized threat. If they waited and the VX were moved—and if they failed to track it—a far deadlier scenario could play out.

That's all the SWAT team needed to hear. They were dedicated professionals who didn't throw caution to the wind—ever—but taking calculated risks was a way of life. If finding and arresting those responsible for the carnage in New York meant risking possible exposure to VX, they were willing to accept and manage that risk.

Sophie and Akil wrapped up their comments and turned the operation over to the SWAT leader. The plan, he explained, was to surround the target house quickly, form a perimeter, then execute an assault on the residence in as short a time as possible. Three blocks from the target the convoy would split into two groups and converge on the house from opposite directions, forming a pincer action.

With everyone briefed, they headed to the target.

Sitting in the back seat of an SUV, Akil gave his gun a cursory inspection. He felt charged up, eager to get the action underway. He knew this was their best chance at stopping the terrorists before more people started dying.

The vehicle they were in was leading the charge. With the target's house less than a block away, Kieslowski turned onto Qasim's street without slowing down. As they made the turn, Akil heard the car tires shudder and squeal. He looked up to see Kieslowski cranking the steering wheel to his right.

They were drifting into the oncoming lane. Having failed to secure his seatbelt, Akil slid hard into the car door, pinning his hand against the armrest. Out the window he saw a panel van rushing toward them, the logo on its side growing larger as they cantilevered toward it.

He braced himself for the impact.

It never came. They had, by some miracle, narrowly avoided the collision.

"Jesus Christ!"

"Sorry!" Kieslowski said. He seemed more amused than upset by the near miss. Akil could see where he'd gotten his nickname from, but found nothing funny about it.

A moment later they descended on Qasim's house without the blast of sirens or flashing lights. FBI vehicles blocked off the street as agents took up positions around the perimeter. They kept their distance, giving the SWAT team plenty of room to work.

The SWAT team was already suited up. They'd use tear gas to try and flush out whoever was inside. If that didn't work, they'd go in from the front and rear of the house simultaneously.

The first canisters of tear gas burst through the big bay window on the main floor. The sound of shattered glass was followed by the *thunk-thunk* sounds of more canisters being fired through the upper windows.

The gas quickly engulfed the house. Using the gas as cover, the assaulters moved into position alongside the front and rear entrances, waiting for the signal to go in.

No one had fled the house. It was possible they had gas masks. Akil was beginning to wonder if those inside had taken their own lives. It certainly wasn't out of the question. As he contemplated that scenario, a series of gunshots slammed into the vehicle inches from where he and Sophie were standing.

They both dove for cover.

"You okay?" Akil yelled.

"Yeah. You?" Sophie asked.

"Yeah."

Akil peered around the front bumper of the car just in time to see the SWAT leader give the signal for his men to go in. He watched as the battering ram hit the front door, causing it to explode off its hinges. A fraction of a second later the assaulters entered, one by one, covering each other as they went.

Akil waited about thirty seconds, then jumped to his feet and ran in a low crouch across the front lawn. He heard several bursts of gunfire come from inside the house as he approached the door. The sound was familiar—a suppressed MP5. SWAT most likely, but there was no way to be sure.

Stepping through the front door with his gun drawn, Akil felt the tear gas begin to burn his eyes. Most of the toxic gas had dissipated, but what remained caused him to tear up. Moving down the hallway he could hear members of the assault team giving the all-clear from different locations throughout the house. In the middle of the hallway, he passed an assaulter moving in the opposite direction with a young girl in his arms. The girl was crying, her eyes as red as pomegranates. Poor kid, Akil thought. What had she done to deserve this?

Akil moved further down the hall, past the staircase, then turned the corner. He came to an abrupt halt. In front of him, at the end of another short hallway, was a man lying in a pool of his own blood. His upper body was sprawled on the carpet, his legs sloping down into an open door-way. Blood spatter covered the wall to his right and extended out into the garage. A gun lay nearby. One of the assaulters and the element leader were crouched down beside the body.

Akil stepped forward and took a closer look at the dead man's face.

"Is it Sayyid?" Sophie asked.

Akil hadn't noticed her follow him in.

"No. It's Qasim."

"He came out of there," the assaulter said, pointing to the garage. "He opened fire. I had to drop him."

Akil marveled at how poised the agent was. He'd just killed a man at point blank range, but you could hardly tell. He had also ruined their chances of gaining any intelligence. The SWAT team had been given strict orders to shoot only as a last resort. Another dead terrorist didn't bother Akil, but dead men told no tales.

Kieslowski came around the corner and stared at Qasim. The element leader stood. "The other man you were looking for isn't here," he said.

Akil looked at Kieslowski and said, "The VX may still be in the house. Who knows, we might get lucky."

Kieslowski nodded. "I'll have my men start looking."

Akil stepped over Qasim's legs and entered the garage.

Sophie followed. "You think we missed him?"

"I don't know. Qasim went down shooting, which means he figured he had no way out. I'm guessing that had something to do with Sayyid."

There was a lot of junk in the garage. Akil waded out into the middle of it, throwing plastic bags and empty cardboard boxes to the side as he went. He looked around the room for anything that would indicate the presence of VX. There were some spray cans along the far wall, their tops smeared with green paint. There was a wooden pallet in the corner, crushed on one side. Something heavy had obviously been placed on top of it or dropped. Bits and pieces of plastic tubing and loose hose clamps littered the floor all around it. There was a jerry can with a splash of gasoline still inside. Tucked in the corner was a welding torch and cylinders of gas.

The individual clues—if they *were* clues—didn't seem to add up to anything obvious?

"There has to be something to indicate that Sayyid was here," Akil said.

He continued looking, unwilling to admit the possibility that Hashemian had given him bogus information. Finally, he spotted something he'd missed when he first entered the garage. Two metal clothes racks were pushed up against the wall that led into the house. They were the kind you found in used clothing stores or costume shops or...

No. It couldn't be.

Akil bent down and grabbed one of the plastic bags he'd tossed aside moments earlier. *Yes, it could.* He picked up another one of the bags, then another. They were the kind made of thin plastic—the kind your clothes were sheathed in when they came back from the dry cleaners. There were dozens of them.

Akil dropped the bags and reached for one of the cardboard boxes. Printed on the side was a name and logo: Excalibur Dry Cleaning.

"Son-of-a-bitch!"

"What?" Sophie asked.

"Sayyid. We just missed him."

"How do you know?"

Akil didn't answer, he was already running toward the door.

Sophie followed in his wake, trying to catch up. "Talk to me," she shouted after him.

"That van we almost hit on the way in. It was a dry cleaning van," Akil yelled over his shoulder. "You see it?"

"Sort of."

"It had green lettering on the side."

"And you think Sayyid was inside?"

"And the VX. Yeah."

Akil reached one of the unmarked cruisers parked out front of the house. The keys were still inside.

"You think he's headed downtown?" Sophie asked.

"Yep."

"What's his plan?"

"He must have some sort of delivery system for the VX. That's what all that crap in the garage is about."

Akil hopped in the FBI cruiser and rolled down the driver's side window. "Tell Kieslowski that he needs to get a chopper in the air right away. We're looking for a white panel van with green lettering on the side. Excalibur Dry Cleaning. As soon as you have eyes on, let me know."

"Will do."

Akil turned the key in the ignition and tore down the street.

116

SAYYID WAS STILL shaking from the near miss.

Years had gone into this operation, begging and cajoling for the opportunity to show what he could do, convincing those that mattered that his plan could be carried out. But all his hard work had nearly been foiled right when he was on the verge of success. Only God's will had saved him and his operation from disaster.

How had they found him?

How did they know about Qasim?

It didn't matter. He'd slipped through the net one last time, and the price America would pay would be far greater than in New York. Thousands would be dead by day's end. Only then would they see how serious he was. Already the attacks against New York were fading from the American consciousness. How quickly their attention shifted, he thought. Another blow against the American psyche was paramount if he wanted the American people to demand action from their government. After today, they would have to make a real choice. And if they chose wrong, others would follow in his footsteps until change came about.

Rolling down his window, Sayyid listened to the helicopter hovering above him. If they were searching for him, they were too late. He could see the skyscrapers up ahead, just across the bridge. Downtown. Home of the Chicago Stock Exchange. The Chicago Board of Trade. Fortune 500 companies. The wealthiest, most powerful nation in the world made manifest on the shores of Lake Michigan.

No one denied that America was a great nation. A super-power. He too had been awed at first. Seduced even. It was an economic empire born of blood and sanctified by the great American myth that still prevailed after all these years: that America was the champion of freedom.

He laughed at the arrogance and the absurdity of it. You didn't become the wealthiest nation on earth—or the most powerful—by championing the poor and defenseless. You applied your leverage and power and you advanced your interests whenever and wherever possible. Now he had come to do the same for his people. This truck, with its deadly cargo, was his leverage—the future of the Palestinian people his only interest.

117

AKIL GRIPPED THE steering wheel, blood hammering at his temples.

He glanced down at the speedometer.

95 mph.

He had tried engaging the car's sirens already, but they weren't working. Another bit of bad luck, he thought, knowing how risky it was to be racing down a crowded city street in the middle of the afternoon without sirens. But if he wanted to catch Sayyid in time, he had no other choice.

Looking back up, he clocked a yellow Volkswagen hurtling toward him. Swerving on instinct, he narrowly avoided clipping the vehicle's back end. One mistake now and his pursuit would end in tragedy. Sayyid's mission would go ahead, unobstructed. Luckily, the vehicle he'd commandeered had been factory-modified for just this type of driving.

The car's radio burst to life with a spatter of static.

"We have him," a voice said.

It was Sophie.

"He's headed south on Union. You were right, he's going straight for downtown."

Akil spotted the street up ahead on his right and slowed significantly. When he got within a car length of the intersection, he engaged the emergency brake and cranked the wheel. The maneuver allowed him to maintain much of his speed as he went through the turn.

Straightening his line, he carried on, passing the cars and trucks in front of him, one after the other, chasing after the van with Sayyid and the VX inside.

Then he spotted the van.

Two blocks in front of him.

A string of green lights allowed him to close the gap even further, but the traffic leading into downtown was getting congested. He'd already been forced to slow to less than 30 mph. Soon it would be stop and go.

Desperate, Akil kept fighting his way forward until a red light stopped his progress altogether. He could hear the helicopter above him now. All it could do was track the van—he was the only one who could stop it. With Sayyid still a dozen cars ahead of him, and with only three blocks to the bridge that led into the downtown, time was running out.

The light turned green.

They barely moved a block before another red light stopped traffic.

Akil was close enough now to see protrusions coming from either corner of the van's roof, but still too far away to tell what they were. He thought about getting out of the car and going after Sayyid on foot, but if the light changed before he got there, he'd be stuck.

Instead, he turned left into the oncoming lane and sped forward. There was a line of cars stopped at the red light fifty feet ahead. He drove straight at them, making up four or five car lengths before slamming on the brakes.

Vehicles turning left onto Union honked their horns as they veered around him. Some of the drivers yelled at him, hands gesturing at him in anger. He ignored them, focusing on the roof of the dry cleaning van. He was closer now. He could see that the protrusions were nozzles of some kind, each one pointed up and away from the roof. He went over in his mind exactly what he'd found in the garage at Qasim's, trying to tie the pieces of the puzzle together: the scraps of hose and the clamps scattered on the floor. The garden hose. The empty pallet. The jerry can. The acetylene torch.

What did they add up to?

If I wanted to cause mass casualties using VX, what would I do? Seconds ticked by as he contemplated how he might kill thousands of innocent civilians, conjuring up different scenarios, turning them over in his head, then dismissing each of them in turn.

The unique properties of the nerve agent limited the ways it could be effectively deployed. A bomb for example—unless carefully engineered and detonated well above ground—would squander most of the VX's deadly potential. And it's natural liquid state was thick, tacky, and not easily dispersed over a large area, especially not from ground level.

Cars kept turning left in front of him. Kept swerving around him. Kept honking their horns in frustration.

Then it clicked.

Clever son-of-a-bitch!

Sayyid was going to release the VX into the air using an aerosol generator. All the clues in the garage fit, especially the empty pallet and jerry can. It was feasible too. With a few modifications to the VX itself, the aerosol generator would be able to atomize the nerve agent and allow it to be released into the air. The colorless and odorless vapor, once breathed in, would kill within minutes. Those whose skin was exposed to the VX would die as well, only slower and more painfully.

A stiff breeze was blowing in off Lake Michigan, he noted. That was bad news. He figured Sayyid planned to drive through the core of the city, releasing the nerve agent as he went. Released as an aerosol, on a day like this, the VX would be swept along the man-made canyons of downtown like a wall of death. Unlike sarin gas or other nerve agents, VX was extremely persistent. It would remain a long-term threat by adhering to the pavement, shop windows, to cars and people's clothing—everything—for weeks. Months maybe. Temperatures near or below freezing would only exacerbate the situation and it was already the beginning of December. The city would have to be shut down. But if Sayyid wanted to inflict maximum casualties, he had to get across the bridge first. He had to reach the downtown core.

When the light turned green, the oncoming traffic didn't move. They were waiting to see what Akil was going to do. That hesitation gave him the opening he needed. He stepped on the gas and accelerated past several cars. Then, at the edge of the intersection, he forced his way between two vehicles, squeezing back into the south-bound lane.

He was one car and one lane away from Sayyid now, but trapped behind a black Escalade. A silver BMW was beside him, impeding his ability to get in behind the van.

He watched Sayyid pulling away, speeding onto the bridge.

Without hesitating, Akil smashed into the silver BMW to his right, causing the front quarter panel to buckle. Debris erupted into the air as the German car jerked right and rolled to a stop at the edge of the guardrail.

Akil pushed past it, ignoring the sound of metal grinding on metal.

At last, he had a clear path to Sayyid. All he had to do now was close the gap and disable the van.

Closing the gap quickly, he moved to within a few feet of the van's rear bumper. Then, adjusting his line, he braced himself as the cruiser collided with the van's back left side.

The van bobbed and weaved, and for an instant Akil thought the PIT maneuver had worked, but his alignment had been off.

Sayyid regained control.

They were at the half-way point on the bridge now, downtown rising skyward in front of them.

Akil lined up the cruiser for another attempt. If he could hit the van hard enough, and in just the right spot, the maneuver would cause the van to spin out of control, and in doing so, neutralize both it and Sayyid. He had to hit the sweet spot though and that was easier said than done.

Zeroing in on the van's left-hand side once again, he accelerated forward. Drawing alongside the target, he judged his car's relative position to the van and calculated the angle he needed. When everything was aligned, he swung the cruiser hard to his right.

The impact, perfectly executed this time, reverberated through his body. Pain exploded in his rib cage. The van—destabilized—swung wildly to its left and swerved across the yellow line.

The van T-boned a pick-up truck traveling in the opposite direction.

Oncoming vehicles braked and piled into one another.

Akil stopped and surveyed the damage he'd caused. It was a chaotic scene, steam and smoke wafting from vehicles that had stacked up on top of each other—debris scattered everywhere. The pile-up on the bridge was mostly fender benders. The van had come to a more violent stop. With its front end crushed, it wasn't going anywhere. He'd prevented Sayyid from reaching the core of the city, ending his weeks-long hunt for the terrorist here on the bridge.

The realization brought a wave of relief and a sense of triumph.

Both were short-lived.

He could see a fine mist escaping the nozzles atop the van. Sayyid had triggered the VX.

Akil undid his seatbelt and swung open the car door. As he exited the vehicle, two gunshots plowed into the cruiser's windshield. Crouching down behind the open door, Akil wondered if it was enough to stop Sayyid's bullets, knowing that it didn't matter, that he had to move, had to get to the van and shut off the flow of VX.

Looking up he saw that the prevailing wind was blowing the VX to the west. Upriver. If he hurried he could get to the van without exposing himself to the mist.

Another gunshot slammed into the car, forcing him to duck back down. The gunfire was coming from the driver's side of the van.

He had to make a move.

Gun in hand, he stepped out into the open and started running toward the back of the van. As he did so, he leveled his pistol at the driver's side door and began squeezing off rounds. He shot methodically. Six shots, six seconds. The goal was not to hit Sayyid, but to prevent Sayyid from shooting back and hitting him.

Reaching the back of the van unscathed, Akil took a knee. He could see the aerosolized VX overhead as it drifted away on the wind. Quick loading another magazine into his gun, he stood up and felt something moist dusting the back of his neck.

Shit!

He didn't have time to worry about the exposure now. Holding his breath, he rotated away from the back edge of the van.

Swinging his arms and body around the corner, he sought out his target. With his feet still in motion, he came face to face with the man he'd been hunting since Thanksgiving. They were less than seven feet apart, both in the open, both with their guns drawn.

Akil felt the impact of Sayyid's bullet almost immediately. It spun him around, slamming him against the van, causing his left shoulder to erupt in fire.

Stunned, it took a moment for him to regain his bearings. He could feel the heat radiating out into his arm, chest, and neck. The ground beneath him was holding though. He was okay. And he'd managed to get off a shot of his own.

Looking over at Sayyid, he saw the Palestinian lying on the ground with a hole in his chest—center mass—the Glock still gripped in his outstretched hand. Sayyid had been hurt in the crash, Akil noted. A large gash had opened up on his forehead and blood had run down into his eyes. The effects of the wound had likely saved Akil's life.

Looking down at his own shoulder, seeing his own blood, he was thankful to still be alive. For the moment at least.

Gathering his strength, Akil stepped over to the Palestinian. His legs felt weak, but he had no problems walking—his body had pumped enough adrenaline into his bloodstream that he'd be good for at least another five or ten minutes.

Akil bent down and removed the gun from Sayyid's hand, then went to the driver's side door and leaned in. He spotted the shut-off valve immediately. It was welded into place beside the driver's seat. He reached over and turned it off, then stepped back onto the deck of the bridge and checked to make sure the VX had stopped flowing out the back.

People were standing by their cars, staring at him. All he wanted to do was collapse, but he had to warn the others. Who knew how much VX had drifted upriver. An antidote—atropine—could save lives if it was administered in time. His own life too.

Akil headed back to his vehicle, glad he'd stopped the worst of it. On the way, he could feel his heart racing and noticed that the pain in his shoulder had begun to fade. That wasn't good. He was going into shock. He thought of Michael. Wanted to tell him that everything was going to be alright. That he wouldn't leave him. Not again. Hoping it was true.

EPILOGUE

IT WAS WEEKS before Akil fully recovered from his wounds. Once he had, he and Michael went to visit the boy's mother, picking up flowers on the way. Parking along the side of the road, Akil took Michael's hand and led him across the damp grass to the edge of Hannah's grave.

They stood there, neither one speaking for a long time. Michael gripped his uncle's hand, not wanting to let go. Finally, with the cluster of flowers held to his chest like a shield, Michael stepped forward. Seeing the tears running down the boy's face, Akil felt his own eyes well up. He sensed that Michael, at last, understood his mother wasn't coming back. Neither was his father. As he watched Michael kneel down and place the flowers on top of the grave, Akil understood too that he alone was responsible for the child's wellbeing now.

A few minutes later the two of them headed back to the car, hand in hand. Akil had been saved from the lingering effects of the VX by a dose of atropine. Not everyone in downtown Chicago had been so lucky. Most of Sayyid's victims had survived, thanks to the quick reaction of emergency services. But dozens had succumbed to the nerve agent and had died. He took solace in the fact that things could've been much worse.

Recovering from his wounds in the hospital, he'd come to terms with the fact his life had changed in ways he could scarcely have imagined only a few weeks earlier. Bill knew it too and had offered him a new position at Langley. Skeptical at first, thinking the new position sounded too bureaucratic, Akil had declined the offer. But Bill, persistent as ever, explained exactly what he had in mind.

I want to build a network of human intelligence in the Mid-East that will rival that of Mossad and SIS. To be successful, I need your help. No one knows the region—the players—better than you.

Akil had been championing a move like this for years.

You'll work out of Langley and answer to me. But more importantly, you'll be liaising with our Arab friends overseas, building bridges. Of course, you'll have to travel from time to time, but it'll be at your discretion.

How could he refuse? It was an ambitious undertaking, one that would require all his expertise. And it meant he could be near Michael and take care of him. Maybe, in time, as Michael got older, he could move back into the field. But right now, what Michael needed was stability, and what Akil wanted—what he had always wanted—was the chance to stay in the game. Bill was offering him both.

Arriving back home, Akil grabbed Michael with both hands and slung him over his shoulder. The boy shrieked, his feet flailing in mid-air as Akil spun him around, slowly at first, then faster and faster. A few seconds later Michael was laughing uncontrollably. Akil hoped the laughter was a sign of healing, or the start of it anyways. His optimism was tempered only by the now familiar ache in his left shoulder. The gunshot wound Sayyid had inflicted on him had healed as well as could be expected, but the doctors warned him there would be no escaping the residual effects. The pain would never go away entirely, they explained, but with time it would diminish.

Time heals all wounds.

Not exactly true, Akil thought. But he hoped, for Michael's sake, there was some truth in the old adage.

Inside the house, Akil set Michael down and told him to go brush his teeth and get ready for bed. Ten minutes later Michael was under the covers.

"Who are we playing again?" Michael asked.

"The Penguins," Akil told him. He had promised to take Michael to the Capitals game tomorrow.

"Can we go early and watch the warm-up?"

"Of course."

"And can we have some hot dogs?"

"You bet."

"And—"

"Hold on."

Michael stopped.

"You need to get some sleep, alright kiddo? We'll discuss the details in the morning."

"Okay," Michael said, disappointed.

Akil leaned forward and gave him a kiss on the forehead, then headed for the door. As he was leaving the room he turned and looked back.

Michael, who had pulled the covers up to his chin, was watching him.

"Have a good sleep," Akil said.

"You can turn the light off if you want."

"Are you sure?" For weeks Michael had insisted on having it left on.

"I'm sure."

"I'll leave the door open, okay?"

Michael nodded.

Akil headed downstairs.

A bottle of Caol Ila sat on the counter in the kitchen with a bow wrapped around its neck. He had found the bottle of single malt on his desk at Langley his first day back at work. It had come with a handwritten note from Bill.

Here's to second chances, kid.
-B

Akil opened the bottle and poured himself a glass, inhaling the aroma. There was a faint hint of honey and cloves accompanied by the smell of peat and lingering smoke. He took a sip, then set the glass down beside that morning's *New York Times*. The picture on the front page showed Anthony Marchetti. The accompanying article delved into Marchetti's sudden resignation as Director of the Central Intelligence Agency and quoted him as saying: "I did all I could to protect this country and pursue its enemies. Now, in order to make room for a new generation, I feel it's time to step aside."

Akil threw the paper in the recycling bin. Everyone knew Marchetti had been asked to resign by the President. Not publicly, of course, but quietly, behind closed doors. The reason he'd been forced out was still a topic of wild speculation in and around Washington. Most would never know the truth. Not all of it. For Akil, it was enough that Marchetti was gone—he just hoped the next appointee would be better suited to the job.

With his glass of scotch in one hand and his cell phone in the other, Akil wandered into the living room. He had promised to give Sophie a call. They had started dating and he was happy to have a woman in his life again. They'd been through so much together it felt as if they'd known each other for years. He'd never met a woman quite like her, but with Michael in the picture, he didn't want to rush things.

Luckily, that wasn't an issue. Both he and Sophie were swamped with work. Their unilateral action against Sayyid, it turned out, had been judiciously overlooked by their superiors. With two bona fide heroes on their hands, the only thing their leaders could do was capitalize on the situation as best they could by praising Akil and Sophie for their initiative, then offering them up to a hungry media as proof that America was being well protected.

Sitting down on the couch, he dialed Sophie's number, eager to hear her voice. As he waited for her to pick up, he found himself feeling something he hadn't felt in years. He felt fortunate, not only to be alive, but for having Michael and Sophie in his life. For having his job back. For all of it.

AUTHOR'S NOTE

Dear Reader:

Thank you for taking the time to read this novel.

Imminent Threat was a passion project of mine and took a little over two years to complete, then longer still to get into your hands. I had a great time developing, researching, and writing the story of Akil Hassan, Sophie Martin, Bill Graham, and Sayyid. I'm excited to have been able to share their story with you. I hope you enjoyed it.

I'm always eager to hear from readers, and I've benefitted greatly, in all sorts of ways, from the feedback so many of you have already given me. I encourage you to write to me directly with any thoughts you might have: daniel@danieldickbooks.com.

As an independent author, I know how important you, the reader, are. Not just to me, but to the countless other independent authors out there. Your encouragement and passion for what we do is fuel to us all and I want to let you know that I appreciate it very much!

If you enjoyed this book, I have one request: please take a moment to write a short review online (even if it's just a sentence or two) or tell your friends about it. Or both! Every review helps, and word of mouth is far more powerful than any ad campaign could be. In the meantime, I'll keep working on the next story.

Thanks again for reading.
Daniel

ACKNOWLEDGEMENTS

I owe a great deal to all those who believed in me and helped support the writing of this novel. It was a marathon, not a sprint, and it takes an entire team to make it across the finish line. The list of people on that team is long and distinguished, including my friends and family, beta readers, colleagues, and many others who contributed in one way or another. You know who you are.

THANK YOU!

Made in the USA
Columbia, SC
25 January 2021

31614713R00195